About Tricia Stringer

Tricia Stringer is the bestselling author of the rural romances *Queen of the Road, Right as Rain, Riverboat Point, Between the Vines,* and *A Chance of Stormy Weather* and the historical sagas *Heart of the Country* and *Dust on the Horizon,* the first two books in the Flinders Ranges series.

Queen of the Road won the Romance Writers of Australia Romantic Book of the Year award in 2013 and *Riverboat Point* and *Between the Vines* were shortlisted for the same award in 2015 and 2016 respectively.

Tricia grew up on a farm in country South Australia and has spent most of her life in rural communities, as owner of a post office and bookshop, as a teacher and librarian, and now as a full-time writer. She now lives in the beautiful Copper Coast region with her husband Daryl. From here she travels and explores Australia's diverse communities and landscapes, and shares this passion for the country and its people through her stories.

For further information go to triciastringer.com or connect with Tricia on Facebook or Twitter @tricia_stringer

T0362960

Also by Tricia Stringer

TRICIA STRINGER

Jewel *in the* NORTH

First Published 2017
Second Australian Paperback Edition 2018
ISBN 978 1 489 24693 6

Jewel in the North
© 2017 by Tricia Stringer
Australian Copyright 2017
New Zealand Copyright 2017

Except for use in any review, the reproduction or utilisation of this work in whole or in part in any form by any electronic, mechanical or other means, now known or hereafter invented, including xerography, photocopying and recording, or in any information storage or retrieval system, is forbidden without the permission of the publisher.

This book is sold subject to the condition that it shall not, by way of trade or otherwise, be lent, resold, hired out or otherwise circulated without the prior consent of the publisher in any form of binding or cover other than that in which it is published and without a similar condition including this condition being imposed on the subsequent purchaser.

All rights reserved including the right of reproduction in whole or in part in any form.

This is a work of fiction. Names, characters, places, and incidents are either the product of the author's imagination or are used fictitiously, and any resemblance to actual persons, living or dead, business establishments, events, or locales is entirely coincidental.

Published by
HQ Fiction
An imprint of Harlequin Enterprises (Australia) Pty Ltd.
Level 19, 201 Elizabeth St
SYDNEY NSW 2000
AUSTRALIA

® and TM (apart from those relating to FSC®) are trademarks of Harlequin Enterprises Limited or its corporate affiliates. Trademarks indicated with ® are registered in Australia, New Zealand and in other countries.

Cataloguing-in-Publication details are available from the National Library of Australia
www.librariesaustralia.nla.gov.au

Printed and bound in Australia by McPherson's Printing Group

MIX
Paper | Supporting
responsible forestry
FSC   FSC® C001695
www.fsc.org

To my Tilbrook aunties,
Barbara and Mary

Prologue

July 1894

There was little comfort in the front room of the Hawker Hotel save the pitiful fire and the frothy ale. A winter storm raged outside. Inside the men huddled together as much for the warmth as due to the cramped conditions. Smoke from the fire mingled with the more cloying fumes of pipe tobacco, but the overpowering smell was of sheep. The men were mostly shepherds with their recent pay packet in their pockets, from which most of them would soon be parted. They were jammed in like sheep in a pen.

For Clem the excitement of coming to town had dimmed. From his vantage point in the corner of the room he knew everyone except for two strangers. He'd noticed them as soon as they'd walked in; they were well dressed, more like city men. He could see they were buying drinks for the shepherds they spoke to. Clem had an uneasy feeling about them, especially the taller man who kept glancing around as if he were looking for someone. Right at that moment the man swivelled his head in Clem's direction. Clem looked away and pressed against the wall.

His friend, Albie, pushed a mug of ale towards him. "Here, drink this. Put a smile on your face." He giggled. It was a silly sound coming from the wiry man who was older than Clem by ten years and had the stamina of several bigger fellows combined.

"Thanks, Albie." He stared into the froth. Clem had never been much of a drinker.

Albie gave him a nudge. "Drink up." Once more he gave the silly giggle. He'd already had a few more mugs of ale than Clem.

Clem nodded his thanks and took a big mouthful of the brown liquid.

"How much of this stuff you reckon we can drink with this money?" Albie patted his pocket, his face contorted in a huge grin.

Clem couldn't help but smile back. "More than you can hold in your belly."

He had already bought himself a warm jacket and some new boots before he came to the hotel but he was fairly sure Albie would spend his whole month's pay there. "Remember you have to be back for work in two days. Old man Prosser will beat you if you're late."

Albie grinned so hard his face was almost split in two by his big wide mouth. "He's gotta catch me first."

Clem shook his head as his friend turned away and went back to a small group huddled by the fire. Albie had been employed by Prosser because of his speed and agility around sheep. His father had been a shepherd and Albie knew the hill country well. He was a sensible fellow when his belly wasn't full of ale.

The rain pounded heavily on the roof, causing a momentary pause in the conversation as everyone looked up. Then the talking resumed, but louder.

More rain was welcome. The years since Clem had arrived in the district had been a time of plentiful rain but there were those who told tales of the terrible drought from several years before.

Clem couldn't imagine it when all he could see was long grass for the sheep and cattle. Trouble was the rabbits were in bountiful supply too and following them came the dingoes that not even the fences kept out. The only way to keep sheep safe was to have men watching them all the time.

Clem glanced around at the faces in the room. Many of them wouldn't have a job if it weren't for the dingoes. It was certainly the only reason Albie had money in his pocket. Ellis Prosser was fussy about the men he employed. They were cattlemen, a close group who didn't mix much with others. With the good seasons and the grass being so thick Prosser had taken on some sheep and he'd also had to take on some extra shepherds.

A young Aboriginal woman slipped into the room carrying a tray with mugs of ale. He knew her name was Mary. He'd met her once or twice at the Bakers' place where he'd worked for almost five years now. She was the daughter of one of their shepherds and was employed to look after the publican's children but sometimes at night once they were in bed she worked in the bar too. Mary gave him a slight nod and moved among the men, handing out the ale, collecting the money and the empty mugs.

Clem noticed the two strangers were closer now. He raised his eyes to the wooden ceiling as thunder rumbled overhead. The pounding on the roof grew louder. The outer door beside him crashed open and a man scuttled inside, bringing the wind and rain with him. The old fellow had to put his shoulder to the solid wooden door to close it.

Clem leaned against the wall as once more the sound of voices fought with the noise of the storm. The smell of wet clothes, pipe tobacco and sheep fouled the air. He shouldn't have come. He much preferred the hill country, even in the rain.

A prickle tingled down his spine. He looked around. The outsiders were moving his way. They came to a stop either side of him. He straightened against the wall. The men were both of average height but one had red hair and mottled skin, while the other was a complete contrast — brown-haired, with skin that had darkened with the sun. He was the one whose piercing gaze had swept the room.

"I am Mr Jones." The dark-haired man held out his hand to Clem. "I am here with Mr Becker."

The redheaded man put his hand forward.

"Clem." Clem couldn't help but stare at the fair hand that clamped his in a quick squeeze. The skin was so pale you could see the blue of his blood beneath. Had Jones said Baker? Maybe this man was somehow related to his employer, Joseph Baker.

"We were told you work in the hill country to the east." Jones continued to do the talking.

Clem gave a slow nod and glanced beyond them, wondering who had pointed him out.

Jones pulled a rock from his pocket and stretched it out on the flat of his hand. "Mr Becker is interested in rocks like this one."

Clem's eyes widened and he leaned in for a closer look. It was like the rock his boss carried in a pouch as his good-luck charm. Clem had seen it once or twice and gathered it had been found somewhere on Baker's land, but he didn't know where.

He shrugged his shoulders. "I've seen a rock like this."

Becker leaned closer, his intense gaze locked on Clem. "Can you show me where? I would make it worth your while."

Clem frowned. He had to concentrate to understand the man's accent.

"Mr Becker is from South Africa. A country a long way from here." Jones glanced around then lifted the rock closer to Clem. "He wants more of this. He would pay you a lot of money to show us where you've seen a rock like this."

Clem swallowed. He'd spoken before he'd had time to think. He met Mary's worried look as she peered between the two new-comers. She gave an almost imperceptible shake of her head.

Clem remembered the promise he'd made to tell no-one about the rock Joseph Baker had shown him one night after a few drinks around the campfire. He looked at his feet. "Long time ago."

"Near here?" Becker clutched the sleeve of Clem's new jacket.

Clem shrugged again.

"Let us buy you a drink?" Jones smiled but Clem didn't like the way his teeth glinted between his fat lips.

"I've gotta go."

He slipped away; both men took a step to follow but he tugged the door open. A blast of cold wet air invaded the room. He stepped out and slammed the door shut on the two hungry faces. The night was miserably cold. He hunched his shoulders against the wind and rain and hurried away into the darkness, glad he'd escaped further questions and even more glad of his new coat.

Back inside, Albie waited until Mary had left the room then he sidled up to the redheaded man with the funny accent.

"I know where there're more rocks like these." The words tripped over his tongue in his excitement. He sniggered. He had never seen the rock his friends said Joseph Baker kept as his lucky charm but he'd heard it was a diamond. Albie wondered how many drinks he could buy with the money these men would pay him to show them the country out in the ranges at the back of Baker's place. Perhaps he'd never go back to Prosser's Run and the evil old man who wielded his whip so freely.

One

May 1895

The pride that had filled Henry Wiltshire's chest was wiped away in an instant. The day darkened around him. "The gall of the man," he hissed. "How dare he?"

"What's wrong, Father?"

Henry had forgotten his son was standing beside him. They'd been surveying the line of horses, carts and wagons wending their way along the track from Hawker. Overhead the afternoon sun was blocked by a thick cloudbank and light rain had fallen earlier in the day — but Henry had thought nothing could dampen his spirits today.

"Joseph Baker has come, and brought his native wife. How dare he think he can mix with decent people?"

Henry glowered in the direction of the man who provoked anger in him by his very presence. When he had first opened his business in Hawker many years earlier, Henry had thought Baker one of the well-to-do pastoralists he would do business with and whose family would be suitable friends. Then Henry had discovered Baker was a native lover. So much so that his second wife was a black woman. She was sitting beside him now. Henry studied the others in the back of the cart. It appeared some of the offspring from his first marriage were with him but, thankfully, of the younger mixed-breeds there was no sign.

"Perhaps they'll soon leave, Father. None of the decent folk here today will speak to them."

Henry tugged at his jacket and smiled down at his son. "You're right, Charles. And we will not allow outcasts like Joseph Baker and his family to mar our day." He drew in a breath and the air was fresh. The earlier sprinkle of rain had seen to that, although the large movement of people and animals stirred up some dust in spite of the damp. "Come, Charles, we have guests to greet."

Henry turned towards the front door of the Far North Creamery, soon to be declared open, built on a plateau several miles from town. The new building in front of him had been constructed from thick wooden beams, and had a cement floor and a gleaming tin roof — it was a testament to his foresight and business acumen.

Both members for their electoral district of Newcastle were attending today's official opening, along with Hawker councillors and as many people from the town and surrounding districts as wanted to come, which of course they all did. He swallowed his annoyance as he once again thought of Joseph Baker and his family. The Bakers had reclaimed the Smith's Ridge property Henry had taken from them when their poor management had left them floundering. Not only that but Joseph blamed Henry for his first wife's death. Today was a significant event for Hawker. Henry's two partners in the venture were also there of course, but Henry was the lead figure, the businessman who had brought it all together. He did not want his fine image besmirched by the appearance of the Bakers.

There were those who had thought him foolhardy to invest such a large amount of money in a venture to make cream in this district. His friend Ellis Prosser had been one, but had rested his case of late. There were many farmers in the Hundred of Arkaba who had dairy cows as a sideline and soon there would be more with the Warcowie country beyond the creamery being subdivided for mixed farming. The region had been blessed with many years of good rainfall, silencing the worry-mongers and lifting the shoulders of the district with enthusiasm. Henry could see the future development of the creamery expanding to include butter.

"The ladies have the afternoon tea in hand, Henry."

He smiled at his wife as she arrived at his side.

"Thank you for supervising, my dear." He looked her up and down. Catherine fiddled with the exquisite lace at her collar. It was pale coffee in colour, a perfect complement to the rich chocolate of her dress. She no longer liked to come out to big social events but he was pleased to see she had done him proud today. His mother had sent up the silk dress, which was topped with a brocade jacket with matching lace at the cuffs. It was the latest fashion and no-one in Hawker would have seen anything like it. Of course after years of trying for another child Catherine's body no longer boasted the lithe shape it had once but even with her broader waist he was proud: she was still a beautiful woman.

He looked over her shoulder. "Where did Charles go? We must be ready."

"He slipped off as I approached." Catherine gave Henry one of the indifferent looks she had taken to bestowing on him when it was just the two of them. "Don't worry, Henry. He knows he must be here. I'm sure he won't be long."

Henry studied her face, which was shaded by a broad-brimmed hat decorated with bunches of ribbon and tulle to take the appearance of flowers. No doubt something his mother had arranged from the milliner next door to her dress shop in North Adelaide. He wondered at his wife's private moments of coolness towards him, and yet she remained dutiful no matter what. He could rely on her to manage the shop, entertain his guests — anything that was required of the wife of a man as important as Henry Wiltshire. And yet he had noticed a difference about her for some time now. Perhaps the loss of so many babies was taking its toll. He certainly rarely shared her bed any more. He wondered if she needed more of the tonic she was fond of.

Now Catherine's lips were set in a small smile as she gazed out at the people gathering in front of the podium. "It's certainly a magnificent turnout." She glanced up at the sky. "I do hope the rain holds off."

He was distracted from the grey sky by the arrival of a carriage drawn by no fewer than four sleek black horses. "The dignitaries are here."

Charles stepped around his mother's wide skirts.

"Good timing, Charles."

"I have been keeping a watch, Father."

Henry nodded his approval at his smartly dressed young son. Charles's voice had deepened of late and he behaved in a dignified manner beyond his years. Not yet a man but well on his way. "Are we ready to show this town how lucky they are to have the Wiltshires as leading business people?"

"Yes, Father." Charles's face lit with pride.

Henry lifted his shoulders, offered his wife his arm and smiled. It was going to be a spectacular day in spite of the Bakers. Charles fell into step behind them and they moved forward together to greet the two men alighting from the carriage.

Joseph eased his horses into a gap near some low trees. Carts, horses and wagons were dispersed in all directions. People had come from everywhere for the grand opening of the Far North

Creamery. They had followed the crowd out from Hawker after spending two nights there. As was often their practice with trips to Hawker for business and supplies, their second wagon was now fully loaded and waiting at the first creek on the way home. After the opening today they would collect it and begin the journey back to Wildu Creek.

The wagon had barely rolled to a stop when William jumped down and helped his two sisters to the ground. "Can we go ahead, Father?"

"Of course. Look out for your sisters."

Violet, only a few years younger than William's twenty, gave a small nod, but Esther, who was younger again, rolled her eyes.

Joseph raised his eyebrows in return. "Don't give your brother any trouble, Esther."

"We won't, Father." Violet smiled sweetly and drew her sister away before she could spout forth with her usual outrage at any inference that she needed minding. At sixteen Esther was no more or less a handful than she'd been at three or seven or any time in her life.

"You mustn't tease her, Joseph." Millie shook her head at him. "It only makes her dig in her heels."

Joseph pulled himself up and frowned at the back view of his three grown-up children disappearing in the throng making its way towards the new creamery building. "It was no joke. I meant what I said. Esther has been known to make a spectacle of herself before. Only last month outside the church she pushed that boy over."

"He was a young man, older than her and being obnoxious. I do believe she was defending me."

"You don't need defending, do you? Surely we've been married long enough to cease being a curiosity."

Millie shook her head slowly at him. "You truly have blinkers." Her big dark eyes, which were usually glowing with joy, were deep pools of melancholy. "We don't come to town that often. A white man marrying a black woman will always cause a stir with some."

"Well, they're not people we spend time with."

"But on days like this everyone is here. We can't avoid those who don't like us."

After helping her down from the cart, Joseph turned her to face him. They had both known what they were doing when they married. At home on Wildu Creek they were so happy, and Millie was usually indifferent to the snubs of others. He took her hands. "What's wrong?"

"I'm being silly. Today I don't have the strength to face those who look down their noses at me." Millie's frown softened. "I think I am tired, that's all."

"I am sorry, my love. You have as much right to be here as everyone else. I am sure the Garrats from the general store will be here and of course Mr Pyman from the saddlery. He has money invested in this venture I believe. They will be kind to you."

"I know, Joseph." Millie slid her hands from his grasp and fiddled with her belt, pulling it in a notch to accentuate her waist. After two children she was still as slender as the day he'd met her and even more beautiful. Her thick dark hair was coiled up onto her hatless head.

"You look beautiful, my dear." He offered his arm and they strolled together nearer the general gathering of people, but Millie pulled him up.

"It's not all about you and me, Joseph." She indicated a group of young people nearby. "It's hard on William and the girls."

Joseph looked to where his son stood with Violet and Esther, talking to several friends from Hawker. He knew his children loved Millie but he understood what she meant.

"I'm worried about our young ones," Millie said. "This new law that's talked of that allows the Protector of Aborigines to remove children of mixed blood from their parents terrifies me."

Joseph grabbed her hands and gave her arms a gentle shake. "It's not law yet and anyway, no-one is going to take our children from us, Millie." He bent to kiss her lips. "No-one."

Her eyes locked with his and Joseph gave a firm nod of his head in return. It was the children of poor misfortunates unable to look after them who would be taken. Not well-cared-for and loved children like his own. Millie was feeling unease at being in such a big crowd, that was all. He looked around.

A murmur and shuffle from the crowd — a group was walking towards the front of the creamery building, led by Henry Wiltshire. Speaking of the devil, Henry was one of those dogmatic people who judged by the colour of a person's skin or the amount of money they had.

Millie fussed at the buttons of the white lace shirt she wore beneath a simple deep brown jacket.

"You look perfect, Millie." He kissed her on the nose.

She giggled and he grinned back.

He took her arm again. "Let's go and see this tomfoolery of a creamery for ourselves. I'd be happy to eat my words but I can't see it being a success in this country."

William and the girls stayed with their friends while Joseph and Millie made their way to the front door. Inside the building was congested but the crowd parted for them. Joseph heard someone hiss. He gripped Millie's hand tightly. He was relieved when Mabel Garrat saw them and beckoned them closer.

"Hello." The older woman smiled, her big round face lit up with welcome. "I thought you'd gone home."

"We decided to stay on for the festivities," Joseph said. "We will leave as soon as the official proceedings are over."

"What a turnout." Tom Garrat shook Joseph's hand and tipped his hat at Millie. "Looks like everyone from the district is here. No customers left in town so we closed the shop to come out for a gander."

"Will you be stocking their cream?" Millie asked.

"Unlikely." Mabel gave a snort. "Mr High and Mighty over there." She gestured towards the machinery where Henry was pointing out features to a group gathered in close. "He will be stocking his own cream I am sure and he won't be letting us have any. We're his best competition."

"Ladies and gentlemen." The local publican used his booming voice to gain everyone's attention. The crowd inside the creamery began to settle and quieten and more pushed in from outside. Those who couldn't fit huddled close to fend off the chill of the afternoon.

"At least it's warm with everyone in together." Mabel tugged her jacket closer. "What a cold May day it is."

"There must be at least two hundred or more here," Joseph murmured.

"You have to be impressed." Millie gave him a nudge. "Anyway it's not just about Henry Wiltshire. He has Mr Button and Mr Pyman as partners in this enterprise, doesn't he? They are sensible gentlemen."

"I would have said so until they threw their lot in with Wiltshire."

Once more their attention was drawn back to the machinery, which began to whir to life. There were murmurs of awe from the crowd as the first gallons of milk surged through the pipes and into the separator.

Henry felt fit to burst with pride. The cream production had impressed the large crowd enough that they gave three rousing cheers at the publican's prompting. Mr Foster, one of their local members, gave a stirring speech, which was followed by another three cheers and then Mr Button spoke on behalf of the three proprietors. Henry revelled in the opportunity to be seen standing beside the two parliamentarians.

He looked from one to the other. "Now that the official ceremonies are over can we offer you a cup of tea, gentlemen?"

"That would be most welcome," Burgoyne replied.

"I'd like to mingle if you don't mind," Foster said. "There are a couple of other locals I would like to speak with while I have the opportunity."

Henry felt a little deflated; Foster set off through the crowd, his stride confident, as if he had already set eyes on someone. Henry turned back to Burgoyne and gave him a broad smile. "Shall we go this way?" He pointed towards the door closest to the refreshment tent that had been set up outside.

"Mr Baker?"

Joseph turned. Mr Foster stood before him. A distinguished-looking man with a thick moustache that turned up at each end, he was a few years Joseph's junior.

"I am Joseph Baker."

Foster held out his hand. "I've been hearing good things about you, Mr Baker."

Joseph was encouraged by the politician's words, but he knew Millie wouldn't enjoy the closer attention they were now receiving from others around them. He put his arm around her and drew her close. "This is my wife, Millie, and three of my children, William, Violet and Esther."

Foster shook everyone's hand. "A fine family."

"I have three more children at home."

"No doubt they are a blessing to you, Mr Baker." He smiled once more in Millie's direction then turned back to Joseph. "I don't want to monopolise your time but I've been hearing good reports about your sheep-breeding exploits."

"Have you indeed?" Joseph was surprised but more than a little proud to be singled out by Foster, who was by report energetic and dedicated in his work.

"I would like to know more."

"Perhaps the girls and I can take some tea while you discuss business." Millie smiled but Joseph could see the uncertainty in her eyes. Nevertheless the three set off, and Joseph turned back to Foster as William stepped closer.

"What would you like to know, Mr Foster? William is proving a most reliable support and my father, Thomas Baker, is also part of our endeavour."

"Your mutton is well recommended, Baker, along with your wool. I was hoping to interest you in the freezing machinery the government has built at Port Adelaide, along with the establishment of a produce depot and agency in London."

"The demand for our meat is strong in South Australia."

"I am sure but we are already exporting poultry, pork and even rabbits. I mentioned the interest in butter that comes from this region. The sweet herbage of the area improves the flavour, as it does the flavour of your meat."

Joseph looked from Foster to William, who had moved closer, then back again. "Do tell us more, Mr Foster."

Henry glared at Joseph Baker from his position near the creamery main door. Baker was in deep conversation with Mr Foster. Henry couldn't imagine what they would have in common. He'd seen the way Foster had greeted Baker's wife — no doubt as a member of parliament he had to be polite. The locals had no such scruples. Henry shifted his gaze to where Millie Baker and her stepdaughters were approaching the refreshment tent. Several people stepped back, parting a way for them.

"They should not be encouraged to spend time with decent white folk," he muttered.

"I assume by 'they' you are referring to the Bakers." Catherine looked at her husband with a steady gaze. "Why does it bother you so, Henry? Millie Baker appears to be a well-mannered woman, who dresses suitably and keeps a fine house from what I've heard."

"She's still a black woman and her children are mixed breed. I've noticed more and more of such people about town as well as full-blood natives."

"Surely if they have money ..." Catherine paused and gave him a superior smile. "They are entitled to spend it the same as anyone else."

"Entitled." Henry huffed. She knew very well the Bakers were some of the most well-off people in the district. His fingers curled into his palms. Most of the other natives weren't so comfortable. "It only gives them excuses to linger."

"Father's right." Charles joined the conversation. "Mr Garrat allows natives in his shop and they're often standing about out the front as well."

"Passing the time of day with their friends." Catherine looked from her son to her husband. "In a similar way to anyone else in town."

Henry glared at her. She had always held a weakness for the down and out but she had never openly contradicted him. "We will not discuss this here." He turned to Charles. "Go with your mother to get some refreshments."

Catherine gave a barely audible sigh but she said no more and took her son's arm.

Henry leaned in to the boy's other ear. "And make sure she ends up nowhere near that woman of Baker's."

Joseph shook Mr Foster's hand and watched as the man moved on to speak with someone else. "I think we should have a cup of tea to warm our bones before we go." Joseph rubbed his hands together. "Millie and the girls have theirs."

They set off together towards the refreshment tent. William glanced around as they walked.

"Looking for someone?" Joseph asked.

William's cheeks had a pink glow. "Not in particular."

"I believe the Prossers are away."

William pulled up and gave his father a penetrating look. "Who said I was looking for them?"

Joseph grinned. William was smitten by Georgina Prosser, their nearest neighbour. They all knew it, as much as he tried to hide it.

"What do you think about Mr Foster's suggestion, Father?" William changed the subject.

"It's certainly worth considering."

"You don't sound eager."

Joseph looked into his son's bright eyes. William had hung on Foster's every word. "Mr Foster has given us much to think about."

Suddenly Henry Wiltshire stepped in front of him.

"How dare you come to this public event and bring your ... your woman with you."

Joseph gaped at Henry. The man was not his friend but he was thrown by the open hatred etched on his face. Henry's son Charles stepped in beside his father, a similar glower furrowing his young face. Joseph glanced around. Thankfully they were a small distance from the nearest people and, he hoped, out of ear-shot. He locked his gaze back on Henry.

"My wife and I are interested in your venture." Joseph couldn't help but lift his lips in a smile. Henry had gone quite red in the face with indignation. "The same as the rest of the district."

"You're not welcome here," Henry hissed. "You and your ..." He flicked his gaze over William. "... tribe."

Joseph ignored the barb. "There was an open invitation in Hawker for all to see."

"An open invitation for decent people. It's distressing for sensitive people. I don't want my wife upset. And how dare you collar the local member? He's a generous man but he would not want to be involved in your sordid family affairs."

Joseph drew himself up. "Mr Foster is a sensible man who sought me out for my opinion on farming matters."

"What?" Henry snorted. "That's preposterous."

Charles mimicked his father and beside him, Joseph could sense William's anger. There was no point in continuing. He wasn't in the mood for Henry's open antagonism and he didn't want to cause a scene that would only distress Millie. "We're leaving now anyway. I've seen enough of this foolhardy scheme of yours."

"Foolhardy, is it?" Henry's voice rose a little and those nearby looked at them. "We will be supplying cream to the district and the rest of South Australia, and then butter. We'll see who's foolhardy then, Baker."

Joseph didn't bother to reply. "Come on, William." He moved off in Millie's direction.

From nearby came the sound of happy laughter. Joseph glanced across to where Catherine Wiltshire was being told some kind of joke by the two visiting MPs. Mrs Wiltshire's eyes were bright and her cheeks were rosy.

So much for being upset, Joseph thought.

Two

April 1896

The night was still but for the crackle of the campfire, the occasional snort of a horse and the murmur of voices. Four men huddled around the flames, their hands stretched to the warmth while their backs felt the chill of the cold night through their coats. Overhead the clear sky was scattered with a million stars and in the east a full moon was sending its glow over the hills, a promise of the silver light to follow.

"It's good to have made home ground tonight." Joseph clapped William on the shoulder and nodded across the fire to his father, Thomas, and his friend Binda. "I have to admit I've had concerns about this cattle venture but a month of droving has done us all good."

Thomas lifted one cheek of his aching backside from the log he was using for a seat and gave it a vigorous rub. "This was not the way I had planned to celebrate my birthday."

Joseph shook his head. "I told you to stay home. Timothy or Hegarty could have come."

"I might be feeling every one of my seventy-year-old bones." Thomas straightened his back. "But I wouldn't have missed this.

It's a while since I went on a droving run." He looked at his grand-son. "I'm grateful for the opportunity to be out here working with my family. This will be a new venture for the Baker clan."

William's weary gaze met his grandfather's. "I'm glad you're here. And I'm grateful you both agreed to take on cattle."

"It makes sense." Thomas opened and closed his hands, stretching his gnarled fingers. "I've always been a sheep man but I only learned about them when I was your age. You have plenty of time to learn about cattle."

"The country here at Smith's Ridge is better suited to cattle. Sheep only do well on here in plentiful times," Joseph said. "But I can't see us having anything but sheep at Wildu Creek."

"Your breeding program has produced a fine breed of sheep suited to the conditions." Thomas looked to William. "I'm sure you will work as hard with the cattle."

"I hope to, Grandpa." His eyes shone in the firelight.

"Time will tell." Joseph stretched and yawned. "Thank good-ness we're home. I've been a long time with my backside in the saddle."

William nudged his father. "Cattle aren't to be rushed."

Joseph gave him a nudge back. "I see you think you're the expert now after only four weeks of owning these animals."

"I've learned a lot at Prosser's Run."

Thomas noted the good-natured smile slip from Joseph's face. They'd all been surprised when William had suggested they take on cattle at Smith's Ridge, but after much discussion and research they'd decided it could be a useful diversification. Joseph had not been able to hide his displeasure when his oldest son had also proposed learning about the beasts from his offensive neighbour, Ellis Prosser.

"Times change." Thomas met Joseph's sour look across the fire. "Forty-five years ago your mother's brothers and I brought the first sheep to Smith's Ridge. So much has happened since then and yet that which is most precious to me is here … family." He looked from his son to his grandson and then to the native man sitting beside him. Binda was only a little older than Joseph and had been part of their lives since he saved Joseph's life as a teenager. "That includes you, Binda."

A high-pitched bellow made him pause.

William grinned. "I reckon one of those bulls is at work already."

Joseph stood up and looked in the direction of the sound but all was quiet again. "Robert's been gone a while."

"He went off looking for rabbits." William turned to the wagon, where their swags were already laid out on the ground. "He's probably slipped back to camp empty handed and into his bed and is dreaming already."

Thomas watched as both his son and grandson started towards the wagon. Robert was the youngest of Joseph's children by his first wife, Clara, and he'd always been treated as the baby even though there were more children since Joseph had married Millie. They had all been extra watchful of Robert since, several years earlier, he'd received a nasty blow to the head and a badly broken leg. It had taken him some time to recover, but at sixteen he was strong and stocky with no trace of those injuries.

"He's not in his bed." William was the first to reach the wagon.

The bull bellowed again, closer this time and accompanied by the low rumble of heavy footsteps. Thomas scrutinised the surrounding bush and Binda took a few steps in that direction. Behind them Joseph and William called Robert's name in unison.

Thomas looked at Binda. "That bull's getting closer."

Binda's eyes were wide. He wasn't keen on cattle and was especially wary of the five large bulls they'd bought.

"What are you shouting for?" Robert appeared on the other side of the clearing, two rabbits hanging from a rope over his shoulder. He carried a thick branch with two sticks like a fork on one end. The rumble of hooves drew closer and the bush parted.

Binda began to run. "It's the black bull."

The huge beast charged into the camp and they all scattered.

Binda was the first to climb up onto the wagon.

"This way, Father, quick," William yelled. He was already climbing aboard.

There were several feet between Thomas and the wagon and, seeing the last man standing, the bull veered around the fire in his direction.

"Father!" Joseph's yell and the sight of the lowered horns galvanised Thomas into action. He made a dash for the wagon and threw himself at it with the heat of the bull's breath on his neck. Joseph and William hefted him up as the bull bunted the side, which shuddered under the force. Thomas's heart was thumping in his chest as he peered over the enraged animal to the place where Robert had been standing. There was no sign of the boy. They were camped a little way from the creek and there were no big trees close by. Thomas scanned the shadows of the bush looking for a sign of his grandson. The bull backed off, pawed the ground and began again with its low moaning bellow. "I can't see Robert." Thomas turned back to the others. Joseph was scrabbling around under the canvas at the side of the wagon.

"What are you doing, Joseph?"

"I'm looking for the rifle."

"You can't shoot it." William grabbed his father's arm just as the bull dealt the wagon another blow. They all lurched with the force. "It's our prize bull."

"Prize bull be damned."

Joseph continued his search, William remonstrated with him and Binda stayed in the corner of the wagon furthest from the beast, which continued to bellow. Only Thomas saw Robert leap from the shadows with his solid wooden stick raised. He grabbed the bull by the tail and hit it across the rump. The blows were forceful and the bull took off across the clearing with Robert still hanging onto its tail with his spare hand, administering more blows with the stick in the other.

Thomas put a hand to his heaving chest. William and Joseph moved either side of him.

"Robert." Joseph's voice held a note of terror. The shadowy bush swallowed beast and boy and the hoofbeats receded along with the sound of the stick hitting its back.

"Dear God, Robert." Joseph was the first to move. The rifle now in his hands, he jumped down from the wagon.

"Father, wait!" William landed beside Joseph and pulled on his arm.

Joseph shrugged him off. "I can't let that mad animal kill your brother."

"William's right." Binda had also climbed down from the wagon. "You can't go running out into the night shooting. Even though there's a full moon you could hit Robert."

"Not to mention setting the whole herd into hysterics." William moved to stand in front of Joseph.

"But I can't just leave Robert." Joseph's voice was full of fear.

Thomas saw movement on the edge of the clearing. "It's all right." He let out a huge sigh of relief. "Robert, you crazy young fool."

Robert stumbled forward into the light thrown by the fire. He still held the stick.

Joseph was on him in an instant, pulling him close in a hug.

"I'm all right, Father." Robert struggled to be free and Joseph let him go.

"What happened?" William asked.

"I held onto his tail and kept whacking him for fifty or sixty yards." The firelight reflected the huge grin on Robert's face. "He just needed to know who was boss."

"I can't believe it." William clapped his brother on the back. "Well done, little brother."

"I'm not so little." He lifted his head high.

"Neither you are." Robert was almost as tall as William and Joseph already and much thicker of frame.

"You've become a man." Binda's voice was full of pride. "You're a good bush fella."

"Someone had to take charge." Robert chuckled. "You four women needed rescuing. I've never seen anything so funny." His chuckle turned into a laugh.

Thomas saw the frowns on Joseph's and William's faces but like him Binda was grinning. He started to laugh, and finally the other two saw the funny side and they all fell back around the campfire, the sounds of their laughter echoing around them as the night settled again.

Robert turned away. "I hope that bugger hasn't tramped my rabbits."

"Robert." Joseph reprimanded.

He raised his eyebrows. "I'm a man now, Father." He stood tall, the flames throwing an even taller silhouette across the bush behind him. "Binda said so."

"By heaven and hell, that you are." Joseph began to laugh again as Robert retrieved his rabbits from the dirt where he'd dropped them.

"Tomorrow's breakfast." He held the catch high.

"A good hunter as well as animal tamer." Binda poked Joseph in the chest.

William gathered the mugs and Binda threw some more tea into the billy. Robert and Joseph added wood to the fire and all the

while the four of them joked and laughed. Thomas felt his chest
swell with happiness. All those years earlier when he'd driven sheep
to Wildu Creek only to find his wife Lizzie unwell and his baby
daughter succumbed to the same illness he had thought nothing
was worth the price, but with Lizzie's help and that of his native
friend Gulda he'd gone on. Now he had two children and eight
grandchildren, and Joseph and Millie were expecting another.

His only wish was that some of the things he'd brought from
England, family heirlooms really, were still in his possession: a
small link to family that he could pass on to his Australian descen-
dants. They'd been stolen from him by a devil of a man, Septimus Wiltshire. Thomas had been duped by the ex-convict of his
money and possessions. Some items such as his mother's pretty
china tea set and her books had been returned by Septimus's wife
Harriet after he died, but others remained lost. He knew his
mother's filigree heart-shaped locket, a gift on her wedding day,
had hung around Harriet's neck when he had seen it last. Lizzie
had advised him to forget about it but it had been difficult with
Wiltshire turning up again and again to cause grief in their lives.

Now Wiltshire's son, Henry, lived in Hawker and ran a business, a place where the Bakers were not welcome. Thomas knew
it all stemmed from their mixing with natives. He had always
worked alongside the original inhabitants of this land and he
didn't care for people who mistreated others simply because of the
colour of their skin.

The happy voices of his son and grandson carried in the still
air. Thomas gazed up at the starry night sky and imagined his
dear departed wife smiling down on their family. *What do you
think of them now, Lizzie?*

"Grandpa?"

Thomas focused again on the young man standing in front
of him.

Robert gave him a gentle smile. "I've made you some tea."

Thomas reached for the mug he was holding out. "Thank you."

They walked back to the fire where the others were already sipping the hot liquid. Thomas felt a chill through his body and he gratefully settled by the flames again. Even though it was early April, the nights had become very cold. The happiness that had filled his chest ebbed away and left a hollow nagging feeling. They'd had no rain to speak of since before Christmas. It wasn't unusual to go for several months without rain but they'd enjoyed seven good years in a row and the pattern of the weather had changed again; he knew it. Drought had plagued them in the past. He prayed they wouldn't suffer in its clutches again any time soon.

"What a night." Joseph lifted his mug into the air. "I hope this isn't an omen of things to come, William."

"Robert's done the right thing. That bull needed to be shown who was boss."

Robert's shoulders lifted and he beamed at his older brother.

"Not that I want you to do anything so foolish again," William added quickly. "That bull was hand reared from a calf and used to humans. Ellis Prosser says hand-reared cattle have no fear of us. That bull could have become dangerous if Robert hadn't taught him a lesson."

Joseph spluttered over his tea mug. "Could have! What do you call charging into our camp if not dangerous? Imagine the damage he could have done to one or all of us if we hadn't made it to the wagon. Your grandfather had a lucky escape."

"Are you all right, Grandpa?" William raised his eyebrows and his look was one of mock worry.

"Never better." Thomas shook off the melancholy feeling. "Plenty of life in this old man yet."

William woke in the grey light of pre-dawn. He lay still, listening to the deep breathing of the men around him. Everyone else was asleep. He'd been woken by a different noise. His immediate thought was for the bull, but there were no angry bellows or thundering hooves, just the shuffles and snorts of cattle and horses and men still asleep. He couldn't help grinning to himself over the events of the night before. His father had been the most upset and fussing over Grandpa. William was quite sure his grandfather was as fit as any of them, even if a little slower these days.

The snap and crackle of fresh twigs on the fire made him sit up. Robert was bent over the fire, set to one side away from the wagon, his rabbits roasting above the flames. William smiled. He eased from his swag and the chill of the crisp morning sent a shiver through his body. Nearby were the prone forms of his father and grandfather but there was no sign of Binda. He was also a very early riser.

Robert grinned at he approached. "Bout time you got up."

William pointed at the billy. "That got some left in it for me?"

Robert poured some of the tea into a mug. William wrapped his cold fingers around the hot vessel. They both huddled close to the fire, watching the rabbit.

"It's going to be different now." Robert's voice was so low William hardly heard him.

"We all have to get used to cattle."

"I don't mean the cattle." Robert's gaze lifted from the rabbit. "With you and Hegarty living at Smith's Ridge and Timothy and Eliza moving in with Grandpa, things will be different at Wildu Creek."

"Now that I'm taking over the house at Smith's Ridge it's only fair that Timothy and Eliza get a decent house to live in. They've worked for our family since before you and I were born." William looked away from his brother's soulful gaze into the flickering flames. He had felt guilty about asking to take over the second family property. Timothy Castles had first worked for his grandfather at Wildu Creek and had become a trusted member of the Baker family along with his wife. After the Bakers reclaimed Smith's Ridge from Henry Wiltshire, Timothy and his wife Eliza had become the managers there. That had been several years back and now William was itching to take charge of something for himself. At Wildu Creek there were already his father and grandfather having their say and not always agreeing about how things should be done, without William adding his bit. He looked back at Robert. "With you all in the big house, Millie has enough to do, and even more with another baby coming. Grandpa is happy to have the company of Timothy and Eliza even though he's not far from the new house, and Eliza seemed keen to take him under her wing. It should all work out well."

Robert turned the rabbits once more. The fire snapped and spat as fat dripped into the flames. "For everyone but me."

William opened his mouth to speak then closed it again. He hadn't given a thought to Robert in this new arrangement. Their father and sisters, Violet and Esther, lived in the grand new house that had finally been finished up the hill behind Grandpa's house. There was plenty of room in it but it was a house full of women. Father's second wife Millie had produced two daughters already.

"Perhaps Millie will have a boy this time."

Robert grimaced. "I don't care about that. It's the work that I want. There are plenty of hands at Wildu Creek. They don't need me. I want to be part of what you're doing at Smith's Ridge."

William saw the hope in his brother's dark eyes and knew immediately how he felt. Like William, he wanted to try new things, different ways. At Wildu Creek Robert's role was virtually that of a shepherd and they employed several of them. Still, he was only sixteen. "You can spend time at Smith's Ridge whenever you like. It's only a day's ride."

Robert sat forward eagerly but they were both distracted by Binda's sudden appearance in the hazy light. He grinned at them, his white teeth a sharp contrast to his dark skin. Another bundle of rabbits hung from a stick he carried over his bare shoulder.

William got to his feet. The sun would soon rise above the hills. "Time to get started." He felt a surge of excitement, his conversation with Robert forgotten as he listened to the first low calls of his herd stirring. "Let's eat and get these cattle home."

Three

William stood on the front verandah of his childhood home, staring out across the sloping terrain to the creek a short walk away. Smith's Ridge had been first settled by his grandmother's brothers, who had been swindled out of it by Septimus Wiltshire. When Septimus perished, his widow, Harriet, had handed the lease back to the Bakers. William had been born there but after his mother died in childbirth, seven years later, Joseph had not managed the property well. To add to their troubles the land had been in drought and Joseph had made the difficult decision to let go the lease and move his family to Wildu Creek.

Smith's Ridge had been taken over by Septimus's son, Henry, who had fared little better than the Bakers. Henry's half-brother, Jack Aldridge, had been installed as the overseer. He had proven to be an evil man. William's hands clenched into fists at the thought of Jack's visit to Millie when the man knew Joseph was away from home. Thankfully he'd never done her any real harm but he'd tried. William took in a sharp breath as he recalled the night of Jack's death, struck by lightning here at Smith's Ridge. William, Joseph and Henry had all been there, brought together by a common enemy. Jack's demise had been the catalyst for Henry to quit the lease for Smith's Ridge and now it was in the hands of the Bakers once more and William had returned.

William shifted his gaze to the stand of taller gums on a rise further on from the house. His mother and baby brother were buried there. He had been just seven years old then. Now he struggled to remember his mother's face. He had left Smith's Ridge as a boy and returned as a man, determined to improve and look after it.

In the front room behind him the murmur of male voices were interspersed with Eliza's softer tones as she encouraged them to eat more of her food. They had made good time, reaching the paddock that was to house the cattle just after midday. Everyone had washed and lingered over a late lunch inside. After spending more than a month on the back of a horse, droving cattle, they had all enjoyed the comfort of a real table and chairs and a roof over their heads.

The front door gave a small squeak of protest as it opened. William turned. His father came to stand beside him. They both stared into the distance.

"Apart from losing your mother I was always happy here." Joseph leaned on the verandah railing, his shoulder touching William's.

"So was I."

They lapsed into silence a moment, each conjuring their own memories, then Joseph spoke.

"This is a fine opportunity for you, son. Hegarty has had some experience with cattle before so he will be a good support."

"When will he arrive?"

"I'll send him on once we get back to Wildu Creek."

"Robert wants to stay."

"I've said he could."

William's heart sank. In spite of the guilt he felt for not wanting his brother to stay, he needed to do this on his own.

Joseph met his look. "But only for a few days. With you and Hegarty here, he can have more responsibility at Wildu Creek." He put a hand on William's shoulder. "This is your venture, son. Robert's time will come." He gave a wry smile. "Besides, I need him home to give some balance to the household. Your sisters like to boss me about if Robert's not there for them to fuss over."

William sucked in a deep breath.

"I'm glad Hegarty offered to come here." Joseph patted his trouser pocket. "He knows to keep an eye out for anyone searching for diamonds."

"We haven't had any trouble since that South African fellow came sniffing around a few years back."

"No, but he did find his way to the bottom waterhole, which is lower down the same waterway where I found this one." Joseph pulled a grubby leather pouch from his pocket and tipped the rock it contained into the palm of his hand. He tossed it from one hand to the other. "We should have it cut one day. Might make a nice piece of jewellery."

William ignored his father's remark. Joseph had made similar suggestions before but William knew he liked to keep the raw diamond as his lucky charm.

"You haven't ever thought about looking for more?"

Joseph gripped the rock in one hand and fixed his steely gaze on William. "I've seen what mining does to people."

His father never talked much about his time on the Teetulpa goldfields but William knew it hadn't been an easy or happy couple of years scratching to find gold to bring them home some money during the drought.

"It would only be us," William said. "We'd take care of the land."

"Others would get wind of it. It's enough we ask your Uncle Binda's people to share their country with us."

William gripped the rail in front of him. He didn't agree with his father's views on natives belonging to this land. "It's our home now. You were born here, I was born here." He stared out at the country stretching out in front of him. He thought of it as Baker country.

Joseph sighed. "Regardless of where Binda's people live we only lease this country."

"And we will keep the lease from now on." William turned and watched his father push the rock back into its pouch.

Joseph lifted a sorrowful gaze to William. "We can't stop other people from staking mining claims here so it's best we leave it be."

William gave a sharp nod. Even though he didn't think of this country as belonging to the natives he had no interest in looking for diamonds. On that he agreed with his father. He lifted his hat and tugged his fingers through his stiff curls. "I still don't understand what would have made the fellow come all this way."

"There are always people searching for minerals and gems. Before I hurried him on his way the South African told me this country was similar to diamond country in his homeland."

"But how did he end up in exactly the right place?"

"Not exactly the right place. The hidden waterhole where I found the diamond is much further along and higher up in a narrow gorge at the farthest boundary of Smith's Ridge."

"Well thankfully that Becker fellow didn't have much of a look around before you gave him short shrift, and Albie no longer works for Prosser. Ellis found him drunk again late last year and told him never to come back. Threatened to beat him if he set foot on Prosser land."

"I don't know how you can stand to be near that man."

"I'm not fond of him but—"

"He has a beautiful daughter."

William gave his father a dismissive look. He was in love with Georgina Prosser but no-one knew that. Not even Georgina. "I was going to say he has an excellent knowledge of cattle. It would be foolish of me not to take lessons from the nearest expert."

"As long as the only lessons are those about cattle."

"Don't worry, Father. Ellis barely gives me the time of day, but because I've shown an interest he can't resist the opportunity to show how much he knows. We speak of nothing but cattle at Prosser's Run." William didn't mention how he tried to continue meeting up with Georgina while he was there. It was never easy but the last few times he'd been checking cattle in the yards close to their house Georgina had come and watched or ridden past a few times on her horse.

"I assume you are intending to inspect the cattle again?" Joseph pushed the battered hat he'd been carrying onto his head. "We'd better get to it before I seize up altogether. The ride home tomorrow already seems very long."

Thomas stayed back at the house with Timothy and Eliza to talk over the logistics of what would fit at the Wildu Creek house and what would not. They would leave with him tomorrow. Binda offered to do a visit to each of the shepherds camped around the property. He would make his way home to Wildu Creek later so it was only William, Robert and Joseph who rode out to check the cattle were settling into their new home.

They reined in their horses on a ridge that gave a view across the slopes below them and thus a good vantage point to cast their gazes over the cattle. The animals had spread out, heads down, munching in the thick grass.

William sat high in the saddle and leaned forward to take in the sight of his cattle in their new home. Their bigger size and russet brown and deep black coats looked so different from the pale brown sheep he was used to. "I will move them to the higher country later and bring the sheep onto the plains. I want to keep them close while they settle in."

"Look at that damn bull." Joseph pointed at the large black bull meandering its way between the blue bushes. "He looks perfectly angelic."

William chuckled. "He certainly didn't give us any more trouble after you dealt with him, Robert."

"He just needed someone to call his bluff. He's happy now."

"They'd all better be," Joseph said. "They've got work to do if we're to recover our investment."

"Someone's coming."

William looked in the direction of Robert's outstretched hand. Two riders were making their way up from the creek, following the fence line.

"It looks like Ellis Prosser," Joseph growled. "What a way to spoil a beautiful day."

William ignored his father's gruff reaction. "He said he might come and have a look once we got back."

"He's quick off the mark." Joseph glared in the direction of the riders. "Who's that with him? It looks like a woman."

William took in the other rider, who did indeed look slight of form.

Before he reached them Prosser waved an arm in the general direction of the cattle. "I hope you didn't pay a lot of money for this dismal lot, Baker," he bellowed.

William heard his father's sharp intake of breath but he barely acknowledged it, or Ellis Prosser. His gaze was only for the woman who rode beside Ellis. Georgina Prosser always took his breath away but today she looked even more beautiful. She wore a crisp white shirt buttoned to the top with a deep red velvet bow tied at the collar and over that a smart tan jacket. Her wild red curls were swept back in another bow and she wore a broad-brimmed hat to shade her pale skin. It was her legs that held his attention. Not that he could see her legs, but she was wearing light trousers tucked into long boots so she could ride the horse like a man. He'd never seen her do that before.

"Hello, William." She smiled brightly at him and then at his father. "Mr Baker."

Joseph moved his horse up beside William's and ignored Prosser altogether. "It's a lovely day for a ride, Miss Prosser. I hope your mother is well."

"Yes, thank you."

Finally he turned his attention to Prosser. "There's little wrong with these cattle that our plentiful country feed won't fix, Prosser. You've made good time coming to look at them. We only arrived back at the homestead a few hours ago."

"One of my men caught sight of you yesterday as you made camp near the creek. I thought I would come and inspect the animals you ended up with. I wouldn't want anything diseased near my prime cattle."

Finally William dragged his gaze from Georgina's pretty smile and found his voice. "These animals are all healthy specimens, Mr Prosser. As Father says, they need some fattening up — that's all."

"Hmph!" Ellis snorted and so did his horse.

William wanted to laugh but he knew it was not the time.

"You didn't rush them?" Ellis peered at him doggedly.

"No. Just as you said, we brought them quietly along and they are quite used to us being around them now."

Ellis harrumphed again. "Good."

"We were just going to walk among them." William dismounted and tethered his horse. "Do you wish to join us?"

Ellis mopped his florid face with his handkerchief. "It's warmer than I expected."

"I'd like to." Georgina slid from her horse.

Once more William was lost for words.

"Why don't we let the younger generation inspect the animals?" Joseph also got down from his horse. He waved a hand at his youngest son. "Robert has a water bag and some mugs. We can sit in the shade while we wait."

"Very well." Ellis looked his daughter in the eye. "Don't be long, Georgina. I want to make home creek to camp tonight. Make sure our own cattle in that region are in good form before we return home."

Georgina's pale green eyes swept over William, her lips turned up in a cheeky smile. "It seems we must be quick." She lowered her gaze. "And yet one mustn't rush when there are cattle about, must one, Father?" She set off. William followed with Ellis's loud snort sounding behind him.

"See to Miss Prosser's horse, Robert." Joseph could tell his youngest son was about to join the walk, but it was patently obvious William was smitten by Georgina Prosser — a fact Joseph thought her father had not yet detected. It took every ounce of his being to be polite to Ellis Prosser but Joseph did it for his son. Georgina might be Ellis's daughter but from the few times he'd met her he'd seen none of the brash aggrandisement and bigotry exhibited by her father. There were few enough young women for William to meet. A short walk alone with Georgina Prosser would be good for him.

Robert brought the water, gave his father a petulant look then saw to the horses.

Ellis continued to mop at his face. "Yes, I think I could do with a sit in the shade. The damned weather is out of kilter. We have cold autumn nights and yet still the heat of early summer during the day."

Ellis settled himself on a flat part of the ridge and Joseph offered him a mug of water. He took a mouthful and wiped his hand across the back of his mouth. "She looks like a man," he snarled. "I knew nothing good would come of this giving women the right to vote. I don't know what this state is coming to. The sooner we form a federal government and put paid to this nonsense the better. Next we know they'll be giving natives the vote."

Joseph swallowed the retort he wanted to make. For his son's sake he would keep the peace. Prosser was such an arrogant man he probably hadn't even thought that Joseph's wife, even though of age, could not vote with the other women because she was an Aborigine.

He tried a different approach. "Surely you're proud to be part of such a forward-thinking state as ours, Prosser. The other states will have to follow suit now."

Prosser harrumphed and continued to glare down the slope.

Joseph followed the progress of his son and Prosser's daughter as they reached the plain and walked on steadily, side by side with an appropriate distance between them. Prosser was right about one thing. Even though her figure was shapely, from the distance and wearing trousers, Georgina could easily be mistaken for a man. However, he doubted that had any connection to her new ability to cast her vote.

"She must be a comfort to you." Joseph did not like Ellis Prosser but he felt a sudden empathy for the father whose two sons had died, one from a native spear wound and the other from typhus on the Teetulpa goldfields. Joseph's first wife had died during childbirth, the baby with her; he understood grief and loss.

"She is." Ellis turned his crevice-lined face to Joseph. "And yet I must send her away."

Joseph inspected his neighbour. "Why?"

Instead of sorrow Ellis's face was twisted in anger. "Because of your son." He spat the words. "I know what he's been up to. Coming around pretending an interest in cattle."

"Pretending!" Joseph's hand curled into a fist, his brief sympathy for his neighbour evaporated. He was aware of Robert moving in close beside him.

"Your gold money might indulge his fancy but I will not." Spittle formed on Ellis's lips. "I hear he's to live at Smith's Ridge now. Do you think my daughter can be bought with a few cattle and a shepherd's hut?"

"Shepherd's hut!" Anger burned inside Joseph with the heat of a summer sun. "Smith's Ridge is a suitable establishment for anyone my son chooses to ask to be his wife." Joseph pushed his face close to Prosser's. "But you can rest assured it wouldn't be the likes of your daughter he'd be asking for the hand of."

"He has been sniffing around her for years."

Joseph glared at Prosser. "He's not a dog."

"He's little better."

"You're the dog, you mongrel." He poked Prosser's barrel chest.

Prosser's lips twisted in an ugly grin. "I think that term is more apt for the brood you're raising with a black woman."

Joseph lifted his arm but Robert was beside him, holding him back. He was momentarily stunned by the strength of his son's grip.

Prosser struggled up, the colour deepening in his face again. The two men glared at each other. They were matched in height but Prosser had extra weight and was a good ten years older than Joseph.

"Get off my land, Prosser, and take your daughter with you. My son is far too good for the likes of her."

Ellis mopped at his crimson face once more. His shoulders drooped and he blew out a long breath. In that instant he looked every bit the miserable old man he was. "Georgina doesn't know but she and her mother leave for England to see family in a month. You keep your son away from Prosser's Run until they're gone."

Joseph felt a wave of sadness for William. Still, it would be for the best. "My son will be all the better without the distraction."

Prosser waved a hand at Robert. "Bring our horses, boy."

Joseph shook his head. "You are our guest but you lack any sense of common courtesy. The horses are tethered but a few steps behind you. Get them yourself." He turned on his heel, afraid if he stayed a moment longer he would punch Ellis Prosser on his big fat nose.

"They look strong and healthy." Georgina paused to look over several cows munching contentedly on the long grass nearby. She looked back at William and a smile lifted her lips. "As you say, time on good pasture will soon fatten them up."

William glanced up the hill to their fathers. "Looks like movement up there. Your father will be wanting you to leave soon."

"He's been almost melancholy of late." Georgina cast her gaze up the hill like William had. "He wanted me to come with him so we could spend some time looking over our own property. We've left a spare horse and supplies back at our first waterhole. We are to camp out three nights. That was how I got him to let me wear these trousers."

William was standing only two feet from Georgina and he liked what he saw. "It makes better sense than skirts."

Georgina laughed. The merry sound sent a warm tingle through William's chest.

"I'm glad you approve."

"Millie used to wear trousers when she worked with father but with the little children and another on the way she tends to stay more at the house these days."

"I envy your big family."

"Really?" William studied her for any sign of teasing.

"It can be so quiet at our house. I miss the noise of my brothers and, though I can't believe I'm saying it, their teasing."

"Perhaps you'll have your own big family one day."

"Perhaps." The wistful look left her face and her eyes sparkled. "But I wouldn't want to become housebound like your poor stepmother."

William's chest filled with longing. He itched to take her hand, pull her close, tell her how he felt, but with her father so near there was no way he could attempt it. It wasn't as if he'd never held a woman in his arms or even kissed one for that matter, but none of them had sparked the desire Georgina did. He loved her. He was quite sure of that. He'd harboured this feeling for so long even before he understood what it was.

Georgina glanced once more up the hill, flipped her hand as if brushing at a fly and knocked her hat from her head. Immediately William bent down to pick it up. She bent too, her hand went over the top of his and he felt a warm tingle as her lips brushed his cheek. He reached for her but she stood up and stepped back. A cheeky smile lit up her face.

"What game are you playing, Georgina?"

"It's not a game." She pushed her hat firmly back on her head. "I've been wanting to do that for a long time but we never get the chance to be alone."

William's heart thumped in his chest. "Do you truly mean that?"

"I never say anything I don't mean."

"Georgina!" She looked around, startled by her father's call.

Ellis Prosser was marching down the hill, leading their two horses.

"Damn it, Georgina." The frustration William felt at not being able to follow up that kiss and the thunderous look on Ellis's face strung him as tight as a piece of fencing wire. He scowled at her.

"It's only the thought of your father hanging me up from the nearest tree that stops me from taking you in my arms right now."

"Time to go," Ellis bellowed.

William had time to give her one last longing look before her father was beside them, thrusting the reins of her horse towards her.

Ellis helped Georgina up then heaved himself up onto his saddle and glared down at William. "There will be no further need for you to visit Prosser's Run."

William blanched. Had Ellis seen Georgina's kiss?

"I've done all I can for you." Ellis wheeled his horse around. It snorted and pranced. "Keep your cattle well maintained and away from mine." He flicked the reins and his horse sprang away. "Come along, Georgina."

William risked stepping up to her. "We must meet again."

"Soon." Once more she gave him a cheeky grin. "I'll send word." Then she too urged her horse on after her father.

William watched, hands on hips, until they disappeared from his sight among the trees along the creek. He couldn't believe it. It appeared Georgina truly returned his affection: a thought that would buoy him until they could meet again. He grinned. Then he would give her a kiss she'd never forget.

Four

Charles Wiltshire scowled at the baby his mother held proudly in her arms. It was tightly wrapped in a soft white blanket; the only thing showing was the sleeping face with a wisp of hair across its forehead.

"Meet your sister, darling." His mother glanced up briefly then cast her adoring gaze back over the baby.

Charles had been surprised by his mother's appearance. She had been rotund and puffy before she'd left Hawker to travel to Adelaide for the last few months of her confinement. The baby was now a month old and his mother's face still looked puffy and pale in spite of the face powder she'd applied. Her dress was not fitted but flowed loosely around her.

"Laura Florence Harriet Wiltshire." His father spoke with reverence. "So clever, my dearest." He placed a hand on Catherine's shoulder.

Charles was already tired of the fuss being made of the tiny snippet of life. "Why does she need such a long name?" He only had one extra name. He was simply Charles Henry after his mother's grandfather and his father.

"She's named after both of her grandmothers," his grandmother Hallet said proudly. "Florence after me and Harriet after your other grandmother. Such an honour."

All three adults bent over the baby. Charles stepped away and looked out of the large arch windows that graced the front of his grandparents' house. He cast his gaze across the sand dunes to the sea. It was a warm afternoon for April — perhaps he could swim while they were staying there. Most of his trips to Adelaide to stay at his grandparents' Glenelg home had been over summer and he'd learned to enjoy the ocean. His mother detested the summer in Hawker so he'd often spent a few weeks after Christmas at the coast. This year his mother had travelled alone to have the baby and he had stayed back in Hawker with his father. It hadn't bothered him. Even though it was often cooler at Glenelg and there was the lure of the ocean, he'd much prefer to help his father with business than spend his time with his mother. At fourteen Charles did not enjoy the fussing and commotion and giggling that went with a female household. Perhaps it was why his grandfather stayed away.

"Would you like some nice cool lemonade, Master Charles?" His grandmother's housekeeper had come to stand beside him with a tray.

"Thank you, Mrs Phillips."

She smiled at him. "What do you think of your new sister?"

"She's a ... baby." Charles couldn't think of a polite word to use for the bundle his mother held.

"Another dear little girl." Mrs Phillips bustled off.

He took a sip of his drink and turned back to the view of the water. His father had said they would only stay a few days and they had yet to call on Grandmother Harriet. Charles was looking forward to that. She didn't fuss and she treated him like the adult he felt he was.

"How are you, my dearest?" Henry looked steadily at his wife. They were finally alone in the upstairs bedroom that was always ready for Catherine's visits. He laid a hand gently on her shoulder then pursed his lips as she shrank away from his touch.

"I am well enough, thank you, Henry." She tucked the baby into the cradle then sat in the rocking chair and fanned her face with her hand.

He bent over his daughter. Her little cheeks were a soft rose pink and her lips like perfect little buds. "She's beautiful."

"She is." Catherine let out a long audible sigh.

Henry yearned to pick up his daughter and hold her close but something about the way Catherine had placed her in the cradle and then tucked her firmly deterred him. He trailed one finger across the baby's soft cheek and her lips sucked in and out but she was otherwise still. "The baby is settling well?"

"She's contented enough."

"That's very good." Henry stood tall and once more studied his wife. It had been a long time since he'd seen her naked but he imagined her body beneath the layers of clothing would be flabby and soft. Not like the firm flesh of Flora Nixon. Henry hardened at the thought of their housekeeper. He hadn't been in her bed for some time either. He would have to rectify that as soon as they returned home.

Catherine put a hand to her forehead. "How long are you staying, Henry?"

"We shall spend two days here. I have some business to attend to and then we will all travel home to Hawker together."

Catherine's hand fell to her side and a frown creased her brow. "It's too soon. I am still exhausted."

"You said the baby was doing well."

"The birth was long and difficult. You know that I had rheumatic fever as a child and the doctor said my heart was not strong.

It is I who have not recovered. I wouldn't have managed without Mother and Mrs Phillips."

Henry clasped his hands to his sides. Catherine had been difficult to remove from Adelaide after Charles Henry's birth fourteen years earlier but she'd been young and inexperienced then.

"I will help you when we get home, and Mrs Nixon will be there."

A strange look passed over Catherine's face. Henry felt his chest constrict. Could she know?

"I need to stay here a little longer."

"Two more days."

"No, Henry. I mean a month or more. I need some rest and I won't get it at home even with Flora's help."

Henry looked down at Catherine. He was not going to have this again. "You will come home, Catherine." He went back to the cradle and carefully lifted the tiny bundle into his arms. She pursed her lips but her little eyes didn't open.

"What are you doing, Henry? You shouldn't pick up a sleeping baby."

"I wish to hold my daughter." He tore his gaze from the sweet little face. "She will be coming with Charles and me when we leave. If you wish to stay longer that is your choice but our son and our daughter will be going back to Hawker where they belong."

Catherine tilted her chin and glared at him. "How will you feed your daughter without me?"

"I will engage a wet nurse."

Her face fell and tears brimmed in her eyes. Henry was pleased to see her small attempt at defiance was short lived. He didn't want a stranger feeding and caring for his daughter but if that was what it took so be it.

Catherine flopped back against the chair and put a hand to her brow. "I can't be ready in two days."

"I am sure your mother and Mrs Phillips will help you and anything extra can be sent up on the train." He kissed his daughter's cheek and placed her back in the cradle. "Now that everything is settled I shall take a stroll to the hotel and enjoy the sea air while I can. Don't wait up for me, Catherine. I shall sleep in the spare room with Charles when I return. Good night."

Catherine stayed in her chair long after Henry's footsteps had faded down the stairs. How was she to face living in Hawker again? The extremes of summer heat and winter cold were bad enough but the dust and the flies and the rancid smells of the town were unbearable. Instead of growing accustomed to it she had come to detest it.

She looked towards the door Henry had closed gently on his way out. The tears that had threatened earlier rolled unchecked down her cheeks. She believed Henry when he said he would employ a wet nurse for their daughter. Since the birth of Charles she had endured miscarriage after miscarriage until for the last few years no baby at all had grown in her womb. Then just when she thought her child-bearing days were finally over, along came Laura.

To carry her daughter to full term Catherine had spent nearly the entire confinement in bed with the exception of the journey to Adelaide two months before the birth. She had also given up her tonic. Her doctor in Adelaide had been worried it was addictive and wasn't helping her confinement. She'd had a terrible time after that. The tonic had been the only way to deal with life in Hawker and if it hadn't been for living with her parents at Glenelg she might have gone quite out of her mind. Now the thought of returning made her heart race and her fingers tremble. Her mother knew she wanted to stay longer but would not openly take Catherine's side against Henry, and her father would agree her place was with her husband even if he didn't like her living in Hawker.

A sigh from the cradle drew her gaze. Catherine felt so much love for the tiny baby it was as if her heart would burst. Laura was a miracle, there was no denying it, and Catherine knew Henry was as delighted as she was to have a daughter. More than delighted: he was infatuated. How had she ever entertained the idea that he would allow them to stay longer in Adelaide? She gripped the padded arms of the old wooden rocker and tried her best to think rationally but like her legs, her mind felt unsteady.

She looked up at a sharp rap on the door. Charles pushed it open without waiting for her response. He crossed the room quickly with a brief sideways glance towards the cradle. He was as tall as Henry these days and looked so like his father, with his thick dark hair and deep brown eyes. He also had a good dose of Henry's confidence with the added brashness of immaturity.

He bent and brushed a brief kiss across her cheek. "Good night, Mother."

"Good night, Charles." She put a hand on his arm but he pulled away and was gone as swiftly as he'd entered.

Catherine closed her eyes. She felt as if her son was lost to her, in the same way that Henry was. He'd grown up so quickly. There were many times over the years when she'd taken to her bed for weeks at a time after the loss of yet another baby or simply from the weight of the melancholy that sometimes overwhelmed her. These days Charles needed her for nothing but her housekeeping skills and even they were not required. Flora Nixon provided that service, just as she did many other things in the Wiltshire household.

Catherine pondered on Flora, who was her dear friend more than she was a housekeeper. They had become close over the years. Flora understood her needs. As Catherine had discovered she also understood Henry's. She'd heard them together one night in the spare bedroom when she hadn't been able to sleep. It had been a shock at first and then a relief. If Henry was with Flora he did not often hanker for his wife's body. Thankfully Flora's children had grown and moved away and her husband hadn't shown up for years. Henry had taken to visiting Flora in her cottage next door. It was a better outcome for all of them.

Catherine had wondered why Flora allowed him to use her so. The woman could have flaunted it but there was nothing about her manner that alluded to the fact that she shared her master's bed. Neither did she act ashamed or subservient. Catherine wanted to ask but that would have opened up a knowledge that was best kept quiet. Flora was a capable housekeeper as well as her dear friend; to lose her would be a terrible blow from which Catherine could not see a way to recover. She did wonder how long Henry had been bedding her. When Catherine thought about it he'd rarely visited her bed for years. It made Laura even more of a miracle, but now she was finally here Catherine would not entertain the idea of ever having another child.

When the doctor had insisted she give up her tonic she'd been in a constant state of agitation. It had taken some time for the longing to fade away. If she went back to Hawker she didn't know if she'd have the strength to get through the days again without it.

Laura snuffled and gave some soft cries. She was no doubt hungry. Catherine rose and tended to her daughter. She watched her delicate mouth and her fluttering eyelids; one tiny hand gripped the soft flesh of her breast. There was nothing more precious. Catherine had loved Charles, she still did, but he no longer needed her; neither did Henry.

Once more she considered the idea she'd had since her daughter's birth that Henry would let them live in Adelaide and simply visit from time to time — after seeing him with their daughter she knew that would not be the case. He might give up his wife perhaps, but not his child. He'd had the same possessive reaction with Charles. Henry had gradually taken her son from her. Catherine would not allow him to take her daughter.

She lifted the sated baby from her breast and placed her on her shoulder. Laura's soft breath blew against her cheek. Catherine leaned back in the chair. She would have to return to Hawker for the time or it would cause a scene, but she would go on her terms. She had no desire to expose the scandalous life her husband lived but it was the only bargaining power she had. She must tackle him now, this very night, before her resolve left her altogether.

Feeling stronger for having made a decision, she placed the baby back in the cradle, changed into her nightgown and sat in the chair waiting for the sounds of Henry's return. As she had suspected he hadn't been able to resist checking on the baby. The creak of the door woke her from her doze as Henry opened it and stepped inside. She hadn't drawn the curtains and the silvery moon afforded some light through the window. Her eyes followed his movements. He bent and kissed his sleeping daughter.

"She's perfect in every way."

Henry's head flew up at the sound of Catherine's voice. "What are you doing sitting there in the dark?"

She took her time lighting the lamp she had left on the table beside her. "I need to talk to you, Henry."

"Surely it could wait until morning. It's late." He turned towards the door.

"We must talk now, Henry."

He was obviously confused by the determined tone of her voice. He hesitated at the door. "I'm sure anything you have to say can be said in the fresh light of day. We don't want to wake the baby."

"She won't wake." Catherine glanced at the cradle. "She sleeps very well."

"I'm tired, Catherine."

She took a deep breath as he reached the door. "So am I, Henry, but I am sure you won't wish to discuss the details of your arrangements with our housekeeper over breakfast with my parents."

Henry's head went up and his back stiffened. He let go of the door handle. The shock she saw in his eyes as he turned gave her some small satisfaction.

He opened his mouth to speak but she rose from her chair and held one hand up to stop him.

"Please don't deny it, Henry. Did you think I was so stupid as not to know about your time in Flora's bed?"

"It was only ... I —"

"Don't waste your breath with excuses. I have endured your adulterous behaviour because of our son and my family's reputation. Besides, it meant you were not bothering me with your ..." she shuddered "... grabbing hands and pathetic kisses and your ..." She waved in the direction of that part of his anatomy she never wished to be near again.

Henry gaped at her.

Now that she'd said her piece Catherine's strength deserted her. Her legs shook and she lowered herself back into the chair. In the silence that followed the only sound was the hiss of the lamp and a loud sigh from Laura.

Henry moved closer to the cradle and looked from Catherine to the baby. "What do you propose to do?" His voice came out in a whisper. Catherine could see the anguish on his face as he studied their daughter.

Her heart beat quickly and tears pricked her eyes. She had to get it all out before her courage deserted her completely. "I would happily leave you, Henry, but I cannot bear the thought of the stain that would mark our children's lives."

He strode across the room, kneeled before her and took her hands in his. "I won't visit Flora again. You and I will be strong together. I need you, Catherine."

She looked down at the man she had once loved and felt nothing but revulsion. She extricated her hands from his. "How could you?"

He dropped his head and shook it slowly. "I have needs and you didn't always want —"

"Don't you blame your weakness on me," she snapped. "How many times have I been with child to give you the children you wanted? How many times did I endure the loss of those babies and the discomforts that brought to my body? And where were you, Henry? Consoling yourself with our housekeeper."

He lifted his head quickly. His dark eyes studied her with a brooding look. "What is it you want, Catherine?"

She held her nerve and looked him in the eye. "To raise my children here, at Glenelg, without you."

"But you said —"

"I cannot have what I want." She cut him off and looked longingly towards the cradle. "It would not be fair to the children. They need a mother and a father." She dragged her gaze back to Henry. "And no scandal."

"I shall end it with Flora and dismiss her."

Catherine pushed him away and rose to her feet as he struggled to keep his balance. "You will not. Flora is my dear friend. I will not speak of this with her — though I need your assurance that you do not force her." She took in a deep breath, closed her eyes then opened them to look Henry in the eye as he scrambled to his feet. "She comes to you from," she swallowed her distaste, "mutual need?" Catherine clasped her hands tightly. She did not want to lose Flora's help and friendship but neither could she abide it if her friend was being forced.

"On my child's life I have never taken Flora against her will. At first she did want extra money ... for her children but now ..."

"That is enough." Catherine closed her eyes and put a hand to her mouth. She must enjoy Henry's attention. Catherine's heart quickened again, remembering an oh-so-brief time when she had too. A small gasp erupted from her lips. She clutched the fabric of her nightgown.

Henry watched her like a man watching a snake.

"You will continue to be discreet with your visits. You will not tell Flora I know about your liaisons and we will never speak of it again." She lifted her chin. "I will return with you to Hawker —"

"Very sensible of you, Catherine." Henry reached for her hands but she batted him away.

"But!" She held up a finger. "You will allow me to visit my family more regularly and stay as long as I like."

He nodded eagerly. "I don't have to be with Flora."

"Yes you must or she will wonder why. Flora must never know that I know about your ... I could not endure it then."

"I do not want to end our marriage." His look was contrite. "It will be as you say."

"I know what matters to you, Henry. Provided you keep your part of the bargain I will always return to Hawker, raise your children, entertain your guests and continue to be the picture of a perfect wife." She lifted her chin even higher and looked down her nose at him. "As I have always endeavoured to be. Do I have your word?"

He licked his lips. "Of course."

"Now leave me please. I shall attempt to get some sleep."

Henry held her gaze but said nothing. He turned abruptly on his heel, kissed his daughter once more and left the room, closing the door quietly behind him.

Catherine pressed her lips together but the shuddering sobs she tried to hold back burst forth, shaking her whole body and forcing her to take refuge in her chair. She had only ever wanted a simple life: surely that had not been too much to ask?

Five

May 1896

"What a fine spread, Henry." Ellis Prosser brushed sausage-roll crumbs from his shirt. "And in honour of a beautiful healthy daughter. Catherine has done you proud. You chose very wisely with your wife. You're a lucky man."

"Indeed." Henry looked over the table laden with food to where his wife sat on a delicate brocade chair holding their newly christened daughter. Several women, including Prosser's wife, Johanna, fussed over them.

Henry puffed out his chest. Even though he had wanted several children, he would have to be content with just the two, a fact he'd come to terms with. He had a good-looking wife who raised them well, managed his home splendidly and turned a blind eye to his mistress. Flora Nixon was handing around a tray of sweet cakes. He cast a quick look in her direction. Yes indeed he was a lucky man. He would love to explain to Prosser just how lucky but that was a secret Henry must keep.

"My family will miss your wife and daughter." Henry gestured to where Charles was talking with Georgina Prosser. "How long will they be away for?"

"The Orient liner leaves Adelaide next week and they will be aboard. I am told the journey takes as long as six weeks. They will stay with Johanna's family near London then move on to Europe. They haven't booked the return journey yet but I imagine they will be gone at least a year."

"That is a long time to be away from you and their home."

"It's for the best. My sons are both dead and, while Georgina has her heart set on taking over the property one day, her mother wants her to have more refined influences." Ellis looked to his wife, his craggy features softened. "Johanna married me not long after stepping off the boat from England. She's adapted to life here very well. We've made our fortune these last few years but she wants to visit her family. I cannot deny her some small reward for her support."

"How will you manage?"

"Hmph!" Prosser picked up his teacup and swallowed the contents. "My manager's wife, Mrs Donovan, will look after me and the house well enough in their absence. Besides, I also think it would be wise for Georgina to travel, expand her horizons." Prosser leaned in closer. "You've heard that young Baker has moved to Smith's Ridge?"

"I had, yes." Henry took a sip from the cup of tea he held and wished it was something stronger. Smith's Ridge held nothing but bad memories for him. He had been glad to hand the lease over to the Bakers but since they had taken it back they had prospered and that irked him. "I also heard he's stocking it with cattle."

"Yes. The young pup spent time with me learning all he could about cattle, or so he said, but he had an ulterior motive."

Henry raised his eyebrows and waited.

"He's been chasing after Georgina."

"What?" Henry's cup slammed back on its delicate saucer. William Baker had grown into a strong, good-looking man with money behind him, but that could not make up for his father taking a black woman as his wife and breeding mixed-race siblings. Henry glanced across at Charles, who sat awkwardly next to Georgina, neither of them speaking. "Surely you wouldn't allow that."

"Of course not. Johanna has been nagging me for years to take Georgina on a tour overseas. The time is suddenly right." Ellis raised his shaggy eyebrows. "If you get my meaning."

"I do."

"Who knows who she may meet on her travels? Whoever he is he'd better be a lot worthier than that Baker pup."

Henry took another sip of tea and looked over at his son again. Charles would be another year older by the time Georgina returned. Still far too young for marriage, but if she didn't find a husband overseas — well who knew what the future might hold?

"Why do you keep looking out the window?" Charles had been watching Georgina twist her head towards the glass at regular intervals. "Are you expecting someone?"

"No." She put her cup and saucer on the side table and brushed at her skirt. "But don't you find all this fussing over a baby claustrophobic?"

"I do." Charles had been trying valiantly to think of something interesting to talk to Georgina about. Maybe if they were away from the adults their conversation would flow better. "Would you like to take a stroll in the garden?"

"I'd like that." Georgina rose from her chair with a speed that startled him. "I'll tell Mother."

Charles was surprised there was little objection from the adults, other than asking them to stay in the house grounds. Then again he was several years Georgina's junior. No doubt they thought of him as a child rather than a possible suitor. Charles gave a secret grin. He'd already tested his manhood with the girl from the bakery. After the first time when they'd been awkward and Charles had failed miserably to perform, he'd made up for it and they'd both enjoyed their fun in the stables at the back of the bakery. Unfortunately that had come to an end recently when the young lady had been sent to work at her uncle's bakery in Quorn. Charles would need to find someone else as accommodating to his needs.

He helped Georgina into her soft velvet coat before shrugging on his own; the day was chilly. He held open the door to let her pass. Her emerald green skirt rustled softly and the faint scent of violets accompanied her. Charles closed the door firmly. He might be Georgina's junior in years but he was more experienced, he was sure. Charles would bide his time and one day Georgina would be his wife.

"What are you doing?" She shook his guiding hand from her elbow as they made their way across the front verandah.

Charles dropped his arm quickly. He would have to remember Georgina was not a simpering woman like his mother. "Watch your footing on the path," he said to cover his mistake. "It's uneven here. Father has plans to make a curved drive around the front so carriages can pull up right at the front door."

Georgina ignored him and made straight for the front gate, where she stopped and looked up and down the street.

Charles faltered. "We should stay in the yard."

She smirked at him. "We're hardly little children, Charles. Where's the harm in a turn around the block?"

"It could rain." He cast his gaze skywards at the grey clouds.

"Stay here if you like." She stepped through the gate. "I'm going for a walk."

Charles looked back over his shoulder. Their parents would expect him to accompany her, so he followed her out onto the path. No-one would even know they were gone anyway. 'Footpath' was a loose term for the uneven surface that had been built up along the front of the houses in the street but he was quickly at Georgina's side.

"Where do you want to go?"

"Just for a walk."

He tried to think of ways to keep up a conversation. "I am to go to Adelaide to school next year. Father says I need something to round off the mix of lessons from Mother and my local tutor."

"I didn't enjoy school in Adelaide. I'd much prefer to have had lessons at home."

"Will you miss this when you're away?"

She gave him a sideways glance. He was tall for his age and they were matched in height. "Not Hawker, but I will miss Prosser's Run." She kept moving forward at a pace, her gaze focused ahead again.

"Imagine all the sights you'll see."

"I can't imagine anything more beautiful than the country right here." She stopped and looked at him. Her breath came fast from walking swiftly; her lips were deep pink and slightly parted, her green eyes were bright and her coppery red hair, loose today, flowed over her shoulders in waving curls. She was the prettiest girl in the district by far. Charles shifted uncomfortably as he felt a surge of desire. She moved off again and he followed.

Georgina continued to talk. "The towering trees along the creeks, the deep reds and tans of the rocks and the brown water roaring after a heavy downpour. The scent of eucalypt on a warm day and the sharp smell of wattle in the spring. The sounds of the birds and then the complete quiet of the night. A summer wind that almost singes your eyebrows with its burning breath and a winter chill so cold the water freezes in the bucket. Mountains that change colour with the time of day and the seasons." She had turned in the direction of the range to the north as she'd spoken. Now she looked back at him in puzzlement. "How can there be anything more beautiful than that?"

Charles didn't know what to say. Trees were trees, rocks were rocks — he'd never thought of them in the way her words described. Perhaps here was a way to connect with Georgina.

"It's hard to imagine there might be," he said. "I wish I lived out of town. The country is much nicer."

Georgina spun around at the sound of hooves. A man rode towards them on a horse and lifted his hat.

"Good day to you, Miss Prosser."

Charles frowned as the rider slid from his horse then turned to face them.

"And to you, Charles."

It was William Baker of all people. Charles inclined his head briefly in reply, annoyed his time alone with Georgina had been interrupted.

"Where are you off to?" William kept his gaze on Georgina.

"We were just out for a walk to take some fresh air. The house was stuffy, wasn't it, Charles?" She asked him the question but she was looking at Baker.

"May I join you?"

Before Charles could object Georgina spoke up. "Of course."

Baker tethered his horse at a post and Charles was astonished to see Georgina slip her hand around the arm he offered.

"I was just lamenting how much I will miss the country while I'm away."

They walked on, Georgina and William chatting as if Charles were not there. Light rain began to fall. Charles stopped but the other two kept walking, engrossed in their conversation.

"I'm going to the house," he called after them.

They paused, looking back at him as if they'd just remembered he was there. A small frown creased Georgina's brow. "It's only a little rain."

Charles puffed out his chest. "It's not the rain." He was not continuing to play the part of a gooseberry and he was very sure Georgina's father would not approve of this chance meeting.

William leaned in closer to her and said something Charles couldn't hear. She looked at Charles with a bright smile on her face. "Would you be a dear and wait for me on the verandah? We can go back inside together. William and I won't be much longer."

Charles pursed his lips. She was using him and it was that smug William Baker who had put her up to it. They were sadly mistaken if they thought Charles was going to be anybody's fool. Georgina may be infatuated by the older charm of William Baker but he was no contender for her hand. Charles would make sure of that. He knew his father would not be pleased to see her walking with Baker and he was sure Ellis Prosser would feel the same ire. He turned on his heel and marched back towards his own street.

William watched Charles stalk off around the corner then he drew Georgina down a small lane between two houses.

"You shouldn't have let him go." He gazed into her sparkling green eyes. "He will no doubt go running straight to your father."

"I don't care." Her look hardened, full of defiance. "We have such a short time together and then I will be gone for nearly a year. I'm so glad you got my message to meet me here. We leave on tomorrow's train."

William saw her lips move towards him but this time he was ready. There was no need for words. He took her in his arms and pushed his lips against hers, relishing the softness of her flesh and enjoying the frisson of excitement it sent through him. His arms pulled her close and she melded against him. He savoured the taste of her, the brush of her hair on his cheek and the faint scent of violets; it felt so right having her in his arms after all this time. Finally, their lips parted. He could see the heightened pink of her cheeks, hear her quick short breaths. She surely felt the same thrill as he did. The rain grew heavier. He pushed her back against a wall and pulled his coat up to cover their heads.

"I can't wait a whole year to be with you." Her words came out urgently between short breaths. Her warm body was pressed against his.

"It won't be easy. But when you come back you'll need no-one's permission to marry."

Her eyes widened. "Marry?"

"I want to marry you, Georgina Prosser. I don't think your father will give his permission so you must be of age."

"You're very confident." Her lips turned up in a mischievous grin. "We've hardly spent any time together."

"You've known me for years. I'm sure we are meant for each other." He lowered his coat and shrugged it back around his shoulders. The rain had stopped as quickly as it began. He gripped her hands tightly and pulled them to his chest. "Surely you feel it too."

The smile left her face to be replaced by an earnest look. He felt the regard of her green eyes keenly, as if they could see inside him. She dipped her head and once more he kissed her.

When next they stopped for breath he eased her away a little. He wanted far more than to kiss Georgina Prosser but he was wise enough to know that could not be until they were man and wife.

"I must take you back before Charles alerts everyone to your absence."

Georgina brushed her lips across his cheek. "I love you, William Baker."

He tucked her hand into his arm and patted it. He felt he would burst from happiness and yet at the same time he despaired at the thought of their forthcoming separation.

"A year is not so long," he said bravely.

She pulled him up at the corner of the Wiltshires' street and turned worried eyes to his. "So much can happen in a year. You won't forget your promise to marry me?"

"Of course not."

They stepped around the corner, walking side by side but with an arm's length between them. Already William felt empty without her touch. His step slowed as Ellis Prosser burst onto the path outside the Wiltshires' gate. He was looking the other way but turned as they approached. Another shower of rain began to fall.

"What the devil do you think you're doing?" He glanced back over their shoulders then back behind him. "How dare you disgrace my daughter, Baker?"

"We were walking and taking in some fresh air, Father."

Prosser reached for Georgina as they drew near and hustled her through the gate. "Go inside quickly before anyone sees you. Thank goodness young Charles had the foresight to speak with me discreetly or everyone would know about your ..." Prosser's ruddy cheeks went a deeper red. He pursed his lips and glared at William.

"We were only walking, as Georgina said, Mr Prosser." William lied to protect Georgina. He cared little for what Ellis Prosser thought of him. "There were three of us but Charles made for home before we could accompany him."

"Save your breath, Baker." Prosser drew himself up. William wasn't sure if he'd be stupid enough to swing a punch in the

Wiltshires' front garden but he was ready just in case. "I told you to leave my daughter alone."

"You're being very melodramatic, Father. Charles and I were out for a walk and we ran into William." Georgina tried to distract him. "Have they cut the cake yet?"

Prosser's shoulders eased but he didn't shift his simmering glare from William. "You're never to see my daughter again." He poked William in the chest with his finger then spun on his heel and put his hand to his daughter's elbow. "Come inside, Georgina. Just as well you're leaving tomorrow. I can't believe you were a part of such ridiculous behaviour." Prosser marched her to the verandah. She twisted her head back to give William one last smile.

"Georgina, wait." He dug in his pocket and pulled out the emerald green ribbon he'd bought for her many years ago. He held it out. "This is for you, until we meet again."

She moved as if to come back to him but her father tugged at her arm and drew her inside. William watched in despair, his eyes on the closing door. He didn't see the movement from his right. Something hard connected with the side of his face, spinning him back through the gate and onto the muddy path, where he dropped Georgina's ribbon. He looked up at the smug face of Charles Wiltshire standing over him.

William frowned and put a hand to his jaw. He couldn't believe the boy had dealt such a heavy blow but he had size on his side and William hadn't seen him coming.

"Get back to the bush," Charles snarled. "You don't belong with decent folk." He ground his boot into the ribbon, covering it in mud.

William struggled to his feet but Charles hurried away.

"It's easy to take a fellow by surprise," William called after him. "One day you can face me like a man and we'll see how well you do."

Charles gave William one last withering look from the safety of the verandah. William took a step towards him and was rewarded with a worried look from the boy, who hurried inside and closed the door with a thud.

William bent to retrieve the ribbon. One end was muddied but he slipped it into his pocket. It was same beautiful green as Georgina's skirt and was the only thing he had to remind him of her.

Six

September 1896

"Don't bother Grandpa, Beth."

Thomas looked into the deep brown eyes of the little girl clasping his hand, hoisted her to his lap and kissed the top of her head. Her thick curls gleamed the colour of dark molasses. She was the oldest of Joseph and Millie's three children and although he wouldn't admit it, his favourite. Born the year after his dear Lizzie died and named Elizabeth in her honour, the honey-skinned baby had been his constant companion from the time she was old enough to be taken on walks. Now as a seven-year-old she was still his shadow, and slipped onto his lap for a chat or a cuddle whenever she got the chance. Her sister Ruth was a few years younger and was a replica of her older sister except for the pale yellow of her hair and her shy manner.

Thomas smiled up at his daughter-in-law. Her deep brown eyes sparkled and a protective hand rested on the baby strapped to her chest. "She's not bothering me," he said. "The children are my greatest joy; you know that."

Millie's smile widened; she gave him a grateful nod and moved back to the bench beside the large fireplace, where Violet and Esther were helping prepare the food. Thomas was so happy his son's older daughters had made the journey to be with them.

The delicious smell of roast mutton permeated the air of the kitchen, which was large by anyone's standards. There was plenty of room for the table as well as a stove and workbenches, and it even boasted a tap fed by a tank on the hill above. High over their heads was a ceiling of pressed tin and beyond that the corrugated iron roof raised to a high pitch far above. The kitchen took up one back corner of the house, which was made of stone Joseph and William had gathered. The back wall was butted against the side of the hill. Two of the other walls separated the kitchen from the washroom and a bedroom. Only one wall faced outside, with a large window, and a wide verandah stretched beyond it. This room would always be a cool part of the house during the heat of summer.

Thomas looked down the long kitchen table. On one of the benches running either side sat William and Robert with Ruth between them. At the opposite end of the table in the other chair, Joseph smiled proudly. His new house was finished at last. It had been years in the making and, though not quite as big as he had originally planned, it was a fine house. The kitchen was large and easily held room for preparation and a table for eating. Joseph had included a dining room but it was not furnished yet.

Millie unstrapped the baby and tucked him into the basket in the corner of the big room under the large glass window. The baby was the reason for the gathering. Matthew was but a few weeks old and the Bakers had gathered to celebrate his birth.

"Come and sit on the bench beside me, Beth." Esther indicated the space beside Robert and put a plate with a decorated meat terrine in front of Thomas as Beth slid from his lap. "Start with this, Grandpa. Millie made it and it's delicious."

"Grace first, Esther." Thomas cast his gaze around his family gathered at the table. The last few years had been good to them. He was worried they faced a tough time again but he didn't want to spoil the day with talk of drought. "We have much to be thankful for."

Once he had finished, they all tried the cold rabbit terrine and the vegetable tart Millie had made before they began on the roast meat and vegetables.

There was much admiration for Millie's cooking. It was certainly one of her many talents. Thomas felt the belt pulled tight around his waist. Since Violet and Esther had left Wildu Creek, Millie had made it her business to make sure he was well fed, as did Eliza. He wasn't complaining but he didn't work as physically hard as he once had. He would soon need to have his trousers let out if he continued to eat every morsel they put in front of him.

"That was delicious, Millie." Violet waved a hand over the now empty terrine plate. "You will have to tell me how you made it."

"And me." Esther added her voice. "I am so sick of rabbit. Edward brings a couple home each day."

"My last gift from Isaac was a pair of laying hens."

The two sisters chuckled.

"You both should be grateful you've married such good providers." Thomas raised his eyebrows. "Others aren't so lucky."

"I didn't marry Edward for his rabbit supply."

"Esther." Violet blushed.

"Don't look so shocked, Violet. I love Edward; that's why I married him." Esther turned her innocent gaze on her sister. "Whatever were you thinking I meant?"

Joseph cleared his throat. "How is Edward since his fall?"

"He's recovered well." Esther's haughty look softened — an accident had nearly claimed her husband before she'd been married a year. "One broken arm and a lot of aches and pains but he was lucky. The gash in his forehead has healed well." She grinned. "It gives him a rugged look."

Both young women had married the year before, Violet to a wool merchant in Port Augusta and Esther to the youngest son of a pastoralist in country north of Hawker. They'd made the trip home to Wildu Creek for this special occasion.

Thomas sat back. Easy conversation and laughter echoed around the table. His stomach was full of delicious food and there was much to be thankful for but it was times like this he missed his dear Lizzie the most.

While the women gathered the plates and cleared up, the conversation around the table turned to a discussion about stock, as Thomas had known it would.

"You have concerns we're overstocked, Father?"

Thomas looked at his only son. Joseph's face was showing the signs of constant work outside in the harsh elements of the Flinders Ranges and yet the lines always made him look like he was smiling rather than weary. After the loss of his first wife, Millie had made him a happy man again.

"I know it's too early to be sure but if this heat continues and we don't get rain we will have little feed for a base mob let alone the huge numbers we have now."

"How are things looking at Smith's Ridge, William?"

"Worse than here. There's little on the plains and slopes for the cattle. I will need to move them to the higher country where there's more natural water, but I've still got sheep up there. Hegarty thinks we should sell them and keep to the cattle."

"What do you think?" Thomas sat back in his chair to ease the ache in his rear end as he asked the question of his grandson. William had absorbed so much in his twenty-one years. He was quick to learn when it came to dealing with animals and he had a natural affinity with the land. He was more level headed than Joseph had been at his age.

"I agree with him. We don't want the lower country to be entirely eaten out and cattle aren't so tough on the vegetation. They will look after themselves better in the higher country. There are some natural springs there."

"My people rely on them."

Binda rarely spoke out when there was a large family group gathered. Thomas saw the look of concern that passed between Joseph and his friend.

"You know we would never allow stock into the top spring." Joseph turned back to his son. "In any case you can't get stock near it. It's inaccessible and if you cleared a way in you would ruin it, and therefore all the downstream pools as well. Not to mention there would be nowhere left for Binda and Millie's family."

Thomas looked around the table at the faces studying William, some with trepidation, some with annoyance. The young man was smart. Thomas could tell he had an idea.

"What are you thinking, William?"

William gave his grandfather a small smile. "I think we should destock as we've discussed. More if the drought does set in — perhaps keep only a few hundred cattle at Smith's Ridge and a similar number of sheep here at Wildu Creek."

Thomas sat back and thrummed his fingers on his stomach. "Thank goodness every house has large tanks now. The last drought left us with barely enough water for ourselves let alone keeping stock alive."

"Both properties have natural springs. Wildu Creek more than Smith's Ridge."

Joseph shook his head. "In country difficult for stock to access."

Binda's wife, Jundala, had been helping in the kitchen. She came to stand behind her husband and muttered something in his ear. He put up his hand in a cautionary manner. She said nothing more but remained where she was, her face turned to the window.

"What if we could redirect the water?"

"What do you mean redirect?" Joseph frowned at his son.

William stood up and went to the window. "We collect the rain that falls on this roof via gutters to the tank and then it flows back down the hill to the tap." He flung his hand in the direction of the tap that protruded from the wall over a large basin where Millie had just finished washing the dishes. "We could do the same kind of thing from the springs. Channel the water to where the stock can reach it."

Thomas recalled the first water trap he had made all those years ago to collect water from the creek near his camp. It had taken a lot of trial and error. His first attempt had been washed away but he'd managed to create a sturdy stage from which he could fill the water barrels. That had lasted several seasons. He felt a surge of pride at William's ingenuity.

"How would you do it?" Joseph asked.

"A series of wooden channels."

"It would be a lot of work."

"What else have we to do but to watch our stock die?"

"It would take the water from my family." They all looked at Binda. His voice was low and his dark brown eyes held a depth of sadness. Jundala put a hand on his shoulder. She spoke several words Thomas couldn't understand but the tone was enough for him to know she was angry. The room fell silent. Even the two little girls stopped their chatter. Tension spread between them, so taut that Thomas felt if he spoke they would all fall apart.

The atmosphere in his new home was suddenly electric. Joseph saw the glare Millie cast her sister-in-law. He glanced at Binda but his friend wouldn't meet his look.

"This is not the time to talk of such things." Millie's voice was sharp as she looked from Binda to Jundala.

Jundala let fly with a torrent of words quick and fast — and full of venom, by the look on her face. Binda stood as Millie replied with equal force. Joseph understood enough of her language to know that what she called her sister-in-law was not good.

Jundala opened her mouth but Binda silenced her with a sharp word.

Once more a quiet fell on the room, thick with unease.

"We wouldn't take all the water." William broke the silence. "It's only an idea, Uncle Binda."

Jundala murmured something and Binda shook his head.

"The idea might have some merit." Joseph thought it time to add his piece. "I wouldn't advise doing anything without planning and of course we wouldn't see your people left without water, Binda."

"Your father's right," Thomas said. "It's an interesting idea, William, but not one to be rushed into."

"We can think on it." Joseph looked from his son to Binda. His friend still didn't meet his gaze. "There's work to be done," he continued. "For the time we will move the Smith's Ridge sheep here for shearing and then decide which we will take south for sale."

"Anyway, what do I know?" Thomas too looked sad. "A man who's lived in this country only forty years. I could be wrong about the dry. Maybe it will rain tomorrow."

"Oh Grandpa." Violet put her arms around his neck and kissed his cheek. "You have learned so much in that time. Where would we be without you?"

Thomas patted her hand.

"We will leave." Binda looked at Joseph.

"You don't have to."

"There's still the cake to cut," Esther said.

"No cake." Jundala's tone was firm. Millie stepped forward and the two women glared at each other. "Thank you."

Joseph's heart was heavy as Binda hugged Millie then said goodbye. Jundala followed him out the door without a backwards glance. The mood was subdued. Millie made a soft tutting sound. Joseph sagged back against the wooden chair. While his family had learned to adapt to this new country he knew the lives of the local natives had been changed forever. He hoped the land was big enough for them all but he wasn't so sure any more.

Beth tugged at William's hand, wanting to be twirled upside down. Ruth took her new doll to show her grandfather and Matthew let out a loud wail.

Joseph felt himself relax as Millie plucked the noisy baby from his bed. "No doubt about this one's lungs. He's either fast asleep or wide awake. No in between."

"He's beautiful," Violet cooed over Millie's shoulder and brushed the baby's dark curls with her hand. She turned and beamed at Thomas then at Joseph. "And there will be a new grandchild for you in the new year."

Esther squealed. "You're with child."

"Yes." Violet's eyes shone and she put a hand to her still trim stomach.

Joseph pushed back his chair and rose to his feet. He hugged his daughter close and kissed both her cheeks. He had a momentary thought of her dear mother, Clara, and her grandmother, Lizzie. How they would have delighted in this moment. "I'm so happy for you, my dear."

"We both are." Millie joined him with their own baby snuggled against her shoulder.

"Matthew will be an uncle before he's one year old." Esther hugged her sister.

"Another baby." Thomas's craggy face was lit in a huge smile.

William came to kiss his sister's cheek with Beth still clinging to his arm.

Robert joined them. Once the excited voices had settled he spoke. "Are we never to eat Millie's fruitcake?"

Millie laughed. "Of course. Come and sit down everyone. The kettle has boiled."

Joseph took Matthew from her and returned to his seat. Cups of tea were handed around, and large slices of cake. He was a very lucky man and yet in the corner of his heart there was sorrow that Binda had not stayed. He had felt things slowly changing between them for a while now — but they had been such good friends for so much of their lives. He hoped they would remain so.

Matthew squirmed in his arms. He looked down at his small son. His hair was dark like Millie's and his skin the colour of honey like his sisters'. Joseph saw this new generation as a blend of the old and the new for this land. They would be the future; he was sure of it. Matthew's little forehead crinkled and he let out a loud wail.

Millie reached out her arms. "I will take him now."

Joseph watched her walk to the wooden rocking chair in the corner, its back to the table so that when she sat in it she had a view out the window. From there she would be able to see the trees along the creek and the back door of Father's cottage, as they'd taken to calling his house since they moved out to the big house.

Joseph glanced around the table at the others, all still engaged in happy conversation. Only Binda was missing. Jundala had lived and worked with the Bakers since she'd become Binda's wife. She'd always been a quiet, shy woman, and a hard worker. She did go for periods to visit her country further north but of course he understood her wanting to be with her family. Millie was quite different; she saw little of her family. She said this home had been built on their country and she was happy with that. Her father, Yardu, had all but disowned her and her brother Binda because of their association with the Bakers.

Joseph felt a gaze upon him. He looked down the table to where William was watching him. William raised his cup and Joseph responded. He couldn't blame his son for the rift that had opened between himself and Binda, and yet William saw things very differently when it came to the natives of this land — he always had. Joseph rolled his shoulders as a shiver rippled down his spine. He had worked hard to create a peaceful existence for his family and his friends. He hoped he could keep it that way.

Seven

October 1896

The bellowing of cattle echoed all around them. William moved Big Red forward to try and keep them steady. The horse responded immediately. Hegarty was doing the same on the other side of the sandy creek bed but there was no holding them. The animals had already got the scent of water ahead. William went with them, trusting his horse to keep out of their way. They'd been working for three days, shifting the cattle from the plains below where no winter rain meant little water and even less feed.

The winter had been bitterly cold with icy winds so dry they made eyes water and exposed skin raw. Now it was well into spring but there was still no sign of rain. Occasionally clouds banked on the western horizon, tantalising them with hope, only to slide south again. William didn't want to believe it but his grandfather's prophecy that they faced another drought was showing all the signs of being fulfilled. He looked up at the cloudless blue sky where the mid-morning sun was already spreading warmth and the promise of another hot day.

The creek narrowed and William urged his horse up a bank and onto a rocky plateau. He slid from the saddle, whipped his hat from his head and dragged his sweat-dampened hair back from his eyes before pushing the hat firmly back in place. Hegarty arrived beside him and climbed down, the saddle creaking as his large frame eased to the ground. From their vantage point on the ridge they both watched in silence as the cattle milled around the large expanse of water fed by a natural spring. They had named it the bottom waterhole.

William knew Millie's people used this spring for water. While the quest for water for his stock was never out of his mind he was burdened by the memory of Matthew's birth party and the idea for diverting the water from the top spring that had caused a rift between his family and Uncle Binda's. As much as the idea had seemed a good one at the time he had come to realise that without those higher, less accessible waterholes, Uncle Binda's people would not be able to survive. He didn't believe it was his problem but they had nowhere else to go.

"The cattle should be all right here over the summer." Hegarty plucked a leaf from a saltbush branch and crushed it in his huge fingers. "Plenty of feed here to last them and, who knows, we might get rain then since we didn't get any all winter."

"Perhaps." William knew it was possible. Summer storms had brought huge rains in the past. "Let's hope you're right."

They watched the cattle a little longer as they drank and milled around the edge of the water, turning it to mud and leaving their prints. William thought again of Uncle Binda's people camped further up in the ranges. He took his horse's reins and called to Hegarty. "I'm going to ride up into the higher country. I suspect there may still be sheep up there."

"Surely the natives and the wild dogs would have taken any left after we shifted the main mob over to Wildu Creek."

"Maybe, but I haven't been up that way for a while." William mounted his horse and looked down at Hegarty. He couldn't explain to the older man the sudden urge that had him wanting to visit the rugged country further east. "You go back to the homestead. I want to do some exploring. If we don't get that rain these cattle are going to need other water supplies before the summer's out. I'll come back this way and check the cattle again before I return. Expect me in a couple of days."

Hegarty gave him a steady look. "You're the boss."

William lifted his hand in a wave and wheeled his horse away. They worked easily together and William liked the older man and respected him, but he wanted to make this expedition on his own; see for himself if there wasn't a way for the natives and the cattle to exist together.

He ducked his head under a low-hanging branch and urged Big Red up a slope between two ridges of brown and black shale rock. He was in no hurry. After working with the cattle he enjoyed letting the horse amble, taking him deeper into the hills but at no desperate pace. It allowed him the luxury of some time to think about Georgina.

It had been several weeks since he'd had a letter from her. Their communication had been tenuous since she'd left. Finding time alone to write to him was difficult for her as she spent nearly every minute with her mother, who she said watched her like an eagle searching for prey. They had spent some of the English summer with an uncle and aunt of her mother's and were now in Europe, travelling to the warmer areas for the European winter. In the spring they planned to travel through Scotland and Ireland. William had written several letters in reply which he longed to send but even if he knew where to send them, her mother was bound to intercept them. Instead he kept the growing pile in a wooden box in his room. His heart ached for her return.

The horse beneath him came to a stop; the terrain around them looked impassable. William knew it wasn't even though he hadn't been paying close attention to the landscape. Now he climbed down and studied the narrow gorge walls and thick trees. He'd come this way before with his father and Uncle Binda, and they had shown him the hidden waterhole where the two older men first met. It had been during the previous big drought and all the waterholes had failed except the one to which he was heading. It was the same place where his father had found his lucky rock, which they had discovered was a diamond.

He led the horse around a large outcrop and on up a narrow gully, and sure enough they came to a small pool where water trickled over the rocks. William scooped up the clear liquid and drank. Nearby his horse took some in too. He looked around and could see signs of animals including the sheep which, barring a few stragglers, had all been moved to Wildu Creek. Thomas and Joseph managed them while William and Hegarty managed the cattle on Smith's Ridge. There were too many sheep for the current conditions and he knew they would soon need to make the decision to sell some off; perhaps the cattle would be sold too if the dry continued.

William tethered the horse so it could reach feed and took some damper from his saddle bag. He leaned his back against the base of a large gum and bent one leg to prop himself up.

A shadow swept the ground in front of him. He looked up to see a large eagle circle the waterhole, then it drifted higher until the branches hid it from his sight. He stepped out from the shade and watched as the giant bird circled again, further away this time. It spent some time focused on the one place before it drifted again and was lost from his sight. Perhaps he should look around. The eagle was only searching for something to eat but if that something was a sheep William would prefer his family have it than the bird of prey. He decided he would scout around and camp the night. Then, since he'd come this far, tomorrow he would go on to the next spring, which was even more inaccessible.

Tomorrow he would visit the camp. With luck Binda and Millie's father would be feeling benevolent towards his presence. While Uncle Binda was a native of the land, he was a man who'd lived much of his life in a white man's world. His father, Yardu, was the opposite, keeping away from the settlers as much as he could. It would depend what mood Yardu was in as to whether William would be welcome.

The horse snorted and shook its head. Time to move on. William took the reins and led the way out of the narrow gorge down into the dry creek bed where he mounted again and headed deeper into the hills.

Yardu heard the excited call of the young men as they returned to camp. They'd caught something big to share. He hoped it would be kangaroo. He had never learned to enjoy the white man's sheep like his family did. The buzz of voices grew louder as the women and children joined in. Everyone would eat well tonight.

There had been no rain. They'd stayed in this summer camp all winter and now there was no purpose in moving. Nearby was one of the last waterholes not polluted by the white invaders and their animals. Sorrow weighed heavily on Yardu. It had been a sad day when his son Binda had found the young white man, Joseph Baker, at the waterhole and brought him back to their camp. Yardu had known then his hope that they would keep some small part of the country free from the white man was futile.

Even his family had been taken from him. First Binda had left to go and live with the Bakers and then Yardu's daughter, Millaki, had run off to work for white people further south before she ended up becoming Joseph Baker's woman. Others had left. Young men who thought they would find something they didn't have here. Some returned and brought the white man's sickness with them, infecting the camp. It hurt his heart to see the change he now accepted he was powerless to stop.

Yardu eased his legs out from under him and used the stick that lay next to him to get to his feet. The pains that wracked his back were not so bad today. He struggled out of the shelter and straightened his aching body just as the young men came through the trees. They carried a large kangaroo suspended on a stick between them. Yardu frowned as his wife called out a greeting. Behind the hunters walked a young white man leading a horse. The children rushed to his side and Yardu watched as the one they called William put his hat on the head of one of the boys.

A shadow over Yardu flowed across the ground to also pass above the fair head of the white man. Yardu stared up at the giant bird circling in the cloudless afternoon sky. It had one black-tipped wing and one white.

"Wildu," he murmured.

The bird dipped again, did one more circle and once again its shadow crossed Yardu and then William before it gained height and drifted away on a current of warm air.

Yardu looked back at William, who was oblivious to the giant bird's presence.

As if sensing Yardu's scrutiny William looked around then lowered his gaze. He called a greeting in a plausible replication of the language spoken by Yardu's people. The old man acknowledged him and felt some warmth for the white-skinned man, who at least showed respect for his elders. Yardu hobbled closer and then faltered as a sharp pain raged up his back. His wife stepped towards him but he put out a hand to stop her. The spasm eased.

William offered the good wishes of his parents then dug in the bag attached to his horse. He lifted out two smaller pale bags and held them out towards Yardu's wife. Yardu knew this was the sweet white grains and the soft white powder the women liked to add to their cooking. He inclined his head and his wife took the bags.

Yardu settled himself in the dirt by the fire, which was already full of coals ready to receive the kangaroo. He waited patiently for the pain to subside and looked up at the brilliant blue sky, where three wildu circled in the distance, gliding effortlessly in the warm air over the mountain. The presence of the birds of prey was not unusual and he took comfort in their company. It was the big one that had come so low, a large male he hadn't seen for a season, that made him look again at the young white man. Wildu had shown the time was right. Yardu's heart ached. He knew his own time in this country was running out. He had done his best to protect his people from the invaders but he knew now it had been futile. Somehow he had to ensure the survival of his people once he was gone. His son, Binda, had turned his back on them and Binda's son had returned to his mother's people. It should be Millaki's boy, but he was too young, and Yardu had little time left. As much as it was against everything he believed, the only hope for his family was to put his trust in the white man who now approached his fire.

William left the camp early the next morning. The heat of the sun was warm on his back and yet a chill wriggled down his spine. The old man was dying. He had said nothing about being unwell. There had been no complaint, but the pain was etched on his face and he had grown weary after much talking. The night before the group had welcomed William and shared their meal with him. The kangaroo had been delicious but he had been careful to only take a small portion, knowing the meat would be needed to feed the community for several days. After also eating little, Yardu had retired early.

William glanced back towards the camp, hidden from his sight by the large rocks and bush. He remembered the first time he'd come there with his Uncle Binda. Back then he'd been a young boy with mixed feelings about the native people who shared his home as Uncle Binda and his family did. He'd resented Binda's daughter Mary most — she often had the job of looking after him. Finally he'd realised it was being bossed by a girl that he didn't like rather than the colour of her skin. His father had married Yardu's daughter after William's mother died, and after that Millie had taught him a lot about the country.

William had felt keenly the dislike that oozed from some of their neighbours and townsfolk. The Bakers were ostracised by some for their cohabitation with natives and for allowing them access to the waterholes and some sheep. William found he no longer cared. They knew who their friends were at least. But now there was a new burden.

He turned west and led his horse back though the creek and over a ridge before he mounted and made his way down to the flatter country. From there he followed a track worn in from many journeys of hooves and wheels towards the Smith's Ridge homestead. It was William's duty now to make sure Yardu's people were safe. The burden of the old man's expectation was a weight he had not asked for and did not want.

Eight

November 1897

"You're very quiet, my dear."

Georgina looked up from the book that lay closed in her lap. Her mother sat opposite her, their knees almost touching in the small space of their shared room. Even though there was a fire, the air still felt cold, and the lamp was lit though it was nearly midday. They had both been reading but Georgina had lost interest.

"I was thinking of home." She had been, and more specifically of her handsome neighbour, William Baker.

"This has been a wonderful holiday to see other parts of the world." Johanna Prosser looked down her pointy nose at her daughter. "Your father expects you to make the most of this opportunity."

"And so I have, Mother. The three months we spent in Europe were certainly interesting and even England has been so different from how I imagined it would be but the winter is so cold and your aunt and uncle have barely enough room for themselves in this tiny cottage let alone for us."

"Uncle Winston has been very kind to take us in. We can't spend all your father's money on hotels."

"I realise that, Mother, but surely it's not fair to burden them. Two more mouths to feed and us taking over their front room." Georgina cast a hand to the cramped space behind her, where the furniture of Aunt Anne's best room, as she called the only living space besides the kitchen, had been moved to the side or shifted out to make room for the double bed that had been borrowed from a neighbour. "Surely you find it cramped."

"I must admit I had thought from Aunt Anne's letters that they had a more palatial establishment."

"It's three rooms in a row of cottages." Georgina gave a snort. "She certainly thinks she's a cut above the lowly relatives from Australia but this whole cottage could fit into our two front rooms at home."

"Hush, Georgina. They might hear you."

"They're both deaf, Mother."

"Uncle Winston, yes, but she can hear well enough when she wants to." Johanna glanced over her shoulder at the closed door. "She won't admit it but I think they're most grateful for the board we are paying and she almost smiled when I offered to buy a turkey for Christmas."

"You want to stay in Birmingham another month?" Georgina felt her spirits dip even lower. The thought of spending much longer in the cramped cottage with her dour aunt was dismal.

"I long to experience one more white Christmas, Georgina. I was only a young girl when my family left England. We will go home in the new year."

Georgina's shoulders sagged. After experiencing snow during their first winter away she no longer gave a penny for it. Sometimes winters at home were cold enough for snow and people in the highest country said it had fallen on the peaks in the past. Give her the crisp chill of winter in the Flinders any day, with the refreshing downpours and the scent of eucalyptus. She closed her eyes: how she missed that smell. Everything here in Birmingham, where her relatives lived surrounded by factories and mills, smelled of cloying smoke and foul drains. The countryside was different, of course, and her few brief experiences of it had been a reprieve from the confines of the town. Everything there was grey, from the weather to the people.

"Don't pout, Georgina. It isn't becoming." Her mother closed her book. "I have a suggestion. I will book us a week in London before Christmas. We can purchase some gifts and go to the theatre."

Georgina would have jumped up from her chair if there had been room for her to do so without landing in her mother's lap. Instead she remained demurely in her place. "That would be delightful, Mother. I liked London. It was so exciting to be there in the summer for Queen Victoria's golden jubilee." She glanced up the commemorative mugs she and her mother had bought. They had pride of place on the mantle. "It would be fun to dress up again."

"Perhaps even to dance." Her mother's voice had a wistful tone.

They both looked round at a sharp tap on their door.

"Come in," Johanna called.

The door swung in as far as the bed then one had to close it to get round. Aunt Anne peered around the door but came no further into the room.

"The post has come." She waved an envelope. "A letter for you, Johanna."

Georgina watched hungrily as her mother twisted around in her chair to retrieve the letter. How she wished she would get some reply from William. She knew he had no way of getting a message to her but a small part of her hoped by some miracle she could have some news of him.

"Would you like a cup of tea?" Aunt Anne asked.

"Yes, thank you, Aunt." Johanna smiled. "We shall join you just as soon as we've read the news from home."

"It's not a very fat letter. I hope it's nothing bad." The old woman's lips twisted sideways, giving the lie to that statement.

"I am sure not. Ellis likes to keep me informed of life at home. I will share it with you when we take our tea."

"Very well." Aunt Anne gave a curt nod and withdrew, closing the door as she went.

Georgina watched as her mother took up the ornate handle of the opener and slit the envelope with slow deliberation. Johanna slid the pages out and unfolded them. Just as Aunt Anne had indicated, there were not many. The crackle of the small fire was the only sound as she read the pages to herself.

Georgina could stand it no longer. She was desperate for news of home. "What does Father say?"

Her mother glanced up. "I will tell you in just a moment, Georgina. Be patient."

Georgina flopped back against the over-stuffed back of her aunt's best chair.

It was taking her mother a long time to read the few pages. At one point Johanna's lips pursed and then within a minute a smile played on her lips. Finally, she laid the letter in her lap and looked at Georgina. "Your father wrote this in our Australian spring. Winter was cold and dry. He is having to sell cattle."

"Some of the older pastoralists were predicting another drought before we left."

"Your father says they're still saying that but one dry winter doesn't make a drought. He's selling a small number to be cautious, and some of the sheep."

"What else does he say? Can I read it?" Georgina held out her hand.

Her mother folded the letter and clutched it to her. "You may not. There are personal things in the letter. Your father misses us of course and asks after you. He is making sure your horse is ridden often and well cared for and in spite of the poor winter we have had a good lot of calves. There was little water in the creek when he wrote but he was hopeful of spring rain."

"We are so far away and letters take so long. Perhaps it has rained, perhaps it hasn't." Georgina stared into the fire. "I wish I was there now."

"He had more to say."

The cautioning tone of her mother's voice made Georgina lift her gaze to the letter again.

"What is it, Mother?"

"It seems our neighbour has taken a wife."

"Which neighbour?" They really only had two neighbours and the Marchants were already married.

"William Baker of course."

Georgina tried to conceal her intake of breath and the sharp pain that stabbed at her heart. "How ... who?"

"I knew your father was right to keep you away from that man. He's taken a woman like his father's." Johanna's eyes narrowed. "A native."

"I don't believe it."

"The apple never falls far from the tree."

"I don't mean that William has a native wife. I don't believe he has a wife at all." She reached out her hand. "You must have misunderstood. Perhaps she's a housekeeper. Let me read it."

Johanna clutched the letter tightly. "It is private, and your father's words are quite clear." Her gaze pinned Georgina. "You've been pining after that man for too long, Georgina. It's time you forgot him and looked for a more suitable attachment."

Georgina felt her arms sag and a loud rushing in her ears drowned out the sound of her mother's nagging voice. William wouldn't have married someone else. He was going to marry her. She had known they would marry since she was a little girl. They were meant for each other. Her parents had done their best to give her a social life beyond the isolation of Prosser's Run — her years at school in Adelaide had provided her with more opportunity and she had met several men on this trip too. She'd even been kissed by one of the more forward Englishmen she'd met on her last visit to London. None of them matched William's rugged strength, his wide smile and the feel of his arms around her, his warm lips on hers. She shivered. She was sure he'd felt as smitten as she had. He couldn't have forgotten her so easily.

"Your father wants you to find a husband who will care for you and be able to take on the responsibility of Prosser's Run. And he wants grandchildren even if they won't bear his name. Grandsons to continue the traditions he began at Prosser's Run."

Georgina snapped from her contemplation. She did not need a man to care for her. William would have been her life partner but she would not have been his property. "Why is it that marrying and providing children are the only things I am good for? I can manage Prosser's Run on my own, Mother. I can employ people to help me. A husband and children would only be a hindrance."

"Don't be silly, Georgina. I know your father has indulged you but it is not fitting for you to take on all that managing a property entails on your own. I wouldn't hear of it." Johanna's lips pursed together. She lifted her chin. "A visit to London will do you the world of good."

Georgina had long ago learned the best way to get around her parents was to appear to do as they wished while quietly working things her way. "Perhaps London will produce such a man."

Johanna clapped her hands together, completely missing the sarcasm in her daughter's tone. "I will contact my friend Mary again. It will be short notice but she may be able to plan a little soiree. We could meet some new people and maybe that nice Mr Durham will be there." Johanna paused and Georgina noticed a glow in her mother's cheeks that couldn't be attributed to the small fire.

Durham had danced with Georgina several times, and had declared himself enchanted by her and her life in Australia. On their last evening together he had kissed her. Georgina shuddered at the memory of his soft moist lips.

Her mother reached out to her. "I know it's a little dreary here but please allow me this extra time. Prosser's Run is our home and once we go back there will be no more trips away for me."

Georgina swallowed her despair at the news of William's marriage. It was not her mother's fault and she was right. It was unlikely either of them would get this opportunity again. Mr Durham was a fine dancer and, as long as he didn't try to kiss her again, he was good company. "Very well, Mother."

Johanna stood and edged around her chair to the door. "I shall make the arrangements now." She smiled at her daughter. "We will have a most enjoyable time and then we can bring some trimmings back to brighten Uncle Winston and Aunt Anne's Christmas."

Georgina tried not to show her despondency at the thought of Christmas in this glum little cottage.

"They have no children of their own." Johanna tucked the letter into the pocket of her thick plaid skirt and smoothed the fabric with her palms. "I am their only niece. I feel I should do my best for them. I shall probably never see them again."

"Of course." Georgina stood, her annoyance eased by empathy for her mother. Johanna was an only child and both her parents had died not long after she married. It was her inheritance that had helped Georgina's father begin his pastoral life, which led them to Prosser's Run. "Do you ever wish your money had been invested in another life, Mother?"

Johanna had manoeuvred around the door and looked back in surprise. "Good heavens no, Georgina. When I married your father my money became his. He has not been wasteful and he's made us a good life. We are enjoying this holiday because of it. You are being perverse today. Why would I want another life?"

The door shut and Georgina was left alone in the small space. Her father had intimated she would eventually inherit Prosser's Run. Once that time came there was no way she would let a man tell her how to manage it or any money that was hers. She closed her eyes and imagined William's handsome face as she had done every day since she left home. A wave of despair washed over her and she sank into the chair. He'd said he would wait for her. She had imagined them working side by side, building a future together. She had been gone a long time. He had obviously forgotten her.

She gripped the padded arms of the chair. She would not give in to despair. She was strong and fit and quite capable of stepping up to manage Prosser's Run when her father was no longer able. She would show him and William Baker she was her own woman and had no need of a man to support her.

Nine

December 1897

"Young Baker is taking after his father." The chair beneath Ellis Prosser creaked in protest as he moved.

Henry took a puff of his cigar and contemplated his guest. Ellis had been a regular visitor since his wife and daughter had been away. Thankfully a guest bedroom had been added to the back of the house beyond the bathroom.

The strong smell of tobacco curled around Henry as he blew out. He watched with satisfaction as a ring of smoke floated across the living room. They had eaten a delightful meal prepared by Mrs Nixon. Catherine had retired early, as she often did these days, and Charles was away from home, so it was just their overnight guest and Henry who sat in their good front room. It had been an extremely hot day but there was a gentle breeze coming through the front windows now the sun was down. "In what way?"

"He's taken a native woman as his wife. My man Swan saw them going in to the church."

Henry raised his eyebrows. "Not necessarily to marry."

"She was on his arm clutching flowers and he in his best suit. Swan says she's living at Smith's Ridge."

"How appalling. That family are not fit to be with decent people." Henry shook his head. "You were right to send your daughter overseas, Ellis. Georgina is better off away from the Bakers for a while. She is such a fine young woman."

"But headstrong. She was quite smitten with young Baker." Like Henry, Ellis blew out a ring of smoke.

"How terrible if she had become his wife."

"Over my dead body." Ellis lurched forward in his chair. "That was never going to happen. I'd rather send her to a nunnery."

Henry raised his eyebrows but said nothing. Ellis was wont to make explosive comments that were sometimes unrealistic. But he did understand his despair at the thought of his daughter marrying William Baker.

"Joseph Baker has disgraced his whole family by marrying that native and now they have three half-caste brats. Although I do wonder how they will fare with the appointment of the new Protector of Aborigines."

Henry sat up. Ellis was on a return journey from Adelaide, where he had gleaned all kinds of information about the affairs of South Australia that had not yet filtered through to Hawker. Henry was keen to learn what he could. "What difference will a new protector make?"

"He might do more about these natives, especially those with mixed blood. I've never been one to tolerate any of them but we are stuck with them. If they are to live among us the only way is to teach them our ways."

"As much as I hate to admit it Millie Baker appears to be a quick learner."

Ellis gave a snort. "Baker has made a bit of a go of it with his wife. She wears proper clothes and I'm told she cooks inside and good English food to boot. He's built her a fancy house — but she'll always be a native and thus so will her children."

"Nothing can change that."

"Well, the talk in Adelaide is of removing half-caste children and sending them to live with white families."

"Surely they'd run away or their parents would find them?"

"No, they would be taken away and no information would be given about where they'd be sent. They'd be raised at a mission or by white families so that they forgot their wild roots."

"Really?" Henry sat back and pondered that.

"Anyway, I have little care for what happens to the Bakers as long as it doesn't involve my daughter."

"Very sensible, Ellis. Nothing good can come of mixing black skin with white or of mixing with the Bakers." Henry nodded sagely. "Have you heard from your wife lately? How is their trip going?"

"The last time I heard from Johanna they had just returned to England after touring France and Italy. My wife has ageing relatives in England and they have no children. She would like to spend Christmas with them and perhaps tour a little more before returning to Australia."

"No doubt they are making the most of such a big journey." Henry sank deeper into his chair. "I hope the same for Charles although of course he is not travelling so far. He's had a successful year at school in Adelaide. Accompanying my mother on her trip to Melbourne and Sydney will expand his knowledge of her business and ours and, I hope, open his eyes to new possibilities before he returns to us."

"I am sure he will learn a lot from your mother. How is she faring?"

"I am glad she took Charles as her companion. Her eyesight is failing."

"Such a shame. Her business must depend upon on it surely?"

Henry sighed. Harriet was being very stubborn and insisting he should sell up and take over her business in Adelaide. She had trained several talented seamstresses and women to manage the shop and wanted him to create a menswear shop next door. Henry had other ideas. If he could get his hands on her money, there was so much more he could do in Hawker. "My mother cannot continue to run her business as she has for much longer. She has taken Charles under her wing, and he is helping her with buying for her shop and ours, but he cannot stay in Adelaide." Once more Henry blew out a perfect ring of smoke. "Our business is expanding and I need him here."

"You are very optimistic. We've had little rain for over a year now. Some think we are going to have another drought."

"There are always the worry-mongers."

"They might be right this time."

"I have made sure my business will not suffer."

"You are wise. There are those who don't pay heed to the warning signs."

Henry studied his friend. Ellis had aged visibly during his wife's absence. He had always been a big man but now his stomach was hanging over his belt and his trademark brown leather vest was open, revealing straining shirt buttons. His once fiery red hair was a faded sandy colour and his cheeks were often florid. So different to Henry, who prided himself on his own appearance. He flicked his gaze down over his silver vest and the grey shirt tucked neatly into his dark trousers. He rarely over-ate and did not over-indulge in liquor as Ellis did. Still, Ellis was a powerful man and a good ally. His say-so had helped Henry onto several committees over the years. The local council position had not worked out — that he had lost his seat after barely a year in office still rankled — but there were other groups who had been pleased to have a man of his standing involved.

"I am sure you're right, Ellis. My neighbour Mr Garrat is not particular with the credit he extends." Henry frowned; he was far more discerning, and he certainly didn't allow natives, or any foreigners for that matter, in his shop. "Did I tell you I have recently acquired another farm near Wilson?"

"Won't do you much good if it doesn't rain."

Once more Henry puffed on his cigar. "I can wait until things improve." He'd got the land in exchange for a debt. It mattered little to Henry when it rained next but once it did he was not fool enough to try to crop the country. Cropping was a fickle business, as those he'd preyed on discovered. Once the seasons improved he would stock his land with sheep as he'd done in the past. That was where the money was.

"You said Charles was buying for your shop?"

"Yes, we are expanding our clothing department."

"When do you expect him to return to Hawker?"

"Quite soon. The last telegraph I had from him reported they were about to leave for Adelaide. Mother was worn out from the travel. He may stay a few days to see her settled before he returns home."

"You will have to let me know when the new clothing arrives." Ellis brushed at his shirt. Henry noticed some dark stains from the red wine they'd been drinking. "I suspect I shall need to buy something new before Johanna returns or she will think I can't manage in her absence."

"You know we always look after your needs, Ellis." Henry smiled and Ellis returned the gesture with a quick nod.

Charles closed the door to the house quietly behind him. His grandmother was resting again. The journey to Sydney and Melbourne and back had taken much out of her even though they had travelled between cities via ship.

The whirring of machines didn't falter as he passed the three seamstresses bent over their work, but pretty Miss Wharton, who was around his age, lifted her gaze from the cutting table and gave him a smile to which he responded with a wink — he enjoyed the blush that crept over her cheeks. Charles stepped lightly into the shop beyond the workroom. He enjoyed being there in his grandmother's business, partly because he felt it was much better run than his father's business at Hawker, but also because the place was full of women, all of whom were charmed by his careful manners and ready smile. He had lived with his grandmother for a year while he completed his studies and he knew her business and her staff well.

The shop was busy with customers. All three assistants were in attendance. Miss Wicksteed, his grandmother's shop manager, gave him a smile and slight inclination of her neatly coiffed head before turning her attention back to one assistant in particular. The young woman had only started in the shop as Charles and Harriet left on their trip and he hadn't had a chance to be introduced.

He moved across the light and airy room to the large window his grandmother had installed by the front door. In front of it was the new mannequin she'd bought in Sydney, already swathed in soft georgette in a palette of colours. No wonder Harriet was tired. She must have worked on the display late into the night after Charles retired. He stood back to admire his grandmother's handiwork. Her eyesight may have been failing but she had an innate flair for colour and style. This display cleverly demonstrated the soft flow of the fabric and the variety of colours available.

There was a clatter behind him. He turned to see the red-faced new assistant holding an empty box. The contents, some large pearl buttons, were now scattered over the counter. Miss Wicksteed drew the customer aside to finish her inspection of some bolts of lace, leaving the assistant to tidy up after her clumsiness.

Charles stepped over to the counter and picked up one button that had fallen to the polished wooden floor on his side.

"Thank you, sir," the assistant murmured.

Charles looked up into the hazel eyes that studied him. The young woman was his age or older, neat in appearance and, while not displaying the usual softer beauty of most of his grandmother's shop employees, she had strong bone structure. Her hair, pulled back as it was from her head in a neat bun, made her look more angular. He held her gaze and she didn't look away as the other young ladies would have. The red flush of her cheeks was fading and he got the impression it had come from annoyance rather than embarrassment.

"Good morning," Charles said. "I am Charles Wiltshire, your employer's grandson."

"Yes." She gave a short bob of her head. "I know who you are, sir."

"And your name is?"

"Edith Ferguson, sir."

"Excuse me, Master Charles." Miss Wicksteed faltered as Charles turned a steely look in her direction.

"I beg your pardon, sir, Mr Charles." Miss Wicksteed corrected herself. "I need to speak with Miss Ferguson in the fitting room."

The shop door opened at that moment, admitting the telegraph boy. He glanced around the room and, seeing Charles was the only male occupant, stepped up to him.

"I have a telegraph for a Mr Charles Wiltshire."

"That's me." Charles took the paper from the lad, who let himself out again.

Miss Ferguson gave him a smile. He studied her again. It wasn't the shy look the other young shop women gave him: she had a gleam in her eye.

"Come along, Miss Ferguson." Miss Wicksteed ushered the young woman away, and Charles watched as both women disappeared through the door into the back rooms behind the shop.

The telegram was from his father. Business was brisk. Mr Hemming wanted urgent leave and Charles was needed at home. He re-read the paper then folded it into his pocket and let himself out into the warm Adelaide day. O'Connell Street was bustling with activity. Too late he thought of his hat but he didn't intend to be long. It was mid-December, dry and dusty. Hawker would be hotter on his return, he knew. Not that he minded the heat; it was his future he wished to contemplate before he joined his grandmother over breakfast. Normally she would be up by now but he suspected her late night had tired her. She had been looking forward to the comfort of her own bed on their return from their travels the day before.

During their trip they had got into the routine of planning their day over breakfast and reviewing their discoveries and purchases over the evening meal. His grandmother always retired early, leaving Charles the evenings to explore the night lives of first Sydney, and then Melbourne. He had turned sixteen the previous September but knew his height and older looks passed him off as a man of nineteen or twenty. It had been a surprising freedom, which he had made the most of, enjoying the delights of late-night houses and bawdy shows that had at first shocked the young man from the bush and then titillated him. He'd sampled a variety of liquor, smoked cigars and of course indulged in the welcoming pleasures of several different women. Not whores, but young ladies who were easily charmed by his ready smile and charismatic ways.

Charles gave a self-satisfied smile. Harriet had been generous with his travel allowance. He had sowed his wild oats and learned many things about the world beyond Hawker. He would be more than ready to beguile Georgina Prosser on her return home — but that was part of his dilemma. His grandmother had asked him to be her right-hand man. Henry was obviously never going to sell up and move to Adelaide, and Harriet was sixty-five and her eyesight was failing. She needed someone to help her and eventually take over her business and she wanted that someone to be Charles. She had put a lot of effort into explaining her business and how she wanted to expand it to include menswear. Charles would be in charge of that and Miss Wicksteed would manage the ladies' fashions with Harriet a guiding hand to them both in the background.

Harriet had put this to him on their last night in Melbourne. She predicted an increase in demand for fine clothes. "The coming of Federation will see many celebrations. Adelaide's gentry will want to look their best," she'd said. She was quite sure the soon-to-be-held referendum would see a unanimous yes vote for the commonwealth bill. "We will be kept very busy."

It was a tempting offer and one to which Charles had given a lot of thought on the boat journey to Adelaide. He knew his grandmother would want an answer before he returned to Hawker, but he was in a difficult position. Charles was keen to expand his father's shop and also the scope of their business. His father was fixated on acquiring land but while Charles thought it good to own property, it was a fickle business, dependent on weather and markets. Better to provide services to the people on the land. His father had done well with the creamery so far. Charles was sure there were other ways they could service the people of the area.

Then there was Prosser's Run. All his father's little holdings were pitiful in comparison to that. When Charles married Georgina Prosser the combination of the Wiltshire and Prosser fortunes would be significant.

And another possible pursuit had arisen from his chance meeting with a South African called Becker while in Melbourne. He had been in a club where scantily dressed young women served drinks, cigars and more. His mention of Hawker had attracted Becker's interest. He was in search of diamonds and believed he'd found signs in the hills beyond the town. Even more intriguing, Becker mentioned he had been removed from the property by the owners: men called Baker. He had other prospects but he was keen to return to the area in the future and needed some reliable local knowledge.

Charles felt a surge of anticipation. If he stayed in Adelaide he would simply be a shopkeeper. Although isolated and small, Hawker offered him a much bigger future.

The morning sun began to beat heavily on his head and he was pleased to reach the corner and turn back into O'Connell Street. Time to meet with his grandmother. He had to convince her of his need to return to Hawker for the time being and yet have her believe he was interested in eventually managing her business.

Harriet Wiltshire looked through bleary eyes at the young woman seated across from her. Miss Ferguson was perched on a fine damask-covered chair in the neat sitting room of Harriet's house behind the shop. Rarely did she admit staff into her home, especially not juniors, but the shop and fitting rooms were all busy and this business needed to be sorted in private.

Miss Wicksteed had just regaled her with Miss Ferguson's latest blunder, the last of several, and now it was up to Harriet to deal with her. The new assistant had only been taken on because of her acquaintance with a staff member who'd recently married and left Harriet's employ. Harriet had regretted the moment of weakness that had allowed her to hire the plain, awkward young woman. She was not like the fine-mannered girls with pleasant looks who

Harriet more usually employed to grace her shop. Still, she had said a month's trial and that time was well and truly up.

"I am sorry about the buttons, Mrs Wiltshire. The catch on the box needs replacing." Miss Ferguson spoke just as Harriet drew a deep breath. "None were broken and the customer wasn't upset."

That was another thing Harriet disliked about the girl. She had already apologised for Miss Wicksteed's list of her mistakes, but Edith Ferguson's tone had been more defensive than apologetic, as it was now.

"I'm pleased to hear that at least, Miss Ferguson."

"It was only a box of buttons."

Harriet pulled herself up higher in her own comfortable chair. The young assistant appeared to be looking down on her. "We agreed to a trial period, Miss Ferguson, but with today's mishap and all that has occurred in my absence, I don't believe you are suited to work in my shop."

"Miss Wicksteed doesn't like me. She doesn't record the other girls' mistakes with such fervour."

Harriet pursed her lips. Indeed Miss Ferguson's tone was almost insolent. No wonder the shop manager had taken a dislike to the girl.

The door from the shop opened. "Ah! Good morning, Grandmother. I see—" Charles stopped beside Miss Ferguson's chair and looked down. "I'm sorry. I didn't realise you had company."

Harriet's irritation dissolved at the sight of her darling grandson. "That's all right, Charles. Our business is finished. If you will gather your things, Miss Ferguson, I am sure Miss Wicksteed will be ready with what we owe you."

"Oh dear." Charles's tone was musical. "Surely you're not dismissing Miss … Ferguson was it? … over a few spilled buttons, Grandmother?" He chuckled and placed a hand on the back of the chair.

Harriet's annoyance rose again. There was little she would deny her grandson but he was yet to learn how to employ and manage staff.

"I'm afraid that is the case, Mr Wiltshire." Miss Ferguson's bottom lip trembled.

"There is more to it than that," Harriet snapped.

The young woman sat forward and gripped her hands tightly together. "I need this job, Mrs Wiltshire."

Harriet shook her head. "I'm sorry, but you are not suited. I will write you a reference. I am sure there will be some kind of shop work for you, but not in my business."

Edith Ferguson's face crumpled and large tears rolled down her cheeks. "What am I to do?" she cried.

"Can't we give Miss Ferguson another chance, Grandmother?" Charles plucked his freshly laundered handkerchief from his pocket and offered it to the young woman, who dabbed delicately at her eyes with it.

"She has had several chances."

"I have no-one," Miss Ferguson wailed. "Without this job my landlord will cast me out onto the street."

Harriet sat back. It was quite possible that was the case but it was not her responsibility. Besides, the young woman gave her the impression she could look after herself.

"Would you be prepared to move to Hawker, Miss Ferguson?"

Harriet's eyebrows shot up at her grandson's suggestion. "Charles, I don't—"

"It's all right, Grandmother." Charles gave her one of his delightful smiles. "It may be the answer for all of us if Miss Ferguson is game. I have had a telegram from Father this morning urging me home, as Mr Hemming must take leave. We are already short staffed and Mother rarely ventures out of the house these days, let alone to the shop. We are on the lookout for a new assistant."

"Is there no-one in Hawker?"

"Not with the kind of training I am sure Miss Ferguson has learned working here."

Harriet lowered her gaze to the young woman, who gave a sob and patted at her dry cheeks with the handkerchief. "Do you know where Hawker is, Miss Ferguson? It is a long way from Adelaide. You are a young woman to make such a journey alone."

"She wouldn't be alone, Grandmother. She can travel with me and, now that the extensions are finished on our house, Mrs Nixon has moved into the new quarters at the back and the small cottage beside it is vacant. Miss Ferguson would have us close by if she needed help."

Harriet forgot about Miss Ferguson and focused on her grandson. She had so enjoyed his company these last two months she had almost forgotten he must return home for the time being.

"I think you should discuss this with your father first. He is the one who hires staff."

"We discussed the need for an extra assistant in our recent correspondence but he has employed no-one yet." Charles crossed the space between them, took her small knotted hand in his large warm one and patted it. "If Father has good staff I will be able to return all the sooner to you. This is the perfect solution for everyone. If Miss Ferguson agrees."

The young woman rose. "I like a challenge, Mr Wiltshire. Thank you most kindly for your generosity. I won't let you down."

Charles patted Harriet's hand again. "There, that's settled."

She blinked, willing her eyes to focus clearly, and peered around his broad arm to her erstwhile assistant. She was sure she'd glimpsed a smug look of defiance on Miss Ferguson's pinched face.

Ten

William shoved the calico-wrapped bread into his bag beside the oranges and the small parcel of meat and picked up his water bottle.

"Thanks, Jessie." He gave the young woman at the other side of the big Smith's Ridge front room an encouraging smile but she looked down and pushed the broom harder across the floor, raising a cloud of dust that made her sneeze.

"Whoa." Hegarty stepped through from the kitchen behind her and she almost dropped the broom.

"A little more gently, lass." He took the broom and demonstrated. "This place hasn't been cleaned properly in quite a while." He looked over the girl's bent head and directed a glare at William.

"Don't look at me." William shook his head. "You wanted a housekeeper."

Hegarty crossed the room and muttered in William's ear as he passed. "Someone who could cook at least."

"Millie's coming over to stay for a while after Christmas. She's going to conduct some lessons." He nodded in the direction of the determined sweeper. "Jessie is a quick learner."

The young woman looked up at the mention of her name, gave William a quick smile and returned to her sweeping. She was very reticent without Clem's presence but her features lit up when she smiled. William could understand what had first attracted his stockman, Clem, who then fell in love and made her his wife.

Jessie's early years had been tough. Her mother was Aboriginal and her father an Afghan. She had drifted between both groups until her parents died within months of each other, leaving young Jessie to move from place to place, always on the outer. She'd been living in squalid quarters, washing linen at a hotel in Hawker, when Clem met her. He'd married her a few months back. Neither of them had family and William had been the only witness at the wedding, where he'd been happy to escort Jessie down the aisle. The young couple had then settled in the old cottage Clem occupied at Smith's Ridge.

William had offered Jessie the job of housekeeper soon after she arrived. Clem's work at Smith's Ridge often took him away from the main homestead and, though Jessie had only ever worked in the laundry at the hotel, she was pleased to have something to do. So far her attempts at cooking had been on a par with Hegarty's and, in William's opinion, not as good as his own, but he had been happy to not have to worry about food preparation any more. He had enough to do.

"I'm heading out to check the waterholes along the Prosser's Run boundary. Clem's due back from the northern run any day."

"With any luck he'll have found a straggler sheep or two. We're in need of some fresh meat."

"I doubt there's any left up there that the natives haven't found." Since his talk with Yardu and the old man's death William had taken on the responsibility of assisting the survival of the group still living in the hills at the back of Smith's Ridge. His father also allowed them the run of the country at Wildu Creek, and the few remaining able-bodied men worked for either William or Joseph.

"I'll go the other way towards Wildu Creek," Hegarty said. "I should be back around the same time as you."

William waved a hand at the remaining food on the table. "Jessie has prepared some food for us to take."

Hegarty raised his eyebrows but crossed to the table to collect his share without a word.

"Can you check that new fence along the eastern boundary while you're there?" William watched as the older man collected the bread and neatly wrapped pickled meat. "That waterhole just the other side of the boundary will be a big temptation for the cattle."

"I'll check it. Have you made up your mind about which stock you're selling?"

William took his hat from the hook by the door and turned back. Jessie had given up on the broom and he could hear her doing something in the kitchen. "When I get back."

"You can't leave it too much longer. The export market won't take poor-quality cattle."

William was disappointed they would have to exit that market. They had done well from selling prime Smith's Ridge cattle and Wildu Creek sheep for English consumption. They had just begun to make some headway with it when weather conditions had adversely affected their stock.

"Those in the south who want to buy still have feed," Hegarty said. "But who knows when this drought will begin to affect them too?"

"It may not."

"No, but best to sell now while cattle are still bringing a good return."

William knew Hegarty made sense but he was sacrificing some of his hard-earned best breeding stock. Still, better to get money for them than to watch them die if the drought continued. "When I get back."

"We should look at the horses too." The gruffness of Hegarty's tone softened. "Those that aren't good as stock horses should go."

William met Hegarty's gaze. They were both keen horsemen, although Hegarty was more interested in breeding racehorses than William, who was developing good stock horses. They'd gone halves in a stallion when they first started working together on Smith's Ridge and the beast had sired several promising offspring, two of them better suited to racing than stock work. They'd built up quite a stable. He was training one fine mare in particular. He'd named her Bella and she was to be his gift to Georgina when she came home. She wasn't a racehorse but William thought her capable of stock work. William knew Hegarty thought the mare an indulgence. He gave a sharp dip of his head. "I'll be back in three days, maybe four. We'll work it out then."

By the time William had saddled his horse the sun was well above the horizon and another cloudless blue sky spread as far as he could see. They had recorded little rain in the last two years and on the plains virtually nothing had fallen in that time. It was definitely a drought, but how long would it last? That was the gamble.

The creeks and the waterholes were dry. Only the permanent springs fed water into pools, and that was not enough for the voracious throats of cattle that required as much as eight gallons each of water a day. Hegarty was right. He did have to make a decision to destock, and the sooner the better.

William had given up on his idea of somehow shifting the water from the more inaccessible springs in the hills. It had simply not been practical and had caused a lot of unrest. It frustrated him to know a ready source of water was available but beyond the reach of his cattle, and yet he knew there were some water supplies he must leave alone.

Inevitably William's thoughts drifted to Georgina. Her last letter had said they would return to her English relatives at the start of the European winter and she hoped her mother would be ready to book a passage home by then. He longed to see her again. To take her in his arms, to kiss her and to finally make her his wife.

It was nearly Christmas. Too soon to expect her arrival even if they had taken the first available passage after her last letter, but he hoped she would return early in the new year.

A noise ahead distracted him from his thoughts. William reined in his horse, startled. Clem was on foot, leading his horse towards him. A man was collapsed over the saddle and from the look of his body he'd been badly beaten.

William climbed down from his horse as Clem came to a stop in front of him. "What's happened?" Blood oozed from the gaping lacerations on the prone man's back, and he moaned. "Is that your friend, Albie?"

"Stupid bugger went back to Prosser." Clem spat the word. "Thought he'd get his old job back. Lucky I was up near the boundary. Saw Prosser's men dump him over your fence."

William's anger rose. "Did Prosser do this?" He looked at the wounds but didn't know where to begin to aid the now loudly moaning Albie.

"That's what Albie said." Clem trickled water into the corner of the injured man's mouth.

William could see blood seeping over his lips. "Where are you taking him?"

"Millie."

William dragged his gaze from the bloodied back where flies were collecting in little black lines. "Wildu Creek is too far. We'll have to take him to Smith's Ridge."

"Jessie's no good with blood."

"We can clean him up. I'll send word for Millie to come to us."

"All right." Clem moved to lead his horse on.

"Wait," William said. "Why don't you ride with him? We can move a little quicker at least and you can keep the flies off him."

"I tried that." Clem shook his head. "Albie screamed as soon as I got up behind. He can't bear anything to touch his wounds. I draped my shirt over him but even that made him shriek."

William rubbed at his eyes. They needed to get Albie home quickly. "We'll have to tie him to the horse, cover his back—"

Clem protested but William cut him off. "We have to, Clem. Then you can ride with me. We'll get back to the homestead quicker."

Clem hesitated.

Albie groaned.

"Come on, we've no time to waste."

Clem nodded and pulled his already bloodied shirt from his saddle bag. William took some rope from his and together, despite Albie's agonised moans, they secured the man to the horse. William was thankful he was riding Big Red. He was a large horse, used to stock work. William had perched orphaned newborn calves across the saddle with him before. Clem was strong but slight of build; Big Red would be able to bear them both home.

Two days later they all sat around the table. The mood was sombre. Albie was sleeping after the care of Millie and her assistant, Jessie. Hegarty was still away.

"Albie's wounds are many," Millie said. "He's been beaten as well as whipped, and lost some teeth. There are most likely other injuries but he can hardly stand the washing and healing treatment I've done already. I can do no more until he's rested." She clutched the sleeping Matthew to her chest. Her normally happy eyes brimmed with tears.

"You've done what you could for him, Millie." William reached up and placed his hand on hers. "Clem and I both agreed you were his best chance."

"I hope it's enough."

There had only been Robert, Millie and the young children at home when William had ridden to Wildu Creek. Millie had gathered whatever she thought she'd need and left the little girls with their adoring stepbrother. Robert would take good care of them and Joseph was expected home that night. With the baby sleeping in a temporary bed, an old crate William had found, Millie had done her best to tend Albie's wounds.

While he had been kept awake by the agony of his injuries he'd told them what had happened between gasps of pain. His money was all gone and he'd gone back to Prosser's Run to ask for his old job back. The evil man — Albie rolled his one open eye every time he mentioned Prosser — had set his men to beat the shepherd and Prosser had finished with his whip. Albie wailed all over again at the recollection and the pain of Millie attending his wounds. He'd been sleeping for the last few hours, much to everyone's relief. They had endured their own agony listening to his distress.

Clem, who had only just sat down after pacing the floor, sprang to his feet again. "I'm going off for a while."

"Where?" A worried look creased Jessie's face.

"Prosser can't get away with this."

"You're going to the police?" Millie's tone was incredulous.

"No. Prosser's a big name. They'll sweep it under the carpet." Clem crossed to the door and reached for the stock whip that hung on one of the row of hooks beside it. "I'm going to give him a taste of what he dished out."

Jessie and Millie both jumped up and Matthew, jolted from sleep, began to cry.

"No, Clem," Jessie pleaded. "There are many men at Prosser's Run. They will do the same to you."

"I must, Jessie." Clem cast a bitter look at William, who was still seated. "They cannot get away with nearly killing a man."

William drew in a breath. He had been thinking about what he should do since they'd first brought Albie home. Clem had a point but the current constable in Hawker was a sensible man. William stood so they were all now upright, even Matthew, who Millie was jiggling over her shoulder.

"You must ride to Hawker, Clem. Tell the constable where you found Albie and what happened."

Clem's dark eyes glittered. "I'm going to Prosser's Run."

"No." William crossed the room to stand beside Clem. "I'll go and see Prosser."

"Your friend." Clem spat the words. "What will you say to him? Good job, Ellis. You've beaten a defenceless man nearly to death."

William was speechless at the venom in Clem's words. It was hard to believe he thought William would defend such a cowardly and malicious act.

"No-one should go there." Millie spoke firmly. "Let the police deal with that man."

William was still looking at Clem. "I will let Prosser know he can't get away with what he's done."

"He will be terrified." Clem put his hands to his hips and laughed. It was a bitter sound.

"Stop, please Clem." Tears rolled down Jessie's cheeks.

A moaning sound came from the bedroom where they had left Albie to rest.

Millie gripped Matthew tightly and crossed the room. "William, you must go to Hawker. Report to the constable and then see if the doctor can come back here with you. I don't think Albie would survive the cart ride to town." She turned to Clem. "You will stay here. I don't like it being only Jessie and me here and I need strong hands to help me with Albie."

Clem stared at Millie, whose stance was determined.

"Ellis Prosser has a nasty temper and he's unpredictable." She waved her hand towards the bedroom. "Albie's wounds are testament to that."

"Please, Clem." Jessie came and took his hand.

He looked from her back to William.

"Millie's right." William felt the fight slip out of him. What would he have done when he got to Prosser's Run? Ellis Prosser would have laughed in his face and there was nothing William could have done about it. "We should tell the constable. He can come this way and see Albie's wounds for himself. Ellis Prosser will receive what he deserves."

Clem gave a snort but Jessie continued to grip his hand firmly. Millie stood ramrod straight beside them. William took his hat from the hook and pushed it firmly onto his head. At the door he turned back. They all watched him. Once more anger at the despicable actions of Ellis Prosser rose within him like hot lava. They were his responsibility. He snatched the rifle from the wall above the door. At the same time Albie's wails grew louder.

"William!" Millie's call was sharp. "Go to Hawker and bring back the doctor. Nothing good will come of seeking vengeance now." Her voice wavered. "Please."

William remembered the night when he and his father had sought revenge on Jack Aldridge. Henry Wiltshire had been there — Jack was his half-brother. It had been a terrible time. Jack had been living at Smith's Ridge then and William had ridden over planning to kill him for his torment of Millie and their family. It had not been so easy to pull the trigger on a man in cold blood, but thankfully the storm had done it for him. Jack had been struck by lightning and died. It had been a terrifying incident. Once more he gave thought to Ellis Prosser, father of the woman he loved. What should he do? He could confront Prosser, but then what?

He turned back to Millie, took in her trusting look, then strode outside into the brilliant sunlight of the hot December morning to get his horse. There would be time later to deal with Prosser but right now there were more urgent issues.

Eleven

Edith took the hand Charles offered as she stepped down from the train.

"Here we are at last." Charles waved grandly in the direction of the sprawl of buildings. "The thriving town of Hawker."

Edith blinked. Dust blew along the platform and mixed with the clouds of smoke billowing from the train. The heat from sun and wind was like stepping into a furnace. She was gratified to see that Hawker had an impressive railway station at least, and she had noted several other solid establishments as the train pulled in.

Prior to their arrival she had been beginning to doubt her decision to travel to Hawker for work. It had been interminably hot and stuffy in the carriage during the last part of the journey across desolate plains. Hawker was not quite what she'd call an oasis, but buildings, trees and streets busy with people, horses and carts gave an air of business. Unfortunately, all this motion stirred up the dust even more.

"It's certainly industrious." Edith adjusted her hat and brushed down her skirt. She was thankful she'd worn her one pale blue shirt over her grey skirt. After the close confines of the carriage where perspiration slipped into every crevice of her body these clothes were least likely to show the dirt that surely clung to her now.

"Ah, here's Father with our transport." Charles took her arm with one hand and gave a big wave towards a man in a dark suit alighting from a cart.

Edith took a deep breath. Charles had defended her against his grandmother and offered her this job. She could have made more of a fuss but it suited her to move away from the city. She had reinvented herself once already when she'd moved to Adelaide. This was an opportunity to begin again and leave Edie Jamieson and her tawdry past behind forever.

Father and son hugged each other while she waited. There was obviously great affection between them and Edith felt a pang of jealousy. Charles had been giving her his undivided attention over the past two days. He turned back to her. "Father this is Miss Ferguson, about whom I sent you the telegram."

Sharp dark eyes appraised her. Edith pulled her face into her most charming smile. She hoped Mr Wiltshire's mother had not also sent a telegram. Edith may have fooled Charles with her tears and desperation but she had the feeling Harriet Wiltshire's failing eyes had seen through her charade.

She need not have worried. Henry shook her hand warmly. "Welcome, Miss Ferguson. We are delighted you have agreed to join us. I hope you won't find it too harsh after working in my mother's delightful city premises."

Edith relaxed. "I'm most grateful for the opportunity, Mr Wiltshire, and looking forward to seeing your shop. Charles has told me much about it."

"Well once we're loaded up we can go straight there."

"Father, perhaps Miss Ferguson would like to see her accommodation and freshen up first. You know how tiring the journey from Adelaide is. First the trip to Quorn and then the overnight wait until today's train."

Mr Wiltshire senior's face crinkled into a smile. "Of course. Forgive my exuberance, Miss Ferguson."

"I must admit I would like to tidy myself, Mr Wiltshire, but after that I am very keen to inspect my new place of employment. Mr Charles has brought so many new ideas which he has also been sharing with me."

Charles guided her to the cart and his father walked alongside them. "We have been looking forward to your arrival, Miss Ferguson. My wife will also be pleased to meet you. She has invited you to dine with us this evening. Your accommodation is right next door."

Two sets of hands helped her up onto the seat. She looked down at the two Wiltshire men, who were beaming back at her.

Edith smiled. "Please, Mr Wiltshire, you are my employer: do call me Edith. Mr Charles does."

"Then I will be Mr Henry." The older man chuckled.

"Thank you both so much. This has been quite an adventure already."

Charles climbed up beside her and there was barely a chance to wave goodbye. She was forced to grab her hat with one hand and the side of the seat with the other as the cart lurched forward. The male Wiltshires were dancing attendance on her but she had yet another hurdle to cross. Mrs Catherine Wiltshire may be more like her mother-in-law and not so easily swayed by a smile or a teardrop.

Edith squinted through the dusty air at the houses they passed, while Charles kept up a banter about who lived where and their importance, or lack thereof, to the community.

A horse thundered past them, coming to a stop at a building ahead, and the rider slid from the saddle.

Edith heard the hiss Charles made through his teeth. "Who is that?" she asked as she watched the man hurry into the building, which she could see as they passed was the doctor's residence.

"William Baker. A man from the bush with few manners as you can see by the way he just barged inside Dr Chambers' rooms. You don't need to worry about him though. We don't allow him or his family to darken the doors of our shop."

They travelled on. Edith cast a quick look at Charles, who had lost his good humour. She risked a glance behind in time to see Baker come outside again and stride off in the other direction.

Charles almost faltered as he rose to his feet when his mother entered the room. She had been resting when he'd called in at the house before taking Edith to the shop. Now as Catherine entered the sitting room where they waited before dinner he was shocked. His mother's face was deathly pale, deeper lines sagged across her once-pretty face and as she drew him into a hug he was engulfed in a wobbly ball of flesh. Her health had deteriorated in his absence but her clothes, as always, were immaculate. Tonight she wore a deep red silk with an open neckline that showed the puffy flesh around her neck.

"You look lovely, Mother," he said as he kissed her cheek.

She smiled at him but her eyes remained dull. "And you have grown into a man during your travels, Charles."

"Mother, we have a guest." Charles deflected her attention to Edith.

Catherine turned to the young lady, who had also risen to her feet. "And you must be Miss Ferguson." They clasped hands. "Please do sit down again while we wait for Henry. You must be so tired, Miss Ferguson. I know how tedious the journey from Adelaide can be."

"It's certainly a long way, but I had the opportunity to rest after visiting the shop."

"And what did you think? Henry said you previously worked in his mother's shop. Ours is nowhere near as grand."

"But it's much more interesting."

Charles dragged his concerned gaze from his mother to Edith, whose face glowed in contrast. She had been enthusiastic during her visit to the shop that afternoon.

"Oh, I hope you don't mind me being so frank, Mrs Wiltshire, but your shop has such grand diversification and Mr Charles has ideas for improvement gleaned from his travels with your mother-in-law."

"Really, Charles? You must tell me all about them."

The door swung open and a small curly brown-headed apparition in white flew across the room and pounced into Charles's lap.

"Laura." He murmured as two little arms flung around his neck and a wet kiss landed on his cheek.

"She's missed you." His mother smiled benevolently — finally her eyes showed some light.

"Chars." The little girl giggled.

Charles set her on the ground and turned her round. "Laura, this is Miss Ferguson. She is going to work in our shop."

Laura's thumb went to her mouth. She did a wide arc around Miss Ferguson and climbed onto her mother's lap.

Catherine patted her back as she cuddled her. "Laura's shy with strangers, Miss Ferguson, but I am sure she will soon get to know you."

"Hello, Miss Laura," Edith said.

Laura huddled closer to her mother's bosom.

"You should encourage her manners, Mother. She's not a baby."

"But still very young." Edith inclined her head to Catherine. "I know how it is to be shy. I was always cowering behind my mother's skirts as a little girl. I am sure we will get to know each other soon enough."

Catherine gave Edith a grateful smile. "And where are your parents now, Edith?"

Edith's lips turned down. "Both gone from this world now, Mrs Wiltshire. I am quite alone."

"Oh my dear, I am so sorry. How sad for you."

Edith's face was drawn. "I have been managing quite well and I am most grateful to have the job at your shop."

"It seems I rescued you from Grandmother's clutches just in time." Charles felt compelled to lighten the moment and was rewarded with a brief smile from Edith.

"You did."

"What's this about your grandmother?" Catherine asked.

At that moment Laura put two hands to her mother's face and turned it to her. "Story, Mama, story."

"Oh my darling." Catherine chuckled and drew the child into a hug. "She speaks well for someone so young, don't you think, Edith?"

Edith remained ramrod straight, perched on the edge of her chair. "I wouldn't know, Mrs Wiltshire. I've had little experience with young children."

Laura clutched the necklace that hung around her mother's neck.

"What a beautiful locket, Mrs Wiltshire." Edith's gaze was on the heart that Laura held.

"It is very special. It has been in the Wiltshire family for a long time. Grandmother Harriet gave it to me when Charles was born." Catherine glanced at him.

Laura wriggled on her mother's lap and clapped her hands. Catherine kissed her plump cheeks. "You are *such* a delight."

Charles blew a silent sigh over his lips. Laura was far too indulged but there was little he could do about the infatuation that consumed both his parents. He always treated her with distance but, in spite of this, Laura sought him out if neither of them was available.

Once more the door opened and Henry stepped into the room. "Ah, good. You're all here. Mrs Nixon tells me dinner is ready." He swept Laura from her mother's lap and planted a kiss on her cheek. "And you are off to bed, my little princess."

Laura wailed.

"She wants a story, Henry." Catherine spoke above the noise.

Henry kissed his daughter and, ignoring her protests, carried her to the door. "Mrs Nixon will read you a story once our dinner is served." He disappeared from the room and the sound of Laura's protests faded.

Catherine struggled to the edge of her chair. "He is so good with her," she puffed. Charles bent to offer his arm and she took it with a grateful smile. "He is a very good father to you both."

Once everyone was seated around the table Mrs Nixon served slices of jellied meat.

"Thank you, Flora," Catherine said. "Have you been introduced to our guest, Miss Edith Ferguson?"

"Yes, Mr Charles brought her to the kitchen when he arrived." Flora inclined her head towards her mistress. Charles noticed she flashed a sharp look in Edith's direction then she glanced from him to Henry. "Enjoy your meal."

"Thank you, Flora," Catherine said again as their housekeeper, cook and general help maid left the room. "Now, I need your honest opinion about this, everyone. I would like to serve it on Christmas Eve. We are expecting quite a crowd so I want to make sure everything is in order."

Charles eyed the jelly-like substance on his plate. "What is it, Mother?"

"Fruity jellied mutton." Catherine took a small taste from her fork. They watched as she nodded her head. "Yes, it has a delightful orange tang and is refreshing. Just what we will need for the heat of Christmas Eve."

They all tried the food and Charles was relieved to find it quite tasty. He noticed his father and Edith finished what was on their plates as well.

"I think we can put that down as a yes, Catherine." Henry patted at his chin with his napkin.

"It was delicious, Mrs Wiltshire." Edith quickly added her praise.

"I can't take all the credit. I came up with the idea and Flora fiddled with the quantities to get it right."

"Well done, Flora," Charles said as she came in to collect their plates.

"I should help." Edith rose.

"There's no need, Miss Ferguson," Flora said. "Enjoy your dinner; no doubt you'll be joining me in the kitchen in future." She strode from the room with her full tray.

"Oh ... I ..." Edith sat. "I hope it's not been too presumptuous of me accepting your kind dinner invitation, Mrs Wiltshire."

Charles noticed her cheeks were a soft pink, whether from the heat or from the small amount of wine she'd sipped he wasn't sure. He hoped she wasn't embarrassed by Flora's brusque response.

"Of course not, Edith." Catherine gave the young woman a radiant smile. "It is so lovely to have guests. We try not to be too formal here."

"It's only fitting you should eat with us on your first night." Charles hurried to add his reassurance. He was fond of Flora but she could overstep the mark sometimes.

"But all the same it would be best if you ate with Mrs Nixon once you begin work." Henry cleared his throat. "Even though we are in the country there are some formalities that should be observed."

Charles didn't know what to say. On the one hand he agreed with his father but on the other Edith already seemed like one of the family to him rather than an employee.

"Oh, I do understand, Mr Henry." Edith looked perfectly calm. "I will be very comfortable in my new accommodation and will take my meals there. Mrs Nixon will have enough to do without looking out for me. I am most grateful for this opportunity." She turned dark eyes to Charles and smiled. "I fully intend to look after myself."

"Good." Henry took a large sip of wine and turned to Catherine. "Now, my dear, who are all these people we are expecting for Christmas Eve dinner? I hope you won't overdo it. You must remember your poor health."

"Have you not been well, Mother?"

"I am perfectly well. Your father fusses."

Charles thought that was last thing his father did, but he didn't contradict her.

"There will be Ellis Prosser of course," Catherine began. "That poor man will be spending his second Christmas alone."

"Any word on the Prosser ladies' return?" Charles asked.

"Ellis thinks in the autumn," Henry said. "It will depend on which ship they can book passage on."

"I am delighted to say Dr and Mrs Chambers and Headmaster Harris and his wife have accepted my invitation to join us. They don't have other family here in Hawker." Catherine tapped her fingers together, a smile played on her lips. "I'm not sure about Sydney and Agnes Taylor; they may still be away. Councillor Hill and his wife and daughters, and of course I invited your creamery partners, the Pymans and the Buttons."

"Really, Mother. Don't these people have their own Christmas functions to attend?"

"We will all have the day itself with our own families, of course, but I thought it a nice gesture to invite special guests to share one meal with us. We are so isolated here in Hawker I would like to begin a new tradition."

"Your mother is doing her best to keep us in the community standing we deserve, Charles." His father gave a disapproving frown. "You should be grateful for her efforts."

Charles noticed a strange look pass between his parents. They were an odd couple these days. They slept in separate rooms. He had the third bedroom and Laura slept in a little cot in her mother's bedroom. When they were alone, just the three of them without Laura, all conversation was directed through Charles, and yet they held regular events such as this, where they were the ultimate host and hostess. He wondered if other families were like his. Lonely and cold on the inside yet showing a bright happy face to the community.

"I am sure it will be a wonderful event." Edith leaned closer to Catherine. "Perhaps I could offer my services to Mrs Nixon. I am a basic cook I'm afraid but I could clear the table and wash dishes."

"Oh that would be marvellous, Edith." Catherine beamed. "Thank you. I am sure Flora would appreciate the help."

"Well that's settled then," Henry said just as Mrs Nixon came through the door, her tray laden with the next course.

"I'm sorry to bother you, Mrs Wiltshire, but little miss won't settle without a good-night kiss from you," Mrs Nixon said as she placed platters of cold meat on the table.

Charles sucked in a breath of annoyance as his mother folded her napkin and rose. He'd forgotten all this bedtime drama while he'd been away.

"She can wait, Catherine," Henry said.

"It won't take a moment. She's probably nearly asleep already." Catherine waved a hand at the food. "Do continue without me. I shan't be long."

Once more Charles noticed the look of annoyance his father gave his mother as she passed.

"How long have you had your business here, Mr Henry?" Edith's question broke the silence.

"Wiltshires have been here as long as the town of Hawker itself, Edith. We opened our doors in 1881 and we've built a fine reputation since then."

"One that will only improve." Charles looked from Edith to his father. "Grandmother would like to support us with the extensions to the shop."

A brief look of surprise crossed his father's face and then he smiled. "Well done, son," he said. "Well done."

Twelve

Henry turned back from the window as Flora ushered in Ellis Prosser. The big man appeared even bigger than when Henry had last seen him, and his face was a florid red. Christmas Eve had been hot from first light, and now it was early evening and no cooler. Outside there was not a breath of wind. Thankfully the thick walls of the house at least kept the temperature lower inside, but it was still warm. Henry stuck a finger between his neck and his stiff new shirt collar and wriggled it in irritation.

"Hello, Henry." Ellis strode across the room, his hand outstretched. "I thought I was running late. Damned horse shed a shoe. Where is everyone?"

Henry shook Ellis's sweaty hand. "We are a small group this evening."

"Oh, don't tell me you've been stood up. Who have you offended this time?" Ellis helped himself to Henry's good whisky and took a swig from the new crystal. It was one of a set, a gift to Henry from his mother for Christmas. Catherine had only placed them on the tray moments before Ellis's arrival. Ellis gave a sharp laugh. "I'm joking, Henry. You've a face like thunder. What's happened? Catherine's parties are famous for their fine food and hospitality."

"As it happens we have been 'stood up', as you say, Ellis."

"Really?" Ellis took another swig and made himself comfortable in one of Catherine's fine chairs. "Whatever for?"

"It seems it's your behaviour rather than mine that has people upset."

The big man spluttered into his glass.

"Once word got out your name was on our guest list we were suddenly not so popular."

"What?" Ellis's huge eyebrows knotted across the bridge of his bulbous nose. "What do you mean, Wiltshire?"

Henry paused. Ellis had helped him with his venture into farming and had stood by him on committees. Their friendship went back a long way. Like Henry, Ellis did not tolerate poor behaviour in employees, although Henry had strong suspicions Ellis was indeed more physical in his dealings. Henry had kept clear of anything distasteful but this last incident was too terrible to ignore. He drew in a deep breath. "It seems you have been reported to the police for beating and whipping a shepherd."

"I ... that's ... " Ellis spluttered into his glass. "I told the constable it was a load of lies cooked up by that lazy bugger who used to work for me." He spluttered some more. "Can't even remember his name."

"Albie, I believe."

"Yes, he's the one. Always drunk when he worked for me. Couldn't do his job, so I sent him packing." Ellis drew himself up, his gaze steely. "That was a long time ago."

Normally Henry would back down from Ellis's dark side but this time he stood his ground. "So you didn't order your men to beat him and then take your whip to him just recently?"

"The constable came to see me about this already. He spoke to me and questioned my men. I told him we'd had a drunk on the property and sent him packing with a flea in his ear, that's all. It could have been that Albie fellow — I don't know. I can't help it if he was so drunk he injured himself later, but I won't take the blame for it."

Henry studied Ellis. He wanted to believe his friend but the stories of the beating endured by the shepherd had been horrific. "The injuries described couldn't have been from an accident. Someone inflicted them."

"You've been listening to gossip, Henry." Ellis jabbed his finger in the air. "Now you can listen to me. I can't believe you would take the word of a lazy servant over mine."

Henry wavered. "The man has not been well enough to say too much to the police up till this point."

"There you are then." Ellis downed the last of his drink. "It's all gossip. You know how this town is."

Muffled voices came from the passage and before Henry could clarify what he'd heard the door opened and Catherine entered. She paused when she saw Ellis; a small frown flitted across her forehead and then she smiled.

"Ellis, I didn't know you'd arrived." She stepped aside. Sydney and Agnes Taylor followed her in. "The Taylors arrived home on today's train and have been able to join us."

Henry saw her lip tremble and he willed her to hold herself together. She had been distressed when their guests had declined one after another, but she had been determined not to spoil their party.

Sydney shook Henry's hand and then Ellis's.

Agnes fingered a shiny new brooch at the neck of her shirt. "We knew we'd be able to catch up with several of our friends in one place if we made it here for Christmas Eve." She paused and looked around. The jewelled drops on the brooch wobbled as she moved. "We are obviously early."

There was another knock at the door. Catherine glanced hopefully at Henry and retreated to the hall.

"It will be a small gathering." Henry crossed to the dresser. "Can I offer you a cold lemonade or a glass of wine?"

Voices could be heard in the hall and before the Taylors could answer Catherine was back.

"The Hills have arrived."

She ushered in the councillor, his wife Anne and their two daughters. Both young ladies were of a similar age to Charles and Henry noticed them looking in his son's direction.

Mrs Hill looked rather pale, perhaps from the heat. As soon as the greetings were finished her husband took her arm and guided her to a chair. Charles and Catherine offered drinks but the gathering lacked the usual geniality of social events at the Wiltshire house.

A hush fell over the room, punctuated by a giggle from the youngest Miss Hill as Charles handed her a glass of lemonade. Even Ellis was quiet. He'd taken a seat in the corner and was glowering at the gathered guests.

Henry cleared his throat and raised his glass to the room. "Merry Christmas, everyone."

The same sentiment chorused around him.

"What pretty dresses your daughters are wearing, Anne." Catherine seated herself next to Mrs Hill. "Is that your handiwork?"

Henry ignored Ellis brooding in the corner and asked Councillor Hill about the progress of the referendum to be held in the new year. The separate states were being asked to vote on becoming a nation and he wanted Councillor Hill's views on the subject.

The conversations were finally flowing when Mrs Nixon came in to announce dinner was ready.

Catherine paled. "Oh, Flora, I forgot to come and tell you we will be ten at table."

Flora smiled. "I've taken care of it, Mrs Wiltshire."

Henry's shoulders relaxed. Flora would have been taking in the arrivals and added the extra settings around the table accordingly. He knew Catherine had fiddled for days with the place names, written neatly in coloured ink and decorated with small red berries. Several were now packed away of course but ten was a good number and the seating wouldn't be so tight.

They crossed to the dining room, where Flora had already set out neat serves of the fruity jellied mutton. From across the table he saw Anne Hill purse her lips as she took in the names either side of hers. She beckoned to her husband.

"I accepted this invitation because you said we should but I will not be seated next to that man." She spoke in a harsh whisper. Her dark eyes swivelled in Ellis's direction.

"Don't fuss, Anne," her husband murmured. "You can have my place." He turned to Catherine. "Sorry to rearrange your seating plan, but I rather thought I would like to sit next to Ellis."

"Oh." Catherine swept up the offending name card. "No ... the ladies are in between ... I had it all arranged."

Agnes and Sydney looked curiously at the Hills and Charles showed the two young ladies to their seats either side of him at the other end of the table.

Henry could see his wife dithering as her careful planning was upset. Catherine was no longer able to think on her feet. She had become an old lady before her time. Today she had chosen to wear a pale pink dress covered in lace and frills. With her pale complexion and ballooning body shape it only succeeded in ageing her further.

"Just a moment," Catherine said. "I'm sorry everyone. I seem to have made a muddle of the seating." She made a move towards the younger people's end of the table.

"And not with my girls." Anne's look was positively thunderous.

Ellis, who was the last into the room, looked over Catherine's shoulder at the paper she held. He'd had several glasses of whisky already. "Am I being removed?"

"Not at all, Ellis," Catherine soothed. "I made a mistake —".

"The mistake was inviting that man." Anne Hill's voice was sharp and clear now.

"What's this?" Ellis bellowed. "Control your wife, Councillor."

Anne's eyes blazed. "Or what, Mr Prosser? You will take your whip to me?"

"My goodness." Agnes put her hand to her mouth.

"What's this about?" her husband asked.

"Mrs Hill has been listening to malicious gossip." Ellis folded his arms across his broad chest. "So much for friends."

"There was an incident during your absence, Sydney." Henry felt it his duty to smooth the waters but he wasn't sure how. Anne Hill had obviously attended under sufferance and could hold her tongue no longer. "A shepherd was badly injured on or near Prosser's Run."

"And I got the blame," Ellis cut in. "I've already been questioned and the constable is satisfied it was not my doing."

"That's not what I've heard." Anne would not let it go.

"Hah!" Ellis snorted and jabbed a finger in her direction. "Gossip."

"Dr Chambers is not one to gossip," Councillor Hill said, supporting his wife. "He treated the unfortunate man, whose injuries were so bad they did not think he would live."

"Nothing to do with me," Ellis roared. The red of his face and neck deepened.

"Dr Chambers was present when the constable questioned the shepherd again just yesterday," Councillor Hill said. "The doctor heard everything and so did the young nurse assisting him."

From there it hadn't taken long for the news to spread. Henry had heard about it from a customer the previous afternoon and by evening the hurried excuses from their guests had begun arriving. They would all have known Ellis Prosser was a likely attendee for Christmas Eve dinner. The Taylors' recent return and Councillor Hill's ambitions for his daughters had provided them with their only guests. Henry glanced across at the two young ladies, still seated either side of his son, and sighed.

"What has this to do with Ellis?" Sydney asked. "He has stated he was not involved."

"Albie, as the injured man is called," Councillor Hill continued, "described in detail what happened to him, where and by whom."

"So the constable will no doubt be paying you another visit." Anne gave a self-satisfied nod.

"The man's a liar if he's blaming me." Ellis's bellow filled the room. He glared at the occupants one by one and finally his angry gaze reached Henry. "It's my word against that of a drunken timewaster."

"One of your men has come forward." Anne spoke again. "You can't buy everyone's silence, Ellis Prosser."

"Oh dear." Catherine's words were a mere whisper as she crumpled to the floor, a bundle of pale pink lace and frills. Silence followed her collapse.

Henry was the first to move. "Catherine." He pushed past Ellis to his wife, who lay still and deathly pale. He reached for her hand as the room suddenly filled with voices.

"See what your bad manners have caused, Mrs Hill," Ellis snarled.

"Mother?" Charles had come to kneel on Catherine's other side.

"How dare you accuse my wife, Prosser?" Councillor Hill roared.

Henry didn't see what happened behind him but there was a thud, screams from the ladies and the sound of breaking glass.

"Stop this at once." Flora Nixon's commanding voice boomed over the cacophony.

Henry glanced around. Flora stood just inside the dining-room door, glaring across the room, with Miss Ferguson wide eyed beside her. They both looked down at Catherine on the floor. Flora rushed to her side. "Edith, wet a cloth please," she commanded.

"I think she's only fainted," Henry said as Flora snatched a nearby cushion and placed it gently under Catherine's head. "We've had a bit of a to-do in here."

Flora looked up. Their gazes locked and for one brief moment Henry saw her gentle look, then just as quickly her housekeeper face returned. She turned to Charles beside her. "We need to loosen her clothing. You should take the guests into the sitting room."

"Offer them another drink," Henry said.

Edith passed a table napkin she had dampened with cool water, which Flora pressed to Catherine's forehead. Charles stood, giving Henry a clear view of Ellis Prosser slumped against the wall in a pool of broken glass. Anne Hill was tending her husband's face, with her two sobbing daughters beside her.

"Should we send for the doctor?" Agnes asked.

"I'll be all right, woman," Ellis snapped.

"Not for you, you big fool. For Mrs Wiltshire."

Catherine's eyelids began to flutter.

"She's only fainted," Henry said. "If you'd all go with Charles to the sitting room he will make sure you have a refreshing drink while we see to my wife."

They filed out. Ellis was the last. He glowered at Henry then glanced down as Catherine gave a soft moan. "Tell her I'm sorry," he muttered. The front door thudded shut a few minutes later.

With the help of the two women Henry managed to get Catherine to her bed.

Thankfully Laura was oblivious to the mayhem that had ensued, fast asleep in her cot in the corner. Catherine was rousing and he left her in Flora's capable hands to return to his guests. Some Christmas party this had been. Somehow he had to smooth waters and continue the meal without the hostess.

The sitting room was empty. He returned to the dining room, where Charles sat at the table alone.

"They've all gone," Henry said, declaring the obvious.

Charles shrugged. "All very apologetic. Leaving with their best wishes for Mother on their lips." He turned his deadpan look on Henry. "Is she all right?"

"She'll have a sore head but otherwise yes. This happened a couple of times while you were away. Dr Chambers seems to think it's brought on by agitation or distress. There's no need to call him out tonight."

"He would be unlikely to come." Charles twisted his lips in a wry smile and slowly poked a fork into the now sloppy mutton jelly. "We may have become unpalatable seeing as we are harbouring an apparent criminal."

"Don't be ridiculous. Of course the doctor would come, but I don't see the need." Henry crossed to the small table that housed the drinks and stopped when he saw the crumpled legs, the wet floorboards and broken glass. The delicate piece of furniture must have borne the full brunt of Ellis's weight in his struggle with Councillor Hill. A small pain niggled behind Henry's eyes. He had worked hard to get where he was. He owned land in the district, his business was thriving and he had used the money it generated to add a servant wing and cellar to his house, which was now the finest in Hawker. His friend Ellis Prosser's behaviour could threaten all he'd achieved.

"Do you think Mr Prosser did beat that man, Father?"

Henry took a breath. "We should leave it in the hands of the constable." He adjusted the tie at his neck. "I need a drink."

Henry left Charles and crossed back to the sitting room, poured himself a whisky and slumped into a chair. What was he to do? This whole business was very nasty and most people appeared to be against Ellis in this. Henry would need to think on it. There had been many times when Ellis Prosser had been a great help to him and there had been a few business dealings between them Henry would prefer no-one else knew about. If this business with the shepherd turned out to be true, Henry's friendship with Ellis could see him ousted from his carefully built position as a leader in the Hawker community.

He took a swig from the glass, closed his eyes and rubbed at the now throbbing pain in his temple.

Thirteen

January 1898

Hegarty brought the loaded wagon to a stop as William, Clem and Jessie came out to meet him. The sun was still only a glow on the horizon. Thin wispy clouds stretched across the sky tinged with pink and the promise of another hot dry day.

"You've made good time," William said as the big man climbed down from the wagon and rubbed his behind with both hands. "I wasn't expecting you until tomorrow at the earliest."

"Nothing to hang around in Hawker for." Hegarty wiped his face with a large handkerchief stained with brown. "The dust is worse there than here. It's as if every fragment of the surface of the plain has been swept into the air."

"We still have some cover here," William said. The drought had set in and they had very little stock.

"You were right to sell off as many cattle as you could, and Joseph was right to do the same with the sheep from Wildu Creek. At least the land hasn't been stripped bare." Hegarty looked back in the direction of Hawker. "Those farmers on the plains have ploughed the land so much, and now there is nothing left to hold the dirt. Even the slightest puff of wind lifts it into the air. Plenty are leaving their land. The price of copper has risen and some of the old mines further north have been reopened. There are those who've gone off in search of work."

William felt the weight of the drought as if it were a physical load on his shoulders.

"We just have to wait it out," Hegarty said. "It can't last forever."

They set to work unloading the wagon. Jessie supervised the storing of the food in the house; William helped carry the items needed for their ever-expanding fence lines to the stone hut up the hill.

When it was done the sun was fully risen, belting them with its relentless heat. They stood in the shade of a tree and Jessie passed around mugs of cool water.

After Hegarty had drained his he patted down his pockets and finally, with a dramatic flourish, he drew something out. "I found you this, lass." He held out one big hand to Jessie.

"What is it?" Clem asked.

Hegarty winked. "She'll know what to do with it."

Jessie took the small bottle, glanced at the label and levered the cork from the top.

The three men watched as she put it to her nose and took a sniff. Her eyebrows raised and her face broke into a beautiful smile. She studied the small label on the front again.

"Ess ... ence of ..." she peered closer "... rose?" She looked up at Hegarty, her eyes wide.

"I'm guessing you probably haven't come across a rose before," Hegarty said.

Jessie shook her head.

"I've heard of them," William said. "Flowers with a rich perfume. My grandmother loved the smell."

Jessie pushed the top back into the neck of the bottle. "I can add it to the soap."

"That was my idea, lass. You could find something to make a pale pink colour too, I'm sure." Hegarty's smile slipped. "But not in the blocks you make for us men. It's for the ladies, that one."

Jessie slipped the precious bottle into her apron pocket then reached up and flung her arms around his neck. "Thank you, Mr Hegarty. It's a very thoughtful gift."

As she stepped back William was torn between laughing at the wide-eyed Hegarty and crying for the young woman who'd not had the delight of sharing and friendship in her life until she married Clem and came to live at Smith's Ridge. Her joy over the small gifts they'd exchanged at Christmas had been wonderful to see.

"I'm going to cook us pancakes for morning tea." Jessie beamed at them all and kissed Clem's cheek. "Would you bring me some wood please, Clem? The box is low." He gave her a nod and set off towards the woodpile as Jessie almost skipped back inside.

William let out a sigh of relief. Her pancakes were better than her scones at least. She made a good job of washing their clothes, keeping the house in order, milking the cow and even plaiting rope, but her cooking had improved little, even after Millie's tutelage.

"Where did you find the essence?" he asked Hegarty as they unhitched the horses from the wagon.

Hegarty looked at him over the back of a horse. "Wiltshire's shop."

William raised his eyebrows. "We don't usually shop there."

"I know." Hegarty undid the harness. "But Garrat is only stocking the basics these days and he's spending a lot of time on the road. I overheard two women talking about the new shop assistant in Wiltshire's and the introduction of more soaps, perfumes and essences." Hegarty shrugged his shoulders. "The new assistant's a woman. I went for a look. Then I had to buy something from her. Jessie makes good soap. I thought she might enjoy making something special for herself."

William grinned. "And the new assistant?"

"Young and shapely enough but barely smiled, mousey hair and rather plain of face."

"You took a good look at her then." William laughed and shook his head as he led the horses away. Hegarty was older than Joseph. He'd never mentioned life before meeting Joseph on the Teetulpa gold fields and then coming to work with the Bakers. There had never been talk of a wife or children. William supposed Hegarty wasn't too old to be with a woman if he chose — not that there was any chance of someone Henry Wiltshire employed becoming friendly with anyone associated with the Bakers. William shook his head to erase the thought.

They ate the pancakes in the big front room. It was just as warm in there as outside but at least they could keep most of the little black flies out.

"Any news from Hawker?" William asked.

"Some," Hegarty replied through a mouthful of dough.

"You mentioned Mr Garrat was out on the road. What's he doing?"

"He has a weekly round taking wagonloads of groceries to farms. Saves them coming in to town."

"That seems like a good initiative if people can pay." William shook his head. "Mr Garrat has always been generous to people in hard times."

"Garrat is a good man but this drought has affected him like everyone else." Hegarty sat back. "Everyone except Wiltshire, of course. While we're all tightening our belts he's building additions to his shop. It looks to be a big change and business didn't appear that busy while I was there. His son Charles was there among the builders giving orders and strutting around like a peacock."

"Like his father."

"But taller," Hegarty said. "Evidently he's been away. Must have been eating well by the way he's filled out. The teamsters in Hawker are all getting work with the copper mines reopening. There's been plenty of loads of new plant and supplies to take out and the first load of ore came in to the rail yards while I was there. Wiltshires have bought two of their own teams. They've even got their name painted on the sides of their wagons." Hegarty sat back. "They certainly don't seem to lack money to splash about and they've got their hands in many things."

William dropped his fork to his empty plate. "Surely there must be other news that doesn't involve the Wiltshires."

"Some." Hegarty glanced at Clem. "Ellis Prosser has been called before the magistrate."

Jessie jumped as Clem's fist thumped the table. "At last."

"It could still be a while. Evidently the magistrate won't get to Hawker for another month or two. Ellis has been confined to Prosser's Run until then."

Clem snorted in disgust. "He should be in chains."

"Prosser won't leave his place," Hegarty said. "He has too much invested there."

Once more Clem gave a snort.

William looked across the table. "At least Albie is walking again."

"He'll be a cripple for the rest of his life." Clem's eyes blazed with anger.

"Let's hope we see justice in the end."

Clem pushed back from his chair. He strode across the room and out through the kitchen, his footsteps the only sound until the thud of the back door.

Jessie gathered their plates. She gave William and Hegarty an awkward smile and left them alone.

"He's an angry young man, that one." Hegarty jerked his head in the direction of the kitchen.

"He cares deeply for his friend." William turned his gaze to the window. "What Ellis Prosser did was sinful. How could one man treat another so badly?"

Hegarty was silent a moment. William continued to stare out the window as motes of dust whirled in the air around him.

"Prosser will get what he's due." Hegarty slapped his leg and stood. "Work to be done." The big man lumbered from the room.

William heard him have a quick chat to Jessie in the kitchen before letting himself out. The thought of Ellis Prosser being brought to justice was a double-edged sword for William. On the one hand he was glad to see the man made accountable for his terrible treatment of Albie but on the other William worried about Georgina and her mother. What would become of them if Prosser were sent to prison?

His thoughts lingered on Georgina. He hadn't had a letter from her for months. He had hoped she would manage to send him a message at Christmas but it was nearing the end of January and no mail had come his way.

A little worm of hope wriggled in his chest. It had been more than a year and a half since they had pledged their love for each other and made their plan to marry. Surely he could survive a few more months.

Fourteen

April 1898

"Oh look, Mother, there are the Wiltshires." Georgina pressed her face to the train window as it came to a halt at the station. "Oh dear, Mrs Wiltshire looks even larger than she was when we left. What on earth is she wearing?"

"Hush, Georgina," her mother reprimanded.

"I wonder who they're meeting?" It was so hard to sit still. Georgina felt as excited as a child to be home at last. She twisted the other way. "I can't see Father."

"Do sit back, Georgina. I'm sure he'll be there somewhere." Johanna Prosser reached across and pulled at her daughter's arm. "You'll crush your new hat."

Georgina flopped back on the seat but kept watch through the window as the train finally came to a halt. She didn't give a fig for the new hat her mother had insisted on buying in Sydney. She had already accumulated so many clothes that would be impractical for life at home.

"Home," she whispered. How good that sounded. Her eyes searched through the hustle and bustle along the station for her father's tall frame. All she wanted was to return to Prosser's Run. It was April already, nearly two years since they'd left. She was tired of travelling and longed to see the country. It had been a shock to see the state of the dusty plains they'd travelled across before reaching Hawker, but it hadn't dampened the enthusiasm she felt on her return.

Now, with the train stationary at last, they both got to their feet and collected their hand luggage. The trunk and several new cases were in the baggage car.

"I hope Father has brought the wagon," Georgina said. "He won't fit all our things in the cart."

"I warned him how much luggage we had in my last letter from Sydney." Johanna smiled at her daughter. "You're right. It is good to be home." She reached up and adjusted Georgina's small russet-red hat. "Let us alight and find your father."

No sooner had they stepped down than Henry Wiltshire was at her mother's side. He removed his hat, his face like stone. "My dear Mrs Prosser." He inclined his head to Georgina. "Miss Prosser."

"Hello, Henry," Johanna said, looking past him. "Have you seen Ellis?"

Henry cleared his throat. "I am here in his place. Catherine is with me. We've come to escort you to our house."

"Is Ellis unable to come?" Johanna asked.

Georgina felt her spirits dampen. She didn't want to spend time with the Wiltshires while she waited for her father. She simply wanted to go home.

"Please come this way." Henry shepherded them towards his wife.

People on the platform watched them curiously. A few they knew gave them barely an acknowledgement and moved on. It gave Georgina a strange feeling.

"Oh, my poor Johanna." Catherine dragged Georgina's mother into a hug.

"Catherine." Henry's tone held a warning note.

Georgina studied Mrs Wiltshire. Up close she looked terrible. Her skin was pale and her once-pretty eyes were dull.

"What is it?" Johanna looked from one to the other. "Where's Ellis?"

Even as her mother asked the question Henry moved them on. A fine new open carriage awaited, almost as sleek as the mare that pulled it. Charles sat sombre-faced in the driver's seat. A chill swept over Georgina in spite of the sunshine. Henry almost tossed them into their seats, though Catherine took a bit more manoeuvring. Finally, all four of them were in the carriage and Henry gave Charles a pat on the shoulder. They set off at a pace, Charles showing no concern for the people who had to scatter out of his way.

"Where is my father, Mr Wiltshire?" Georgina spoke up, as her mother seemed to have lost her voice altogether.

Henry leaned forward and almost landed in their laps as the carriage bounced over a particularly large rut. He looked from Georgina to her mother. "I'm sorry to have to tell you, my dear." He took her hand and Catherine sniffed loudly into her handkerchief. "Ellis is gone."

"Gone?"

"He's passed."

"Passed?"

Fear gripped Georgina. "Are you saying my father is dead?"

Catherine let out a sharp cry.

"Yes." Henry croaked.

"He can't be." Johanna shook her head in disbelief. "I had a telegram from him before we left Sydney. He was looking forward to our return."

"And so he was." Henry patted her hand. "I dined with him only a few weeks ago and he was delighted to know you would soon be home."

Georgina turned a baleful look on Catherine, who was sobbing openly now. It was hard to think. "What happened?"

"Your housekeeper, Mrs Donovan, found him in his chair just two days ago. The doctor thinks it was his heart."

"No." Johanna shook her head. "Not Ellis."

Georgina glared at her mother. They should never have stayed away so long.

The carriage turned from the street into the Wiltshires' front yard, where a track covered in gravel swept in a curve to their front door. Charles brought the horse to a stop and was quickly beside the carriage to help them down. He guided his sobbing mother inside and Henry took Johanna's arm. Georgina was left to trail behind. Her heart thumped loudly in her chest and all other sounds faded as if she were in a bubble.

Charles came back to take her arm and she let herself be led to a chair in the Wiltshires' sitting room. Their housekeeper was there pouring cups of tea. Mr and Mrs Wiltshire were missing; it was Charles who made sure they were comfortable. There was no conversation. Georgina turned to her mother, who sat as if in a trance, all colour gone from her face, her own new hat slightly askew. The cup of tea beside her sat untouched, as did Georgina's.

Henry joined them. He murmured something to the house-keeper, who left, then he sat beside Johanna. He took both her hands in his and rubbed them gently. "Catherine will be back to sit with you soon. You know we held Ellis in high regard. Whatever we can do to help, you can count on us."

Johanna looked at him. She opened her mouth but no sound came out.

"I think the ladies should drink their tea, Father." Charles picked up the delicate cup and saucer from beside Georgina and put it in her hands. "This has been a terrible shock for you."

Georgina raised the warm cup to her lips and sipped the sweet black tea. It slid down her throat, spreading warmth through her chilled body. She watched as Henry helped her mother do the same. The room was quiet except for the rustle of fabric, the soft chink of cup on saucer, the tick of the large clock on the mantel. Soft footsteps sounded outside and the door opened; Catherine came in. Although still pale she was composed. She crossed the room, placed a gentle hand on Georgina's shoulder then went to sit on Johanna's other side. She took the teacup and saucer Henry had been trying to coax Johanna with and urged her friend to sip the tea.

Henry got to his feet. "Perhaps we should leave you ladies for a while."

"I must see him." Johanna had found her voice.

"Of course you shall," Catherine soothed.

"We were not sure of your wishes. Mrs Donovan has ..." Henry cleared his throat "... taken care of him and I have the undertaker on standby. It was just as well you were due home today. The funeral will need to take place soon. Would you like me to arrange for him to be brought here? He could be buried in the Hawker cemetery."

"I ... I ... " Johanna looked from Henry to Georgina. "I don't know."

"You need to rest." Catherine put down the cup and took her friend's hand. "I've had Mrs Nixon make up a room for you. Things will be clearer in the morning. You may stay as long as you wish."

Henry cleared his throat again. "We can't wait too long, Catherine," he murmured. "It's already been two days."

Johanna hunched forward and began to sob. Catherine wrapped her in her arms while Henry stepped from foot to foot.

Georgina could stand it no longer. Her mother had lost all sense of direction. It was up to Georgina to take charge now. "Thank you for your kindness, Mr and Mrs Wiltshire. We will stay just to catch our breath. Then we must return to Prosser's Run. Father would want to be buried there."

"But you will not make it home before dark, even if you leave now," Catherine said.

"We often have to camp overnight between here and home, Mrs Wiltshire."

Charles, who had remained silent since first offering the tea, stepped forward. "I will come with you."

Georgina took a good look at Charles for the first time since their arrival. She'd noticed how much taller he was but he was also stronger: she'd felt it in the arm he'd put around her to guide her inside. She was six years older and yet she felt small beside him now.

He smiled, a gentle curve of his lips, though with sorrow in his eyes. "I will do whatever I can to help you through this terrible time."

Georgina was determined she would not be dependent on a man but she took his suggestion as a genuine offer. She glanced at her mother. Her sobs had ceased, but she was staring vacantly as if she were no longer in the room. There would be no help there.

"Thank you, Charles." Georgina felt strength return. "I think it would be best if Mother stays here a little longer, but I would like to set off for home as soon as possible."

"I will look after Johanna," Catherine said.

Georgina glanced down past the huge leg-o-mutton sleeves of her maroon and white striped dress to the skirt, which floated out around her in thick folds. Her mother had insisted on her buying it before she left London. Now the tight S-bend corset was cutting her in half and the style of her outfit was both out of place and impractical in Hawker. Their tour now felt like a frivolous indulgence, and the life she'd led for nearly two years was receding from her mind. She was thankful that she had convinced her mother to allow her to buy some of the new-style tailor-made suits that were now in her trunk.

"My smaller case has something more practical for horse travel."

"All of your luggage should be here soon," Henry said.

"Would you like me to drive you to Prosser's Run in our carriage?" Charles asked.

"I'd prefer to ride if I can borrow a horse. Mother can come out in the carriage in a day or so."

"I'll arrange it," Charles said.

Georgina sucked in a breath then let it out softly. "You've all been very kind." She turned to Henry. "I'd like to meet with the undertaker before I leave, Mr Wiltshire."

"Of course. I will send for him straight away." Henry gave Georgina a thoughtful look. "Why don't I send the driver and wagon on the way to Prosser's Run now? Then he will be ahead of you and he can set up camp along the way so you will have somewhere to rest tonight. I will make sure he has something for you to eat and you can set off again at first light."

Georgina tried to keep her emotions in check. All this kindness was undermining her resolve to stand on her own two feet. "Thank you."

Henry made for the door. As he opened it a sweet little face peeped around the frame. "Laura, you must go back to Mrs Nixon."

The little girl evaded her father's hands and made a dash across the room for her mother.

"Is this baby Laura?" Georgina felt a small lift of spirits at the distraction.

Catherine put one arm around her small daughter and hugged her close. "Yes, this is Laura."

"She's not a baby any more." Charles frowned at his little sister.

Georgina was not particularly entranced by small children but she was surprised by his gruff tone. "She's such a pretty little thing."

Henry strode back across the room and scooped his daughter high into the air. She became a squirming giggling bundle of white frills and lace. "We celebrated her second birthday just last week."

"How lovely."

They all turned to look at Johanna, who had lifted her hands towards Laura.

"May I hold her?"

Henry lowered his daughter gently to Johanna's lap.

Catherine held Laura's hand. "She can be shy with people she doesn't know."

As if to discredit her mother's words, Laura stared up into Johanna's face, then she gently put her two little hands on the woman's cheeks and smiled.

"Oh," Johanna whispered. "What a darling girl."

Beside her Georgina heard Charles exhale sharply. She looked at the Wiltshire parents gazing adoringly at their little girl and had to bite her lip to stop the sudden sob that surged up her throat. She was all alone. Her big strong father was dead and her mother, lost to Georgina in her grief, was finding solace in a child's smile. An arm went around Georgina's shoulder and she looked up into Charles's caring gaze. He was little more than a boy and could be irritating and arrogant, but right now she could do with a friend. She gave him a grateful smile.

Fifteen

May 1898

William reined in his horse at the end of the track that led to the Prossers' homestead. He took a deep breath and cast a look around the yards and stone buildings that skirted the fence constructed around the house. There were horses in a yard further beyond it, some milking cows chewing on some blue bush branches that had been placed in their enclosure, and the usual birds flitting between the leaves of a large gum over his head, but there was no sign of human life.

He had arrived back at the Smith's Ridge house late the day before to find a travelling hawker sharing the news: Ellis Prosser was dead from a bad heart and his funeral had been that day. The two Prosser ladies had arrived home just in time to attend. William's own heart had both leaped and bled at the news. He was excited Georgina was home at last but saddened for her at the loss of her father. It had been too late to ride to Prosser's Run then. He'd slept fitfully then risen when the sun was only a smudge of light on the horizon to wash and dress in his good shirt and set out for Prosser's Run. The tatty emerald ribbon was in his pocket and with the bunch of wildflowers Jessie had gathered in a calico bag attached to his saddle, he'd made the distance between their two homes in good time.

Today he was nervous. He hadn't seen Georgina in so long and hadn't had a letter for several months. What if she had changed her mind about her feelings for him? He glanced around once more. All was quiet. He might have thought no-one was home but for the puffs of smoke he could see from the kitchen chimney. He knew that part of the house. Ellis had twice invited him into the kitchen for a cup of tea before the journey home back in the days when the older man had been sharing his knowledge of cattle. Now William walked his horse towards the front of the house, where there was a low verandah. He dismounted and patted his horse's neck. Big Red was a fine animal and the offspring of the same mare and stallion who had produced Bella. But he would not mention the mare today. There was much to share and discuss, so many things he longed to tell her, but today was about offering support in her sorrow. He tethered Big Red to a rail beside a water trough, slid the flowers from the calico bag and walked across the last short piece of dirt to the gate.

The hinges squeaked loudly behind him as he shut it again. His footsteps crunched up the rocky path and echoed across the wooden verandah. Everywhere around him there was silence.

He lifted his hand to knock at the door but it opened. His heart thumped. There before him stood Georgina. Her red hair was swept back from her face and pinned up at the back in a mass of curls. She wore a black skirt in a much straighter style than he was used to seeing and a soft grey blouse that buttoned to a small collar that stood up around her neck. She looked even more beautiful than he remembered.

"Hello, William." She was the first to break the silence that hovered around them like a blanket.

He swallowed, suddenly awkward, not knowing what to say. He thrust the flowers towards her. "I've come to offer my condolences. My family all send their sympathy ... to you and your mother."

She took the bunch without looking at the arrangement of bright pink and white flowers.

"The flowers were gathered by Jessie, my—"

"Mother is still in bed." Georgina lifted her chin and pulled back her shoulders. "We held the funeral two days ago."

"I'm sorry I missed it." William hadn't exactly expected her to fall into his arms but he thought she might show some sign of pleasure at his arrival. Instead she was stiff and unwelcoming. "I've been working at the far side of Smith's Ridge, building fences. I only heard about ... I only got the news on my return last night."

"You must be tired." Neither Georgina's voice nor her face gave away any emotion. "Would you like a cup of tea before you leave?"

William's heart thumped. "I had hoped ..." The words died on his lips as one of her eyebrows raised and she gave him a hostile look. He shook his head. He knew grief did strange things to people but he hadn't been expecting this. "I don't want to bother you."

"Which is exactly what you're doing."

William was stunned by the sight of Charles Wiltshire coming to a stop beside Georgina. He had the appearance of a boy who had just climbed from his bed and quickly pulled on his clothes.

"You promised you would stay in bed and rest this morning, Georgina." He put a hand on her shoulder.

William thought he saw a small flash of irritation in her eyes but she turned her face towards Wiltshire. "I couldn't sleep. There is much to do."

William couldn't believe what he was seeing. The younger man's hand on her shoulder was possessive, intimate. "If there is anything I can do ..."

Georgina glanced back at him and this time her face registered the pain of her loss.

"Thank you for coming. I'll tell Mother you were here." She slipped from under Charles's hand and disappeared into the house.

"We're managing fine thanks, Baker." Charles curled his lip. "We don't need anything from your kind of people."

William's fists clenched at his sides. "What do you mean, my kind of people?"

"Native lovers. Not worthy of decent folk like the Prossers and the Wiltshires."

"You arrogant pup." William's voice exploded.

Wiltshire simply laughed.

Disbelief and anger surged through William at seeing this young upstart by Georgina's side. He recalled all the times the Wiltshires had besmirched his family with their snide remarks and smug smiles and then he remembered the punch Charles had given him before Georgina left.

Charles's hand shot forward to push William in the chest. William's reaction was swift. He landed his own punch, right on Wiltshire's nose.

Charles staggered backwards, one hand to his face, the other clutching at the wall. He stared at William in horror.

"You bastard," he bellowed.

William watched as blood seeped from around Wiltshire's fingers and trickled down his chin.

"What's happened?" Georgina was back. She took in Charles's bloodied face and turned to William. "Did you hit him?"

William rubbed the palm of his hand over his sore knuckles. "I did."

Charles groaned and leaned heavily against the wall. "A sneaky punch, that's all. Caught me off guard." The words came out muffled by his hand.

William couldn't help but smirk. Then he saw the anger in Georgina's eyes and the humour left him. She reached for the door handle.

"You should go," she said and firmly closed the door in his face.

William had plenty of time to think on the journey home. He cursed his stupidity for hitting Wiltshire, even though the smart-mouthed brat deserved it. William shouldn't have lost his temper but he couldn't deny the part of him that had enjoyed wiping the smile off Wiltshire's face. The only problem was Georgina's open disgust with his behaviour.

William shook his head. He didn't understand any of it. He'd set off that morning expecting to offer his condolences and be welcomed by Georgina. He'd hoped to have the opportunity to tell her how much he loved and had missed her, offer her any assistance he could, but she'd been distant right from the start. And what was Wiltshire doing there, looking as if he belonged?

When he reached the top gate, a small gap in the fence that divided their properties, William stopped to drink some water. He stood in the scattered shade of some ragged gum trees and looked back in the direction of the Prosser's Run homestead. It wasn't visible, of course, but he pictured Georgina's sad, beautiful face and his heart ached more. He took the ribbon from his pocket and slipped it through his fingers. It had lost some of its colour and was tatty on the ends, and there were a couple of stains where it had been ground into the mud by Wiltshire's boot, but it was the same emerald green ribbon William had bought for Georgina all those years ago.

He held out his hand and a gust of wind blew it to the ground, the green bright against the brown and red of rock and soil. How stupid he'd been to believe she would wait for him. Once more he glanced in the direction of her home. The day had turned

murky. There was dust in the air. He should ride north along
the fence and check the bottom waterhole. It still held water and
was just beyond the fence line. With a purpose now he bent to
retrieve the ribbon and took it to the fork of the nearest tree. He
wound it tightly between two branches then stepped back and
looked at the bow. If he were ever tempted to cross this point it
would be a painful reminder to keep away. William shut the gate,
mounted his horse and turned his back on the gusting wind and
Prosser's Run.

Georgina bathed the blood from Charles's face and gave him a
cool cloth to press to his nose. The whole time he muttered about
William and his lucky hit. Georgina murmured and soothed but
she was numb inside. Since the news of her father's death and her
mother's inability to deal with even the simplest things, Georgina had taken charge. She had been grateful for the help Charles
offered but the day before, as Henry was preparing to leave, he
had delivered more devastating news. It had been another terrible
blow to hear of her father's supposed treatment of a shepherd and
that he had been preparing to appear before the magistrate.

This morning she had seen William arrive outside and for a
moment her battered heart had rejoiced at the sight of him. Just
as quickly all feeling had seeped away. He was no longer her William but someone else's. She would have almost preferred he was
dead like her father. Then at least she could have mourned him.
Seeing his long lean frame, his handsome face full of concern for
her, had been the final blow.

The groans and complaints Charles made assaulted her ears.
She let go the cloth she was rinsing and it floated in the basin. The
water, pink with blood, seeped into it. She watched mesmerised
as the fabric was sucked below the surface and slowly sank to the
bottom.

"Georgina?"

She turned to Charles. By the look on his face he must have spoken before.

"I said I would instruct Donovan to have that man thrown off the property if he ever sets foot here again."

She stared at Charles. His pompous manner and his attempt at acting older than his years erased her small gratitude for his help.

"Thank you for everything, Charles, but I can manage from here. Your father needs you in Hawker and Mother and I need some time alone to adjust."

The pain of his nose was apparently forgotten as he jumped to his feet. "I can stay a few more days." He tried to take her hands but she pulled them back from his grasp.

"That won't be necessary."

His face showed puzzlement at the coldness of her tone. She couldn't help herself. She wanted him gone.

He gave her a tight smile. "You need some time. I understand. I'll leave you alone for a while but not for long. Two women out here is not a good thing."

"We're fine." Georgina shook her head. She felt as if she was talking with a mouthful of marbles. "Mr and Mrs Donovan are here, as well as Mr Swan and several shepherds."

"Well." He pursed his lips. "Yes. I can see you're very tired." He patted her shoulder before she could evade his touch. "You take some time to rest. Let the Donovans look after you and I will return in a week to see how you're getting on."

"That won't be necessary, Cha—"

"I insist." He shot her a concerned look. "Others may have deserted you in your time of need but I will look out for you."

She sucked in a breath. Henry Wiltshire's news the day before had been simply awful but it had explained why, apart from the short notice, so few people had attended her father's funeral.

Supposed friends had turned their back on them. She spun on her heel and left the room with as much dignity as she could muster. There was no sound from behind her mother's closed bedroom door as she passed. Georgina let herself in to her own room, shut the door and fell across the bed. She didn't even have the energy to unbutton her boots. In spite of her exhaustion large tears rolled down her face and her body was racked with sobs.

When at last the terrible shuddering subsided and her tears had dried she hugged the soft pillow under her head, longing for sleep to claim her, but it wouldn't. Finally she dragged herself from the bed and rinsed her face in the cool water of her bedroom basin. She gently patted it dry and inspected her reflection in the mirror. Sad eyes looked back at her from a pale face. She tucked some of the larger curls that had escaped her bun back into place, took a deep breath and opened the door. She stepped quietly along the passage. Still no sound from her mother's room but she could hear noises from the kitchen. She glanced around the door. If it was Charles she was ready to send him on his way. She couldn't stand the thought of his self-important voice assaulting her ears again. She was relieved to see it was only Mrs Donovan, who was busy at the fireplace.

"Hello, love." Mrs Donovan gave her a smile. "You look done in. I've just boiled the kettle. How about a cup of tea?"

"Thank you." Georgina crossed the room and sat at the table facing the window. "I'll take one in to Mother later."

"Already done it." Mrs Donovan put a mug of tea in front of Georgina. "And I coaxed her to eat one of my pikelets. Got to keep your strength up at a time like this."

A plate of warm pikelets, dripping butter and dollops of dark plum jam, appeared beside the mug. Georgina's stomach rumbled. She couldn't recall eating anything that morning.

She had been forlornly looking out the front window, watching, for what she didn't know, when she'd seen William approach.

Knowing he was lost to her had been the final blow. The life she had imagined with him had been obliterated.

"Drink up, Miss Georgina." Mrs Donovan bustled past. "I'll be out tangling with the washing if you need me. There's a pile of bedsheets to deal with. Oh and young Mr Wiltshire left an hour ago. He says he'll be back in a week or so." She gave Georgina a sympathetic look but didn't wait for a response. She closed the door gently behind her.

Voices wafted back to Georgina from outside.

"Decisions have to be made." It was Mr Donovan's voice. Her father's right-hand man.

"Give them some time," Mrs Donovan replied.

Georgina listened. All was quiet then she heard the murmur of their voices as they moved away.

Steam wafted from the big mug of tea. Georgina sighed and wrapped her hands around it, seeking the warmth for her chilled fingers. No doubt Mr Donovan wanted to talk about stock but she didn't feel ready for that yet.

She took a sip of the tea. It was hot and sweet and she felt it doing her good. Now Charles was gone she could think more clearly. She had inherited Prosser's Run. There were provisions for her mother of course, and other requirements. Her father had wanted to maintain control even from his grave. She pressed her fingers to her lips. She hadn't imagined this was how she would take over the property. Since the deaths of both her brothers, her father had always said the place would be hers once he was gone. She had thought that would take place in some distant time, not just after her twenty-first birthday.

He had used her love of Prosser's Run to get his way, keeping her from William when she'd declared her love for him, sending her overseas with the promise she could have more say in running the property once she came home. Georgina shook her head. No doubt he had thought she would forget her love for William and find some other more suitable man. As it turned out, neither had happened.

The bunch of wildflowers sat in a jug on the dresser. Mrs Donovan must have found them and put them in water. Georgina would have thrown them out. How dare William bring flowers plucked by his wife's hand and offer them to her? He had said Jessie; it was a pretty name, and no doubt she was a pretty woman.

Georgina put a hand to her chest as the pain of William's betrayal returned. It was silly to torment herself with images of him with someone else. She was determined to make a life without him but every now and then a crack in the wall she'd built around her heart reminded her he wasn't forgotten. Seeing him today had been a shock but she had survived it. She'd prefer not to see him again, but they were neighbours. At least she hoped it would be a long time before she did.

Georgina thought back to the provisions her father had put in his will. One was that her mother was to remain in the house and be provided for. Of course she would look after her mother. It angered her, however, to think it put her mother in the position of becoming a tenant in the place she had made into a home for her husband and children.

Georgina drained the last of the now cool tea and put the mug back on the table with a thud. Another provision was that she wasn't to marry without her mother's consent until she was thirty or the property would be sold and Georgina would receive nothing. That rankled even more. Not that she had plans to marry anyone now — she was not going to become anyone's property — but if by some chance she did decide to marry she wouldn't be seeking anyone's permission to do so.

There was a clatter outside. She looked to the window, where a brown light filled the sky. The wind had picked up, carrying dust from the plains with it. Drought had taken hold in her absence. Donovan had said there were decisions to be made. She stood up and felt the tug of her skirt as it hooked on the chair leg. She jerked it free. The first thing she would do was change into the pants she had worn before her trip away, then she would meet with Mr Donovan and see what work needed to be done. Georgina lifted her head and strode from the kitchen.

Sixteen

November 1898

Catherine shifted her weight against the pile of pillows behind her on the bed. No matter where she sat she didn't feel comfortable, and every breath was a struggle. She turned her blurry gaze to the window. She could see dust had coloured the air and it frightened her. The last dust storm had made breathing even more difficult and the doctor had warned her that her heart and chest weren't up to it. There had been little he could do for her and she'd resorted to taking an extra draught of her medicine. At least that relaxed her.

Her gaze shifted back to the bedroom and to the little bottle on the table beside the lamp. She had resisted taking the special tonic in the first few months after Laura had been born but she'd been so miserable back in Hawker she'd finally succumbed. The doctor in Adelaide had warned her it contained laudanum and was addictive, but she no longer cared. It was the only thing that got her through each day. Her promise to Henry to act as the perfect wife and mother had come at a price.

She struggled upright and poured herself a dose, appalled at the tremor in her fingers. The medicine slipped down her throat and she lay back just as the door burst open.

Laura flew into the room with a book clutched in her hands and Flora Nixon close behind her.

"Mama, Mama."

"I'm sorry, Catherine." Flora's face was full of concern. "I hoped you would be sleeping."

"I couldn't get comfortable." Catherine reached her arms to her daughter, who climbed up on the bed beside her.

"Story, Mama."

"Your Mama is very tired today, Laura. Why don't you tell her what we've been doing instead?"

"We made cake." Laura slid from the bed. "I get you some." She dashed across the room again.

"Bring the one on the plate," Flora instructed then turned her kind gaze back to Catherine. "How are you feeling?"

"Not so good." Catherine felt her lip wobble. She sucked it in. There was no point to self-pity but she worried what would become of Laura if anything happened to her.

"Have you had some medicine?" Flora crossed to the bedside table.

"Yes, I've just taken it."

Flora sat on the edge of the bed and took her hand. "Then you must relax and let it do its work. It looks like another of those nasty dust storms is on its way and you know what the doctor said."

Catherine took strength from the gentle squeeze of Flora's warm hand. "Thank you. I don't know what I'd do — what we'd *all* do — without you."

Flora gently brushed some loose hair from Catherine's face. "You are a very special woman. I am so lucky to have found work here."

"And I am lucky to count you as my friend."

They looked at each other a moment. Two women from such different backgrounds who had been brought together in unusual circumstances, who yet had maintained a true friendship.

Catherine fought to keep her composure. She felt so teary today. "I couldn't have survived without you, Flora. Living here in Hawker, managing this house and ... life in general."

Flora shook her head and her grip on Catherine's hand tightened. "You know, don't you?" she whispered.

"Know?" Catherine tried to smile. "I know you have been a wonderful friend."

Flora's usually expressionless face crumpled. "How can you be so kind? Knowing that I ... that your husband and—"

"Hush, Flora. There is no point in talking now." Catherine had vowed never to speak of Flora's liaison with Henry, but their lives had become so entwined; both Henry and Catherine depended on Flora.

"At first it was purely a business arrangement." Flora lowered her head.

"I understand the things we do for our children ... but ..." Catherine had partitioned away any thoughts of her husband and Flora for so long it was as if she was asking about someone else's life. "Your children have long been grown and able to look after themselves."

"I ... I had grown used to Henry's attentions, and the comforts of living in your house. I never imagined myself in your place, but I did think that perhaps you didn't enjoy his attention in the ..." Flora waved her hand "... the bedroom like I did." She looked back at Catherine, her eyes wide. "You must think me wicked."

Catherine shook her head. "I am surely so also for not putting a stop to it."

"It is impertinent of me to ask, I know, but if you knew about it, why didn't you?"

"You were right." Catherine dragged in a breath. "While my husband was with you he no longer bothered me. I am not so naive as to think he wouldn't have sought some other company if you had not been … available. At least I knew he was with someone good, someone trustworthy."

"Oh, Catherine."

"There's more." Catherine looked directly into Flora's eyes. "If I had left Henry it would have been such a scandal. I couldn't put my family … my children through that. Instead I used that knowledge to make Henry give me some freedom. He allows me visits to Adelaide each year with Laura. So you see, we have both been wicked."

Flora put her head to Catherine's hand and kissed it. "You and I — things are so strange and yet …"

"It is what it is." Catherine sighed and closed her eyes. "We will speak of it no more." Her eyes flew open again as she struggled for breath. She put her other hand over Flora's. "You must promise me," she whispered, "if anything happens to me you will take care of them."

"I will continue to take care of you all." Flora slid her hand over Catherine's as if they were playing a children's game. "Nothing's going to happen to you."

Catherine smiled and felt her troubles slip away. The elixir and Flora's presence were working their magic.

Laura walked carefully back into the room. She balanced a small cake on the plate she held in front of her but it wobbled precariously. The two women who were the centre of her life stopped whispering together and smiled at her.

Flora came to help her but Laura stepped around her.

"I made it for you, Mama."

"Thank you, my darling."

Laura was especially pleased to see her mother smile so the lines around her eyes crinkled. She didn't like it when her mother sounded breathless. Now she looked a little better. Laura clutched the bedsheet that covered her mother and used it to pull herself up onto the bed.

"Why don't I make a cup of tea to go with it?" Flora left them together.

Catherine put an arm around Laura and drew her close. She pressed her nose to Laura's hair. "You smell so sweet. How lucky I am to have you," she whispered.

Laura reached for the locket that always hung at her mother's neck. It was a pretty heart and Laura loved to hold it. Catherine put her soft warm hand over hers.

"This locket belonged to your great-grandmother, and your Grandmother Harriet gave it to me." Catherine took a breath. "It will be yours one day."

Laura gazed into her mother's adoring eyes. Today they didn't sparkle. "Don't be sad. I love you, Mama."

Catherine kissed the top of her head. "And I love you, my darling."

Laura's ear was pressed close to her mother's chest and she could hear the wheezing rattle she knew meant her mother was having a bad day. Catherine shifted away and took a deep breath.

Laura looked up. Her mother's smile was gone, replaced by a fearful look.

"Mama?"

"Hello, my two lovely ladies." Henry came into the room.

Laura gripped her mother's hand.

"What is it, Catherine?" Henry's voice was full of concern behind her.

"Nothing." Catherine fell back against the pillows. "Please take Laura."

"Of course." Henry put his hands around Laura's waist but she struggled to evade his grip.

She put a hand to her mother's cheek. "Story, Mama," she pleaded. Stories always made Catherine feel better.

"I ... I'm sorry my darling ... later." Catherine gasped.

Laura was whisked into her father's strong arms. Over his shoulder she got one final glimpse of her mother. Catherine lifted a hand to her lips and pretended to blow Laura a kiss but her hand fell back and her eyes closed before they were out the door.

Edith folded the last of the fine cotton ladys' nightdresses into the box and closed the lid. Why anyone would spend such a ridiculous amount of money on something they wore to bed she could never imagine. Certainly she had no idea who would purchase such garments there in Hawker but they were among the items Charles had ordered to stock the new extension.

The bigger room next door was to be for clothing, haberdashery and manchester only. The original shop, where she and Mr Hemming were busily checking new stock between serving customers, was to be for groceries and hardware items. Mr Hemming would serve there and Mr Henry would maintain his refurbished office in the back. She was to serve in the new section and Charles would supervise both shops — at least when he was in town.

She gave a small sigh. These last six months Charles had spent his time between Prosser's Run and his grocery-cart deliveries. She'd hardly seen much of him at all but she had to be patient. Edith would bide her time. She'd had her sights set on marrying Charles Wiltshire from the moment she first met him in his grandmother's shop.

The unknown was Georgina Prosser. It was laughable really. He was a boy compared to the older, more cultured Miss Prosser. Edith couldn't imagine Georgina falling for Charles but he was certainly smitten with her. Edith had seen Georgina on several occasions when she'd come to town to purchase supplies. Miss Prosser was always smartly dressed, favouring the narrower gored skirts she had no doubt brought back from overseas. Edith thought them eminently more practical than the volumes of material that swished around her as she moved about the shop. She had resolved to make herself something similar but in a more sensible serge fabric.

"You may take your lunch now, Miss Ferguson." She looked across at Mr Hemming. The customer he had been serving had left and they were alone in the shop. "I don't think there are many people about today."

Nor any day over the last month, Edith thought, but she kept it to herself. She only hoped the Wiltshires could ride out the terrible drought that had descended on the land. "Thank you, Mr Hemming. I shall go back to my cottage."

Hemming glanced towards the window. "It's become quite dull out there. I don't like the look of it. If the wind comes up you are to take the afternoon off and stay home."

Malachi Hemming was her senior but she didn't like taking instruction from him — especially now that she was to be in charge of the new shop virtually alone. She thought herself on an equal employment footing with Mr Hemming, but she hid her chagrin.

"Mr Wiltshire will expect me to be here. There is still much to be done if we are to open the new shop before Christmas."

"If that turns into a dust storm out there, no-one will be afoot this afternoon, not even Mr Wiltshire, and we have time to shift the stock. Christmas is still nearly two months away."

Edith cast a nervous glance at the window. The sky did look brown. There had been a bad dust storm only a few weeks earlier at the end of October. She had found it quite terrifying and the aftermath had been horrendous, with everything needing to be cleaned. "Very well," she said. "I will be watchful of the weather."

She took her umbrella and her bag and walked through to the remodelled room that was to be a waiting area for Mr Henry's office. Where once there had been a window there was now a door into the new adjoining shop. The door was closed and two wooden chairs and a painting on the wall were the only furnishings in what had once been the Wiltshires' sitting room. Mr Henry's office door was open, his desk tidy, but there was no sign of him.

She continued on through the back of the premises, which had also undergone some remodelling to join the new shop. Much had changed since Charles had given her a tour of the original shop, which he said had been both a home and business place for his parents when they first came to Hawker. Now the Wiltshires lived in the biggest and most beautiful home in town. Edith liked to imagine herself living there instead of the little cottage next door. One day she was sure it would be so but for now she watched and listened and learned as much as she could about the town, the people and especially the Wiltshires. If she was to become Mrs Charles Wiltshire one day she had to be prepared.

Outside the men who had been sawing and hammering at the new verandah roof had downed tools and were gone. She put her umbrella up but the wind tugged it and threatened to blow it inside out. There was already so much dust in the air the November sun was no threat to her complexion, so she folded the umbrella again and, putting her head down, she hurried towards her little cottage. By the time she reached it the wind was blowing so hard she struggled to shut the door. She looked down in dismay at the

brown dirt that had accompanied her inside. Mr Hemming had
been right. It was to be another of those awful storms. She placed
her umbrella and bag inside her bedroom and moved from room
to room, checking all the windows and doors were secure. When
that was done she went to her little kitchen, stirred the fire to life
and set the kettle to boil. Outside the wind buffeted the walls,
rattled the roof and moaned at the gaps around the windows.

Edith shivered even though the day wasn't cold. The sound was
what frightened her. It was an evil noise and it brought with it the
terrible brown dirt that seeped into every nook and crevice. She
watched the window fretfully until the kettle boiled and then,
thankful for something to direct her gaze away from the glass, she
poured the boiling water into the teapot.

"Edith!"

She jumped at the call from beyond the back door and then
again as someone thumped on the wood.

"Edith, are you there?"

It was Flora Nixon's voice. Edith frowned. Flora was the one
person in the Wiltshire household she hadn't been able to charm.
Sometimes Edith took her meals with Flora in the big house if she
had helped with serving guests. She could rarely get much conversation from the older woman, who was very good at keeping
her own counsel.

Edith slid the bolt and opened the door carefully, bracing herself behind it to stop the force of the wind whipping it backwards
and slamming it into the room.

"You must come, quickly."

Edith bridled at the command.

"Mrs Wiltshire is sick. I must sit with her while Mr Wiltshire
goes for the doctor and we need someone to look after Laura."

Edith peered past Flora at the dust and rubbish flying through
the air.

"Quickly." Flora had already turned away.

Edith edged out the door. It took all her strength to shut it and when she turned she was appalled to see the day was so dirty Flora was already lost from her sight. Edith put her head down and hurried along the path that led from her back door to the Wiltshires'. She knew at least inside their solid stone home, the sounds of the storm would be softer. The wind whipped her hair from her bun. She was pleased to reach the shelter of the roof that spanned the large U-shaped courtyard at the back of the house. Today the wind rattled the tin and swirled dirt around the courtyard.

Flora was waiting to close the door behind her as she walked into the calm of the large kitchen. Edith blinked. The dust made her eyes water and she brushed the grit from her cheeks.

"Help yourself to some food." Flora waved her hand towards the big table, where a tart and some bread and cheese sat beside a freshly baked cake. "I will go and fetch Laura. You will have to think of some way to keep her with you." Flora's face hardened. "She cannot be with her mother. It only upsets them both."

"What's wrong with Mrs Wiltshire?" Edith dared to ask. Charles's mother had not been in good health when Edith had first come to Hawker and in the last month Mrs Wiltshire had not visited the shop or left the house at all from what Edith gathered. She hadn't seen her mistress in that time.

"Her chest is bad." Flora said. "This weather makes it so much worse. She struggles to breathe ... and it puts strain on her heart."

Tears brimmed in the normally steel-faced Flora's eyes before she turned away and walked briskly up the passage.

The tart looked good. Edith cut herself a slice and took a mouthful. The pastry was perfect and the vegetables were soft but not overcooked.

"Here's Miss Ferguson." Mr Wiltshire came into the room carrying a squirming Laura in his arms.

"Hello, Laura." Edith smiled but the little girl buried her face in her father's chest. Edith kept the smile on her face to hide her annoyance. The child was spoiled and rarely did anything she was asked. Edith was happy to do most jobs the Wiltshires requested of her but looking after Laura was not something she enjoyed.

"You must stay with Miss Ferguson." Henry's voice was sharp.

"Not Edie, want Mama," the little girl cried.

"Mama is resting." He forced Laura into Edith's arms. "You must stay here."

Edith hung on to the struggling child.

Henry gave them a worried look then strode away, shutting the door that led to the passage and the front of the house. Edith heard his footsteps recede and then the squeal of the wind and the thud of the front door closing.

Laura's knee caught her in the stomach.

"Stop it," Edith snapped and placed the child firmly on a chair.

Laura tried to wriggle away but Edith held her firmly to the seat.

"You must stop this nonsense, Laura. Your mother is very sick. You will only make her feel much worse."

"Mama." Tears flowed down Laura's cheeks.

"Your mother doesn't want you." Edith stood back and glared at the child. "Stop those tears. Everyone is too busy to fuss over you. You will stay here with me."

The little girl looked at her through big round eyes, her thumb in her mouth, then quick as a flash she slid from the chair and ran around the table. Edith moved to block the passage door but the child went to the bedroom that opened from the kitchen.

Edith crossed to the partly open door. There was nowhere Laura could go from there. It was probably best just to leave her alone. Easier for Edith at least. She paused: perhaps she should check. She pushed the door carefully. It swung open to reveal a room darkened by deep brown curtains drawn across the window. The light from the kitchen gleamed off the polished rosewood head and base of the large single bed. It was neatly made with a plain tan cover draped all the way to the floor. Edith raised an eyebrow at the sight of one small foot poking out from beneath it.

To the right of the door was a set of hooks with a coat, a jacket and a hat and beyond that a small gentleman's wardrobe in rosewood to match the bed. This was Charles's room. Edith stepped inside. Over the bed hung a painting of horses against a lush English-looking landscape. A large chest of drawers took up another corner and beside it on a stand sat a wash jug and bowl. Edith looked over her shoulder and listened. The only sound was the distant roar of the wind.

She went to the drawers and picked up one of the leather-bound books lined up along the top. "*The Adventures of Sherlock Holmes.*" She read the title softly and ran her fingers over the stiff cover. Edith had learned to read but she had never owned her own book. She looked greedily at the other titles then flipped open the pages of the tome she held in her hands and breathed deeply. The paper had a luxurious smell. It was also stiff. Inside the front cover there was an inscription to Charles from his parents, dated two Christmases prior. She looked at the pristine pages and doubted Charles had read the book.

There was a scuffle behind her. She replaced the book and returned to the door. Laura could stay under the bed for all she cared but someone might come in and discover Edith's dereliction of her duty.

She looked around the kitchen for inspiration and her gaze lighted on the cake on the table. Mrs Nixon may be standoffish to Edith but she could cook and her cakes were always so light and delicious.

Edith turned back to the bedroom. "I'm so hungry," she announced. "I think I shall have some of Flora's cake." She left the door wide open and crossed to the table where she cut a slice of the honey-coloured sponge covered in jam and cream. It did indeed look delicious. "Oh." She groaned as loudly as she could. "It's so good. I shall have it all for myself."

Instantly there was a scuffle from the bedroom and Laura appeared at the door, her hands tucked behind her back. The ribbon that had been holding back her curls had come undone and hung in a long pink tangle to her shoulder. "You can't eat it all," the little miss declared.

Edith pretended to be surprised to see her. "Good heavens, I thought you had gone."

Laura crossed the room and stood on the other side of the table. "I like cake please, Edie." She spoke so sweetly Edith was almost fooled into thinking she was a well-behaved child.

"Very well." Edith picked up the knife again. "But you must wait here with me until your father returns for you."

A small frown crossed Laura's face as she looked from the cake back to Edith. She lifted a book out from behind her back and placed it on the table. "And a story."

Edith reached across to pick it up. The book was so well read the cover felt soft in her hands. A story was something she could manage and enjoy at least. She flipped open the book to the title page. She gasped, snapped the book shut and glared at Laura. "Where did you get this?"

The little girl had a mouthful of cake and appeared to have forgotten the book already. Edith gripped the well-thumbed book tightly, the title, *The Romance of Lust*, still dancing before her eyes. She flipped the book open and felt her heart quicken as she read.

"Chars."

Warmth spread across Edith's chest, up her neck and over her cheeks. She looked at the child. "This book is your brother's?"

Laura nodded emphatically. "Read me a story."

"Where did you get this?"

Laura shrugged and the ribbon flopped over her shoulder.

"Was it under the bed?"

"Yes." The little girl smiled. "Story please," she said sweetly.

Edith stood and sucked her lips tightly over her teeth. There was no doubt what Charles spent his time reading. The little bit she had read had set off a strange tingle in the pit of her stomach. It seemed bizarre that the young man in the book who was describing a sexual act was also named Charles.

"Story, Edie."

Edith put her hand to her chest and looked at Laura still happily eating the cake. "I'll find a story," she said.

She glanced towards the back door and then to the internal passage door. Both remained firmly shut and no footsteps could be heard. She went back to the bedroom, slid the book under the bed and searched for something more suitable. Among the others on the chest of drawers she found a copy of *Fairy Tales told for Children*. She gave one more glance around the darkened room, pulled the door shut behind her and took the fairy tales with her to sit beside Laura. She began to read and tried not to think about the book that was Charles Wiltshire's choice of reading matter.

Once she was a few pages into the story Laura climbed onto her lap. Outside the storm raged, the wind so thick with dirt it eventually began to seep into the air around them. The little girl grew heavier and heavier and her head flopped back against Edith's shoulder. Edith closed the book and placed it on the table. The child was asleep in her arms. What was she to do with her now? While she had been reading she had heard the sound of doors closing, footsteps and murmured voices from beyond the hall door. No doubt the doctor had arrived. She didn't want to take the child that way. She was familiar with the dining and the sitting rooms but she had no idea in which of the two large bedrooms that led off the main hall Laura slept.

She decided to lay the little girl on her brother's bed. Laura rolled into a ball as Edith placed her on the cover. She looked so small in the middle of the large masculine bed. Edith stood over her a moment. Once more the house was quiet inside and the wind continued its relentless wailing and buffeting outside.

From beyond the kitchen she heard a thud and a wail that was suddenly cut short. Edith glanced at the sleeping child then, pulling the door behind her, she crossed to the door leading to the passage and carefully opened it a crack. She put her hand to her mouth at the sight before her. Mrs Nixon had her arms wrapped around Mr Henry, who appeared to be sobbing. It could easily be that the housekeeper was offering some kind comfort to her master but Edith saw more than that. Mr Henry's arms were wrapped tightly around Flora, his face was buried in her shoulder and breast and she held him equally tightly. Flora kissed his cheek as someone did a lover, not an employer.

Edith drew back in shock, gently pulled the door closed and released the handle with great care so as not to make a noise. She was astounded by what she had witnessed. Poor Mrs Wiltshire lay sick on her bed and her husband and housekeeper were behaving like paramours just outside her door.

She had just returned to her chair and composed herself when the passage door opened and Mr Henry entered the kitchen, dishevelled but alone. His cheeks were flushed and damp. He looked at Edith as if he didn't know who she was then walked around the table.

"Where is Laura?"

"She fell asleep so I laid her on Mr Charles's bed. I hope that was the right thing to do."

Henry looked from the bedroom door to Edith. "Sleeping, yes, that's best."

He sat down. "Charles isn't here?"

"No, Mr Henry." She frowned. "You surely remember he is away overnight with the grocery cart."

"Yes, that's right."

Suddenly he clutched his head in his hands and let out a moan. Edith got to her feet, fearing some illness had come over him.

"Are you well, Mr Henry? Perhaps you have caught your wife's complaint." She flinched as his elbows hit the table.

"Dear God," he moaned.

Edith hovered opposite him, not sure what to make of everything she'd seen in the last little while. She looked fearfully at the kitchen window. The dust outside was still too thick to see very much. It was much nicer in the Wiltshires' solid kitchen than in her cottage but she was concerned about her employer's strange behaviour. "Should I go now, Mr Henry?"

"Go, stay. It doesn't matter." He looked up at her through red-rimmed eyes. "My wife is dead."

Edith gasped and clutched at her collar.

"She's been struggling for a while now. Her heart couldn't cope, the doctor said."

"I'm so sorry." Edith pressed her fingers to her lips to hold in her own wail. Mrs Wiltshire had been kind to her.

"Not as sorry as I." Mr Henry groaned again and gave her such a wild look Edith feared for his sanity.

Flora Nixon came into the room on quiet feet. She put a firm hand on Mr Henry's shoulder. "You must be brave, Mr Wiltshire." She spoke to Henry but her gaze locked with Edith's. "Your wife was very ill. The doctor said there was nothing more you could have done. I will make some tea."

"Shall I do it?" Edith found her voice.

"No, thank you, Miss Ferguson. It was good of you to look after Laura." Flora looked around.

"She's asleep on Mr Charles's bed."

"Very well. Thank you again. The doctor has kindly offered to call on Mr Hemming and inform him of the sad news."

Edith saw Flora flinch as if she were hurt, then the older woman pulled back her shoulders and went on. "I am sure Malachi will find Mr Charles when the weather improves. You can return home now. I will see to the family."

Edith looked at the rigid form of her employer, and then at the woman who appeared to have taken charge.

"Very well," she said. "Let me know if I can do anything else." She moved to the door.

"There will be a mess to clean up tomorrow."

Edith turned back.

"You will need to be at the shop early to clear up after the storm has blown itself out."

Edith straightened. It was hardly the housekeeper's place to give her instructions regarding her work at the shop.

"Yes, thank you, Edith." Mr Wiltshire lurched to his feet. "The shop may have to remain closed but there will be much to do."

"Very well, Mr Wiltshire." She bobbed her head. "Once more my sincere condolences on your loss. If there's anything else—"

"We will let you know." Flora's words and her glare cut Edith off.

As she let herself out into the courtyard Edith thought she heard a gentle murmur from Flora to Henry, but the dust and the noise of the wind assaulted her and her only concern became getting home safely.

Seventeen

Charles stood on the edge of one of the several large shades erected beside the church where his mother's funeral had been conducted. Thankfully there had been a gentle breeze during the morning and the shade had provided some protection from the sun. He tugged at the starched collar of his new shirt and felt the weight of the black jacket on his shoulders. His father had insisted they wear the dark wool fabric though it was more suited to the chill of winter. All around him the ladies and gentleman of Hawker and even some less salubrious residents were dressed in similar black or dark shades. It was a very large gathering.

Georgina walked among them, offering a plate of sandwiches to some ladies. He was grateful to her and to her mother for acting as hostesses. His father had assumed Flora Nixon would take charge but Charles had explained that was not seemly. Flora had been put in charge of catering of course and Edith was there to help. Along with Mr Hemming's wife they had made sure there were plenty of refreshments for the mourners.

Charles glanced through a gap in the crowd. His father was seated between Mrs Prosser and the doctor's wife, and Mr and Mrs Taylor stood close by. Henry appeared to be joining in the conversation. Charles had helped his father with many things since Catherine's death. He had been mystified at the strength of his father's grief. His parents had lived separate lives in many ways, and yet his father had been almost inconsolable.

Charles rolled his shoulders and kept the glum look on his own face. It wouldn't do to look bored but that's what he was. So many people had offered their condolences and told him what a kind woman his mother had been, but they hadn't had to put up with her vague days, her dithering and in the last few months her inability to manage the simplest of tasks. It shouldn't surprise him that his father looked to Mrs Nixon for help. She held the household together.

"Ah, Mr Charles."

Charles turned to accept the outstretched hand of his father's business partner, Mr Button.

"We haven't had a chance to offer our condolences."

Mrs Button gave him a sad smile. "Your mother was such a kind lady."

"Thank you." Charles tried to sound suitably sad.

"Where is your dear little sister?"

"Mrs Hemming offered to stay at home with her."

"Very sensible. She won't understand all this, poor little darling." Mrs Button dabbed her cheeks with her handkerchief. "Not even three and she's lost her mama."

"Father and I will take good care of her."

"Oh, of course." Mrs Button's eyes brimmed again. "I didn't mean—"

"Please have some refreshments, won't you?" Charles excused himself and headed towards Georgina, who was now standing on the edge of the crowd sipping a cup of tea.

It was enough to put up with continued sad words and small talk about his mother but when they brought up his sister, Charles found it hard to remain calm. He blamed Laura for his mother's demise. For as long as he could remember his mother had tried to have another baby. She had been so caught up in that she hadn't had time to devote to her son. He'd learned to stand on his own feet and when help was needed Charles sought his father.

Finally his mother had produced another child and that child, Laura, had worn her down until she could no longer leave her bed. And yet Catherine had continued to pander to Laura, insisting the child sleep in her room, and reading her stories for as long as she had strength. So devoted had his mother been to her youngest child it had been some time since he'd had more than a simple hello or goodbye from her. In fact the last time they'd had a conversation had been his birthday two months earlier and even then he recalled they'd been interrupted by Laura wanting to give him some ridiculous gift she'd made with the help of Mrs Nixon. He banished thoughts of his mother and sister as he came to a halt beside Georgina, who was a very different kind of woman.

She welcomed him with a conciliatory smile. "You look worn out, Charles. Let me get you a cup of tea."

He was up to his ears in tea but he allowed her to get him one anyway. He enjoyed having Georgina fuss over him the way she had since she and her mother arrived two days earlier. They had been busy with preparations but he had found himself seeking her out, craving her undivided attention. His mother's death had been a timely event. He had seen less and less of Georgina in the last few months. She had taken over the running of Prosser's Run with relish. It kept her busy and she never invited him to visit. At least the funeral had been an excuse to spend some time with her again.

"Here you are." She placed the cup and saucer in his hands. "Nothing like a cup of tea. I drank so many after father died I felt as if I sloshed when I walked, but they did help me get through each day."

Charles took a sip and smiled as if the tea had lifted his spirits when in fact he'd much prefer a nip of his father's whisky. It was enough for him that Georgina stood close beside him, and he imagined her doing so as his wife. He had been so pleased to see her come out to the carriage dressed smartly in a dark suit with a wide skirt for the funeral. Her thick coppery hair was highlighted against the white collar of her shirt and the black of her silk jacket. Even in the dark clothes of mourning she looked so much better than when she wore the trousers she preferred for work on Prosser's Run. Once they were married he would insist she got rid of them.

He put a gentle hand on her arm, savouring the opportunity to be close to her. "Thank goodness for you and your mother."

"It's the least we can do for friends." Georgina glanced in her mother's direction. "The circumstances are not of our wishing, but it has been good for both of us to be here. To mix in the community again. After Father's death it was … Well it's simply good to be able to spend time here."

He bent closer, inhaling the sweet delicate scent she favoured for special outings, and desire surged within him. He hadn't found a suitable woman with whom to release his urges since his return from the east. A man of his position in the community had to be discreet. He curled his fingers into his palms and focused on Georgina. "I hope you can stay for a few days, and your mother of course."

"We have already spent two nights under your father's roof. Mother may wish to stay longer. I am sure Mrs Nixon will appreciate the help and our shepherd Mr Swan will accompany her home whenever she is ready. I must leave early tomorrow morning."

"You can't ride alone."

Georgina flicked her steely gaze over him. "Of course I can. I regularly ride from town to home alone. Good heavens, Charles, you do it."

"But I—"

She raised one eyebrow.

"I know what a long journey it is, that's all." Charles thought her foolish to ride alone but he didn't add that.

"Thank you for your concern." The sweet smile returned to her face. "The cart is too slow for me, and I have a good horse. I shall be home well before dark."

Charles had no words to change her mind, although things would certainly alter in the future. He was seventeen now. In less than a year he would eighteen and in a position to make her his wife. Up until his mother's funeral Georgina had kept him at arm's length. No doubt she was still recovering from the death of her father, which had been far more of a shock to her than his mother's death had been to him.

"I should help Mrs Nixon gather the plates and cups." She studied him earnestly. "Will you be all right? I suppose men are different but I remember how bouts of sadness would suddenly overwhelm me after Father's death. Even now they come from time to time."

"I would prefer your company a little longer." He swallowed the excitement he felt at her proximity and gave her what he hoped was the appropriate sad face of a man who had just lost his mother. "But I know Mrs Nixon will appreciate your help and I should go and check on Father. He will be tired from all the people wanting to talk to him."

"It's certainly been a big funeral. You must be so proud of how well your mother was regarded." Georgina lifted her chin, took his cup and saucer and stacked them inside hers. "I will see you at your house later." She turned away to collect more crockery.

Charles knew she would be remembering the small group that gathered to lay her father to rest. All the same he smiled at her departing figure, partly because she was so lovely and partly because he had a plan to involve Georgina in his life more and more.

There was a string of events that would see him mixing with the Prossers and spending time with Georgina, beginning with Christmas Eve dinner. Some might have thought the annual gathering wouldn't happen this year but his father would understand the importance of going ahead with it. They should continue their new tradition of inviting important members of the community, especially after the debacle of the previous year, when Ellis Prosser's presence had put people off. Then there was the cricket match in January, and in February his father would need assistance entertaining the Hawker Vigilance Committee, of which he was now chair. It was his duty to provide supper and some entertainment for their annual general meeting.

Charles knew he could find an event at least once each month for which they could conceivably require the assistance of the Prosser ladies. That, along with visits to Prosser's Run, should put him in a position to offer her marriage by his birthday in September next year. In the meantime, he needed to find an outlet for the passion that had built within him.

"Is everything going well, Mr Charles? I hope you're getting enough to eat."

Charles looked down at Edith Ferguson, who carried a platter of meat-filled pastries.

He took two of the warm delicacies and then bit into one. It was delicious. Edith was regarding him closely. She had always taken a close interest in him. Perhaps …

"Thank you, Edith." He glanced around. There was no-one near them. "This is delightful." He waved the second pastry in front of her. "Did you make it?"

"No. Mrs Nixon is the queen of the kitchen."

"Ahh!" Charles was inspired by her coy glance at him. "Your talents lie in looking after the shop, for which I must thank you.

Times are difficult with the drought but you are doing a wonderful job. I do hope you know how much we appreciate your help." He gave her one of his most charming smiles.

Edith gave him an equally delightful smile back and moved on to serve the food to others.

Charles lifted his shoulders, feeling very pleased with himself. While Edith wasn't as pretty as Georgina she wasn't unappealing. There was no-one to look out for her and she was close at hand. He stepped out to collect his father with a spring in his step, but was careful to replace his smile with the solemn look of a son filled with sorrow. There was nothing to be gained by letting people think he didn't suitably mourn his mother.

Mrs Prosser retired as soon as the last of the dinner guests had left so that it was only Georgina who sat with Henry and Charles at the table. While he and his father enjoyed a whisky, Charles was pleased Georgina accepted a second glass of the white wine he had imported from Victoria.

"Just a small one," she said. "I have an early start tomorrow."

"You are still determined to leave us so soon." Charles tried to look glum.

"We have been here three days. In any case, Mother is staying on."

"It's good of her." Henry shifted in his chair. "We don't want to impose on your kindness too often but I do hope you and your mother will continue to assist us in the future." Now the funeral was over he appeared more alert. Charles had been glad to see him playing the perfect host over dinner.

"Assist?"

Georgina inclined her head in Henry's direction. She had swept her hair into a twist on her head and Charles took in the pale skin of her neck, the tilt of her chin and the soft pink of her cheek. He had to clench his hand to stop himself from reaching out to touch her. Georgina was exquisite.

"We hope you and your mother will join us for Christmas." Henry rolled his shoulders as if shifting a load. "We entertain many guests and now ... without my dear wife ... we are two men alone. I do want our gatherings to still have the genteel guidance of a woman's touch."

Henry's gaze flicked in Charles's direction then back to Georgina. Charles exhaled softly. Thank goodness his father was truly coming to his senses. He had come to realise what a good match Charles and Georgina would be and he was doing his bit. Much better Henry should ask the Prossers to assist them than Charles.

"Surely you have Mrs Nixon."

"Mrs Nixon is an accomplished housekeeper, but she is not a hostess." Charles was quick to add his piece. He had noticed his father deferring to their housekeeper in several instances after his mother's death. It was important he didn't continue the habit.

"You would be our guests as usual," Henry said. "It will merely be the additional matter of presiding in the drawing room, and liaising with Mrs Nixon as you might your own housekeeper while our other guests are present — if, of course, that prospect is an attractive one. I haven't asked your mother yet but I do hope you two ladies would do us the honour of being hostesses for our Christmas Eve dinner."

Georgina sat back and folded her hands in her lap as she considered the suggestion. "I would be happy to as long as Mother agrees. We will do it together."

"That's settled then." Charles took a sip of his whisky, pleased at her response.

"Now there is something I need to ask you two gentlemen to help me with."

"Of course, we will do whatever we can," Charles said.

"Perhaps you should wait and hear my request first." A small crease lined Georgina's brow. She took a deep breath. "It's to do with the terrible business with my father's shepherd."

"Nothing was ever proved," Henry said.

"I have been conducting my own enquiries." Georgina looked pained. "Unfortunately there seems to be some truth in the allegations."

Henry drew himself up. "Ellis died before he could have his say in court."

"I have tracked down the man who spoke up about the beating. He is no longer in our employ but I remember him as always being trustworthy in the past."

"As are all your father's employees, I am sure," Charles said.

Georgina turned to him. There was a deep sadness in her look. "Yes but my father was a commanding presence. They may not have always felt ... free to speak out."

"Neither should they." Henry harrumphed. "Ellis was their employer and he looked after them well."

"Loyalty is important, I grant you, and it is for that reason I wish to assist the fellow. It must have been difficult for him to speak up. I've spoken with Donovan about this. I can't have the informant back at Prosser's Run — the other men won't work with him. However, times are difficult, and I'd like to help him find another job."

"You want me to employ him?" Henry shook his head.

"Or perhaps find someone who will."

"How is he with bullocks?" Charles looked from one to the other.

"He is certainly used to cattle and he would have worked with our bullock team at some stage."

"I would like to take on another team." Charles spoke to his father now. "Our transport business has plenty of work with the mines. It is doing much better than other aspects of our business at the moment."

"We don't want to bore Miss Prosser with such talk." Henry raised his eyebrows at Charles and then turned back to Georgina. "Leave it with us and we will see what can be done."

"Thank you, Mr Wiltshire, but there is one more thing I need your help with."

"If we can." Henry's tone was reserved now.

"It's to do with the shepherd himself. Albie, I believe his name is. I hear his injuries have left him crippled." The lines across Georgina's brow deepened. "I still find it hard to believe my father would have been so deliberately cruel. He is not here to defend himself but from what I have ascertained he had some hand in the affair." She took a breath. "I would like to recompense Albie in some way, if that were possible; I'm not sure how."

Henry pushed back his chair and stood. "Does your mother know about this?"

"We have discussed it. Like you she was disconcerted at first, but she has come to see my point of view."

"Really, Georgina. I don't believe it is necessary."

"But very admirable, Father." Charles could see Georgina was determined and the best course of action was to take her side. "Why don't I see what I can do to get some money to him?"

"Oh thank you, Charles." She rewarded him with her beautiful smile.

Henry gave a slight shake of his head. "I think it's time to retire."

Georgina rose and Charles jumped up to pull back her chair. "Thank you both," she said. "Good night."

Charles watched her elegant movement as she left the room. Once the door closed behind her his father spoke.

"You'll have your work cut out bringing that young woman into line, Charles."

Charles grinned. "But what fun it will be, Father."

Eighteen

Edith walked quickly down the lane behind the shop. Hawker was a small town in comparison to Adelaide and Sydney and she especially noticed this in the early mornings when few others appeared to be afoot. She hated it: it gave her an eerie feeling and brought home just how far from most of the world she was living.

Mr Hemming would not be in first thing. He had opened the shop for the afternoon after Mrs Wiltshire's funeral the day before. Edith had helped all day with food and cleaning up, first at the church and then at the house, where dinner was provided for close friends. Now Hemming was to be given a few hours off and it was up to her to open.

At least she'd had the chance to speak with Mr Charles on a couple of occasions. He had been very attentive and she found herself blushing under his gaze. Not because he looked at her; it was the thought of the book hidden under his bed.

Edith had never been with a man, though there had been several close calls not of her choosing in the back rooms of her mother's ale house in Sydney. Edith shuddered and tugged her jacket down over her waist. She had escaped that life and her sights were firmly set on a much better one.

Her final encounter with Charles before she retired the previous night had left her restless. Mrs Nixon had been taken up with Laura, who kept waking and calling for her mother, and Edith had done the last of the dishes alone. He'd found her turning down the lamps and had offered to walk her home although it was hardly more than twenty steps from his back door to hers. Edith wasn't sure if she'd imagined his hand brushing her cheek as he'd reached up to help her into her jacket. They'd walked side by side, then, at her door, he had hesitated and the light of the moon had illuminated his face. She'd seen on it the same desire that had emanated from the men who tried to grope her back home.

Seeing that look from Charles had taken her by surprise, then given her some satisfaction. He had taken notice of her. She was more than just a shop assistant. Edith didn't flatter herself that he wanted anything other than to bed her. That didn't matter. He was at least interested in her as a woman. It was the first step and she would plan the next very carefully.

She had spent a restless night pondering what to do about that interest. Finding herself awake early and unable to go back to sleep, she had risen, dressed and eaten a simple breakfast of bread and tea. Then with nothing to do at home she had decided to go to the shop. It was well before opening time but there were still boxes to pack for removal to the new shop. That's if they were to go ahead. She had helped Mr Hemming clean up after the dust storm but little else had been done since Mrs Wiltshire's passing.

Sounds ahead of her in the lane made her pause. Who else was about this early? She clutched the collar of her shirt and pressed into the fence behind the Wiltshires' shop. Living in the back room of the ale house and then travelling the long journey alone from Sydney to Adelaide, where her first accommodation was little better than the cess pit she'd left behind, she had learned to be always on her guard.

The noise continued but came no closer, so she edged forward. There was a wagon in the lane ahead behind Garrat's shop. She let out a breath. It was only Mr Garrat. She could see his bulky form hefting something onto the wagon, which was already piled with wooden crates. There were potatoes in one crate and onions in another. It was very early to be making deliveries, but what the Garrats did was of no concern to her. From what she gathered they were struggling to keep their business going.

Edith let herself in the gate and put the key in the lock of the back door. Once more she paused and put her hand to her chest. The door was not locked. She pushed it open, just a little, and listened. There was a shuffle. Her heart was thudding. She looked behind her, wondering if she should go and get Mr Garrat. She was paused on the threshold when a figure stepped from the shop into the office towards her. Edith gasped.

"Oh, it's you, Edith." Charles grinned. "I didn't mean to startle you."

She dropped the hand that had been at her mouth and took in her employer's dishevelled hair and his rolled-up shirt sleeves. "Mr Charles. I didn't know you would be here."

"I couldn't sleep so I decided to begin work early."

He smiled at her and she felt warmth spread up her chest to her cheeks. She was not imagining the guile in his look.

"I couldn't leave all the work for you, Miss Ferguson. You have done so much for my family over the last week. I am most grateful."

He loomed over her, accompanied by the smell of perspiration and something spicy.

Edith stood her ground and met his look. "I came in early because I knew there would be much to do."

"Did you indeed?" His eyebrows raised at her boldness.

Edith put on her sweetest expression. "Is there something in particular you would like to me to start with, Mr Charles?"

Charles groaned, put one hand on the wall behind her and leaned forward. The swiftness of his response startled her just for a moment.

"Are you unwell, Mr Charles?" Edith feigned a concerned look. "Mr Garrat is just outside in the lane loading his wagon. Should I call him?"

She watched the struggle of emotions on his face. He dropped his hand, stepped back and hung his head. "Please forgive my strange behaviour, Miss Ferguson. I am overwrought. What with losing my mother and the work needing to be done ready for the new shop opening I am quite overwhelmed."

"Please don't trouble yourself, Mr Charles. Grief does terrible things to us." Edith put on her saddest face. "I've lost both my parents. I know how it can affect you."

His head whipped up. "I'd forgotten you are quite alone."

She lowered her gaze. It might not have been exactly true but it may as well have been. Her father had been some man her mother had bedded and never seen again, and she used the term "mother" lightly when she thought of the woman who had raised her. Edith's life had been a misery until she had escaped and taken a coach to Adelaide. When she had last seen her mother she had been drinking herself to death; perhaps she already had. Edith preferred to think so.

"That must be very difficult. Is there no other relative you can turn to?"

She shook her head.

Charles frowned. "I know it's not polite to ask your age but you appear so young to have no family to support you."

"I am eighteen." Edith drew herself up. "Quite capable of looking after myself."

"Of course, I didn't mean to imply —"

Edith let her face soften. "Please don't concern yourself, Mr Charles." She moved ahead of him towards the shop. "Now let us tackle some of these jobs before it's time to open the doors." Edith resisted looking over her shoulder but she couldn't help but smile at the sound of his footsteps following her. It was a dangerous game she was playing but one that would reward her with a fine prize if she happened to win.

Charles stepped outside into the small backyard behind the shop and took a long deep breath. Georgina had left very early that morning and he had been up to see her on her way. She had even allowed him to kiss her cheek.

The softness of her skin under his lips and the sweet scent of her violet cologne had driven him wild with desire. He'd come in to the shop as soon as she was out of sight. He had planned to work off his frustration and then Edith had arrived.

He swore under his breath. He had moved too fast with her. If he was to groom her for his bed he would need to be more careful. Finding out she was alone with no-one to turn to had been a useful piece of information. He hoped it would mean she could be more easily influenced by him. Working alongside her he'd been able to think of nothing else and he'd had to find an excuse to come outside for a moment.

He crossed to the gate and looked in the direction of Garrat's. The lane was empty now but Edith had said Garrat was loading a wagon. When he'd questioned her on it she had insisted it wasn't the usual small cart that he used for his grocery deliveries. Garrat could have been doing anything with the wagon but Charles was curious. A couple of his customers had mentioned Garrat visiting their farms. They were further out of town than the older man usually went with his cart. He'd better not be trying to encroach on the Wiltshires' delivery round.

Footsteps sounded behind him and he spun to see his father approaching.

"Hello, Father. It seems none of us could sleep this morning."

Henry stopped and looked him up and down. "You have the appearance of a labourer."

Charles grinned at his father's neat suit and high collar. Even on the hottest day he dressed so formally. "That's what I've been this morning. I have shifted a lot of the boxes into the new shop."

"Yes, the new shop." Henry's face fell. "Your mother will not be here to see it."

"I am sure she's watching over it though." Charles did his best to sound reverent. He needed Henry to be at his best again. Business in the current climate was difficult. Luckily their interests went beyond the shop, but it would take the two of them to manage it all.

"Tell me, why have you made these changes here at the back?" Henry waved his hand towards the high rafters that now began to span the space between the back of the old shop and the back of the new. "You told me you wanted a verandah, not a shed."

"The structure was damaged by the storm. I had to deal with it ..." Charles didn't want to upset his father more but they had to get on with things. "It was the day after Mother died. I didn't want to bother you but what had been started had been partly dislodged by the storm. It was not safe, and a decision had to be made." He looked up at the construction that would eventually be roofed with tin, high over his head. "I decided it would be better to have a structure we could also bring the wagons under. It gives us a place to load and unload for both shops undercover."

"And the cost?"

"I had to make some adjustments but I am sure you will be happy. When you feel ready we can go over it."

"I have no appointments this morning. Make some tea and we will discuss it in my office." Henry moved ahead to the door then he turned back. "And please clean up and replace your necktie at least before you join me."

"Of course." Charles watched his father take one more look around and then enter the premises. The old man had aged visibly this last week. There was extra grey in his hair and his face was permanently creased. Charles knew he needed his father's help and business knowledge but he had to prepare himself for one day taking over. In the meantime, he knew the extra loan he'd managed to extract from the bank, simply awaiting his father's signature, would be easily repaid. Besides money for the new roof, he had got enough to purchase a third team and wagon.

During the week he'd received more good news. Becker had decided he was going to return and he wanted Charles's help to get to the land where he believed there were diamonds. From what Becker had told him back in Melbourne, Charles was sure he'd been talking about the high country on Smith's Ridge. It was very helpful that the land in question could be easily accessed from Prosser's Run. There might be a drought but that didn't deter him. It only provided opportunities. The Wiltshires would soon be back in the black. Charles turned to follow his father inside, whistling as he walked.

Nineteen

Piercing squeals filled the air as Joseph led William into the cool of the kitchen. He was amazed at the sight of his two youngest daughters chasing each other around the table, their faces and clothes dotted with flour, while their mother sat at one end of the large kitchen table feeding Matthew.

"What's this?" he bellowed. He was tired from being in the saddle all day and the sound of their squeals hurt his ears. They stopped at his voice. Matthew slid from his mother's lap and toddled towards Joseph.

Millie rose and quickly readjusted her shirt at the sight of William behind him. "They are just letting off some energy."

"William!" Beth and Ruth chorused and ran to their brother.

Joseph winced at the high pitch of their call. "Perhaps they need some outside time."

"It's very hot." She dismissed his comment and moved towards the stove. "Binda and Jundala left after you this morning so with Timothy and Eliza away it's only us for the evening meal. Would you like some tea or a cold drink?"

"We'll have tea in a while. The worst of the heat is gone."

"I'm so glad you came to us for Christmas." Millie gave William a wobbly smile. "We all miss you very much."

"It has been good to be here." William smiled back at her and patted his stomach. "The food was remarkable as usual."

"I've packed some leftovers for you to take back to Smith's Ridge."

"You shouldn't have, Millie. You've got a big enough family here to feed."

Joseph moved closer. "You're wasting your breath, son."

Millie placed a kiss on her husband's cheek. Her dark eyes still shone even though he knew she was tired from weeks of preparation for their Christmas festivities. "We have plenty to share, don't we, Joseph?"

"You are always able to conjure it up, my love, even in these tough times."

"We are much luckier than many of those poor families trying to live on the plains." Millie smoothed the white tablecloth and straightened the candelabra that was set in the middle of the large table. "So much to be thankful for." Her gaze shifted to her children, who were scrambling around the adults' legs.

"Why don't we all go down to the outside room?" William suggested.

"Yes, yes." The girls squealed and hopped up and down. Matthew echoed their cries.

The children took one of William's hands each and pulled him towards the door. Matthew's strong little arms wrapped around Joseph's legs; he scooped up his son, who immediately clasped his father's cheeks with his chubby hands. Joseph felt a wave of contentment. He was so fortunate to have seven healthy children, but Matthew was a particular delight to him. He swallowed the lump in his throat. "Outside it is." Joseph looked over the little boy's head to Millie, who was watching her daughters disappear through the door.

"Don't go far," she called after them.

"They will be safe with William and me, Millie." Joseph winked at her. "Don't fuss."

She sighed and he was pleased to see her shoulders relax. Ever since they had heard some children of mixed parentage had been taken by the Protector of Aborigines and placed in a mission, Millie had become extremely fearful for her children. No matter how much Joseph tried to reassure her, she kept a constant watchful eye on them and would not take them in to Hawker.

"There's still some Christmas punch." Millie smiled. "Shall I bring that out with some bread and meat? We can all eat early with the children."

"Sounds like a good idea, my love. I'll tell Father."

"No." Millie shook her head. "All the festivities have tired him. He's only just gone off to have a rest. I'll call him when I come."

Joseph left her to the food preparation and, carrying his youngest son, he followed after his oldest. Once more he felt a wave of pride sweep over him. In spite of the drought he felt truly blessed.

William, Joseph and Robert had been out all day, checking the nearest waterholes, where there was nothing but dust. William had wanted to have a look around, as he hadn't been back to Wildu Creek since shearing in September. Thomas had said he'd stay home — Joseph suspected it was the energetic children who had worn him down rather than the Christmas festivities. No doubt Thomas preferred his cottage. It was much more peaceful there.

Joseph and William settled under the remaining gum tree overlooking the dry bed of Wildu Creek. So many family occasions had been celebrated out there in what his mother had called her outside room, although they hadn't used the area much of late. The old wooden furniture his father had made was still there, with the exception of the table. The last few years had taken their toll. The gums had lost branches and finally one had come down during a big dust storm, crushing the table as it fell. The trunk had fallen down the bank and it was there the girls climbed while Joseph bounced Matthew on his knee.

Joseph sat back in his chair and looked across at William. Hegarty had returned to Smith's Ridge after Christmas but William had stayed on after being implored by his younger siblings to spend longer with them. Even though they'd been together they'd had little time for talk alone. He knew how miserable William was over Georgina Prosser's rejection, and Joseph had some news on that front — though he didn't know where to begin in telling it.

"How are your cattle?" he said instead.

"Little better than your sheep looked today. I don't know when or if I'll be able to supply beef to the export company again."

"No point in worrying about that now. We just have to hang on. The drought can't last forever." Thomas would have smiled had he been there, hearing his words repeated. "How are the waterholes looking?"

"We will soon be down to just the two in the rugged hill country. We can get cattle into the lower one but not the top hole."

"Binda and Millie's family still rely on that."

"I know, Father." William's face was grim. "I could barrel out some of the water but it would only be a temporary measure. The cattle would soon need more … Anyway there's more to it than stock needing water."

Joseph frowned and let a struggling Matthew slip from his arms to toddle after his sisters. "Ruth. Beth. Watch out for your brother." He watched as Beth lifted the little boy to her hip, then he turned back to William. "What is it? Do you need to move some cattle to Wildu Creek?"

"You've got your own stock to water."

"The sheep are up in the higher country close to the springs. There's still some water lower down."

"I don't know what to do. Many have lost stock. I can't imagine how we will avoid the same." William put his head in his hands. "Thousands of sheep dying and many cattle as well."

"Some have let the animals eat the land bare and then think they will get good rain every year. We've taken better care of our country. We're surviving because we have some bush left." He leaned across and clapped his hand on William's shoulder. "Hope and pray. That's all we can do now, son."

William pointed towards Joseph's shirt pocket. "You're still not tempted to look for diamonds?"

Joseph's hand covered the lump in his pocket that was the rough diamond. He locked his gaze on William's. "I've told you I won't. I've seen what mining fever does to people and to the land."

"We have done well because of the gold you found."

Joseph stood and began to pace. "Yes." He stopped and turned back to William, who was still watching him closely. "I have taken the riches from the land and used them for our benefit, so why shouldn't I do it again?"

William stood, a frown on his face. "You wouldn't ..."

Joseph shook his head. "I can't say I've never thought about looking for diamonds but that's all it's ever been, a brief thought." He went back to his chair and sat. William did the same.

Joseph sighed. "There are times when I hate myself for it."

"For what?"

"Double standards." Joseph stared out across the dry creek. "I mined gold without a thought for what it did to the land and yet when it comes to this country I can't bear the idea of people crawling all over it, desecrating it in search of riches."

"You can't even be sure there are more diamonds around the waterhole. That rock could have come from anywhere. Yardu's people used to travel long distances to trade. Who's to say some-one didn't pick it up and carry it with them only to discard it later?"

Joseph looked at his son. "Whatever the case no-one will search that country in my lifetime."

William's gazed shifted towards the mountains. "Nor mine," he murmured. "I made Yardu a promise."

"What? When?"

"I visited the camp before he died. He insisted I look out for his people."

"Yardu talked with you? He rarely spoke to me."

"I'm not sure I understood all that his translator said but it boiled down to me being the caretaker of Smith's Ridge and of the people who live there."

"Well, I'll be. So that's why you won't try to divert the water." Joseph scratched at his beard.

"It's not a job I expected either and, apart from making sure they have food and water, I can't see what else I can do. It's mostly only old people left at the camp, and I know little of their ways — but at least they can remain in their country."

"I wonder for how long." Joseph thought of the stories he'd heard about natives being moved to missions and reserves. He could understand Millie's fears for their children.

"I don't know what Yardu really expected of me but I will do my best to see that those who remain have food and are left alone."

Joseph put a hand on his son's shoulder and gave it a squeeze. "You're a good man, son."

William lifted his head and stared down at the creek bed to where the children were playing. Joseph felt for his oldest son. At least at Wildu Creek there was his father, Timothy and Eliza, Robert, Millie and the little children. They had each other to lean on in these tough times. It must be lonely for William and Hegarty at Smith's Ridge, with only Clem and Jessie as company.

"How are Jessie and Clem?" Joseph asked. "I'm sorry they couldn't visit for Christmas."

"They'll come once I get back to Smith's Ridge. Clem wants Jessie to stay here to have the baby. Millie has offered to help when the time comes."

"Who will housekeep for you then?"

William gave a wry smile. "It will be back to me and Hegarty."

They both jumped to their feet at the sound of a piercing scream from below. The two girls were on their hands and knees, heads down, Matthew's chubby legs poking out from beneath them. Joseph scrambled down the bank, his heart thumping in his chest.

Ruth looked up at him, tears rolling down her cheeks. "We found a lizard and we made it a little yard."

Beth held up a small lifeless body. "Matthew squashed it."

Joseph let out a sigh and took the squashed lizard. "We'll bury it. I'm sure Matthew didn't mean to hurt it."

William watched his father pick up Matthew and placate his daughters. The children certainly kept him busy. "Do you need help?"

Joseph gave him a defiant look. "I think I can manage."

The little group crossed the creek and made their way up to the other bank where similar burials had taken place for treasured animals over the years.

William turned away as Robert crossed the flat space of land towards him carrying a table.

"Millie said we're to eat out here tonight."

William took one side of the table. "You should have called me."

"Do I look like I need help?" Robert's tone was sharp but his face bore a grin.

They placed the table on the flat under the tree and William tested to see if it was steady. "We'll have an arm wrestle later to see who's strongest."

Robert's grin widened. "If you're up to it."

William stood tall and hoped his brother wouldn't remember the challenge. Robert had grown into a big man with broad shoulders and it was quite possible William might come off second best to his little brother these days.

They were both distracted by squeals and yells from across the creek. Joseph was coming back with Matthew on his shoulders and the two girls clung to his legs, one balanced on each of his boots. It would be a slow journey.

"Is it my imagination or have our younger siblings become a little wild of late?" William asked.

"Millie's very protective of them. It's been worse since the news of those children north of Hawker being taken away from their mothers. The little ones are hardly allowed out of the house unless one or more of us are with them."

"Surely those children were in a different situation. They needed care."

"They had mothers who loved them and did their best for them. The fathers had to go away for work." Robert turned his big chocolate brown eyes on William. "Just like our father did the last time there was a drought. Imagine if someone had come and taken us away?"

William pursed his lips. It wasn't the same. The children who were taken must have been in need of help — but he didn't want to argue with Robert.

"Here we are." Millie appeared beside them with a tray loaded with cutlery, mugs and a jug of punch. A tablecloth was tucked under her arm. She darted a look at the children as they called to her, then she waved. "Let your poor father walk and come and get a drink." She glanced from Robert to William. "Would one of you mind going back for the food, please?"

"I'll go." Robert was off before William could reply.

Millie smiled. "He's such a help to me in the house. He cooked the kangaroo-tail soup we had last night."

"My little brother cooks?"

"He's mastered a few meals."

There were more squeals from the creek as Joseph sank to the dirt and the children piled on top of him.

"And he's so patient with the children. I think they're beginning to wear your father down." She went to the edge of the bank. "Beth, Ruth. That's enough now. Leave your poor father alone."

William watched the little girls scrabble up the slope and thought about his young giant of a brother and his place in this big family. William had Smith's Ridge, as he'd wanted. His father had said Robert's time would come but with Thomas and Joseph thankfully both in good health, when would that be? Robert probably got little say in the running of Wildu Creek.

The girls came to a stop in front of them, smiling sweetly. Their hair was awry and sprinkled with dirt and leaves, and their white pinafores had turned brown.

"Look at you both. Off you go and wash, quickly." Millie clapped her hands and the girls ran giggling across the yard.

"Hello, Grandpa," they called as they passed Thomas coming from his cottage.

Joseph came up the bank with Matthew. "I think we might need to go and wash as well."

William watched Thomas ruffle the little boy's hair as he passed. How he longed for a family of his own, but that was not to be.

Millie had spread the cloth on the table and was busy setting things out. William took a seat under the tree beside Thomas.

They both stared into the distance towards the mountains. There was little green in the landscape; only greys and browns as far as the eye could see.

"It's good to be out here," Thomas said.

"Lots of happy memories, Grandpa."

"Mmm," Thomas murmured. "And some not so. But that is life. We must always look forward. Your grandmother taught me that."

"You spent a lot of time on your own before you married Grandma." William thought about the stories of his grandfather's early days. "It was a big thing to come out here all alone."

"I suppose so but I wasn't alone for long. There was Gulda and your great uncles and your grandmother of course." Thomas shifted his gaze to William. The skin around his eyes was lined with wrinkles that turned up and always made him look as if he was smiling even when he wasn't. "It was my great fortune that Lizzie agreed to be my wife."

A wave of loneliness swept over William and he looked back to the mountains.

"How's Prosser's Run looking?"

Thomas's question surprised William. He stiffened.

"I hear the young lady has taken over the management with Donovan's help."

"I believe that's the case. I only know what I've seen over the fence. Their country looks much like Smith's Ridge." He had not set foot on Prosser's Run since Georgina had sent him away. The country on the other side of his fence was even more barren than his own and there was no sign of stock.

"No doubt they suffer like the rest of us." Thomas nodded his head. "Ellis Prosser had a lot of faults but he understood this country better than many."

"Yes, but he treated some people very badly."

"True." Thomas nodded again. "And he's not alone in that sadly. So you haven't been over to see how the Prosser ladies are faring?"

"No." William knew he sounded churlish but Georgina had made it quite clear he wasn't welcome.

"When I was in Hawker before Christmas Mrs Taylor couldn't wait to tell me how much time Charles Wiltshire and Miss Prosser were spending together."

William's fingers curled into his palms but he said nothing.

"I can't imagine what a sensible young woman like Miss Prosser could find interesting in that pompous boy."

"Perhaps he doesn't have any competition." Millie handed them both a mug of cold punch. Her face was serious but William saw the twinkle in her eye.

"Mrs Taylor also asked me about your wife, William." Thomas raised his eyebrows. William lurched forward and nearly choked on the mouthful of punch he'd just taken.

"Fancy you taking a wife and not telling us."

Millie was grinning now. It was obviously a joke between them.

"I don't have a wife," William spluttered.

"Well of course we know that." She chuckled.

"It seems the gossips of the district have invented one for you," Thomas said.

William looked at the pair of them laughing at his expense and decided to join their game. "Who is this imaginary wife? Hegarty wouldn't look good in a skirt."

"Perhaps … Jessie?"

William leaped to his feet. If it had been anyone but Millie who'd suggested he take another man's wife he'd have hit them. "People are saying I have taken my friend's wife?"

"They probably don't know she's Clem's wife." Millie stroked his shoulder. "No-one would have seen any of you together."

"You attended their wedding, perhaps someone saw you and got the wrong end of the stick. And it's no secret there's a young woman living at Smith's Ridge." Thomas grimaced. "You know how the gossips like to make a story much more interesting than it really is."

William was speechless. He felt a heat that was due to more than the lowering sun. "How dare they besmirch Jessie's reputation?"

"And yours," Thomas added.

"I don't care what people think of me." Anger bubbled up inside him. It was ironic that once he had cared very much about what people thought. Since Georgina had left to go overseas and then her rejection of him he had attended few community activities. He went to town only when necessary and he didn't linger there. What he did care about was kind-hearted Jessie being caught up in gossip about him. "How can I fix this?"

"I'm not sure you can," Thomas said. "Eventually the truth will out."

"It might help if Clem took his wife to town now and then." Millie lifted a mug from the table and took a sip. "They haven't been to Hawker since they were married."

"Jessie doesn't like town," William said.

"Neither do I, but I think we will have to convince Clem they need to buy some things for the baby."

"What things?" William knew Clem had already made a small cradle and Jessie had been busy sewing.

Millie shook her head. "Doesn't matter what things."

The sounds of the children returning mingled in the air with the deeper voices of their father and Robert.

Millie moved to organise the food Robert carried.

"And perhaps you need to visit your neighbours."

William looked at his grandfather but Thomas was gazing out over the valley again. What did it all mean? William's thoughts were in turmoil. Is that why Georgina had turned him away; she thought he'd forgotten her and married someone else? His hopes soared and then just as swiftly plummeted. There was no doubting Charles Wiltshire was in her life. That wasn't gossip; he'd seen them together with his own eyes. It appeared bloody young Wiltshire was trying to claim her.

There was a gasp. "William sweared."

He looked down at Ruth's shocked face. He hadn't realised he'd spoken out loud.

"Swore," Joseph corrected. He gave William a stern look then when the little girl turned away he winked. "I gather Millie's told you about the latest gossip."

"Why didn't you tell me sooner?"

"We only heard ourselves on your grandfather's return from town before Christmas. There hasn't been a chance since you got here. Something to think about though, isn't it?"

William looked around at the adults, who were all now watching him.

He was blushing, and they were enjoying it.

Joseph clapped him on the back and grinned. "Time to eat, son."

Twenty

William stood on the ridge above the Wildu Creek houses and sheds and looked over the country spread before him. Bathed in the yellow light of early morning the land was grey, appearing fresh and yet tired all at once. He had planned to return to Smith's Ridge that day but after the revelations of the previous evening he had decided to stay one more night.

He had slept fitfully, his mind busy with thoughts of Georgina. A window of hope had opened up and he couldn't shut it. But on top of that, and of more urgency, was the question of what to do about his stock. William knew he had to take most of his remaining cattle south if he was to save them, but had he left it too late? He would need help to do it and his thoughts had shifted to Robert.

At the first signs of light that morning he had dressed and slipped from his father's house to climb the ridge. Buried nearby were his grandmother and two of her babies. He'd climbed a little higher past the graves and perched on a large deep red rock, watching the light spread over the land before him as he pondered.

After their dinner by the creek, he had talked at length with his grandfather, father and brother. Sheep were different from cattle but they faced the same problems with the drought. Much had been discussed but it was his decision to make.

Further off in the hills to the right, two eagles circled lower and lower. Something had attracted their scrutiny. He hoped it wasn't one of his father's sheep — and that thought helped him make up his mind. The sun crested the hills behind him, lighting up the landscape, highlighting the browns, dull greens and deeper purples, which had all looked grey before.

William rose, stretched his arms over his head and let out a long breath. He had arrived at a decision about the stock at least. What to do about Georgina he was not sure, but it would come to him, he knew. He made his way down, noticing fresh puffs of smoke from both his grandfather's chimney and his father's before he lost sight of the smaller house behind the bulk of the newer one. In the big kitchen Millie was busy at the fire. Joseph held Matthew on his knee and Robert sat beside him. There was no sign of the little girls.

"Good morning." Joseph gave William a sleepy smile.

William suspected that his father's rest, like his own, had not been peaceful. Joseph had his own worries with his property. William only hoped what he was to suggest wouldn't add to them. He seated himself at the table opposite Robert.

"You look like a man with something to say." Joseph sat Matthew on the floor with a pile of wooden blocks and focused on William.

"I've decided to leave two bulls and some cows in the high country at Smith's Ridge. The remaining stock I will walk south."

"I agree you should try."

"It will be a slow trek, searching for feed and water."

"And if you make it with cattle still alive?" Joseph only put into words what William already knew. The cattle could all die on the journey.

"Sell them if I can or find agistment." William looked his father firmly in the eye. "I'd rather that than watch them slowly die."

"You will be gone from home a long time."

"Yes." William shifted his gaze to Robert. "I was hoping you would come with me, Robert."

"Of course." Robert's face lit up with a grin then he glanced at his father. "If you can spare me, Father."

"There are enough of us here to look after the sheep." Joseph clasped a hand on each of their shoulders. "It will be a difficult journey but if anyone can manage it you two can."

William felt pride at his father's confidence in them.

"Will you take Hegarty also?" Joseph picked up the mug of tea in front of him.

"I hope he will agree to stay and look after the remaining cattle with Clem. Rex, one of the men from Yardu's camp, has helped us out before. I was hoping he would come with us."

"I think you're right. Clem can help Hegarty. The two of you with an extra stockman can manage the trek south. I may need to do the same with the sheep, but I will have plenty of help. I can afford to wait it out a little longer, see what the new year brings."

Robert rose to his feet. "When do we leave?"

William grinned. "Slow down, little brother. There are things to be done first." He looked back at Joseph. "I will go back to Smith's Ridge tomorrow."

"Good. Let us enjoy one more day together as a family," Joseph said. "Millie, I think we should have a picnic lunch."

Millie came and placed a hand on Robert's shoulder. "A special day." She beamed at William. "We could take the wagon and go further down the creek to the stand of big trees."

Beth and Ruth appeared beside their mother. Their hair tousled from sleep, they were momentarily silent as the adults made merry around them.

The next morning it was a much more subdued group that gathered in the early light to farewell William and Robert.

"Go safely, sons." Joseph said solemnly as he shook their hands in turn.

"Send word from time to time if you can," Thomas said.

William could see tears welling in Millie's eyes as she clutched Matthew to her. Beside her the two little girls sobbed, imploring William and Robert not to go. He kissed his stepmother's cheek and tickled Matthew's chin then hugged his little sisters and turned once more to his father.

They shook hands and William mounted his horse, leaving Robert to make similar farewells. To a chorus of goodbyes, the two brothers rode away from the house, towing with them a third horse loaded with Robert's belongings and food from Millie.

They were silent, William already thinking about what needed to be done to prepare to shift his cattle south, and Robert deep in his own thoughts.

"I hope you won't regret your decision to join me." William finally spoke as they rode through the first of the gates between them and Smith's Ridge. With no sheep in this part of Wildu Creek the gate was left open.

Robert looked across at him, his face solemn. "Thank you."

"What for?" It wasn't the response William had expected.

"For taking me with you. There is little for me at Wildu Creek."

"There will be little at Smith's Ridge if we can't keep the cattle alive."

"But at least we will be doing something, rather than waiting and watching."

William nodded, thankful Robert felt the same way he did and pleased to have his brother as his companion for the work ahead of them.

It was late afternoon when they had their first sight of the house at Smith's Ridge. The smoke from the chimney wasn't the only sign of life: there was a cart drawn up at the back of the house and someone moving around it.

"Looks like Clem is making ready to leave," William said.

Clem was lifting the small cradle he had made into the back of the cart. He held up a hand in acknowledgement of their arrival. "Good to see you, Robert," he said as William and Robert dismounted. "I hope it's all right to borrow your cart, William?"

"Of course." William looked around, uncomfortable now after the gossip he'd heard. He only hoped it never reached Clem's ears. "Is Jessie well?"

"Yes, but anxious. Her time is still two months away but I would like to set off for Wildu Creek so she can be with the women."

"Jundala's away visiting her people. She should be back in a week or so."

"Millie will take care of Jessie," Robert said. "She's looking forward to another baby to fuss over."

William looked around. "Is Hegarty here?"

"No. He's with the cattle. He expected you home soon so he sent me back to help Jessie." Clem reached for the reins of Joseph's horse. "Let me see to the horses. Jessie will want you to have a drink inside and try her latest cake."

William was sure the edges of Clem's mouth twitched. "Thank you."

Robert was first down the path. He hadn't tasted Jessie's attempts at cake before.

"There's something else."

Robert kept going but William turned back to Clem.

"Someone's been around the bottom waterhole."

William raised his eyebrows. "Someone?"

"A man who wears boots."

"Someone passing by wanting water?"

"Bit out of the way for that. Whoever he was he dug a few holes and scratched around."

Irritation prickled William's neck. "Fossicking?"

"That's what I think. The cattle messed up most of the tracks but I found where he tethered his horse. I'd say he was there some time in the last few days."

"Since Christmas?"

"Maybe. I followed the tracks for a while. They were headed back towards the northern boundary."

"Prosser's Run?"

"Could be whoever it was came from that way."

"Does Hegarty know?"

"I told him to keep a watch out."

"Good." William took off his hat. Even though the sun was still hot the breeze through his wet hair cooled his head. "It will be just Hegarty to keep a watch for quite a while. Robert and I are going to take most of the remaining cattle south."

"They're only going to die here."

William slid his hands around the brim of his hat. "I was hoping, once Jessie's had the baby, you might come back and help him out. He'll go crazy up there by himself and he'll need supplies."

"When are you going?"

"As soon as we can."

Clem shook his hand. "Once I get Jessie settled I'll come back. Can't have big old Hegarty starving to death."

"Thanks, Clem."

"You want me to unload this horse?" Clem ran his hands down the neck of the horse that had carried the pack and bags.

"Put everything on the back verandah. We'll sort it out. You go whenever you're ready."

Clem started to untie the bags from the back of the horse.

William held out his hand. "Thanks again, Clem, and good luck with the baby."

Clem gave it a quick shake then he grinned. "You'd better go in for some cake. Don't want Robert to eat it all."

Twenty-one

Hegarty and Robert waved William off from their vantage point on a rocky ledge above the waterhole where several cattle were drinking. The spring-fed hole was deeper on the far side, then it spread out in a large arc and along the creek until a bank of sand blocked it from ranging further down. The brothers had ridden to find Hegarty at first light. William had explained the plan and Hegarty had been in agreement. He and Robert would start rounding up the cattle they thought most likely to survive the journey south.

William had questioned Hegarty but the older man had found no sign of the tracks Clem had followed. Cattle had tramped the ground around the waterhole and there was no longer any indication of human digging or of their trail, but William was keen to look for himself.

He pushed his hat firmly onto his head and walked his horse on, searching the ground as he went. The day was warm but puffy clouds drifted across the blue sky, helping to hold back some of the sun's heat, and a breath of wind cooled his forearms below his rolled-up sleeves.

There was a natural trail from the waterhole down the creek, across rocks and then between the lower hills to the gate in the fence between Prosser's Run and Smith's Ridge. William had avoided this part of the property for a long time, but today he rode with a mixture of hope and dread in his heart. Had the South African man, Becker, returned, or had someone else been looking around? And if it was someone else, who? And did it mean Georgina had been complicit in the search if the person had come from her property or had they simply followed the curves and grooves of the land over both properties? And what of Georgina? Had she listened to gossip and so thought him a married man? Is that why she had turned her back on him?

So many questions played through his mind. By the time he reached the gate he had no answers and a dull ache in his temple. The gate was firmly shut. The ground around it was baked hard, with little plant life strong enough to survive on this windswept part of the hill. He could see no sign of anyone having passed this way in recent times. He looked in the direction of the stand of trees where he had tied the ribbon. From his position he couldn't tell if it was still there or not. He was torn between wanting to check and knowing he must see to his cattle, but he had already wasted the best part of the day. He slid from the saddle. It was foolish but he couldn't resist going to see. The ribbon had been a symbol of his love. Now he had some splinter of hope, he wanted the ribbon back.

He opened the gate and walked his horse to the stand of trees. A flutter of movement caught his eye and there was the ribbon, faded and even more tatty now, but still firmly tied in the tree. He was startled by a gunshot. Big Red pulled back, and William reached up to pat his neck. He reassured the animal and turned his gaze in the direction of the gully, from where the shot had come. A second rang out. He tethered Big Red in the trees and set off on foot. Beyond the trees the barren terrain sloped sharply. William kept his head low as he climbed over the rocky peak that bounded the next gully. A shadow passed over him and he squinted up at a large eagle circling overhead.

He lifted his head cautiously and took in the scene below. Three men stood around a dead cow. One was Swan, who worked for the Prossers. The other two had their faces obscured by their hats but from his clothes and stance one of them appeared to be Charles Wiltshire, and the third — William caught his breath. She might be wearing trousers like a man but it was Georgina Prosser.

"Stand back please, Georgina." The tone Charles used was commanding rather than tender. "Swan and I can deal with it."

Georgina put her hands to her hips. Her gaze lifted skywards as if she were saying a prayer and before William had time to duck away she had seen him.

"William?" Her voice wavered.

Charles spun around. "Baker? What are you doing here? This is not your land."

"I don't believe it's yours either, Wiltshire." William stood to his full height. He glanced back at Georgina. "I was checking the fence line. I heard shots."

She took two steps towards him. "The animal had a broken leg. We had to shoot it. We'll salvage what we can carry."

William saw longing rather than resentment on her face, but with Charles right there and Swan, he was in no position to speak with her. He thought desperately for something to say.

"There's been some damage to the fence," he blurted.

"Where?" She took another step closer.

Charles glowered at him. Swan paid no attention; he was bent over the dead cow, busily working.

"Near the gate. I can show you."

"There's no need, Georgina," Charles growled. "Swan and I can see to it later."

"But you're busy here. I'll be out of the way if I check the fence."

William thought there was a hint of mockery in her tone but Charles didn't seem to notice.

"Very well, but don't be long."

This time William saw indisputably the flash of anger that crossed Georgina's face. She clambered up the gully to stand beside him and without a backwards glance strode down the other side and off in the direction of the fence. He followed, desperately trying to think of an excuse for lying to her.

She stopped in the shade of the first gum tree and waited for him to catch up.

He came to a halt beside her, drinking in the green of her eyes, her pink lips and small upturned nose sprinkled with pale freckles.

She looked back at the hill that hid the men from her view. "Not the way we had planned to celebrate the new year but we couldn't leave the poor animal to the wild dogs and eagles." She swept a strand of hair back from her face and smudged dirt across her cheek. William longed to reach out and brush it away.

"Is that today?" He had lost track of the days since Christmas.

"Tomorrow it will be the new year. The last of this century." She looked back at him. "Which way?"

William could only stare.

A small frown creased her brow. "Where is the damage, Mr Baker?"

The sharp tone of her voice broke the spell she had cast over him. Mr Baker, she had said.

He took off his hat and looked her in the eye. "There isn't any."

She lifted her chin. "Then why did you say there was?"

"I wanted to tell you ... well, I thought perhaps it was the gossip—"

Georgina raised one eyebrow. "Please state your purpose, Mr Baker. I must get back."

"I'm not married." William blurted it out and watched the disdain spread across her face.

"You have brought me here to discuss your sordid living arrangements."

"Aah!" William pressed his hand to his head.

Georgina flinched, watching him warily.

"I have no living arrangements. At least not what you are thinking."

"How do you know what I am thinking?"

"You've heard the gossip."

"I don't listen to gossip. If you are referring to your liaison with your ... the native woman you live with, I got that direct from my father, in a letter, before he died."

"The old bugger."

"I beg your pardon." Georgina drew herself up and the light was back in her eyes. "If you brought me here to besmirch my father I won't stay and listen."

"I don't care what your father thought of me, Georgina, but it matters what you think."

He grabbed her hand. She snatched it back.

"I've heard enough." She made to move away.

"No." He put an arm to the trunk of the tree to block her path. "I need to clear the honour of my housekeeper, who doesn't deserve the injustice of the story made up about us."

She continued to glare at him but at least she didn't try to walk away.

William dropped his arm. "Jessie, who is married to Clem, lives in the quarters at Smith's Ridge with her husband and keeps house for Hegarty and me. Your father wanted to keep us apart.

He probably started the rumour that had me married to our housekeeper ... my shepherd's wife."

"Your shepherd's wife?" Georgina reached behind her for the trunk of the tree and leaned against it.

"I've never looked at another woman since I asked you to marry me, Georgina. And I have never stopped loving you."

Her mouth opened in a small 'o' and her eyes glistened with tears. Above her head the ribbon fluttered. William took a small step closer and leaned towards her.

"Georgina!"

William frowned at Charles Wiltshire striding over and Georgina let out a small sigh.

"Are you all right?" Charles took her hand. "What game are you playing, Baker?"

William met Wiltshire's baleful look with an equally menacing glare, clenching his fists at his sides. What was it about Charles Wiltshire that always made William want so much to punch the boy's nose?

"Simply rectifying some untruths. No doubt your family were involved in the spreading of the gossip."

Charles puffed out his chest. "I don't know what you're blathering about but you are on Prosser land and not welcome here."

"You're not a Prosser so you have no say in it," William growled.

"We are very good friends. Since the loss of Mr Prosser, my father and I have been helping the ladies." Charles shifted his hand to Georgina's shoulder. "We are very close."

William ignored him and locked his gaze on Georgina. Her eyes were sad and her mouth opened just a little but she didn't speak.

"Swan has collected what he could from the dead animal, Georgina, and loaded the spare horse. We should return to the homestead or we will be late for the new year's celebrations. Your mother will be worried."

Still Georgina remained where she stood.

"I have to go away for some time," William said quickly. "I'm taking cattle south. We leave tomorrow."

Charles gave a snort. "They'll die before you get them there."

William ignored him. "Can I call on you when I return?"

"You cannot," Charles huffed.

Georgina let out a sharp sigh and shook herself from his hold. Her white blouse draped softly to her waist where it was tucked into her trousers. The soft fabric rippled in the breeze and a lock of her red hair drifted to her neck. William drank in her beauty and ached at the sight of her bewildered look.

"How long will you be gone?" she asked.

"Several months at least." William wished with all his heart he didn't have to go and leave her.

She darted forward and kissed him. He'd barely tasted the sweetness of her lips than she pulled away again.

"I shall look forward to your return."

"What? Georgina, you can't be serious." Charles hopped from foot to foot.

"We all have obligations." Georgina gave William a look of such longing he wanted to take her in his arms right then, but she turned and walked quickly away.

Charles jabbed his finger at William's chest. "I don't know what story you spun for her, Baker, but if you make it back from your ridiculous trek you keep away from Georgina and Prosser's Run. Do you hear me?"

William's arm came up. Charles jerked backwards and lurched away. He lost his footing and fell on his backside. William looked down at him then he continued the lift of his arm and pushed his hat to his head. "You're a bit jumpy, Wiltshire." He grinned.

"And don't you worry about me; I'll make it back and it will take more than a boy like you to keep me away from Prosser's Run."

He looked over Wiltshire's prone form to Georgina, striding away. She didn't look back and soon disappeared beyond the rise of the hill. Charles was muttering profanities and trying to get himself up. William gave him a mock salute and walked away to retrieve his horse.

Georgina listened in silence as Charles raged on about William. They were riding side by side, heading for the homestead. Swan would be slower, leading the packhorse loaded with as much of the dead cow as they could take. Wild animals would get the rest. Charles went on about William's terrible temper and how he had threatened to hit Charles again.

All Georgina could think about was William and what he'd told her. He wasn't married or living with a woman. She still found it hard to believe after all this time of shutting him from her mind.

"Baker lacks any kind of common decency." Charles's complaint broke into her thoughts. She was tired of his grumbling. She urged her horse forward. Her beautiful Duchess was ageing but needed little encouragement to lengthen her stride and break into a canter.

"I'll see you at the house," Georgina called over her shoulder. She suppressed a smirk at the confusion that registered on his face. Charles Wiltshire really was a pompous ass.

Duchess picked up the pace. Georgina turned back and focused on the ride, confident Charles wouldn't try to match her speed. He was a good horseman but she had seen the way he had hobbled back from his meeting with William. He'd climbed gingerly onto his horse, saying William had caught him off guard and pushed him over. She grinned now, no longer able to contain her contempt. Whatever William had or hadn't done to Charles she didn't care.

She should have sent Charles away and spoken to William alone, told him she did still love him. Instead she'd pecked him on the lips and almost run away, overwhelmed by her feelings and the further despair at yet another thing her father had been guilty of. Not as terrible as his injury to the shepherd of course, but that he should lie to her — not to mention compromise her happiness so profoundly — was another damning chink in the image of the man she had thought a wonderful man and father.

And then there was her mother, so dependent on Georgina and such a worrier. Even when Georgina rode out that morning with Swan, Johanna had fussed. The Wiltshires were staying for new year and it had been to oblige her mother that she'd agreed to let Charles accompany them to check the cattle. Now she wished she hadn't.

Not only had he messed up the shot on the poor injured cow, so that she'd had to take the gun and finish it herself, but he'd spoiled the small opportunity she'd had to talk further with William. Now she had to be content with the memory of their brief kiss until his return. She slowed Duchess as she approached the gate near the horse yards, then reached down and patted the mare's neck.

"Thank you for the ride," Georgina said. Her father was no longer there but she still felt pressed from all sides. It had been so refreshing to fly across the ground as if she was free just for a short time.

Twenty-two

February 1899

William looked down at the dead cow. Already a million flies crawled over its hide as the February sun crested the hills and sent the force of its scorching heat over the land. Once more he questioned his decision to walk them south. It was the third cow they'd lost in as many days.

Robert got down from his horse and bent over the animal. "This one's struggled since we left Smith's Ridge. I didn't think it would make it this far."

William shook his head. Like Robert he knew exactly which cow it was. He regularly walked among his cattle rather than riding and encouraged Robert to do the same. The animals had settled to the journey and moved on quietly and steadily. He was sad to lose another.

"But why now?" William scratched the thick beard on his cheek. "For the first month there was barely any feed or water for them. Now the country at least offers something to feed them and enough water and they're dropping dead."

"Perhaps they were already too worn down to recover."

William looked at the scattered bush around the shallow water-hole. In among the low grey and green shrubs were the browns and blacks of his cattle, heads down, eating. He sighed and turned back to the dead cow.

"We'd better drag it further away. It's too close to the water."

They set to work together. William was so grateful for Robert's calm good sense and his strength. He had got to know his younger brother all over again during their time on the road and he was proud of the man Robert had become.

Once they'd moved the cow Robert got out his knives. "Roast beef again for dinner?"

William raised his eyebrows. There was barely any meat on the poor animal.

"I might be able to find a few mouthfuls from his rump." Robert bent over the cow and began his grisly work.

William left him to it. Rex would already have a fire going. William was thankful the older man had agreed to come with them. He hadn't reckoned on how hard it would be on the road. It would have been too difficult with just Robert. The first week had been the worst, before the cattle and the three men had settled to the routine of constantly moving on. Sleep had been almost nonexistent and food intermittent. They had only dozed briefly in the saddle, keeping one eye on the cattle, who would spread out looking for the sparse feed.

They had followed the edge of the ranges heading south rather than cross the plains, where he knew there was no feed or water. Now they'd come to country that had received some rain in the last few months, by the look of the grasses and bush around them. He had thought his decision to move the cattle south had been a good one until they started dropping dead.

He mounted his horse and set off on a slow loop around the herd, but the rumble of wagon wheels pulled him up again.

The road that led south was only a little further over from their current position. Often they caught sight of a wagon or a coach passing by in the distance. Now he heard the whistle of a bullocky and through the bush he saw the top of a loaded wagon making its slow journey. William was used to living a solitary life but he couldn't help watching the wagon until it was lost from his sight. They had seen few people on their travels but now they were close to the road and camping near waterholes they would often have some fellow travellers nearby. William had taken special notice of the wagons carrying loads from the mines. It was work when there was little else. He pondered the wagons and horses idle at home.

Then thoughts of home turned his mind to Georgina. During the long hours in the saddle he had plenty of time to think about her. Just when they'd found each other again he'd had to leave. He closed his eyes and conjured up a picture of her in his head — her red hair, her green eyes looking longingly at him, the taste of her lips — and he tried to imagine what she might be doing at that exact moment.

A cow bellowed and William's eyes flew open. Just ahead of him a young steer was wedged between the forked branches of a tree.

He slid from his horse to make a closer inspection. The young animal had put its head through the gap, no doubt to reach some leaves, and when it had pulled back its head had got stuck in the fork. Unable to move forward or back, it was panicking and in danger of strangling itself. William walked all around. Somehow he had to raise the steer high enough to get its head out. He was pleased to see Robert riding towards him.

"I wondered what all the noise was about." Robert lifted his hat and scratched his head.

"You're just in time." William waved to the far side of the beast. "You put your shoulder to him on that side and I'll take this side. If we can lift him he should be able to pull himself backwards."

Robert gave William a doubtful look but did as he was asked.

"Ready?" William called. The terrified animal struggled against him.

"Yes," came Robert's muffled reply.

"Lift!"

The animal slid up the tree far enough to free itself and skittered backwards. William was knocked to the ground, landing spread-eagled across some rocks that dug into his hip and buttocks.

Robert stood, hands on hips, laughing at him.

"All right," William grumbled. "Enough."

His brother extended a hand, the grin still on his face.

"Thanks." William accepted the offer and felt Robert's strength as he pulled on his arm.

"Will you be all right while I get the roast cooking?"

"Of course." William brushed leaves and dirt from his clothes.

"Only I don't want you falling over and hurting yourself more." Robert's grin widened.

"That's enough from you." William tried to walk with some dignity to his horse even though his hip and backside ached. "You get back to your cooking. I'll keep an eye on things here."

Robert returned to his horse, swung into the saddle and gave William a mock salute. "See you in a few hours."

William waited until his younger brother was out of sight before he climbed gingerly onto Big Red. He winced as pain shot down his leg, shifted until he found a more comfortable position and resumed his watch of the cattle.

When he returned to camp that night Robert had the meat and potatoes cooked and Rex had already eaten. He set off to watch the cattle and William took his place.

"There's gravy." Robert indicated a tin on a rock at the edge of the small cooking fire.

William peered at the brown liquid and his stomach rumbled at the delicious smell of it and of the meat Robert was forking onto his plate. "You have many talents, little brother. I'm looking forward to you living at Smith's Ridge when we return."

"I'm not coming to be your cook." Robert gave him a baleful look.

"I could do with one." William gave him a wink and a nudge. "But you're not so pretty in an apron."

Robert snorted and shoved William's plate at him before bending to pick up his own.

The night was warm and they sat a distance from the fire, William with a little more care for his bruised backside. They had taken a couple of mouthfuls before Robert spoke.

"I have news from home."

William looked up from his plate. "How?"

"There were some teamsters at the waterhole earlier who were extremely pleased they'd found me. They're travelling from the north and passed through Hawker. One of them knows Father and he asked them to pass on his message if they saw us. He's talking of setting off on the road like us. There's been rain in the south and he's found someone to agist some sheep."

"It makes sense." William took another mouthful of meat. He was a little disappointed. He had hoped the news would somehow be from Georgina. He wondered again where she was right now and what she might be doing.

"Who will Father take with him?"

William looked up at Robert's question.

"Droving the sheep?" Robert said.

"Binda and Timothy I expect. Grandpa would be the best one to remain at home."

"You don't think they'd all go?"

William shook his head. "The three of them could manage. We're only three."

"And look how tired we are. Anyway, cattle are easier than sheep on the road."

"He might take another of the men from the camp. Did the teamster have any other news of home?"

Robert shook his head. "Only that the reason Father was in Hawker was to bring Jessie to Mrs Ward's home to have the baby."

"Why would they do that?"

Robert shrugged. "I didn't ask him."

"I wonder where Clem is?"

"Maybe he's gone back to Smith's Ridge."

"I hope so. I feel bad leaving Hegarty there alone."

William put his empty plate at his feet and eased back against a fallen log. He knew Hegarty could look after himself, but it could get lonely out in the hills with no company and only a basic hut for shelter.

Once more Robert cut into his thoughts. "How long do you think we'll be on the road?"

William shrugged his shoulders. "Unless we can find someone to agist the cattle we'll have to keep doing this. Moving them to the long stretches of crown land where there's feed and water." He held Robert's gaze. "I told you we could be gone a long time."

"I'm not complaining. I'd rather be on the move and have to cut up the occasional cow than watch sheep drop dead and pick wool off their carcass." Robert's usually cheerful look was serious. "It's just that I've been thinking I won't go back with you when you return to Smith's Ridge."

William looked up. He studied Robert. "Why not? You're not upset about the cooking are you? I was only teasing."

Robert shook his head. "I've been thinking I might join the volunteers preparing to assist the British."

"Why?"

"They want men with good horse skills."

"For the unrest in South Africa?" William couldn't imagine why Robert would involve himself in a fight that had nothing to do with Australia.

"Well, yes. It might come to nothing but it would be an adventure and give me something to do. If this drought continues, which it seems it might, there is nothing for me at home. I am tired of being a shepherd and ..." he looked at William's empty plate "... a house help."

William studied his brother. He understood his frustration. Robert had always been an extra, and never his own man. "What if there was something else you were needed for at home?"

"You don't have to invent jobs for me, William. I know how tough it is for everyone."

"This is not just for you. And it would help us all. I've been thinking on it for a while."

"What is it?"

"With the mines reopened there is much freight work. We've got horses and a good wagon with nothing to do and it's the same at Wildu Creek. We will have time on our hands."

Robert studied William with interest.

"You can be in charge of it," William hurried on, determined his little brother should stay safely home rather than becoming embroiled in a war half the world away. "It would keep us busy and make some money. What do you say?"

Robert picked up their plates and unfolded his large frame from the ground. He looked down on William. "Certainly worth thinking about."

Twenty-three

March 1899

Charles watched the young woman crossing the road in front of him like a cat would watch a mouse, then he too crossed the road and followed at a discreet distance. He had heard that the mixed-race woman who had lived with William Baker had given birth to a child at The Gables. Mrs Ward, who ran the lying-in home, didn't seem to mind what type of person stayed under her roof.

He pulled back beside a wall as the young mother glanced over her shoulder, pulled her bundle closer and hurried on her way again. Jessie was her name and he was sure he knew where she was going. It was late afternoon, nearing the end of another hot March day. Most people were inside so they were alone in the street and for that reason he had to stay a long way back. Even though she moved with haste she wasn't moving all that quickly. Charles had no trouble keeping her in sight.

He hoped she would prove very useful. He'd found out about her through his latest useful helper: Charles had a young grocery delivery boy who was more than happy to accept extra coin to be his eyes and ears.

When the boy had passed on the information about the latest resident at The Gables, Charles's curiosity had been piqued, and then an idea had come to him. A way of tarnishing William Baker in a way that would make Georgina reject him for good. It was a desperate plan but if it paid off he'd at least have a better chance at making her his wife.

Charles had paid the young boy who carried the groceries to The Gables to whisper in Jessie's ear that the Protector of Aborigines was in town. Then he'd waited and watched. Charles had taken a guess that she would be fearful for her new baby and he'd been right, by the look of where she was heading. She made her way to the track that headed east of Hawker, keeping to the shadows and the fence lines.

Sure now she was trying to go home, Charles doubled back, retrieved his horse and took another track. He was guessing she'd make for the first decent patch of trees to find herself a place to spend the night and he was planning to be there before her.

By the time he saw the young woman stumbling in his direction he was already set up and waiting for her. Jessie gasped as he moved out of the shadows in front of her. She clutched her baby tightly and jerked her head from side to side, searching with wide eyes. The bag she carried over her arm swung against her hip.

Charles stayed where he was and extended his hand. "Please don't be alarmed. I was resting here in the shade and I saw you coming along the track."

She stayed rigid on the spot, only looking down when the baby began to cry. It was a tiny sound, so pitiful.

"What are you doing out here in the heat?" Charles asked sympathetically. "You look exhausted. I was having a drink of water. Can I offer you some?"

The young woman licked her lips but shook her head. The baby's cries grew louder.

"Please, I have a saddle bag against a trunk." Charles waved in the direction of the trees. "Come and sit in the shade a moment. Tend to your baby. I promise I will keep out of your way."

She lifted the baby higher, pressed her lips to its head and jiggled it, all the while watching Charles.

"I'll get you some water." He took a chance and began to walk back towards his horse. He hoped she'd take up his offer. If not she wouldn't get far.

He took the flask from his saddle bag. When he turned she was standing close behind him. He offered the drink and she took it. As she drank he studied her. She was pale skinned for a woman of mixed blood. Short in stature and round of face. She had dark shadows under her eyes but was otherwise quite pretty. He watched as a dribble of water trailed from the corner of her mouth and on down her neck.

She thrust the flask at him and took a step back. The baby continued to wail.

He indicated the space under the tree where he'd made a rough seat. "Perhaps you could look after your baby here in the shade. I promise I will go and leave you in peace for a while."

Before she could answer he turned and walked away through the trees until he felt sure she wouldn't be able to see him. He waited a few moments then crept back a little way. The back of her head was visible through the trees. He let out a breath. So she had sat. He would give her a chance to settle the baby then he would return. For now he moved a little closer, where he had a good view of her from behind, and waited.

When he saw her lay the baby on the ground in front of her and begin to rewrap it in the blanket he sauntered back towards her, making a small enough amount of noise so as not to startle her.

She stood as he approached and he offered the water again. This time she took several gulps before she handed it back.

"Thank you," she said.

Charles glanced to the west where the sun was lowering in the sky. "It will be dark in an hour or so. Are you travelling far?"

"I have a distance to go. I will sleep out. I'm used to it."

"But not with a baby surely?" Charles carefully extended his hand and placed it gently on the tiny head. He could feel the pulse through its skin under his hand, so fragile. He didn't remember Laura being this tiny. "Is it a boy or a girl? It seems so small."

"A boy. He came early but he's getting strong now."

Charles let his hand fall away and he peered closer at the young woman. "You're Jessie, aren't you? From Smith's Ridge?"

She nodded, her gaze wary again.

"I'm glad we've met. I've something I need you to do for me."

She swayed and he grabbed her arm. He hoped she wasn't going to pass out on him. She'd given birth a week earlier but the word from his grocery boy was that she'd had a long difficult labour. It had been the reason she'd been brought in to The Gables. The baby was the wrong way around. Charles didn't want to dwell on the hideous thought of a woman giving birth.

"Sit down."

She did as he suggested, dropping her bag to the ground first. He made as if to assist her but snatched the baby from her arms instead.

Jessie let out a frantic cry.

"Shh now." He held one finger to his lips and the baby to his chest with his other arm. It felt almost weightless. "I'll hold the baby while you listen."

She tried to get up but he pushed her back. Her head thudded against the tree and now her look was fearful.

"Where are your family, Jessie? Why haven't they come to get you?"

Hope flashed in her eyes. She looked past him towards the track. "They're coming soon. I said I'd meet them here."

Charles let the baby slip a little. Jessie gasped and reached up her hands.

"The truth now please, Jessie." Charles glared at her. "Where are your family?"

"I left the home early." Her shoulders slumped but she didn't take her eyes from the baby. "They're not coming for another week."

"And you were going to walk all that way. Dear, dear. I can take you in my cart."

She transferred her gaze to Charles. "You don't have a cart."

"Not here. But back in town. All I need is for you to do something for me."

Jessie shuddered and pushed herself back against the trunk of the tree. Charles saw the horror in her eyes.

"Good heavens, woman," he snarled. "I'm not going to touch you. There's something else I need from you."

"Give me my baby," she snapped.

"It's about him, actually." Charles adjusted the baby a little higher in the crook of his arm. "He's safe with me for the moment. But if I give him back to you he may not remain safe. I don't know if you've heard of the Protector of Aborigines."

Her face registered fear.

"Ah." Charles smiled. "I suspect you have. My father and I are well acquainted with the man. Mr Harrison is his name. He dines at my family home when he's in Hawker."

Charles began to pace, patting the baby gently. Jessie didn't take her eyes from him.

"I could easily tell him about an irresponsible mother who doesn't look after her baby properly, a child with mixed blood."

"I can look after my baby." Jessie struggled to her feet and took a step towards Charles. "Give him back to me."

Charles let the baby slip a little. Jessie cried out again.

"Sit down," Charles growled. "One word from me to Mr Harrison and your baby will be taken away."

Jessie sat, shoulders slumped. "What is it you want?"

"I need you tell my friend Miss Prosser who the father of your child is."

"Clem?"

"Come now, Jessie. You've spent a lot of time under your employer's roof. He has a liking for brown skin. He had his way with you, didn't he?"

"Mr *Baker*?" Jessie shook her head violently. "I've only ever been with my Clem."

"That's not the right answer." Charles gave the baby a little shake. It squirmed and gave a tiny bleat of a cry.

"Don't hurt my baby." Jessie's lip trembled.

"No harm will come to either of you so long as you do as I ask. Do you understand?"

"Yes," she whispered.

Charles moved closer and stood over her, the baby just out of her reach. "I need you to explain to Miss Prosser that William Baker forced himself on you and then swore you to secrecy so the baby could be passed off as your husband's."

She gaped at him, her mouth a large hole in her round face. "Why?"

"Why is none of your business. If you do this for me, I will take you and your baby home and make sure Mr Harrison never hears about him." He leaned closer. "Do you understand, Jessie?"

She nodded. Tears brimmed in her deep brown eyes.

"No need to cry. I simply want to keep you and your baby safe. Only Miss Prosser and I will know. You can go home to your husband and live safely with your baby."

"I've never met Miss Prosser."

"She is coming to Hawker tomorrow. I will take you back with me now. There is a room attached to the stables where you will be comfortable for the night. I will bring Miss Prosser to meet you and then I will deliver you home safely." He held out a hand to help her up. She steadied herself then reached for her baby. "You must be convincing or I will not help you."

"I will." The tremble of her lips belied her words.

Charles kept a secure arm around the child just for a moment then let her take him.

"And Jessie, if you were ever to tell Miss Prosser a different story," once more he placed his hand on the baby's small head, "well, you know what would happen, don't you?"

Jessie cocooned the tiny body of her baby against her chest. She turned her big brown eyes to Charles. Tears streaked her cheeks. "Yes," she whispered.

"Good." He smiled benignly. "You look exhausted, poor thing. Just as well I found you and offered you a bed for the night." Charles repacked his horse, all the while keeping a wary eye on Jessie, but she simply stood, blank-faced, cuddling her baby. Once he was done he took the baby again, helped her onto the horse then handed the child to her. It had been a very successful day. Now all he needed was for Georgina to call in tomorrow as she had promised and for Jessie to do her bit and all would be well.

"Charles, you're acting very strangely." Georgina frowned at him as he guided her towards the stables at the back of the Wiltshires' house. "What is all this about a new horse?"

He stopped beside her just outside the stable door. "Please forgive me, Georgina. There isn't a new horse. I told you that so you would come with me."

Georgina pursed her lips. Charles was an annoying boy and nothing had changed since her last visit. She put her hands to her hips. "What's this about then?"

"I'm afraid I've discovered something that may be distressing for you to hear."

"Is that why we've come to the end of the yard? In case I get distressed?" She laughed but Charles simply lowered his gaze. The smile he usually had for her was replaced by a sombre face.

"What is it, Charles? You're worrying me."

He took her hands in his. Georgina thought to snatch them away but he was acting rather strangely and she didn't want to upset him so she left her hands in his.

"Tell me."

"It's about William."

She couldn't help the gasp that escaped her lips. "Has something happened to him?"

"I have no idea."

Georgina snatched back her hands. "Then what is it, Charles? I'm not in the mood for games."

"This is about his ... his household."

"What do you mean?"

"I know he has denied living with his housekeeper and he may have been truthful in that —"

"Charles, I won't stand here and listen to you defame William."

"Let me finish please, Georgina. I do not take any pleasure from this. I am only thinking of you and your good name."

"Tell me then." Georgina folded her arms. Charles always enjoyed a drama. No doubt he'd heard some more gossip.

"William has fathered a child."

Georgina began to laugh. "Where did you hear such a thing?"

"I knew you would find it hard to believe so I've brought you here to meet the mother and her child."

Georgina fell silent. She glanced around. "Where is this woman?"

"I've asked her to wait out of sight. I didn't think you would want a public display."

Right now Georgina could smack the self-righteous look from his face. "Well then?"

He pushed open the stable door. A young woman, little more than a girl really, stood just inside, a baby in her arms. Her clothes were simple but clean and her hair was pulled back into a rough bun. The colour of her skin announced her mixed parentage.

"Jessie, this is Miss Prosser." Charles reached out and put a gentle hand on the baby's head then turned back to Georgina. "Tell her what happened to you. What did William Baker do to you?"

The woman met Georgina's look. There was pain in her eyes.

"He ... he forced me." Jessie kissed the top of her baby's head.

Georgina sucked in a breath. There was a loud whooshing sound in her ears. William could not possibly do such a thing.

"And the baby?" Charles wagged a finger at the child clutched to Jessie's chest.

"It is his."

Georgina drew a breath and closed her eyes. Charles had been right. She would never have believed his word but the woman was another thing. Why would she lie? Georgina lifted her chin. In her chest a pain stabbed as if a knife had been driven through her. "If this is true we must tell the constable."

"No." Jessie's eyes filled with fear and she backed away.

"Georgina, you mustn't be so cruel," Charles said.

"If William has hurt this woman he must pay."

"And if he is brought before the magistrate what is to become of the baby?"

Georgina turned to Jessie as she began to sob.

"Please, Miss Prosser. I am married. My husband thinks the baby is his. He is a white man but I am of mixed race. If people find out Mr Baker is the father the protector will take my child."

"Surely not." Georgina looked to Charles.

He hung his head and held out his hands. "We could speak to him, but I think there would be such public outrage the child would be removed."

"Please, Miss Prosser." Jessie grasped her arm. "I'm married to my Clem. He will be a good father. I don't want to lose my baby."

Georgina felt as if the breath had been sucked out of her. Darkness zoomed in. She clutched at the arm that went about her, to steady her. She opened her eyes and took in the concern on Charles's face.

"I have offered to give Jessie a ride home to Smith's Ridge," he said. "It is her wish that this is kept quiet. Only harm will come from making it public."

Georgina's thoughts were in turmoil. She couldn't connect what she had heard with William. Not the man she knew, or thought she knew. But then she'd thought she understood her father and there were things in his life that had shocked her. She hardly knew the adult William. They'd been apart a long time. "Very well." She raised her eyes to meet Jessie's gaze. "I am so very sorry for what you have suffered."

Edith was curious. She'd seen Charles coming out of the room beside the stables the night before when she'd been coming back across her yard. Now in the gloom of pre-dawn he was going in there again. She detoured from her path to conduct her morning ablutions and let herself in the gate to the yard. The morning was crisp and still. Stepping lightly, she glanced towards the U-shaped extension on the back of the house, where Flora Nixon slept. There was no sign of movement so she kept on until she reached the storeroom door, which was slightly ajar. Edith pressed herself to the wall as she heard Charles speak.

"I will come back and collect you once I have loaded my wagon with supplies, Jessie."

A baby gave a cry and a woman's soothing tones followed.

Edith frowned. Why would he have a woman and child in his storeroom?

"You've done very well, Jessie," Charles continued. "You've kept to your end of the bargain, and as long as you tell no-one the truth I will keep to mine. The protector will not find out about your baby as long as Miss Prosser keeps thinking he is Mr Baker's child, and he will be safe."

Edith longed to peep in the small window in the wall. Who was this Jessie Charles was blackmailing? A door creaked from the direction of the house. Edith froze. Behind her Charles continued to speak softly to the woman inside the storeroom. Across the yard the door to Flora's room slowly opened. There was a vegetable garden and some small shrubs between the stable and the house. Edith eased down to a crouch against the stone wall and hoped Flora wouldn't look her way.

Someone poked a head round the door but it was not Flora Nixon. Edith watched Henry Wiltshire emerge from the room. His hair was dishevelled, his clothes crumpled and he carried his boots in his hands. Without even a glance in Edith's direction he hobbled across the courtyard and let himself in the kitchen door.

Edith relaxed against the wall. Henry had probably been visiting his housekeeper's bed for years. How disgusting. Poor Mrs Wiltshire.

"I will be back soon." Charles's voice was louder. Edith pushed off the wall and scuttled around the side of the building.

The door dragged open then closed and footsteps retreated across the yard. Edith let out the breath she'd been holding. She peeped around the corner. The yard was empty. She crept back around the corner and couldn't resist putting her face to the little window. A young woman sat on the edge of a crude bed. She cradled a tiny baby in her arms and she was sobbing. Edith's heart melted at the sight of such despair. She thought of her own mother and what she'd been driven to. Edith didn't want that for herself, or anyone else. She pulled away from the glass and walked quickly back to her own yard.

Once in the safety of her cottage Edith shook off the sadness she'd felt for Jessie, whoever she was, and allowed herself to smile. She did not know yet how the knowledge that her employer slept with his housekeeper and that his son was blackmailing a woman to lie about her child's parentage would be useful, but she stored it away, knowing someday it would be.

Twenty-four

May 1899

The room was heavy with silence as the three men gathered in Henry's office pondered the devastation of the situation. The room was not spacious yet it was usually comfortable enough for Henry to conduct his business. Today it felt crowded. His business partners, Mr Pyman and Mr Button, sat opposite him. Henry rested his elbows on his desk and touched the tips of his fingers together. Pyman shifted in his chair, staring at some point on Henry's desk.

It was Button who broke the silence. "So, we must close the creamery."

"There is nothing more that can be done to save it?" Henry wasn't one to throw good money after bad but there were their investments in buildings and plant to think of. He had a lot of debt still to recover from this venture.

"There are simply not enough cows left in the district, Wiltshire." Pyman rose and strode to Henry's office window, where he stared out at the May day.

Henry knew he would be able to see little from that window except for the wall of the building next door and a glimpse of the cloudless sky.

"We can perhaps sell the plant to recoup some money," Button said.

Henry certainly hoped so. Between the creamery and Charles's ventures their finances were stretched well beyond the comfortable position Henry had built up in the years before this drought.

Pyman turned back from the window. "It's the men who worked for us I feel for."

"They'll get something else." Henry dismissed Pyman's concern. Of more irritation would be the people who had thought them foolish to open the creamery in the first place. The I-told-you-so brigade would be going to town at their expense. Henry did not like failure. He thought of the huge crowd that would gather later in the month for the annual Hawker races. "Can't we keep it going ... just until the end of the month?"

"There is nothing to be gained from delaying." Pyman shook his head and returned to his chair. "It's tough for the whole district."

"And I'm not sure other jobs will be easy to come by." Button leaned in. "It's to remain in this room for the time but I have it on good authority one of the flour mills will be closing soon. So we won't be the only ones laying off workers."

"It's important we do what we can for the men and their families," Pyman said.

Henry ignored him. Pyman was a fool like Garrat, giving credit to people with little thought for his own business.

They were interrupted by a knock at the door.

"Come in," Henry called.

The door opened to reveal Edith carrying a tea tray.

Henry stood and glanced at the small clock on his desk. "Ah, Miss Ferguson. Right on time. I thought you might need some refreshments, gentlemen."

The other two glanced at each other as they stood.

"Thank you, no." Pyman shook his head. "I must return to my shop."

"If our business is done for today there are other matters I must see to." Button made for the door and Pyman followed.

"We will speak again soon." Henry turned from their departing backs to Edith, who had set her tray on the corner of his desk. "It seems it is only to be one for tea then, Edith. Would you care to join me?"

"Oh." Edith glanced towards the door. "Mr Charles is watching the shop so that I could prepare the refreshments for your guests."

"Then there's no hurry to return. I am sure my son is quite capable of taking care of business."

"Well, yes, of course … it has been a busy morning."

"That's some good news at least." Henry flopped back in his chair.

Edith hesitated over the tea things.

"Please do keep me company. Charles will manage."

"Very well, Mr Wiltshire, thank you. I would be glad to be off my feet for a minute or two."

Henry studied Edith as she set out two cups and poured the tea. She wore a crisp white high-necked blouse tucked into a black skirt. The skirt had several gores and was narrower than the wide skirts still favoured by most of the local ladies. Edith's hazel eyes were her most redeeming feature, given her sharp pointy nose, narrow chin and high forehead, made more severe by the tight pull of the bun high on her head. Not the most beautiful young woman, but she was quick to learn and definitely an asset to their business. Charles had chosen well.

She placed a cup and saucer on the desk in front of him.

"Please take a seat, Edith, and tell me how you are finding the shop? We have had little time to talk these last few months."

Edith perched on the edge of the chair Pyman had recently vacated and lowered her cup and saucer to her lap.

"I believe business is going well enough, Mr Wiltshire, considering the current difficulties many people face."

"We've cut back on the amount we stock but we still maintain a good selection."

"Your range is superior to anything else Hawker has to offer and that is certainly appreciated by your more discerning customers but ..."

"But?"

"Not many can afford the quality you provide. It's grand stock of course."

Henry liked the hint of pride he heard in her voice. "And you've arranged it all so well."

"I do enjoy dressing the mannequins for the windows." Edith's smile smoothed the sharpness from her face. "Having one for men's clothing as well as ladies is a wonderful addition."

"You make a good job of it, my dear." Henry gave her what he hoped was a melancholy look. "My dear wife used to be so good at that kind of thing."

"You must miss her terribly."

Henry lowered his gaze to his cup and took a sip of the tea. "I do." He certainly felt glum today but it was more about the creamery closing and his mounting financial burdens than mourning his wife's passing. However, appearances were important, and he must continue to act the part of the grieving widower for some time yet. It had only been four months. Catherine's death had been a shock when it happened but he had recovered his composure in the weeks after. Business kept him busy, Flora had been a comfort in all ways and then there was his sweet little Laura, such a delightful child. The Prosser ladies had stepped in when he'd needed a woman's touch with entertaining — thank goodness Charles had organised that — and life went on. He rarely thought of Catherine any more.

"… and she would have loved the winter umbrellas we've just received. They are tartan instead of black."

Henry looked up. Edith was still prattling about his wife. "The new stock is all unpacked then?"

"Yes, Mr Wiltshire."

"I will place an advertisement in the paper."

"There are so many lovely items. We have some luxurious leather gloves with fur at the cuffs and—"

"You pick what you think best for the advertisement and let me know."

"Yes, Mr Wiltshire."

The door of Henry's office opened.

"There you are, Edith." Charles raised his eyebrows at his father.

"Miss Ferguson has been informing me of the latest stock arrivals, Charles." Henry inclined his head to Edith, who was now busy tidying the tea things.

"I have some customers who would prefer a woman's expertise." Charles folded his arms and leaned against the doorframe.

"Of course, Mr Charles, I'll be right there."

"Leave the tea things," Henry said. "Charles can join me now. We have some things to discuss."

"Very well." Edith walked briskly from the room but at the door she slowed; she had to edge past Charles, who still lounged in the doorway, a smirk on his face.

Henry took in his son's cheeky gaze. He would have to speak with Charles about his rather familiar behaviour with Edith.

Henry knew Charles felt frustration over his lack of progress with Georgina Prosser, but he had to bide his time. While a dalliance with Edith would no doubt release his physical needs it would inevitably cause difficulties. Henry thought of Flora Nixon and how lucky he had been to keep his marriage and his mistress. He wasn't sure Charles was capable of being as discreet as such a situation would require. Nor did Edith necessarily possess Flora's forbearance.

Anger simmered just below the surface but Charles swallowed it and smiled instead as he opened the shop door for a couple loaded with grocery items. His father had just given him a ticking off. Well that's what it had felt like, as if he were still a little boy to be chastised. Charles closed the door and glanced towards the arch that led to the emporium. Through the gap he had a glimpse of Edith, bent over the counter measuring out some fabric. Henry's warning to steer clear of her only made Charles desire her more. His father was an old man now and might be happy with a celibate life but there was no way Charles could be.

Then there was the other news about the creamery. Charles knew it hadn't been doing well but to have it close was not only a business loss but an embarrassment. The Wiltshires had a reputation for good business. Charles did not want anything to tarnish that.

He patted his pocket, where the telegram from Becker was safely stored. The claim had been lodged and Becker was on his way to Hawker. Becker was also sending a letter of intent care of Charles to hand on to the Bakers. Charles wasn't at all concerned about them. They were on leased land and the letter was merely a formality. He had much more important things to think about. Along with his carrier business he had high hopes that diamond mining would improve their prospects.

The door opened with a tinkle of the bell and Mrs Taylor bustled into the shop.

"Good morning, Charles. My goodness, what's put that big smile on your face?"

Charles gave a short bow and extended his hand towards the counter. "It's always a pleasure to have you in our shop, Mrs Taylor."

"What a delightful young man you are." Mrs Taylor's eyes sparkled and she leaned closer. "I do hope the equally delightful Miss Prosser will be on your arm at my dinner on Saturday evening?"

"We are expecting Georgina and her mother to accompany us." Charles kept his face locked in the smile but underneath he groaned. Dinner with the Taylors was about as exciting as watching a bicycle race. However, it did mean that Georgina would be in town for a few days and that was something to look forward to. "I will see you on Saturday, Mrs Taylor."

Charles stepped out from the open door of the shop to the verandah. The sky was bare of cloud except for a few white wisps on the horizon, and, though the sun was warm, the wind had a sharp chill to it. There had been a sprinkle of rain the previous week; a teasing amount barely enough to settle the dust. Clarence Brown rode by on his bicycle, giving Charles a cheery wave as he passed.

"Damned bicycles," Charles muttered. Several people had taken to riding the contraptions around Hawker and even beyond. His father insisted they should be present at the upcoming annual bicycle sports: the local gentry always attended to witness the events even if they didn't ride themselves. Henry had even suggested Charles learn to ride a bike and that perhaps they could sell them, but Charles was having none of it. A bicycle was of no use to him in his carrier business or his trips further afield to Prosser's Run.

He waited for a horse and buggy to pass then crossed to the other side of the road where he could look back at the shop. He liked to do this from time to time. His father's original shop still bore the name of *Hawker General Trader and Forwarding Agent* but it was the black letters on the white paint of the other shop roof that he admired. *Wiltshire & Son Emporium* had a fine sound to it.

A wagon drawn by two horses with a third tethered behind drew up in front. He smiled, adjusted his tie and strode back across the street. Georgina was already climbing down from the wagon but he made it in time to assist Mrs Prosser.

"What a pleasant surprise," he said.

"We are a day early." Mrs Prosser brushed at her skirts and readjusted her hat. "I hope it won't be an inconvenience."

"It's never an inconvenience to have the two delightful Prosser ladies under our roof."

Mrs Prosser patted his cheek and smiled but Charles had caught a glimpse of Georgina's raised eyebrow from the other side of the wagon. She was obviously not in the mood for small talk. He ignored her and offered Mrs Prosser his arm. Together they walked around the horses and stepped onto the shop verandah.

Charles smiled at the lady coming out of his shop with several parcels in her basket. Mrs Maynard was a good customer. Her husband was an auctioneer and forwarding agent as well as a councillor and she was, though a Catholic, well regarded and on several committees. Her return smile withered when she saw the Prosser ladies and she hurried on her way.

"Are you sure you want to be seen with us, Charles?" Georgina's tone was sharp. "It seems some people still judge us for my father's poor behaviour."

"They will come round in time, I am sure."

Johanna sighed as they watched Mrs Maynard stop across the street to talk to the doctor's wife. "I always thought Martha Maynard such a kind person."

"Never mind, Mother." Georgina slipped her arm though Johanna's. "We know who our real friends are at least."

Charles was glad to see her turn a warm smile in his direction.

"Yes." He rubbed his hands together. "And we have been looking forward to your visit."

"The ride in was pleasant," Georgina continued. "We made good time and camped at First Creek last night."

"We were amazed there was no water in it." Mrs Prosser said. "We've had some rain at Prosser's Run."

"Not such a grand amount, Mother, but enough to refresh the small quantities remaining in the waterholes."

"That is good news," Charles said. "We have not been so lucky here, I'm afraid — only a few drops, and there's been no word of rain from other parts of the district."

The wind plucked at their jackets and Charles ushered the ladies inside, glad that Mrs Maynard's snub had been brushed aside.

Georgina went straight to Miss Ferguson, who waited behind the counter with a welcome smile. The Prossers had not come to town for the opening of the emporium the previous December and this was only the second visit Georgina had paid.

"I have worn out my last pair of riding gloves, Edith."

"Oh what perfect timing, Miss Prosser." Edith indicated a display further along the counter. "We have a delightful new leather range just arrived."

"The wind outside is bitter, Charles." Mrs Prosser remained at his side. "It's much more cosy in here."

"A sign of another cold winter ahead." He continued the conversation while keeping an eye on Georgina, who was exclaiming over the gloves.

"We have already been to the house and unpacked. We have an appointment at the bank and Georgina wanted to call in here of course." Mrs Prosser leaned in closer. "She's so serious these days with the weight of managing Prosser's Run. My daughter is not always one to show it, but she always likes to see you, Charles."

Charles wished her words were true but he had made little progress with Georgina since their encounter with Baker on New Year's Eve. He found it devilishly frustrating.

Georgina and her mother were spending three days in Hawker and as usual they were to stay with the Wiltshires. Henry had planned a special dinner to entertain the visiting magistrate and the Protector of Aborigines on Friday night, and there was the Taylors' gathering on Saturday night. Mrs Maynard was not the only person with a long memory. Few other people invited the Prosser ladies into their homes.

There was plenty of opportunity to be with Georgina, if only she would let down her guard a little. Despite the news she'd received regarding William being the father of his housekeeper's child, Charles knew Georgina still harboured some hope for Baker's return. Somehow Charles had to convince her that he, rather than that uncouth scoundrel, was the man for her.

Twenty-five

September 1899

Clem looked down at the baby in his arms and felt his chest swell. His son had grown robust in the six months since his early arrival. They had named him Haji after Jessie's father. Clem liked the sound of it, the way it rolled off his tongue. It was a good strong name.

Haji gave a small cry and Clem glanced in Jessie's direction. She was busy at the fire, making them some tea. It had been a bitterly cold night and the rays of the September sun were slow to warm them. Clem pulled the blanket tighter around his shoulders and snuggled his son closer.

"Shh, little one." He kissed the soft brown curls on top of his son's head. "Your mother is busy."

They were making their way to the bottom waterhole, where Clem would stay for a few weeks. Hegarty had already left for Smith's Ridge and would journey on to Hawker. He'd been up there in the ranges watching over the remaining cattle for two months since his last break.

Jessie had been eager to come with Clem: she didn't want to be at the house alone. Having the baby had changed her. Before

Haji came along she had stayed at Smith's Ridge on her own quite often but since the baby she always had a look of terror if Clem said he was going anywhere without her. Clem wondered if Millie's fears of having her children taken away had influenced Jessie. Not that he minded Jessie's company — and he was pleased his son would learn from an early age how to live in the bush.

He smiled now as his wife came towards him with a steaming mug of tea and a hunk of damper.

"I will take him now," she said as she exchanged the food for her son.

The bellow of a cow made Clem pause. He listened but there was no further call. The sound had come from further below them but it was hard to judge the direction. The bottom waterhole was only a short distance down the ridge. The place he'd chosen for them to stop and make a fire was more sheltered, with the side of the ridge arcing inwards to form a cave-like curve over their heads. There were several big trees and a small sandy plateau void of cow dung. There was room for horses and a small camp that would serve them well while they waited for Hegarty's return.

"We will make our camp here," Clem said. "It's not far to the waterhole and the cattle shouldn't bother us."

Jessie settled on the ground against the trunk of a tree with the baby.

"It's pretty here."

"I'm pleased you like this country like I do." He sat beside her to finish his tea and damper then collected the large water bag from his saddle. "I'll go and check the waterhole and refill this while I'm there." He bent to kiss Jessie's head. She smiled back at him and he set off on foot to make the journey down the ridge to the waterhole.

He came across a young bull scratching its scrawny rump on the branch of a tree. It stopped on his approach and eyeballed him. Clem froze. He was happy looking after sheep but he had never overcome his wariness of cattle, especially bulls, which he regarded as unpredictable. The bellow of a cow sounded loudly from beyond the bull. The ragged animal ignored both the call and Clem and went back to its scratching.

Clem took a longer path through the bush and came out on the other side of the creek that broadened into the waterhole. Once more he came to a sudden stop at the sight before him. A man was bending over the deep section of the waterhole, filling a bucket. A distance either side of him was a crude fence running from the waterhole to the high creek bank. Beyond him on the bank above were a tent, a small wagon and three horses tethered under some trees. Two young cows stood on the opposite side of the waterhole a few feet from the shallow water; once more one of them bellowed. The man ignored them and took his bucket back to a table Clem hadn't noticed before. It was set up in the shade against the base of the creek bank and piled high with rocks. No doubt this was the fossicker they had seen signs of several months earlier.

Clem crossed the creek around behind the waterhole and came up on the other side. The man was so intent on his task, washing rocks and inspecting them closely, that he didn't hear Clem's approach.

"You shouldn't be here."

The rock he'd been examining dropped with a thud and he jerked his head up. This time it was Clem's turn to be disconcerted. The pale-faced man staring at him was the South African he had met in the pub several years earlier. What had been his name? Becker. There was no doubting the red hair and the pale skin.

Becker glanced around then regained his composure and raised his eyebrows. "I was told this land belongs to William Baker. Who are you?"

Clem felt the muscles in his arms twitch. "I work for William Baker." He scanned around at the shovels and buckets and pegged-out ground. Becker was doing more than fossicking. He was conducting a mining expedition. "You have no right to be here."

"I have every right. I am Heinrich Becker." He drew a paper from his pocket. "And I have a legal claim to search for diamonds here." He waved the paper at Clem. "Can you read, man?"

Clem drew himself up. He was not going to be insulted by someone who came to thieve from this country. He waved his hand at Becker. "You can't stay here. You are keeping the cattle from the waterhole."

Becker shrugged his shoulders. "Not my problem. My claim includes the waterhole. I could fence the whole thing if I wished but I don't mind if the cattle drink from the other side. If they cause me trouble I shall extend the fence. I sent your employer a letter regarding my intent to search here. Take it up with him." He turned back to his rocks.

Clem watched. It had only been a week since he'd last been that way to tell Hegarty he could take some leave. In the time Clem and Jessie had taken to arrive the man had come and set all this up. Clem looked around. There was an air of permanency about the place. Hegarty had constructed a crude hut further up the hill, but even that looked temporary. Not like Becker's camp, with its water barrel beside the tent, table and chairs and built-up fire with a pile of wood stacked beside it. A lot of work had been done by one man.

A scream sent a surge of terror through Clem. It was Jessie. His feet were moving before the sound died. He ran up the dry creek bed and scrambled over the ridge and down the other side to the place he'd left her.

Jessie was pressed against the tree with the wailing Haji clutched to her chest. Relief flooded her face as he raced towards her.

"What's wrong?" He put his hand out and she fell into his arms; the baby squashed between them protested even more. "What happened?"

"There was a man." Jessie's words came out in gasps. "He's gone now."

Clem lifted his gaze and twisted to get a better look around. There was no sign of anyone. He gently moved Jessie back and held her at arm's length. He looked from her to his son. "Did he hurt you? Haji?"

She shook her head. "He gave me a fright and that startled Haji. I shouldn't have screamed." She began to jiggle the baby, singing a song softly in his ear to calm him.

Clem frowned. He thought back to his meeting with Becker and the work that had been done in a short time around his camp. There were three horses tethered. They could have been pack-horses or perhaps there was another man.

Haji had stopped crying and Jessie had stopped pacing. He looked at the fear on her face. "Did you know the man you saw, Jessie?"

She shook her head again but he had seen the veiled look in her eye. It surprised Clem. He'd never thought Jessie would lie to him.

He put a gentle hand on her shoulder. "Who was it, Jessie?"

She wrapped her arms tightly around the sleeping baby. "He'll take Haji away."

"Who will?"

"The protector."

Clem scratched his head. "You saw the protector here?"

"No."

"Jessie, I don't understand. There is a South African man down at the waterhole and he has a paper to say he can search for dia-monds. He's made a camp that he couldn't have done in the time on his own. Someone is helping him. It may be the man you saw. You have to tell me."

One large tear rolled down Jessie's cheek. "It was Charles Wiltshire."

Clem blew out a breath. William would not be pleased to find a diamond miner camped at the waterhole but he would be very angry indeed when he found out Charles Wiltshire was involved.

Jessie gulped in a breath.

Clem turned back to his wife. "Wiltshire can't harm you, Jessie. Why are you so frightened of him?" He put a hand under her chin and carefully tilted her face to him. "He brought you home after you had the baby." A terrible thought crossed his mind. "He didn't … harm you?"

Jessie shook her head violently, shaking his fingers away. "No, Clem."

"Then what is it?"

She wouldn't look at him.

He put his hands on her shoulders this time. "I will look after you, Jessie. He can't harm you."

"Not me," she whispered.

Once more Clem frowned. His sweet Jessie was talking in circles. He took in the shielding hand she had placed on Haji's head. "Why do you think the protector would take Haji away?"

She lifted her fear-filled eyes to him. "Mr Charles said."

"Why did Wiltshire threaten you?"

She looked away again. "He's not a nice man. He wanted to scare me, that's all."

"You should have told me, Jessie."

"What could you do? We don't have any say. Men like him can do what they want." This time when she looked at him her eyes were full of sorrow.

"We have good people like William and Joseph Baker. They would speak up for us."

"They can't stop the protector taking children from their mothers."

He put a gentle arm around her shoulder and placed his hand over the one she rested on their sleeping son.

"If anyone came for Haji there are plenty of places we could hide him." Clem hugged her tighter. "But no-one will come for him, Jessie. Some children were taken, but there was such an outcry it hasn't happened again. Besides, there is no reason for Haji to be taken. You are a good mother and I am never far away."

They stood huddled together for a while then Clem eased himself away.

"What are you going to do?" Jessie's look was still fearful.

"Round up what cattle I can find and move them back down to the plain. The small winter rain has raised some feed and there are a couple of waterholes with water. It should be enough to keep them alive until William comes back, then he can decide what to do."

Jessie clutched at his sleeve. "You're not going to look for Wiltshire?"

"Not now. I'll talk to William about it." It annoyed Clem to wait for William but he knew there was little he could do about either the mine or Charles Wiltshire without William's help.

He looked in the direction of Becker's camp and then north. He was confident Becker wouldn't find more of the rock he desperately sought. The diamond Joseph had found was from the hidden waterhole. Once the full heat of summer hit, Clem was sure Becker would pack up and leave. They just had to be patient and wait.

Twenty-six

William lifted his weary head and stared in bewilderment. Big Red came to a stop beneath him. Not only were there cattle in the creek bed, but there were pockets of water for them to drink from. A young brown bull strolled to the edge of a waterhole. It was one of the cattle he'd left in the higher country. Only the older black bull and ten cows had been kept closer to the house.

Obviously there'd been some rain in his absence. Small patches of grass, like threads of silver and green, spread across the slopes he'd just crossed. There'd been no water in the lower region of Wildu Creek where he, Rex and Robert had parted company, but here, closer to the Smith's Ridge homestead, there were all the signs of at least some winter rain.

He thought of the cattle he'd spent months shifting steadily south until he managed to find agistment for them. Perhaps he should have waited — but then it was only September. The summer was ahead of them and if there was no further rain the small amount of water and grass would soon be taken up by the few remaining stock.

Nonetheless he felt happier knowing that there'd been some little relief from the drought there in the hills. He urged Big Red on up the slope to the track that would lead them to Smith's Ridge. They passed more cattle along the way and finally the homestead appeared ahead with smoke wafting from the chimney. At least a sign that someone was home, perhaps Jessie.

Bone weary but glad to be home at last he slid from the saddle, stretched his arms out wide and then rubbed at his behind. What a journey it had been. Now all he wanted was a bath and some hot food. He patted Big Red's neck and removed the saddle.

"You need a few days off as well, old boy." He smoothed the horse's rump then led him into the fenced yard where there was a full trough of water and some hay in a box. "Take a holiday."

"You made it."

William swung his tired body around; Clem was standing at the gate. He was shirtless, his hair hung to his muscled shoulders and his hands rested firmly on his hips.

"Good to see you, Clem." William held out his hand and Clem shook it. "I notice we've had some rain."

"A little."

"You shifted the cattle back from the hills?"

"Most of them. Hegarty's up there, now looking for any we missed."

"How's Jessie?"

"Well."

"And the baby?"

At last there was a flicker of a smile on Clem's face. "I have a son. Haji."

William clapped a hand on Clem's shoulder. "Congratulations."

Clem looked past William to the track he'd just ridden in on. "Robert isn't with you?"

"He went on to Wildu Creek. We heard Father had also gone south with the sheep. Robert wanted to make sure everything was all right at home."

"That's good. Are you hungry? We've just eaten but there's some pie left." This time he did smile. "Jessie has learned a lot more about cooking while you've been gone."

"I'll wash up and join you inside." William began to walk on to the wash house.

"William."

Clem's call made him look back.

"There is a lot to tell you."

William nodded. Clem was naturally serious but his expression left William in no doubt the news wasn't going to be good.

Inside the house Jessie gave him a welcome hug and Clem proudly lifted the sleeping baby from his basket.

"He's a fine-looking fellow." William traced a finger across one soft little cheek. The baby pursed its lips and let out a sigh.

Clem put an arm around Jessie and they both looked adoringly at their child. A pang of longing overtook William. Would this be him and Georgina one day? He was anxious to ride over and see her but knew he had to come home first and find out what had been happening in his absence. He'd ask Jessie to cut his hair and he needed a proper wash and some fresh clothes before he set off to find the woman he loved.

"Sit down, William." Clem handed over the baby to Jessie and waved at the table, which was set with cutlery and a large serving of pie and potato.

William did as he was bid and tucked into the food. The pastry was crunchy but soft, and the meat inside delicious. He smiled at Jessie. "Thank you. This is good."

"You're welcome."

Clem sat opposite William and waited for him to finish.

Jessie put two mugs of tea on the table and left the room. Finally, William sat back and took in Clem's serious expression. "I'm guessing you haven't got good news."

"A man called Heinrich Becker has put a claim on the land around the bottom waterhole."

William opened his mouth but before he could speak Clem continued. "It's the same man who came here several years ago looking for diamonds."

"Damn!" William thumped the table with his fist. "I thought it was too easy to get rid of him the first time. Did you try to move him on?"

"No point. He has staked his claim. Hegarty has been up there and inspected the document thoroughly. We can't move him off."

"I lease this land. He can't do that without letting me know."

"Says he sent you a letter."

"Did he?" William glanced at the small pile of mail that had accumulated in his absence.

"I've seen nothing since you've been gone." Clem shrugged. "He said he gave it to Charles Wiltshire to hand on."

"Becker has poor taste in couriers." William scratched at his cheek through his rough beard. "The bottom waterhole, you said? I don't expect he will find diamonds there."

"Becker doesn't appear to move far from his claim."

"So we have to wait it out until he gets sick of looking and leaves."

"Maybe. Only I think he has a partner who might not be so easy to get rid of."

"Who?"

"Charles Wiltshire."

William leaped to his feet with a growl. "What's that buffoon got to do with it?"

"Jessie saw him near the waterhole when we first discovered Becker and from the look of Becker's camp he had to have had help. When Hegarty got a look at the claim Becker had folded the bottom of the paper below his name but there was something else written there. Hegarty thinks it could have been Wiltshire's name. I suspect that's why Becker sent him the original letter of intent."

"Damn the man." William slapped his thigh. Dust puffed from his trousers. "I've got to have this out with him."

"What good would that do? Hegarty says the paper is legal." Clem glared at him. "You can't change anything."

William sank back to the chair and put his head in his hands. He suddenly felt so tired he could barely longer hold himself upright.

"Drink your tea." Clem picked up one of the mugs and took a mouthful. He watched while William did the same.

The liquid was hot and sweet.

"There's more."

William lifted his gaze to meet Clem's serious expression.

"Becker has fenced part of the waterhole."

"What?"

"That's why we brought the cattle back here. We had just enough rain to raise some grass and put water in some of the closer holes. They will be all right for the moment but if we don't get rain before summer …"

William's fist thumped the table. "How can he fence a waterhole? Our stock depend on it."

"If he doesn't find anything I don't think he will last through the heat of the summer. He'll give up and leave and we can take the fence down."

"I can't believe Charles Wiltshire will give up so easily."

"I'd rather Wiltshire kept away for another reason." Clem glanced towards the kitchen door and lowered his voice. "Jessie is terrified of him."

William couldn't help but glance at the door like Clem had. "Why?"

"For some reason he frightened her with talk of the protector taking Haji away."

"Why would he do that?"

"I don't know. Jessie gets upset at the mention of Wiltshire's name."

"He's up to something."

"Sneaking around making mine claims?"

"Yes, but what has that got to do with Jessie?"

"I don't know. She gets so upset I haven't tried to ask her again."

"No-one would take Haji."

"I don't believe so, but Jessie is terrified."

William staggered to his feet. "I'm going to see for myself what's happening at the waterhole and if necessary I'll speak to Wiltshire."

Clem stood and shook his head. "You don't look like you're capable of anything more today. Nothing will change between now and tomorrow. You should sleep."

Every inch of William ached and his eyelids felt like lead. He knew Clem was right. "I'll set out at first light tomorrow."

"I'll see to your horse."

Despite the turmoil of thoughts that plagued him William slept heavily and woke just as the first glow of the sun's rays lit his bedroom. His first thought was of seeing Georgina and then he remembered the South African and his claim. William dressed in fresh clothes and ate quickly, listening as Clem confirmed everything he'd said the night before. While Clem spoke William glanced several times at Jessie, but she wouldn't meet his gaze and kept herself busy with the fire and the baby. Only Clem came out to see him off on his way to find Hegarty.

The sight of cattle moving towards him was the first indication Hegarty was close. Several hollow-looking beasts trudged slowly along a dry creek bed. William skirted up onto the small plain above the bank and caught sight of Hegarty at the rear. The older man saw him coming and was out of his saddle immediately. They shook hands warmly.

"Good to see you home again, William."

"Clem tells me there's been some trouble."

"Not trouble exactly." Hegarty swept off his hat and dragged his fingers through his thick dark hair. "Becker has a legal claim to search for diamonds. Nothing any of us can do about it."

"Clem says his claim includes the bottom waterhole."

"That is a sticking point."

"And that Wiltshire may be involved."

Hegarty's weathered face wrinkled deeper in a frown. "It could have been his name listed on the bottom of the form but I didn't get a clear look. I'm guessing Wiltshire is the reason Becker accessed the claim without coming over your land. He came in through Prosser's Run instead."

William gazed in the direction of his neighbour's property. Surely Georgina wouldn't have been a party to it.

Hegarty gave a snort. "Doesn't matter how he got there, anyway. The claim says he can search that piece of land and he has the law on his side to access it no matter what you may think."

William turned back to Hegarty. "It's struggle enough to survive here. Why can't people mind their own business?"

The older man looked off into the distance. "Because they think they'll be rich beyond their wildest dreams."

William knew Hegarty was thinking of his own mining days. He recalled the conversation he'd had with Joseph at Christmas. "But surely the lives of people and animals are more important."

"Mining does strange things to people." Hegarty inhaled deeply and his eyes focused on William again. "Clem and I thought the best thing was to move the few remaining cattle closer to the homestead while there's some feed and water there." He waved at the cattle in the creek bed; they had come to a stop, picking at whatever bit of foliage they could find. "I was just going to stop and boil the billy for some tea. Why don't we both take a break? Tell me about the journey south." He bent to collect some sticks.

William glanced beyond him in the direction of the waterhole.

"Don't trouble yourself over the South African. He's not going to find anything of consequence where he is. Anyway, he has other worries." Hegarty set about making a fire. "When I spoke with him he was concerned for the unrest near his home. I've half a mind he'll be gone before the year's out."

"And Wiltshire?" William started the fire while Hegarty got the makings for their tea from his saddle bag.

"It takes stamina to stick with mining. He won't want to dirty his hands or waste his time if there's no quick result."

William thought about that as he prodded the fire to life. He hoped Hegarty was right. The drought still lingered — even though there'd been some rain it had only given a small respite and there was no sign of further falls. William couldn't afford for his stock to be without one of the last remaining waterholes of any significance.

"If you don't think there's any point in me talking to him I will continue to Prosser's Run."

"I thought you weren't setting foot on the place again?"

William sank to his haunches and positioned some rocks either side of the small fire to support the billy over the flames. "I spoke with Georgina just before I left to go south. I think we cleared up the misunderstanding that the gossip-mongers were embellishing."

Hegarty's big face split in a grin. "Good for you."

"You haven't heard how they're faring?"

"I've only seen Swan once or twice in your absence. He's the manager now. The Donovans have left along with a couple of their shepherds. Prossers have lost a lot of stock. Didn't move any south. Like everywhere else there's little to do but to try to keep the last animals alive long enough to see out the drought."

Once more William looked in the direction of Prosser's Run. He had to see Georgina and make sure she understood there was no other person he could love more than her.

He stood and waved away the second mug Hegarty set out. "I'll drink with you when I get back. I have to make Prosser's Run before dark."

Hegarty smiled. "Fair enough."

William strode to his horse, lifted his hand in farewell and set off.

The sun was low in the sky by the time he had the homestead in sight. There were several horses in one large yard near the stables and cattle in another yard beside the shearing shed. None of them paid him any mind as he walked his horse past. No smoke puffed from a chimney or light shone from a window of the homestead. He didn't bother to dismount. The whole place had a deserted air. He rode past and noticed a small wisp of smoke escape from the chimney of the smaller dwelling beyond the main house. It was a smudge of grey against the golden orange sunset and the only sign of human presence.

The door flung open as William approached and Swan stepped out, a rifle in his hands.

"It's your neighbour, William Baker."

"I know who you are." Swan didn't lower the gun. "What do you want?"

"I've come to call on Miss Prosser."

"You're not welcome here."

"I think that's your employer's decision, not yours."

In the gathering gloom William could make out the sneer on Swan's face.

"Correct. Mrs Prosser has made it quite clear you are not to set foot on Prosser's Run." Swan raised the end of the rifle.

William rolled slightly as his horse shifted its weight beneath him. "Miss Georgina is expecting me."

"Is that so?" Swan's face contorted into an ugly grin. "That would be why she left two days ago to attend Mr Charles Wiltshire's birthday celebration in Hawker."

Anger burned in William's chest. Bloody Wiltshire was always getting in his way.

Swan waved at him with his gun. "Get off the property."

William drew in a breath then realised he at least knew exactly where Georgina was. He turned a smug smile on Swan. "With pleasure, Mr Swan, but be careful how you speak to me. Fortunes often have a way of changing and work is hard to come by."

Swan frowned. He opened his mouth then closed it again. William gave him a curt nod and turned his horse in the direction of Hawker.

Twenty-seven

Charles stood on the front verandah of their family home, his father on one side and Georgina on the other with her mother beside her. The party to celebrate his eighteenth birthday was a grand affair and no expense had been spared to ensure it would be a night to be remembered by the dignitaries of the district.

Carriages and horses, carts and people on foot streamed into their circular driveway and made their way to be greeted. All manner of people were attending. Charles was proud that no-one had refused the invitation to the party, in spite of the Prosser ladies' attendance. He thought it a good sign of the Wiltshires' standing in the community.

Lanterns hung from the verandah eaves, and brightly coloured ribbons were tied to each pole. It was a balmy night and the partygoers had the choice of enjoying the evening outside on the verandah or going inside via the new French doors into the dining room. The table in there was laid with a lavish supper, prepared by Mrs Nixon with help from Edith. There were also the delightful tones of the new piano. Henry had bought it for Laura's lessons, but tonight the teacher, Mrs Butler, was playing for their enjoyment.

Charles was pleased Laura had been sent to stay the night with the Hemmings. This was a grown-up party and he didn't want his little sister spoiling it with her silly antics, though they inexplicably charmed any other adult in her vicinity.

Mr and Mrs Button greeted Charles then moved on to speak to the Prossers. Charles had a moment before the next group stepped forward. He smoothed his moustache, patted the natty bowtie at his neck and ran his hands down the soft dark brown velvet of his jacket. His grandmother Harriet had done a fine job with the suit. Underneath the jacket was a satin vest and he wore tan trousers cut in the latest narrow-fitting style.

Beside him Georgina looked like a princess. She had taken his breath away when she joined him before the first guests arrived. She wore a dress of white lace. Scoops of lace were gathered around the low neckline and draped down her arms. The bodice nipped in to show off her tiny waist and the lace fell in three tiers in a flowing skirt. Her hair was piled high on her head in tight curls and her lips and cheeks glowed a soft pink. She was exquisite.

"Charles." His father interrupted his reverie.

Councillor Hill, his wife and two daughters were waiting to be welcomed. Charles smiled and extended his hand to each. The two younger ladies were prettily dressed but were no match for Georgina.

He smiled at her as the Hills moved on. The Prosser ladies had continued to be regular guests throughout the year. Georgina had not sought his company but neither had she turned him away. Tonight, encouraged by his father and her mother, Charles planned to ask her to marry him. He was eighteen now and his business was improving in spite of the drought. His prospects combined with hers would make them a formidable couple.

Edith appeared, carrying a tray of drinks. Her pale pink gown was much more fetching than the usual drab colours she favoured.

"Thank you, Edith." Georgina smiled sweetly as she took a glass. "My goodness, Charles, champagne." She lifted the glass and took a small sip. "How enjoyable. I haven't tasted it since Mother and I were in France."

Charles took a glass and Edith moved on. He took a sip and tried not to wince at the sour taste. He didn't see why people wasted their money on the stuff but his father had insisted they serve it tonight.

He offered Georgina his arm. "Let's mingle, shall we? I want everyone to see how magnificent you look tonight."

"Charles." Georgina lowered her gaze and took another sip of champagne. Her cheeks went a little pinker and when she looked at him again her eyes sparkled. "It's nice to have the opportunity to wear a dress. This is one I had made on our travels and I haven't worn it since. There's little need for lace at Prosser's Run."

"Then I'm so glad we have an excuse to celebrate tonight."

She smiled and raised her glass. "Happy birthday, Charles."

He bent forward to kiss her. She averted her head so quickly his lips barely brushed her cheek.

"Look, Mrs Nixon has made some of her delightful savoury puffs. I am famished, I must say. Let's try some."

Georgina set off to see Flora. Reluctantly Charles followed. Now all he wanted was for the party to be over so he could take Georgina in his arms and kiss her properly.

"This war between the English and the Boers sounds rather serious." Dr Chambers spoke gravely. "Did you get much of a feel for what might happen when you were in England, Mrs Prosser?"

"That was some time ago now, Doctor." Johanna took a sip of the drink she clasped in her gloved hand. "And our last few months were spent in Birmingham, where the main topic of conversation was the new museum and art gallery — which Georgina and I both enjoyed while we were there."

"But there was also talk of the possibility of war, Mother." Georgina had escaped Charles for a while and then found herself caught up with a group of very young ladies, all discussing what they were wearing and ogling him. Georgina had extricated herself and joined her mother, who was with a group of adults talking on broader topics.

"Such a depressing subject." Johanna gave her daughter a withering look.

"Nevertheless it must be discussed. Even though we are in the bush we should still keep up with what's happening in the world, don't you think, Dr Chambers?"

"Do you think Britain will want our young men to help?" Mrs Button's concern for her four strapping sons saved the doctor from coming between mother and daughter.

"Great Britain is still our home country, Mrs Button," the doctor replied.

"War hasn't actually been declared yet, has it?" Her question took on an anxious edge.

"We will be the last to know out here." Mr Wood gave a superior smirk. He was newly arrived from Melbourne to fill a position in the Hawker pharmacy, but Georgina thought he would not be there for long with that attitude.

"Are we a little too dull for you here, Mr Wood?" Georgina's question drew another raised eyebrow from her mother.

"Oh, no, Miss Prosser … not at all." Mr Wood's cheeks went pink and he fiddled with his necktie.

Georgina felt immediate remorse, and gave him a charming smile. All she longed for was to be home again at Prosser's Run. Life in the bush — as city folk loved to call it, even though there was hardly a blade of grass in sight let alone a bush — would be a bit dull for a city man.

"How are you settling in, Mr Wood?"

"I have enjoyed my first two months here, Miss Prosser."

"It must seem very quiet after Melbourne life," Johanna said.

"It's quite a … different way of life."

Georgina smiled at Mr Wood's diplomatic answer.

At that moment, Mr Hemming, who was dressed in a dapper dark suit and in charge of serving drinks for the night, stepped up to their group. Georgina noticed Mr Wood was quick to empty his glass and put it forward for a refill.

Dr Chambers led the conversation again once the glasses had been charged. "It seems you Victorians were as eager to vote yes to Federation as we were here in South Australia, Mr Wood."

"There is certainly much enthusiasm about Australia becoming a commonwealth. I think Alfred Deakin's speech was a turning point in the Victorian campaign."

"Yes, I read a summary in the newspaper. He spoke very well."

"Victorian manufacturers are ready to share their expertise with broader markets."

"Goodness." Georgina couldn't help her teasing tone. "Do you think they will even send their goods as far as Hawker, Mr Wood?"

"Well of course they will, Miss Prosser." Mr Button had missed her attempt at light humour altogether. "It should help our local wheat farmers and even perhaps our one remaining flour mill if these jolly tariffs are removed between states."

"If it will mean the removal of the Victorian stock tax I will be well pleased," Georgina said.

"You must be one of the few pastoralists in the district with cattle left to sell, Miss Prosser." Mr Wood looked at her over the top of his glass.

Georgina noted the twinkle in his eye. Touché, she thought. "No, Mr Wood. Like everyone else we have but a few cattle we are desperately trying to keep alive until this terrible drought breaks. But when it does—"

"Oh look." Johanna turned away. "Mr Wiltshire is asking for our attention. I think it's time for speeches. Come along, Georgina."

She gave Mr Wood a parting smile and followed her mother to where Henry and Charles stood beside the piano. At least Mr Wood had added a welcome diversion to the evening. She glanced back but he was lost in the gathering crowd. Georgina sighed. Now she had to stand dutifully in front of everyone while Henry Wiltshire sang his son's praises.

Charles was beaming at her as she approached. "I'm so glad you're here, Georgina. You've made tonight so special with your presence."

There was such an eager note in his voice she felt a pang of guilt over her attitude. She swallowed her irritation, smiled back at him and took her place at his side.

Twenty-eight

William's bravado with the Prossers' manager began to evaporate as he rode towards the woman he had hoped to make his wife. He tried not to think about the possibility of her being attracted to Charles Wiltshire but the younger man had seemed to have some kind of hold over her when they'd last all been together. Perhaps in William's absence Georgina had somehow been converted to Wiltshire's way of thinking. William gritted his teeth. Of course Georgina would be at Charles's birthday. The Prossers and the Wiltshires were friends. It was natural that they should attend each other's family events.

Once he made the road that led to Hawker, William tried to block the jumble of thoughts that churned in his head and concentrate on the journey ahead. Thankful for a near-full moon shedding clear light, he pushed Big Red hard to cover the distance quickly. He wasn't sure what he'd do when he arrived in Hawker. It would be well after midnight, but at least he would be able to look for Georgina first thing in the morning, arrange some kind of meeting and see how she felt about him. He prayed she still wanted to see him.

William eased Big Red to a trot as the first houses came into view, then he leaned forward in the saddle and patted the horse's neck. "We've made good time."

At the end of the Wiltshires' street William paused, surprised to see a horse and carriage pull out of their yard.

He turned up the road and, as he approached, he could hear voices raised in farewell. When he drew level with the house he took in the festive lanterns and ribbons. Chairs had been set outside and through the glass of the front window he could see more lights blazing. Tonight must have been the celebration for Charles's birthday.

William watched from the other side of the road as the last visitors stepped away from the verandah to their waiting cart. He sucked in a breath. Georgina was standing between her mother and the Wiltshires as they raised their hands in farewell to the guests. William drank in the sight of her like a parched man would take water. There was a lantern above the door and one on each of the poles either side of where she stood. Her hair was high on her head, revealing her elegant neck, and the dress she wore fell softly around her like petals. She had the appearance of an exquisite flower. He slid from the saddle and tethered his horse, and without taking his eyes from her he crossed the road.

"That was the most wondrous evening, Henry." Johanna Prosser smiled from their host to his son. "A birthday celebration to remember always, Charles."

"It was certainly a grand turn-out," Henry said.

"I am sure I spoke with everyone here." Johanna's eyes sparkled. "It's so good to be able to hold one's head up."

"And why shouldn't you?" Henry said. "You and Georgina are most deserving of your place in our society."

"Thanks to your continued kindness. Without your support we would still be shunned because of what Ellis —"

"Mother." Georgina put a restraining hand on her mother's arm. "Let's not spoil the evening with sad memories."

"Of course not." Johanna turned back to Henry. "I do hope you will excuse me. It's very late and I fear I am not as young as I used to be."

Henry stepped forward and offered his arm. "Nor I, Johanna. Let's leave the young ones to it, shall we?"

Georgina bristled at the wink he gave his son. What did that mean?

Johanna took Henry's arm then reached up and patted her daughter's cheek with her other. "Don't stay up too late, my dear."

Georgina smiled through gritted teeth as they swept inside.

The door closed and she turned to Charles, ready to wish him good night. Her feet ached from standing all night in the dainty satin shoes with their high heels, her body felt constricted by the corset she was no longer used to wearing, and she was tired of small talk. He distracted her by taking her hand.

"Let's take a walk in the garden before we retire."

Georgina swallowed her sigh. "Very well." She let him slip his hand under her elbow. It was his birthday after all. She only had to be nice for a little longer and then she could return to Prosser's Run.

He drew her from the verandah and away from the brightness of the lanterns. They stepped across the gravel of the circular carriage track. Charles walked her on along the path that led towards the front gate between the neatly clipped lavender bushes. Somehow these hardy plants had survived the lack of water. Where the path curved around a Rubenesque statue, he stopped and turned to face her.

"I would like to talk to you, Georgina."

Her heart sank. Not more talking. She was tired. "It's very late, Charles."

"This won't take long."

He took her hand in his. She fought the urge to snatch it back as he raised it to his lips and brushed it with a kiss. She blamed her mother for this. She had insisted Georgina be nice to Charles. The Wiltshires were friends and influential and Johanna had maintained her daughter should cease being churlish with Charles. Once Georgina had emerged from her shock at hearing of William's child she had given in. There was no way she would ever have a husband but she was wise enough to know there were times when having a suitable escort was useful.

"I am eighteen now, Georgina."

Charles scrutinised her with a desire she regularly noticed in his gaze. A shiver ran through her.

"It has been a wonderful night," she said lightly, "but it's getting late."

He ignored her diversion. "I have been waiting for this night for another reason." He took both her hands in his and got down on one knee. "I would like you to do me the honour of becoming my wife."

Georgina gasped. Not just at the horror of his words but at the man who had appeared behind him. His hair hung in long tousled waves to his shoulders, where his white shirt was a contrast to the weathered darkness of his skin. William took another step and now she could see the desperation on his face, the longing in his eyes. Her heart leaped at the sight of him then realisation hardened it.

"What are you doing here?" she mumbled.

"What?" Charles looked around in surprise and jumped up. "Baker!"

William didn't take his eyes from Georgina. "You can't possibly be going to accept this ludicrous offer?"

"How dare you, Baker? Get off my property." Charles puffed out his chest.

William still ignored him, his gaze fixed on Georgina. "I love you, Georgina. That has never changed."

Georgina put a hand to her chest. She felt as if the air had been sucked out of her. "How can you declare your love for me and yet father a child with another woman?"

She watched the expression on his face change to outrage. "There is no other woman. I thought we cleared up that rumour."

Georgina glanced at Charles, who had stopped his blustering. "I heard it from the woman herself. She had the babe in her arms and said you had ... you had forced yourself on her." Once more the pain of it stabbed her like a knife.

"Who is this woman?"

Georgina sucked in a breath and lifted her chin. "Her name was Jessie. She said you forced yourself on her."

"She *what*?"

"Get off my property, Baker."

Charles had found his voice again. He gave William a shove. Georgina's heart broke to see the man she'd thought she loved stagger backwards, a look of puzzlement on his face. Charles grabbed her by the elbow and marched her back to the front door.

Someone had turned down the lamps and no light shone from the front room. "Georgina, please." Charles's tone was gentle. "You must listen to me. Come and sit down."

She allowed him to guide her around to the side verandah where the chairs had been neatly lined up against the wall, but her heart was with William.

William had wobbled backwards until the fence had pressed hard into his back. The air was gone from his lungs and his mind spun with images of Jessie and her baby, how she had hardly met his eye when he'd been home.

"Mr Baker?" A voice whispered from the garden and a shadow moved, taking on the shape of a woman.

William's eyes narrowed. "Who are you?"

She glanced behind her then back at William. "Edith Ferguson," she whispered. "I work for the Wiltshires."

He scowled. "Has Charles sent a woman to see me off?"

She put a finger to her lips. "Please keep your voice down, Mr Baker. Mr Wiltshire doesn't know I'm here. My only intention is to help you if I can."

"How can you help me?" William's words rasped from his throat. He still found it hard to breathe.

"I know why Jessie told Miss Prosser her baby was yours."

He straightened and sucked in a breath. "Why? How?"

"The how doesn't matter, but I know Mr Wiltshire — Mr *Charles* Wiltshire — threatened to have her baby removed by the protector if she didn't keep to her story that you had ..." Edith squared her shoulders. The soft taffeta of her dress rustled as she leaned closer. "That you had forced her, and the baby was yours."

A growl came from deep in William's throat.

Edith glanced behind her again. "Please, Mr Baker. No-one must know it was me who told you."

"Why have you?"

"The Wiltshires are my employers and I am very loyal to them. However, I don't like injustice."

William gave a snort. "You shouldn't be working for Wiltshire then."

"It's Jessie and her baby who concern me. They should not be used in this way."

The murmur of voices carried on the breeze. William turned towards the house and with a rustle of fabric Edith disappeared through the gate.

What was he to do? He couldn't exactly storm into the house. All the same he walked in the direction of the front door. When he reached it he hesitated. Once more he heard voices, closer this time. He walked to the corner and there at the other end of the verandah was Georgina sitting on a chair with Charles kneeling at her feet. He strode towards them. They both looked up in surprise.

"You bastard, Wiltshire."

"William."

He ignored Georgina and snarled at Wiltshire. "Tell Georgina the truth about Jessie's baby."

"She knows the truth."

"Your version."

William turned to Georgina, who was regarding them both with dismay. "He blackmailed Jessie into telling you that story."

"Blackmailed ... why?"

Georgina looked from one to the other of them.

"Don't listen to him," Charles growled. "He'll stop at nothing to get his way."

"You are describing your own actions, Wiltshire. You're the devil to frighten poor Jessie so badly. She lives in fear daily that the protector will take her child away." William glanced at Georgina. "The child fathered by her lawful husband, Clem."

Georgina's face paled. "Charles?"

"You're too good for the likes of Baker, Georgina." Charles turned his back on William. "I have asked you to marry me."

William looked over Wiltshire's head to the face of the woman he loved. Was he too late?

Georgina stood. "I am not going to marry you, Charles."

"A union of Wiltshire and Prosser. What a team we would make." Even now there was pride in Wiltshire's voice.

She shook her head. "I was never going to marry you. Our friendship was only for our families' sake but now, I never want to see you again."

"You would believe Baker's word over mine?"

Georgina's gaze met William's. He was relieved to see she did believe him.

"I would take the word of the man I love over yours any day."

Charles fell at her feet. "Please, Georgina. I'd do anything for you."

"Stop it, Charles. I've had enough of your theatrics. Have you no shame for what you've done to that poor girl and to William's name?"

Charles scrambled to his knees. "Baker's name was worth nothing before I came along." He glared at William with a look of pure hatred. "And that won't change. If you align yourself with him your life will be a misery."

Georgina stepped around him and took William's arm. "I think we need some fresher air."

"You'll be nothing in this town without me, Georgina. People have only accepted you because of your connection with my family." Charles's threatening words rung in their ears as they walked away.

Every sinew in William's body was tightly strung. The brush of Georgina's arm against his sent a charge through him. When they reached the middle of the garden he stopped. She turned to face him.

"I'm sorry for what you've been through," he said.

"I'm sorry I doubted you." She looked him squarely in the eye. "I never will again."

He reached for her and she was in his arms in a second, her lips soft and warm and sweet beneath his. The scent of her violet cologne mingled with the lavender on the breeze, and the silvery light of the moon shone over them as they clung to each other. Finally, he eased away. "We have to think clearly and I can't do that with you in my arms."

She cupped his cheek with her palm. "I never want to lose you again."

He covered her hand with his. "You won't, but if we keep that up I am afraid I won't be able to stop."

Her eyes shone wickedly in the moonlight. "Don't then." She leaned forward to kiss him.

"No, Georgina, you must return to the house."

"What?" She took a small step back, her eyes searching his face.

"Dearest Georgina, I want you to be my wife and for us to be together always."

"And I want you to be my husband forever."

"It will be my honour." He took a deep breath. "But tonight you must return to your mother. Life will be difficult enough for you being married to a Baker; we mustn't add fuel for the gossips. My bed will be under a tree somewhere. You must stay here."

Georgina slipped her arms around him and kissed him, then rested her head on his shoulder. "William Baker, you are an honest and honourable man. I've known that since I was a girl." She looked up. "Once again I am sorry I allowed Charles to colour my judgement."

"Don't spoil this brief time we have with his name. He is nothing." William's breath was ragged in his throat. "When will you go home?"

"As soon as I can. I don't want to spend any longer than I have to under the Wiltshires' roof. And I suspect after my rejection of Charles I will no longer be welcome."

"Then I will come and visit you at Prosser's Run in three days. I must ask your mother's permission."

"I know you think you should but I doubt she will give it."

"I must ask." He pressed his lips to hers then eased her firmly away. "You go in, Georgina. Right now my thoughts are anything but honourable."

She gave him that wicked look again, which did nothing to calm the raging desire within him.

"Very well. I'll do as you ask this time, but I must warn you, William, I have become used to giving my own instructions."

He grinned back. "I look forward to seeing more of that."

She blew him a kiss and turned back along the path. Warmth filled his heart as she walked away. At last she would be his wife and make him the happiest man in the world.

Twenty-nine

Edith waited until the other two were out of sight then she stepped onto the verandah and hurried to where Charles was flopped on the floor.

"Oh, Mr Charles." She crouched down beside him. "What has happened?"

She saw the surprise register on his face as she leaned closer and cradled his head to her chest.

"Are you all right?" Edith put on her sweetest, most breathless voice. "Should I go for the doctor?"

She felt him relax and nestle closer against her breasts. "No, Edith. That won't be necessary. I tripped." He cleared his throat. "Perhaps a little too much to drink."

She smiled over his head. When she'd left William Baker she'd gone through her yard, into the Wiltshires' back yard and along the wall. From her vantage point in the shadows she'd seen the whole confrontation between William, Charles and Georgina. Charles had still been on his knees when the other two walked away but he'd thrown himself to the verandah floor in a rage. She patted his cheek. "Perhaps you'd better rest here a moment then I can help you inside."

"Thank you, Edith. You're so very kind."

Once more Edith smiled as he turned his head slightly so his forehead was against the plump flesh of the top of her breasts just above the neck of her dress. She had spent more money on the fabric for this dress than she'd spent on anything in her meagre wardrobe, but it had been worth it. She was much more well-endowed than the slim Miss Prosser, an asset she hoped would help Charles to forget the woman he had planned to marry and focus on the one he would marry.

"It's not been quite the ending to the evening I had hoped for," Charles complained into her dress.

"That's all right, Mr Charles." She stroked his cheek. "Every cloud has a silver lining."

"Not this time, Edith."

"Has something happened?"

"Miss Prosser has turned down my offer of marriage."

"Good heavens, what an ungrateful woman." Edith put a hand to her mouth. "Oh, I'm sorry, Mr Charles," she gasped. "I should not have said that."

"Perhaps not, Edith." He pulled away and studied her so closely Edith was worried he would be able to read her thoughts. "But I agree with you."

She cast her gaze to the ground. "Any sensible woman would know what an exceptional offer you were making and accept at once."

"Well, she has missed her chance." Charles tugged at his jacket and drew in a deep breath. "I really should retire."

"Of course, Mr Charles. Let me help you."

Together they got to their feet, Edith making sure she brushed against him as much as she could. She offered her hand. "You've had a bit of a shock. Let me walk with you."

A small shudder went through her at the lecherous look she saw on his face. She would have to be on her guard.

"I do feel a little wobbly." He leaned on her arm and whispered close to her ear. "Thank you, Edith."

They went in through the French doors. Edith left him a moment to close them then returned to help him cross the room. She knew he could easily manage alone but she was glad he accepted her help. In the hall he hesitated. Opposite was the door to his father's bedroom. It was closed, and Edith wondered if Henry was within or sharing Flora's bed.

They continued on, walking softly towards the kitchen, which was lit only by the light of the moon through the window. Charles hesitated at his bedroom door then swayed against her.

"I'm feeling suddenly light-headed, Edith. Would you mind helping me take off my jacket and boots?"

"Of course not, Mr Charles."

He moved forward and sat heavily on the edge of his bed. She closed the door then lit the lamp. She looked down, remembering the book he kept hidden. She had taken any opportunity she could to read parts of it, and made herself very aware of the kinds of things she would need to do to keep his interest. Some of it disgusted her but Edith was determined she would do whatever it took to become Mrs Charles Wiltshire.

Her cheeks were warm as she turned back and kneeled at his feet, knowing he would be looking directly down at the flesh of her cleavage. She removed his boots then carefully slid his socks from his feet, allowing her hands to caress his skin.

He gave a small groan.

Edith looked up. His eyes were closed, a look of pleasure on his face. She slid one hand over his trouser leg and his eyes flew open. She stood and leaned forward, her fingers brushing his neck as she undid his bowtie.

"And now your jacket."

Her breasts were almost in his face as she eased one arm and then the other from the soft fabric.

"Edith," he groaned.

"Are you in pain, Mr Charles? Perhaps you hurt yourself when you fell."

"No." His voice was a throaty whisper. His arms went around her and he tumbled backwards onto the bed, drawing her on top of him. The bulge against her thigh left her with no doubt she had raised his desire. She had to be very careful now or all could be lost. She struggled but his arms were like a vice around her.

"Mr Charles, what are you doing?" Her heart pounded in her chest.

"Oh, Edith. How I need you." He pressed his lips to hers.

She nipped his lip with her teeth and his eyes widened in surprise. It was enough for his grip to loosen and she scrambled to the floor.

Edith didn't have to create the shocked look she gave him. She had been surprised at his strength. "Surely you would not take advantage of an employee, Mr Charles."

He sat up and glanced past her to the door. She noted with satisfaction the discomfort on his face. "Edith — my dear Edith. I am so sorry." He stood and gently took her hand and pressed it to his lips. "I don't know what came over me. Please forgive me."

"That's all right, Mr Charles. You've had a shock tonight and a fall." She lowered her lashes. "It's just that I hope you don't think I am the kind of person who would indulge in ... behaviour only for married women."

"Oh no, of course not, Edith. It was your beauty that overwhelmed me for a moment."

"You know I would do ... *anything* for you, Mr Charles, but ... well, I am not a woman of the street."

Edith bit back a smile as he sank to his knees. "Dear Edith, please forgive me."

"Mr Charles." She traced her fingers down the stubble of his face to his chin. "Please don't distress yourself. There is nothing to forgive."

He took her fingers, kissed them and stood up. Once more Edith was a little nervous at the size and strength of him as he stood so close.

"I must go now. My goodness, it will be morning in a few hours."

"Of course." He looked her in the eye, took her hands and raised them to his lips again. "But tomorrow we must take tea together."

"It's Sunday, Mr Charles. We have church."

He lowered his hands but she let him keep hers in his grasp.

"In the afternoon. I'll collect you in the cart and we can have a picnic."

"But what will people think? I'm an unmarried woman. I can't be seen out alone with a gentleman."

A small frown flitted across his brow and then he smiled. "I'll bring Laura. She can be our chaperone."

Edith delayed her reply, letting him think she was considering what to do, but she already knew her answer.

He jiggled her hands in his. "I promise to be on my best behaviour."

"Very well." She gave him her sweetest smile and withdrew her hands. "Until tomorrow then."

At the door she looked back. His face was twisted in a mix of desire and frustration. She gave him a coy smile, slipped through the gap and closed the door behind her. She moved on quiet feet to the dining room and let herself out the French doors. If she was seen, she could say she had simply been working late cleaning up after the party. Edith knew more than anyone how easily secrets

could be discovered and she was going to keep her name clean
until she was safely Charles Wiltshire's wife.

As soon as the door closed behind Edith, Charles flopped back
onto the bed and put his hands to his head. He groaned. It was
a guttural sound. His plans had been thwarted by the damnable
William Baker. Georgina was lost to him now. Charles knew he
was no match for Baker in her eyes. He had been in the deepest
doldrums when Edith had appeared. In that low-cut dress she had
clasped him to her and it had taken all of his strength to hold himself back. Once she came with him to his bedroom he had nearly
let go and taken her to his bed there and then.

Edith had been shocked by his behaviour and rightly so. He'd
had to work quickly to reassure her but at least he had a new quest.
If not a wife, then at least someone to warm his bed. Edith was
not beautiful or refined like Georgina, but she had plump breasts
and a trim waist and knew who her master was. That nip of his lip
had been to get away from his grasp, and yet Charles had thought
it almost playful. Edith was more than a simple shop assistant.

He got back to his feet and punched his fist to his hand. He
was not the slightest bit sleepy in spite of the lateness of the hour
but he was tired of the celibate life. Now Georgina was out of his
reach he would need to find someone to fulfil his desires soon or
he would have to make a trip to Adelaide to find an accommodating woman.

He rolled his shoulders and undid his vest. Perhaps a trip to
Adelaide wasn't such a bad idea. He should call on Grandmother
Harriet, thank her for her birthday gift and see how she was faring. He had avoided going because he knew she would want him
to stay. Perhaps if things didn't come about with Edith quickly he
would make the trip.

He also had to take supplies to Becker and spend some time working with him to learn what diamonds looked like and how to find them. Charles smiled. He had been pleased to hear how upset Baker's shepherds had been at the taking over of the waterhole. It gave him some satisfaction. Charles would continue to look for diamonds on that claim and Baker would have to do without one of his natural waterholes. That would teach him to think he could steal Georgina Prosser.

Stripped of his clothes, Charles pulled back the covers and slid into his bed. He pictured William Baker's smug face and drifted off to sleep thinking of more ways to wipe that smile away.

Thirty

William spent a restless few hours in his swag on the edge of town and was pleased to see the first rays of the morning sun. His immediate thoughts were of Georgina and what she might be doing. A flock of birds wheeled overhead and flew screeching towards Hawker as he set a billy to boil. He wished he was seeing her again immediately to confirm the events of last night were not a dream, but there would be no point to him showing up at the Wiltshires'. No doubt there would be enough turmoil there this morning without him adding to it.

He had told Georgina he would arrive at Prosser's Run in three days and that's what he would do. In the meantime, he had much to achieve before he was prepared to ask for her hand officially.

He chewed on some pikelets Jessie had packed for him as he watched the water begin to bubble. How to tackle the problem of Jessie herself was one of them. He was sure Clem knew nothing of what she had said to Georgina and William didn't want to make life worse for the poor girl. He would have to find a way to speak with her alone. He also wanted to go to Wildu Creek and let them know what was happening. He wasn't sure if his father

would be there but it would be good to see his grandfather and
Millie and the children.

William packed his swag while he waited for the tea to cool.
He was impatient to be on his way. He rubbed Big Red's nose and
patted his neck. "You've been a good friend, old boy."

The horse tossed its head in response.

"And we've got my gift to Georgina to get ready."

He hadn't even been home at Smith's Ridge long enough to
check the remaining horses. No doubt Bella would need a brush
down before he took her with him to Prosser's Run. He and
Robert had taken spare horses and others as packhorses on the
drove south but they'd been sold before the return journey.

William took up his mug and downed the tea. His stomach
rumbled but there was no time to waste — and anyway, once he
got to Wildu Creek Millie would ply him with food.

Robert was still at Wildu when William arrived. He was working
with Thomas on repairs to the cowshed. William climbed from
his horse and went to inspect their work.

Thomas's handshake was firm and his smile wide. "It's good to
see you. Robert has been filling me in on your journey south. I
hope your father also has some success."

William shook Robert's hand and turned back to his grandfather.

"Have you heard from him?"

"Millie had one letter but they'd only been gone a month.
We've heard nothing since. Gulda and Timothy are with him and
Eliza has gone to do the cooking."

William gave a snort. "Someone to cook. What we would have
given to have someone preparing meals for us."

"You had me." Robert gave a wry grin.

"I know, but it was an added burden to cook after a day in the
saddle."

"Rex took his turn," Robert said. "He was able when it came to kangaroo."

"I'm glad you took Rex. He would have learned a lot on that journey," Thomas said.

"He taught us a thing or two as well when it came to finding something to eat," Robert said.

"Have you been to the house?" Thomas asked.

William glanced in that direction. "Not yet."

"Let's down tools then and take some refreshment." Thomas retrieved the hat he'd perched on a post. "Millie and the children will be pleased to see you."

"I can't stay long," William said as they walked. "I must get—"

"William!"

His words were cut short by Ruth's scream. She was coming from the direction of the chicken yard, and the wooden bucket she had been carrying fell to the dirt as she flew towards him, arms outstretched.

William hoisted her to his waist and gave her a hug. "Hello, Ruth. I hope there were no eggs in that bucket."

"No." She shook her head.

"Hello!" The call came across the yard.

William looked at the house, where Millie stood just outside the back door with Matthew on her hip. Beth pushed past her mother and hurried along the path.

They all began talking at once, wanting to know how he was and how long he was staying.

"Let the poor fellow inside to sit down first." Thomas ruffled Ruth's hair.

"Are you hungry?" Millie asked.

"Famished."

"I've some pickled mutton and a fresh apple pie. There is even a small amount of cream."

"Sounds good." William reached for Matthew but the little boy ducked his head to his mother's shoulder and gripped her tightly.

"He hasn't seen you in a while." Millie's smile didn't reach her eyes. "Come inside, everyone."

Thomas offered to take Matthew as Millie set out plates, but the child would have none of it. He clung desperately to his mother.

"You're such a big boy now. Are you three already?" William smiled at the child, who lifted his head long enough to peep at his oldest brother.

Millie gave William a tired smile.

"He must be heavy," William said.

"He's only shy with visitors." Millie tugged a loose strand of hair back behind her ear with her spare hand.

Behind her Robert gave a barely perceptible shake of his head.

"Sit by me, William," Beth called.

"No, by me," Ruth objected.

"I'll sit in the middle." William's concern for Millie and Matthew was soon lost as he was submerged in the joy of being with his family again. There was such a babble of happy voices around the table and Millie kept setting out food. Finally, when all the tales had been told, he sat back in his chair and cleared his throat.

"There's something more I'd like to tell you."

A hush fell around the table at his serious tone. All eyes turned in William's direction.

"I have asked Georgina Prosser to marry me and she has accepted."

He was immediately surrounded and received a slap on the back from Robert and a handshake from Thomas. Millie hugged him tightly and planted a kiss on his cheek and the girls squealed in delight. Matthew, who had finally been brave enough to leave his mother's arms and sit at the other end of the table, watched in puzzlement at all the fuss.

"When will the wedding be? Your father won't want to miss it." Millie glanced anxiously at the door.

"He might have to, I'm afraid. Georgina and I have been apart for so long we don't want to wait any longer." William hoped that was what Georgina thought. "We haven't discussed a date yet. We'll have a party when Father gets back."

That brought another round of eager voices.

Once the excitement died down William spoke again. "I have to get back to Smith's Ridge."

The little girls wailed in chorus.

"You'll stay longer won't you, Robert?" Millie gave him a worried look before she handed William a bag of food to take with him.

Robert came to stand beside them both. He looked at William. "I thought I'd stay until Father returns."

"Of course." William felt there was something here he was missing but he followed Robert's lead. "There are three of us at Smith's Ridge for a small number of cattle."

"And they seem to think I'm too old to manage the few sheep we have left here." Thomas looked from Robert to Millie. "However we are low on supplies and I think I can manage a trip to town to collect them."

"Can I go with you, Grandpa?" Beth asked.

"And me," Ruth added.

"If your mother agrees."

Everyone turned to look at Millie. William could see genuine fear in her eyes.

"They will be safe with me," Thomas said firmly.

"I'll think on it," Millie said and the two girls squealed with delight.

William kissed the tops of their heads. "I must go. Thank you, Millie." He waved at Matthew across the room and shook his grandfather's hand.

"I'll see you off," Robert said and followed William across the yard. He glanced back to where the rest of the family waved from the back door. "Grandpa is not as strong as he used to be no matter what he says and there's still a number of stock here to feed and water."

"And Millie?"

Once more Robert glanced in the direction of the house. "She's so nervous, and you've seen how Matthew is. Grandpa says she hides him if ever a stranger ventures this way. She's terrified the protector will take him and even the girls. It seems to be worse since Father left. I think that's why Grandpa's glad to take the girls into town. They never go anywhere or see anyone."

William gritted his teeth. "Damn the protector. It's shameful to see Millie so fearful and it can't be doing Matthew any good to be even more isolated."

"He's just getting used to me. At least Millie will let him come outside if I am here."

William put a hand on his brother's shoulder. "There's no rush for you to return to Smith's Ridge. We can look into the transport idea later."

"I've been thinking on that." Robert gave a wave towards the shearing shed. Beside it was a wagon up on logs of wood. "I've been working on the wagon. There were some wheels needed fixing."

"Good for you." William mounted his horse. "Are there any of the local people about?"

"Yes, from time to time a few help with the sheep in return for some food. Jundala's gone home to her family while Binda's away."

"If anything … well if you need help send word with one of them. I'll come straight away."

"We'll see." Robert grinned. "Sounds like you're going to be busy for a while. Let us know when there's a wedding."

William gave his brother a wave and turned his horse in the direction of Smith's Ridge. It would be dark well before he arrived but with the moonlight Big Red would get him home safely. He had told Georgina three days and one was nearly gone already.

William heard the sounds of the fire being stirred to life in the kitchen. He hoped that meant Jessie was in the house and perhaps alone. When he'd finally reached the homestead the night before he'd heard Hegarty's snores coming from the front bedroom. William had crawled into bed and slept like the dead. Now his head throbbed and his legs felt like lead. The occasional snort from the next room told him the older man was still asleep. William sat up and took a deep breath. He needed to speak with Jessie before he could do anything else.

He peered in the small mirror over the chest of drawers. His hair was a tangled mess and his face was covered in the growth of three days. Certainly not the look he wanted to present to his future mother-in-law. He hoped Jessie could help him with that.

"Jessie?"

She spun from the fire. "William. I didn't know you were home." She glanced towards the back door. "I was going to make bread while the baby is still asleep but I can come back later." She edged away.

"Jessie." William put his hands out wide, palm up. "Please. I need to talk with you about Charles Wiltshire."

Her eyes widened and she swayed.

William stepped forward but stopped as she gave him a baleful look and braced herself against the back of a chair.

"It's all right, Jessie. I know what he made you say. I won't let him hurt you or Haji."

Tears rolled down her cheeks and she began to sink. William drew out another chair and eased her onto it. He pulled out one for himself and sat beside her.

"I want you to know that both Georgina and I are sickened at what Charles made you say."

"She knows it's not true?"

"Wiltshire's lies have been exposed. Georgina will have nothing more to do with him."

Jessie's hands trembled in her lap. "He said if I ever told Miss Prosser my story wasn't true he would ..." tears coursed down her cheeks "... he would get the protector to come for Haji."

William placed a hand over hers. It was cold and soft beneath his roughened skin. "We have exposed his lies, Jessie. Haji is safe."

Jessie doubled over. She dragged her hand from his and clasped her head. "I'm sorry, William." Her words were muffled against her chest. "I did a terrible thing."

"You must not blame yourself." William put a gentle hand on her back. "Charles Wiltshire is the one who must take the responsibility."

Jessie lifted her head and stared at William. "Clem will be so angry."

"I don't advise keeping secrets, Jessie, but this doesn't involve Clem. We will speak of it no more and it will be up to you if you want to tell him." He withdrew his hand and gave her a tender smile. "He won't hear about it from me."

Jessie drew a handkerchief from her apron and wiped her nose and her eyes. "I have been so frightened."

William thought of Millie's haunted look. His fingers clenched.

The wail of a baby carried from outside.

"Clem." Jessie jumped to her feet, wiped her face and hurried back to the fire.

William moved the chairs back under the table and sat at the head just as Clem came in carrying Haji, who was bellowing lustily.

Clem hesitated when he saw William. Jessie took the baby and slipped off outside with him.

"I didn't think you'd be back so soon." Clem crossed to the fire, where the kettle was beginning to steam.

"Nor I." Hegarty stumbled into the room, his eyes bleary. He scratched at his thick beard. "That boy of yours has a hearty set of lungs, Clem. I hope there's enough water in that kettle for all of us."

Clem poured tea into three mugs and they all settled in around the table. The other two men looked to William.

"Georgina Prosser is to be my wife," he blurted.

He received a vigorous handshake from Hegarty and a clap on the shoulder from Clem.

"Congratulations," Hegarty added. "About time."

"Where will you live?" Clem asked.

William paused. "Here." He hadn't thought past Georgina's becoming his wife.

"You'll be needing that front bedroom then." Hegarty grinned.

"Won't she want to stay at Prosser's Run?" Clem asked.

William looked from one to the other. He had always slept in the middle bedroom since returning to Smith's Ridge. The front bedroom held the memory of his mother's death. Even so he'd given no thought to living arrangements. Only that they'd be together at last. "To be honest we've discussed nothing beyond getting married."

"When's the marriage to take place?" Hegarty asked.

"As soon as possible." William stood. "I am going to Prosser's Run tomorrow to ask Georgina's mother officially." He turned away from the look Hegarty gave Clem and a small worm of unease wriggled inside him. There was so much still to decide.

"Well, what say we give this place a spruce up?" Hegarty leaned back and his chair squeaked in protest. "I'll move my things to the shearer's quarters: no-one will be needing them for a while. The big front room could do with a clean-out — it hasn't been used for so long. I'm sure Jessie would give us a hand to add a feminine touch to the place. What do you say, Clem?"

Hegarty's enthusiasm brought a responding smile to Clem's face. "I'll see to the cattle this morning then come back and lend a hand."

"Thank you." William felt his good spirits return.

"No time to waste." Hegarty lumbered to his feet. "We've got a bridegroom and a love nest to prepare."

This time Clem grinned as William's face heated.

Thirty-one

Georgina relaxed in the saddle at the first sight of Prosser's Run homestead through the trees. She was very tired but the prospect of home lifted her spirits. Behind her the small cart followed, loaded with their bags and a small amount of supplies. It was driven by her mother, who had hardly spoken a word in two days. The weight of her silence weighed on Georgina but she knew it wouldn't last. Her mother would have plenty to say once they reached home.

Swan sauntered across to meet them as they arrived at the back of the house. Georgina wasn't as fond of Swan as she had been of Mr Donovan. She didn't find him as easy to work with. It was a pity the Donovans had left, but someone had to go in the difficult times. He'd found work in the south and Mrs Donovan had been pleased to be closer to her children.

Swan helped Johanna down from the cart.

"Thank you, Mr Swan. Has everything been all right here?"

"Still the same, Mrs Prosser. That bit of rain has saved us for a while. No more cattle lost."

"That's a blessing at least."

Georgina slid from Duchess's back.

"I'll take her for you," Swan said. "How was the birthday?"

"The Wiltshires' usual overindulgence." Georgina handed him the reins and undid the small bag attached to the saddle.

"It was a wonderful affair," Johanna gushed. "And most enjoyable."

"I thought you had planned to stay in town longer," Swan said.

"I would like to have but …" Johanna shook her head. "It was not possible. Can you unload the cart, please, Mr Swan?"

"I'll give you a hand," Georgina said. Anything to delay her mother's wrath.

"I am going inside." Johanna gave her a steely look. "I am quite exhausted, however we do need to talk. Don't take too long."

Georgina helped Swan unload the cart. Right now she wished her mother was still the reticent lost soul she'd been after Ellis's death. It had been a relief to see her slowly emerge from those terrible months of inconsolable grief. Georgina felt a little guilty: it had been the trips to Hawker to assist with the Wiltshires' social life that had helped her mother recover. Now they would no longer be welcome. Georgina hoped planning a wedding would give her mother something else to occupy her time for a while.

Once the cart was unloaded Swan led the horses away. Georgina paused on the low back verandah of the house. She removed her favourite broad-brimmed hat and took a mug of water from the jug her mother always sat by the door in the shade.

The late-September weather had become warmer again in the last week. The cattle would soon make short work of the grass that had grown after the minimal winter rain. Once again it would become a daily battle to keep them alive.

Georgina replaced the mug, wiped her hands down her shirt and over the legs of her trousers and went inside.

Johanna had changed her clothes and sat at the kitchen table. In the centre was a plate with cheese and pickles and beside it some slices of the bread Flora Nixon had given them before they left. It had been a hasty and quiet departure. Only Henry had seen them off.

"Sit down." Johanna indicated the space opposite her, where another place had been set.

Georgina sat, steeling herself for the tirade that she felt sure was to come.

Johanna's voice was low and calm. "You know how disappointed I am, and the Wiltshires of course, that you have refused Charles's offer of marriage."

Georgina opened her mouth but her mother put up a hand.

"Let me finish. I want you to think carefully on this. It's not too late to change your mind and for Charles to change his."

"Change his?" Georgina's brow wrinkled in a frown.

"He told his father the morning before we left how he no longer thought you a suitable companion. It's no wonder, the way you treat him sometimes — and look at the way you are dressed."

"My clothing has nothing to do with it, Mother. Charles asked me to be his wife and I refused him."

"For William Baker."

"I would have refused Charles regardless."

"He's a fine young man with good prospects."

"How can you side with him, Mother? He is so much younger than me, and full of his own importance — and he treats some people so badly."

"A few natives."

"Not only the natives, no. And they're people, like you and me."

"Hmph!" Johanna clasped her hands together and looked away.

"He's sneaky as well. He allowed that diamond miner to use our land as a way to get to his claim and he told me his father's name is on the claim. England is at war with South Africa and Charles is in cahoots with a South African. Where is your patriotism, Mother?"

"Sometimes you have to turn a blind eye to small imperfections."

"Small imperfections! Charles is a pompous ass."

Johanna drew in a sharp breath. "You're being very foolish, Georgina." She picked up a paper that sat neatly folded beside her plate. "I didn't think I would have to resort to this but I see I must make you see sense. Have you forgotten the terms of your inheritance?" She waved the page at Georgina. "If you marry before your thirtieth birthday you must have my consent or you will lose Prosser's Run." Johanna glowered at her. "I do not give my consent for you to marry William Baker."

Georgina rose slowly to her feet. "If you make me choose between Prosser's Run and William, I will be very sad." She placed her hands on the table, lifted her chin and fixed her mother with a hard look. "But make no mistake, Mother. I will choose William Baker."

She was rewarded by the colour draining from her mother's face.

"William should arrive here by early afternoon tomorrow, and I expect you to receive him civilly and listen to what he has to say." Georgina stood tall.

There was little sound, bar the crackle of the fire.

She glanced at the food. "I'm not hungry. I'm going for a ride."

"You must take—"

"On my own. I shall be back before dinner." Georgina strode from the room.

The sun shone brightly through her window the next morning. Georgina had slept deeply in spite of the turmoil in her head. There were so many things she and William hadn't discussed. Her head felt heavy from sleep, but in spite of everything her heart felt light. Today she would see William again. She bounced from her bed and took extra care with her washing and dressing.

She buttoned up a white blouse with ruffles at the neckline. Her hands hovered over the previous day's trousers. She hadn't cared what anyone else thought about her clothing — and William had said the trousers were sensible. Still, Georgina put them aside and took one of the narrower gored skirts she'd had made in England from her wardrobe. It was a muddy pink, feminine without being too pretty, and of a lighter fabric for the warm days they'd been having.

In the kitchen her mother was already at the table with some damper and a cup of tea.

"Good morning, Mother."

Her mother gave her a brief glance then returned to her meagre meal.

Georgina sat and dished herself some porridge from the bowl on the table. Breakfast was obviously to be endured in the same silence as the previous night's dinner. Her mother ate without speaking. No doubt adding to her poor temper was Georgina's late appearance.

Since Mrs Donovan had left, Johanna had done most of the cooking, but it was usually Georgina who cleaned out the stove each morning and set the new fire. She'd slept in and it was obvious from the marks on her mother's apron and the smudge on her right cheek that she had tackled the job herself.

Georgina oversaw all the stock work — this had functioned well for them. Now she wondered how her mother would manage on her own. No doubt Swan would relish the opportunity to take more control. Then there were the finances: another role Georgina had taken on since her father's death. Her mother had little idea of how much it took to run the property, and relied on her to manage the money, or lack of it.

Georgina finished her porridge and carried the bowl to the bench. She turned, her hands on the board behind her. She took a deep breath. "Perhaps you should look at employing a cook or a cleaner, Mother."

Johanna took a deep breath of her own and sat back. "You tell me there is barely enough money left to pay the staff we have. How am I to afford a housekeeper?"

"I didn't mean a housekeeper. Just someone who could help out around the place."

"And who will I find out here to do that?" Johanna stood. "And before you say a native, you can stop." She drew herself up. "I will not have them in the house."

"Suit yourself. But if I am not here I don't know how you will manage."

"Where will you be?"

Georgina clicked her tongue. "I am going to marry William. You are denying me access to Prosser's Run so I won't be here to help you."

"And where are you to live?"

"At Smith's Ridge." Georgina faltered. The only time she'd been to the house there was as a little girl and it had been William's mother's funeral. It had not been a happy day.

"It's beneath you, Georgina, and there are natives living there."

"I have work to do outside."

"Dressed like that."

"I really can't win with you, Mother, can I?" Georgina glanced down at her ruffled muslin blouse. "I will be checking the horses while I wait for William." She glowered at her mother. "The air is fresher in the stables." She strode to the back door.

"Don't waste your time watching for Baker. I doubt he'll turn up."

Georgina turned. "Why not?"

"He's not a reliable man, is he?"

"How can you say that? You barely know the man William has become."

Johanna slapped the wooden surface of the table. "And what do you know of him? It's not as if you've spent any time with him. Not like you have with Charles."

They glared at each other. Georgina wanted to say she knew William was a good, kind man with arms she felt safe in and lips she felt caressed by but it would only alienate her mother more.

"I've spent enough time with both men to know that Charles is a despicable boy and William a fine man." Georgina softened her tone. "Please, Mother. Hear him out. That's all I ask." She spun and let herself out into the warm morning, shutting the door firmly behind her.

The few hours till noon stretched out interminably, even though Georgina kept herself busy. She didn't go in for lunch but positioned herself near the stable door where she had a good view of the track that led to the house. There had been no sign of Swan or any of the shepherds all morning. No doubt they were out checking the cattle and the waterholes.

Georgina spent the time brushing down Duchess and the two other horses in the stable. She had donned the apron she kept on a hook inside the door and stopped herself from doing the muck work, at least until William had been. And then what? She couldn't think past the moment when she would see him again. Once more she glanced along the track. Would he make an impression on her mother or would it all be a waste of time, as she had thought?

The sun passed its zenith and Georgina grew more and more restless. She knew which way William would come and she decided to ride out to meet him. She saddled the now gleaming Duchess and perched herself side saddle, a position she detested. Duchess was happy to be outside and eager to trot. Georgina headed her along the track then turned cross-country towards the trail William would follow.

She was surprised to realise she had reached the large stand of gum trees that zigzagged the edge of a dry creek bed with no sign of William. She had thought she would have met him by now.

Her spirits rose when she made out the shape of a horse and rider through the trees. The horse was stationary, a second rider-less horse beside it, and then she realised there was a third horse with a rider ahead of the first.

Georgina frowned. She recognised both riders. One was William and the other was Swan. She gasped as she realised Swan held a rifle pointed at William. She urged Duchess on. Both men looked around at her approach.

"Swan, what are you doing?" she called. "Put down that gun."

Swan frowned and lowered the weapon. She glanced from him to William.

"It seems you no longer want to marry me," he said.

"What? Who told you that?"

"Swan."

"I have my orders," Swan growled. "You shouldn't be here, Miss Prosser."

"What orders, and from whom?"

Swan glowered at her.

"Out with it, Swan, or you can find yourself a different employer."

"Mrs Prosser."

"When did she give you these orders?"

"First thing this morning."

Georgina's shoulders sank. The small hope she'd harboured that her mother would accept William evaporated.

"I think you can put the gun away now, Swan." William climbed from his horse and walked to Georgina's side. "I'm sorry. I'd hoped I could speak with your mother but it seems she's determined to stop me."

Anger flooded Georgina's veins. "Swan. Go back to Prosser's Run and tell my mother her plan didn't work. When ... *if* she wishes to speak sensibly with me, she will find me at Smith's Ridge."

"Georgina." William's voice had a cautionary tone.

Swan didn't move.

"Mr Swan," she growled. "There is nothing more for you to do here. Return to my mother and give her my message."

Swan glared at her a moment longer then pushed his rifle into its holder and turned his horse back along the trail.

"Georgina, what do—?"

She slid from her horse and into William's arms, cutting off his protest with her lips on his. Her arms slipped around him and suddenly he was hugging her tight and kissing her with such passion, she melted against him.

Finally, they drew apart.

"I should take you home." William looked at her with longing. She pressed herself to his chest again and wrapped her arms tightly around him.

"To Smith's Ridge," she murmured into his shirt.

"You can't, Georgina. If you don't care about your reputation I must care for you. Of all people I know what life can be like once others think the worst of you."

"They have already looked down their noses at me for being Ellis Prosser's daughter. The opinion of small-minded people matters little." She looked up at him. "Surely we can find some-one to marry us soon."

"Without delay." William took her arms in his strong hands and gently eased her away from him. "Until then you must return to Prosser's Run."

"I will not."

"The arrangements at Smith's Ridge are not suitable for—"

"I will sleep in your stables if I have to."

His lips twitched. "Georgina, we don't exactly have 'stables' at Smith's Ridge."

"Then I'll build one." She lifted her chin and looked him squarely in the eye. "I am not going back to Prosser's Run. There is nothing there for me now."

"Your mother."

"My mother will not give her permission for me to marry you. I held some small hope she would come round but it's obvious that optimism was futile." Georgina wrenched from his arms and turned to look along the trail to her old home. "Without her permission I lose my inheritance."

"What?"

"My father's will states if I marry before my thirtieth birthday without my mother's permission I get nothing." She turned back to William and held out her arms. "I come to you penniless and in the clothes I am wearing. Are you sure you still want me?"

It took William two steps to reach her and wrap her in his arms again. He kissed her cheek and she closed her eyes, inhaling the earthy scent of him, the man she loved.

"It matters nothing to me, Georgina," he said gently. "But Prosser's Run is your life blood. We could wait—"

She threw back her head and glared up at him. "William Baker, don't you dare suggest we can wait five years, nearly *six* to be married. Take me with you to Smith's Ridge immediately. We have a wedding to plan."

"Very well." He smiled down at her and her anger evaporated. "Come and see." He took her hand. "I have a gift for you."

He led her past his horse to the second: a good-looking mare with a gleaming tan coat and dark mane.

"Who is this beautiful lady?"

"Bella."

"That's a fine name." Georgina whispered in Bella's ear. The horse shook her head.

"What? You don't think so?" Georgina chuckled. "She's truly beautiful."

"Like the woman who will ride her." William put an arm around Georgina's waist. "She's especially good working with cattle."

"Duchess will be pleased about that. She's not fond of cattle work." Georgina ran a hand down Bella's neck then turned back to William. "She's magnificent, thank you."

"If we are to make Smith's Ridge before dark we must set off." William gripped her hand tightly. "Are you sure this is what you want?"

"You are what I want."

He held her gaze and then gave a quick nod. "Very well. Until we are married we must work out some kind of suitable living arrangement."

She stood on her toes and kissed his lips. "Don't take too long."

Thirty-two

October 1899

Charles drew his handkerchief from his pocket and wiped his brow under his broad hat. His ride across the plain had been hot enough but the hill country at the back of Smith's Ridge was even worse. Not a breath of wind stirred and the air in the gullies was oppressive. He was pleased to see there was still water in the spring beside Becker's camp. The man had been sitting at a table in the shade of a large gum. He looked up and got to his feet as Charles approached.

"Good to see you, Charles," he said.

Charles dismounted and shook the older man's hand.

"I see you've brought supplies." Becker indicated the second horse Charles had led in. "I hope you've also brought a swag."

"I planned to stay a few days."

"You will need to stay longer than that." Becker pushed his hat back on his head. His pale skin had turned red with the heat in spite of it. "I am returning to South Africa."

"Why?"

315

"War has been declared. I must return to defend my home from the British devils."

Charles pursed his lips. He didn't give a fig about the squabble between the Brits and South Africa. He wanted to find diamonds. "I can spend some time here but I have other businesses to run."

"Then you will need to find another man to help you. The rules in relation to the claim say there must be someone working it. If not you then an employee."

"When will you come back?"

Becker shrugged. "I do not know." He turned and walked back towards the table he'd been working at. Charles followed, leading the horses. He tethered them and crossed to where Becker was bending over his work. An assortment of rocks littered the table in heaps of varying sizes. Buckets of water stood on the ground beside the table and a large sieve was propped nearby.

On the table one small pile of rocks glittered in the sunlight slanting between the leaves of the gum tree high overhead.

Charles reached for one. "Are they diamonds?"

"No." Becker shook his head. "I've found no diamonds here, although there are definite similarities between this place and my diamond mine at home."

"Surely you've found something."

"It is a needle in a haystack process. The shepherd who first brought us here was sure this was where Joseph Baker found his rock."

"And you're sure that rock is a diamond?"

"Several people were only too happy to describe it to me, including your father." Becker scratched at his thick red beard. "I was able to follow the trail to a merchant in Sydney, who authenticated the rock. That's what brought me this way in the first place, and once I saw this country I knew there could be diamonds here." Becker looked around. "It's strange though. If Baker found the diamond here why didn't he stake his own claim?"

"The Bakers are definitely peculiar people. There would be no explaining it." Charles looked at the waterhole and then further along where the creek narrowed. "Unless this isn't the place and they have staked a claim elsewhere."

Becker shook his head. "This is the only diamond claim in this area. There were gold claims further north and copper of course but no diamond mines."

"Well then, Mr Becker." Charles rolled up his sleeves. "You'd better show me what to do and then I shall have to return to town and find someone who will work here for me."

Becker began to wash a pile of dirt. "I've been using this sieve. It uses less water to do it this way. I've been mindful that the Bakers also need the waterhole for their cattle."

"Isn't it included in the claim we made?"

"Yes, but—"

"Then damn the Bakers." Charles waved his hand in the air. "They have other waterholes."

Becker raised his eyebrows but turned back to his sieve. "You need little experience to look for diamonds. They can be any shape."

Becker began to explain. Charles wondered whether the Bakers really were stupid or playing it smart. If they knew there were diamonds on their land and they didn't want them or want anyone else to find them, it's possible they wouldn't stake a claim. It would be an admission there were diamonds to be found.

Two days later Charles set off at first light to return to Hawker, with a promise to Becker he'd return in a week to relieve him. Now that he was eighteen his name was on the claim instead of Henry's — his father had been happy to offer it as a birthday gift.

Charles had no intention of spending long periods of time doing the thankless work Becker had shown him. Charles was pondering who he might hire in his stead when he saw a horse and rider going through the boundary gate to Smith's Ridge. The man was towing a second horse loaded with bags. Charles recognised the rider as he drew closer. He was one of the shepherds from Prosser's Run.

Charles was on the Prosser's side of the fence but he hadn't planned on meeting anyone. The man had seen him though and reined in his horse so Charles continued on towards him. It didn't matter that he should be seen. Everyone knew he had interests in the mine now anyway.

"Hello, Mr Charles."

Charles raised his hand in a small acknowledgement of response.

"Didn't expect to see you out here."

"Where are you headed?" Charles could see now the second horse appeared to be loaded with personal effects, a case and a large patchwork bag, rather than food items.

"Mrs Prosser sent me to take these things to Miss Georgina."

"At Smith's Ridge?"

"That's right. She lives there now." The man's face split in a big grin. "Going to marry William Baker. Are you going to see Mrs Prosser?"

"No." Charles pulled himself up straight in the saddle. "I've been doing business. I'm on my way home."

"Just as well you keep away today. Mrs Prosser's not a happy lady." The shepherd began to laugh. He kicked his horse into motion and the sound of his merriment floated back to Charles as he rode away.

Anger boiled in the pit of Charles's stomach. Georgina was a fool to marry Baker and even more so to be living with him before the formalities were conducted. If they ever were. She was an embarrassment. He'd show her. Charles would find himself a wife who was much more suitable than Georgina Prosser.

By the time he arrived home it was dark; there were no lamps lit at the front of the house. He rode his horse down the side, where light shone from the kitchen window. Once he reached the stables he could see a lamp had been lit there and also at the back of the house. His father's carriage and the black horse that drew it were missing. Charles removed the saddle from his horse and filled up its hay box. Weary from the heat of working at the mine for no result and the long ride home, he dragged himself across the yard to the back door.

His head hurt from thinking over possible men he could employ to continue working at the mine and, more importantly, trying to think of a suitable woman to be his wife. The only eligible young women paled in comparison to Georgina. He was furious that the more he struggled to keep the evaluations from his mind the more he saw her pretty face.

He flung open the kitchen door with more force than he'd intended.

"Oh, Mr Charles." Edith had been sitting at the table, her head bent over a book, but she stood quickly at the sight of him and snatched up the book. "I didn't know you were expected home."

"I didn't give Father a day. I wasn't sure how long I'd be."

Edith stood quivering by the chair she'd almost knocked over in her haste to get up.

"Edith, you look quite flushed. Are you unwell?"

"I am perfectly well, thank you, Mr Charles." She put her hands behind her back and edged away from the table. "You startled me, that's all."

He glanced around. "Why are you here? Where is everyone?"

Edith turned to the jacket she'd placed on the hook behind the hall door and slid something into the pocket. "Your father had a meeting and Mrs Nixon wanted to attend a musical evening at the church, so I've been enlisted to sit with Laura." She smiled at him. "Shall I make you some supper?"

"That would be very kind, thank you."

Edith lit another lamp and carried it into the pantry. She came back with a tray loaded with bread, cheese and some kind of tart.

"Mrs Ferguson showed me these in case I got hungry. It's a cheese and onion tart, I believe." Edith set about preparing the food for him.

"How was the shop today?"

"Still rather quiet. I did a lot of tidying."

Charles slumped onto a chair and leaned back in it. None of the Wiltshire ventures were faring well at the moment. The swish of Edith's skirt distracted him. He thought back to their picnic the week before. It had been a most enjoyable afternoon, even though Laura had demanded their attention most of the time. Charles was pleased Edith hadn't given in to her like most other adults. He also liked the way she looked at him. Her gaze was full of innocence and yet sometimes there was the hint of something else lurking below her smile.

She put a plate of food in front of him and some cutlery.

"Won't you join me?"

"Oh, no thank you. I told Mrs Nixon I ate before I came over. I'm not hungry."

"A drink, then."

She opened her mouth but he cut her off. "I won't take no for an answer." He got up and, lifting the small lamp she had left on the bench, he made for the pantry. "I am sure there is plenty of wine left over from my birthday," he called back as he inspected the shelves. Several bottles were lined up. He took one and returned to the kitchen to find an opener. He was pleased to see Edith had set out two glasses. He poured the wine and they both sat. She cut herself a slice of bread and a piece of cheese.

"Just to be sociable." She smiled. Her hair, swept back from her face in a bun, shone in the lamplight.

He raised his glass and took a sip. She did the same.

"Mmm," she said. "That's quite nice, isn't it?"

"Have you not tried riesling before?"

"Oh no." She looked at him across the table, her cheeks a softer pink now and her eyes glittering. "I've never really had much opportunity to drink wine, or any other liquor for that matter." She took another sip. "This is most enjoyable."

Charles was suddenly struck by her attractiveness. She did not have Georgina's beauty but there was something about her. He studied her over the top of his glass as he took another sip. Edith was an obliging mix of innocence and kindness and she was always interested in what he had to say. He thought of the way her fingers had caressed his skin when she'd removed his socks and boots. She had no idea, of course, of the sensations that had caused within him.

"Do eat up, Mr Charles. You must be very hungry."

Edith put a small piece of bread into her own mouth. He held his breath as her delicate pink tongue slowly retrieved a crumb from her bottom lip. She took another sip of her wine and he drank a larger slug of his. Why was he only now realising what had been right in front of his face? He had thought he could take Edith as his mistress but she was far too good a woman for that. She might be an employee but she was a fine young woman with no-one else in the world to look out for her. Charles would be able to mould her into the perfect wife. He ate on in silent contemplation, tantalising himself with images of guiding Edith in the art of the bedroom.

A sudden crash surprised him.

"Oh, dear." Edith lowered her gaze to her shirtfront. "How clumsy of me. I have spilled my wine." She took the top of her shirt between her fingers and flapped the fabric. When she stopped the white material clung to her breasts, revealing the pink flesh above her chemise.

"Can I get you a cloth?"

"Oh, no. It's so wet. I have my jacket here and it buttons up the front." She gave him another of her sweet smiles and picked up the small lamp. "May I use your bedroom to remove my shirt and put on my jacket?"

"Of course." Charles stood, wanting to go with her, but restraining himself at the door.

Edith collected her jacket and went into his room. She turned, looked him in the eye and slowly closed the door between them. He let out a soft groan and flung himself back in his chair. Dear Lord, she was the most desirable woman. He wanted to be the one in there removing her clothes.

He looked at the glass she had dropped and wondered how she could have spilled so much on herself. Then he stood, picked up the bottle and refilled both their glasses.

Edith studied herself in the small mirror. The jacket was a serviceable dark grey but the design was shapely. The buttons stopped barely halfway over her breasts, which were pushed up by her corset and covered only by the lace of her chemise. She tugged the jacket lower and loosened the highest button, which sat at the middle of her breasts. The slightest movement and it would slip open.

She smiled and glanced down at the floor beside the bed. What a start Charles had given her when he came in. She had not expected him home. Reading that book had made her feel brazen.

What would have happened had he discovered her reading his secret book? And she had just read a most salacious chapter.

She put her hands to her cheeks and practised her coy look in the mirror. When she had been asked to babysit, Edith had not expected it would involve yet another opportunity to ensnare Charles. She straightened her shoulders, making the button strain dangerously close to slipping open, took up her damp shirt and left the room.

He was waiting for her just outside the door. His eyes were greedy for her. Aware of his scrutiny, she put a hand to her chest.

"Your wine, mademoiselle." He inclined his head and she giggled.

"You do have a way with words, Mr Charles."

"Dear Edith." He offered his arm to walk her back to the table and she giggled again.

He seated her in the chair then, gripping the back of it, he bent over her shoulder. She shifted in her chair to give him the view she knew he was seeking.

"I did enjoy our picnic last Sunday." He spoke softly, close to her ear.

A little shiver ran through her. "So did I, Mr Charles. It was most delightful." Her words came out in snatches between breaths.

Then he was beside her, kneeling at her feet. The swiftness of his movement surprised her. He clasped her hands in his and looked up at her, desire written all over his face. "Dearest Edith. This may come as a surprise to you, but I have the deepest feelings for you."

She paused for a heartbeat, then leaned forward. "Oh, Mr Charles." The button slipped open and she saw his eyes widen and focus on her breasts but she kept her gaze on him, pretending she hadn't noticed. "I had no idea. I had imagined my feelings were one sided," she gasped.

He groaned and finally lifted his gaze to hers. "Dearest Edith, would you do me the honour of becoming my wife?"

She looked him squarely in the eye, took one of his hands in hers and raised it to her breast where she pressed it firmly to the bare flesh. "I would be delighted, Mr Charles." Once more she made sure her words came out as a soft whisper, although after reading that book and feeling his warm hand gently squeezing her breast this time it was not so much of an act.

"Edith, dear Edith." He leaned closer and pushed his lips over hers and his other hand joined the first, and he tweaked her nipples through the cotton chemise.

Her pulse raced as his lips traced a line down her neck while his fingers worked at the buttons of her jacket. She arched her neck back and thrust her breasts forward, eager for his touch now.

"Chars?"

Edith's eyes opened. Laura was standing just inside the kitchen, the hall door open behind her. She clutched a rag doll to her chest, her little eyes bleary and her hair in disarray. Charles jumped to his feet and spun around, hiding Edith behind him. She redid the buttons of her jacket with trembling fingers.

"What's the matter, Laura?" His voice barely hid his annoyance.

"Want Mama." The little girl began to cry.

"Oh for pity's sake," Charles groaned.

Sure she was tidy now, Edith stood. "Let me," she said. She brushed Charles with her arm as she passed and picked up the little girl. "Did you have a bad dream?"

Laura nodded her head.

"Come along, I will sit with you."

"But Edith ..."

She turned back, amused at the pouting look he gave her. "You must be very tired, Mr Charles. Why don't you turn in? Perhaps we could take Laura on another of those picnics on Sunday."

She turned and carried Laura back to her bed. For once she was thankful for the child's appearance. Who knows how she would have extricated herself from the tricky situation in the kitchen. She didn't want to give Charles too much leeway: just enough to keep him wanting more until she became his wife. Edith smiled as she pulled the covers over Laura, whose eyes were closed again already. Tonight she had had a formal proposal from Charles. It was the first step. Edith knew the offer came from desperation and he could change his mind in the cold light of day. She had to keep tempting him in her direction. And then there was Mr Henry. She doubted he'd be happy to learn his son had proposed to their shop assistant, but she had something up her sleeve if he proved a problem.

Edith looked smugly at the now sleeping Laura. "I do believe I shall be your sister-in-law, Laura," she whispered. "Very soon, I hope."

Thirty-three

"Jessie, he's such a dear little babe." Georgina looked up from the baby she bounced on her knee to the young woman kneading dough on the crude table surface.

Jessie paused from her work and looked up. Her lips lifted in a smile and her eyes matched the sentiment. Georgina was relieved to see she was making some headway with William's young housekeeper. It had been awkward at first. Jessie had still been so distressed over her lies and Georgina had to be careful only to reassure her when Clem wasn't around. That wasn't hard at the moment. All the men were off with the cattle.

"You'll have a baby of your own once you marry Mr William."

"I never wanted children … but now…" Georgina sighed. "If we ever get married. This waiting for the travelling priest seems to go on forever."

Jessie's smile widened. "You've only been here two weeks."

"Don't tell William, but that's been more difficult than I thought. Seeing him every day and not …" Georgina put the baby back on the floor and wiggled a wooden toy in front of him. "Not being his wife is worse now than when we lived apart."

Jessie chuckled this time. "Why do you think he keeps finding reasons to go off for days at a time? Clem says he's working very hard so he can fall asleep exhausted at night."

"I know. It's my fault. I insisted on coming." Georgina stood and paced the small kitchen of Jessie's hut. "But I will not go back to my mother. Not that I'd be welcome anyway. Sending those clothes to me was her final farewell."

"I'm sorry." Once more Jessie paused over her dough and this time her look was wistful. "I miss my mother, especially now I have Haji." She glanced down at the baby gurgling happily on the floor. "She would have loved him."

Georgina felt a pang of guilt. "What a terrible daughter I am. I have a mother and I've turned my back on her."

"It's not easy to give up family for the man you love, but that's what my mother did, and that love made her very happy."

Georgina paced again and then gripped her head in her hands. "Oh! I feel like a caged animal."

"Why don't you go for a ride?" Jessie glanced to the window. "It's a beautiful morning."

Georgina's spirits lifted. "You wouldn't mind?"

"You don't have to ask my permission."

"But I'm supposed to be practising my bread-making skills."

Jessie stood up and arched her back. "Your mind is on other things today." She chuckled. "And I don't think there's much you will learn from me when it comes to cooking."

"It's something I've done little of in recent years. We were travelling and then when we came home ... well there was Mrs Donovan and Mother."

"I am happy to cook for everyone." Once more Jessie chuckled. It was such a happy sound. "Thankfully I've improved a lot since I first came here."

"I'm good at cakes."

"And I'm not."

"We'll be a team then."

They grinned at each other like conspirators but the sound of horses made them both look towards the door.

"I thought the men were away all day." Georgina's excitement that William might have returned early was marred by the sight of Jessie plucking Haji from the floor and the frightened look on her face.

Outside she felt a surge of relief as she recognised William and Clem's horses at the back gate of the homestead. "It's all right. It is our men."

The women walked down the path to the main house.

"They must have gone inside already." Georgina walked around the horses to see William and Clem bending over a man lying in the shade of the verandah.

"What's happened?"

They looked up. William walked towards her, his face full of concern. Over his shoulder Georgina could see the anger on Clem's face.

"It's Albie. We found him down in the dry creek. He must have been camped there a few days. He's drunk. So inebriated we can barely rouse him."

"Albie?" Georgina peered at the man who lay prostrate on the ground. "Is that the man—?"

"Your father almost killed." Clem's words came out in a growl. "And he might as well have. Look at him now."

Georgina gasped.

"Clem." William's tone held a warning. "Georgina is not responsible for what happened."

"I'm sorry." Clem's shoulders slumped. "It's hard seeing him like this."

"Clem." Jessie moved closer to her husband. "We should do what we can to make him more comfortable." She turned back to Georgina and William. "Will you take Haji? Clem and I will look after Albie."

"Put him on my bed." William waved towards the bed he'd been sleeping in since Georgina had arrived. It was tucked behind a hessian wall at one end of the verandah.

Georgina extended her arms for the baby and Jessie turned back to help Clem.

"I'll get clean bedding." Georgina hurried into the house, relieved to be out of the warm sun and away from Clem's despair. She had just returned to the kitchen with a blanket and some bed-sheets when Jessie came inside.

"We'll need to wash him first," Jessie said. "Clem and William are trying to get some water into him and remove his clothes." Jessie took the bedding. "Can you heat some water?"

"Of course."

Georgina hurried to her task, glad to have something else to do. As she paced back and forth waiting for the water to boil she felt Haji go heavy in her arms. She took him to the front bed-room, which she had spent most of the last two weeks redecorat-ing, and laid him on the bed.

When she returned to the kitchen, William was there filling the wash bucket from the kettle.

"Is he going to be all right?" Georgina grasped her hands tightly together, anxious for the man, who'd looked as if he could be dead.

"I hope so. Clem's tried to help him before, but Albie's been drinking more and more since his beating." William shook his head. "He's got no job. I don't know where he's getting the money." He took the bucket and strode back outside.

Georgina gripped the edge of the table. She felt suddenly sick. "Dear God." She remembered asking the Wiltshires to make sure Albie was taken care of. No doubt the payments they'd agreed on were still coming from the Prosser account.

By the time William came back inside she had set the table with food and the kettle was boiling again for their tea. She shot up from the table. "How is he?"

"Sleeping still but clean and comfortable at least. We'll keep trying to give him water and then once he's awake we can begin some food."

"We've done all we can for now." Clem stepped through the door.

Jessie followed him into the kitchen. She glanced around. "Where's Haji?"

"Sleeping," Georgina said. "I've just checked on him. Please, everyone sit down. There's cake and the kettle has boiled. I need to tell you something."

William sat. He looked to Georgina. "What's this about?"

Jessie made the tea and Clem took a seat at the table.

Georgina swallowed the lump in her throat and sat beside William. "It's my fault Albie has the money to spend on liquor."

"How?"

"I asked the Wiltshires to make sure he was … taken care of."

Clem stared at her. "You did?"

Georgina glanced at him. "I should have seen to it myself."

"And you think that would have made a difference?" William's question was delivered in a quiet tone. His eyes full of love for her. "You weren't to know he would spend the money on drink."

"It was my responsibility."

Clem's fist thudded on the table. Georgina jumped.

"Albie is a man," he said. "He should be able to take care of himself."

"Nobody made him spend the money on drink." William's voice remained calm.

"He can't work," Clem said. "He has been very sad."

"Perhaps he felt the drink washed away his troubles," Georgina said. "It's all my fault."

"We can't undo what's done." William gripped her hand.

"I'll stop the money." She sucked in her lip to stop the tears that brimmed in her eyes.

"But then he would have nothing." Clem's whispered words were followed by silence. They could clearly hear the sound of birds and the creak of tin in the breeze outside.

It was William who spoke next. "We're all sorry for what happened to Albie, Clem. We can't go back and change it but maybe we can do a better job of helping him to heal inside so he doesn't drink himself half to death."

"How?" Clem turned a sorrowful gaze on William.

"I don't know." William shook his head. "Maybe if we get him back on his feet we can find ways to help him."

There was a groan and a coughing noise from outside.

"I'll go and sit with him a while." Clem got to his feet.

"I'll come with you." Jessie glanced towards the front of the house.

"It's all right, Jessie." Georgina tried to smile. "I'll listen for Haji."

As soon as they were outside she turned to William. He looked at her with such love, the tears she'd been fighting rolled from her eyes. He held out his arms and she flung herself against him. "I'm so sorry," she sobbed.

He rocked her as if she were a child, gently patting her back.

She sat up and wiped her eyes with her handkerchief. "I didn't realise."

"Shh," he soothed. "I probably would have done the same, had I been in your shoes. The thing is to work out what to do now."

"I should stop the money."

"Perhaps."

"Oh!" Georgina put her hand to her brow. "Once the Wiltshires set it up I arranged with the bank to make the money available. I'll have to go into town. I'd hoped not to go until after we were married."

"Albie won't be going anywhere to collect anything for a while. There's no rush to go to town — but in any case it might be possible sooner than you think."

Georgina wiped her cheeks and took in the grin on William's face. "Have you some news?"

He slowly took an envelope from his pocket. "I met the mailman this morning before we found Albie."

Georgina bounced in her seat. "What is it?"

"The travelling priest is calling at Wildu Creek next week, and he is happy to conduct our marriage."

She gripped his hands. "Truly?"

"Truly, my dear Georgina. That's if you don't mind being married at my parents' home."

"I don't care where it is as long as we are married soon." She pressed her lips to his and he kissed her back. She pulled away. Being so close to him without being able to share more was tantalising. "I want to be your wife right now."

"One more week."

"I can't stand it," she groaned.

"Nor I but—"

"One more week." She cut him off. "And not a moment longer."

Thirty-four

Edith knew it would happen as soon as Charles was away. That morning he had left for the mine and she had been on tenterhooks ever since. Now it was almost closing time — Mr Hemming had been ordered to watch both shops and she'd been summoned to Mr Henry's office.

She took a breath and gave a sharp rap on the door.

"Enter."

Edith did as she was bid. Mr Henry's head was bent over a paper he was reading. She crossed the room and didn't wait for him to look up. Boldly, she sat in one of the high-backed chairs he reserved for his clients. She folded her hands in her lap and waited.

Finally he looked up, and his eyebrows rose at the sight of her already seated. "Don't make yourself too comfortable, Miss Ferguson. I won't keep you long."

She met his look squarely. "I have the end-of-day tally to complete, Mr Henry. I don't have a lot of time myself."

Henry pushed back his chair and crossed to the small window with its view of the building next door. He cleared his throat. "My son has imparted some difficult news this morning, Miss Ferguson."

333

Edith said nothing.

He turned to look at her. "It seems Charles has asked you to be his wife."

"Why yes, Mr Henry." Edith smiled sweetly. "I was so surprised but delighted indeed to accept. Isn't it wonderful news?"

Henry shifted from foot to foot and rubbed his hands together. "Yes, well ... you are certainly a fine young woman, Miss Ferguson. I am sure you will make someone a good wife one day."

"I beg your pardon?" Edith feigned surprise.

"My dear Miss Ferguson. You have been an asset to our business but I think it is time for you to move on."

"But—"

"I will give you a glowing reference, of course." Henry hurried back to his chair, picked up his pen and looked at her. "It's just that I cannot have my son and heir marrying our shop assistant."

Edith met his gaze; she lifted her chin. "I think there's been some misunderstanding, Mr Henry."

"No misunderstanding." Henry looked at the paper in front of him. "You cannot marry my son. Of course I have here a tidy sum to help you recover from your despair at having to refuse his offer." He picked up an envelope and placed it in front of her. "You do understand what I'm telling you."

Edith allowed the smile she'd been holding back to spread over her face. "I understand very well, Mr Henry. I think it is you who has misunderstood. I will most certainly become Mrs Charles Wiltshire. Very soon, as it turns out. Charles is anxious we don't delay our union."

Henry's eyes bulged. "You will not marry my son." There was a threatening edge to the words he pronounced slowly, as if she was someone who couldn't understand English.

"Dear Mr Henry." Edith leaned in, her tone equally condescending. "I will be marrying Charles and you will give us your blessing, unless you want the district to know about your ... arrangement ... with your housekeeper."

Edith watched as Henry struggled with the news she'd delivered. Suddenly he drew up his shoulders.

"I see you will stop at nothing less than blackmail to get your hands on my son."

"And I see you don't deny your liaison."

"You're no match for me, Miss Ferguson. I am prepared to weather a small storm that may arise if people find out I took comfort from my long-standing devoted housekeeper after the death of my dear wife."

Edith met his smug smile with one of her own, hiding the turmoil within. "Mmm. Perhaps there are some who would forgive that." She clasped her fingers together on the desk to hide their tremble. "But, like me, Mr Henry, I think most of the people who currently hold you in high standing would be appalled to discover Flora Nixon has been your mistress for a long time. Even while your wife was very much alive."

Henry pushed back his chair and stood. His dark eyes glittered. "How dare you make such accusations?"

Edith remained seated but held his look. Everything depended on her making him believe her. She drew up her shoulders. "I have lived with your family long enough to notice comings and goings."

Henry's gaze faltered.

Edith pressed her point. "Mrs Nixon has a very convenient bedroom. So easy for you to slip from the house. Especially when you and your wife did not share a bedroom."

He slumped back into his chair. Edith let out a silent breath.

"We've been very discreet."

"Secrets never last, Mr Wiltshire."

"Charles doesn't know about ..."

"I don't believe so."

"Flora Nixon is a good kind woman. I won't have her hurt."

Edith bit her tongue on that one. Flora had always held herself in high regard. Too high as far as Edith was concerned, but her time would come. "Your secret will stay with me, providing—"

"Providing you marry my son."

"Precisely."

Henry let out a long sigh. "Very well, Miss Ferguson. You may marry my son with my … my blessing."

Edith rose from her chair.

"I don't know what your exact motive is Miss Ferguson, but you had better truly love my son and make him happy."

"Don't worry, Mr Henry. I do love your son … very much." Edith stopped short of winking at him but her gaze was suggestive. "*Charles* will not be seeking another woman's bed while I'm alive."

Henry gaped at her.

She leaned forward and whisked up the envelope he'd placed in front of her. At a quick glance there was a large number of notes inside. "How kind of you to give me some money for my trousseau. And now I must return to the shop for my end-of-day duties. Good evening." Edith turned on her heel and swept from the room.

Henry sat staring at nothing long after Edith had left. How had it come to this? He couldn't believe he was being blackmailed by a chit of a girl. So many times over the years he had inveigled items, deals, properties from people, and she had beaten him at his own game.

He could call Edith's bluff, send Flora away, but what would become of her? His affection for Flora was very real. She was a reliable sensible woman, and a wife to him in more ways that

Catherine had ever been. Laura depended on her as well. Flora
was the constant female presence in her young life. Henry did not
have the heart to hurt either of them by sending Flora away. He
would have to go along with Miss Edith Ferguson for now. But
he'd keep his own eyes open for any opportunity to be rid of her,
Charles's wife or not.

Henry glanced down at the ledger open on the desk in front
of him. He shifted the demand for payment he had received from
one of their interstate suppliers and looked at the columns of red
figures. Thankfully the separate book Charles kept for his transport business was in the black, although how long that would
last with the money he was putting into his search for diamonds,
Henry didn't know. Charles had set off that morning with two
men he'd employed to replace Becker and speed up the search.

The closure of the creamery had cost Henry a lot, and the
extensions to the shop had come to more than Charles had managed to extract from his grandmother. He sighed, shut the dark
leather cover of the book, rose and took his jacket from the back
of the chair. Money was slipping through his fingers.

Now, not long after the cost of the birthday celebration Henry
had planned for Charles, there was to be the cost of a wedding.
He wondered if Harriet would travel to Hawker for it. If it was to
be soon, as Edith had suggested, it would take part in late spring
or early summer. His mother wasn't so strong any more and Catherine's parents were certainly beyond making the journey. Not
that they ever had while Catherine was alive, so he didn't imagine they'd be interested now. Once Charles had set a date Henry
would write to them.

He returned the ledger to the bookshelf, pulled down the blind
and let himself out the back of the shop. Mr Hemming and Miss
Ferguson would close up. He turned up his collar and walked
slowly along the back lane. The weather had been sunny in the

morning but the late afternoon had turned chilly. The dull sky matched his mood. With Charles away for a few days he had been looking forward to relaxing in Flora's company. Now the anticipation was spoiled. Edith was obviously sneaky. He felt as if he would always be looking over his shoulder.

The ring of a bell made him look up.

"Watch out," came a sharp call.

A young lad wobbled around Henry on a bicycle.

"Sorry, Mr Wiltshire," the lad called over his shoulder. "I'm still learning how to drive this thing."

Henry watched as the boy and bicycle careered on along the street. He had wanted Charles to ride a bicycle, learn about them and stock them. Perhaps in their current economic circumstances it was best that idea hadn't been taken up. Still, Henry did think perhaps bicycles would eventually become more popular and certainly cheaper to run than horses.

He turned and made his way to the front gate. A swish of the sitting-room curtain gave Laura away and his spirits lifted. There was a fumbling sound from the other side of the front door as he put his key in the lock. The door opened to reveal his dear little daughter. Her face glowed and her shining hair had been pulled back with a wide pink ribbon. She gave a little clap of her hands.

"Papa," she cried.

Henry scooped her into his arms. A soft kiss landed on first his left cheek and then his right. He kissed the top of her sweet-smelling head and smiled. No matter what happened he had his little Laura to sweep away his cares with her smiles and her kisses.

"Good evening, Mr Wiltshire."

He looked over Laura's head to Mrs Nixon, who was walking towards him along the hall, a gentle smile on her face.

He glanced back at Laura. She was three and a half now and perhaps getting to an age where she might begin to notice the closeness between her father and his housekeeper. And in light of Edith's revelation perhaps he needed to be more careful even in his own home.

He gave a curt nod. "Mrs Nixon."

She paused. Her face reset in the expressionless look she maintained for times when they were not alone. "Would you care for some refreshments now?"

Henry looked at his daughter, now studiously trying to undo the tie at his neck.

"I think I shall dine early tonight, Mrs Nixon. I shall eat with Laura and then perhaps I shall retire early as well. I've had a busy day." He met Flora's expressionless gaze. "I need a good night's sleep."

"Very well, Mr Wiltshire. Will you eat in the kitchen or the dining room?"

Henry paused. When Charles was away Henry often ate in the kitchen with Flora and Laura. It was always a happy occasion.

"The dining room."

She gave a slight inclination of her head. "I will have it ready for you soon."

Henry watched sadly as Flora made her way steadily back along the hall. He lamented the day Charles had brought Edith Ferguson into their lives. She had ruined everything.

Thirty-five

William stood in front of the golden wattle arch and waited for his bride. The scent of the little yellow flowers was so strong it had set the reverend sneezing and they'd had to move slightly forward of the pollen-laden decoration.

Robert had built the arch while Thomas went off in the cart the previous day to gather the wattle the two men had then woven through the structure. Inside the house were several bunches of wildflowers Millie and the little children had gathered. The rain that had fallen several months back now had been enough to encourage some flowers

Once more William put his finger inside the collar of the new white shirt Millie had made for him. It was mid-morning but already quite warm even though they had some shade from the house. He glanced around at the small group of family and friends gathered: Clem and Jessie holding baby Haji, and Hegarty looking the cleanest William had ever seen him in a brown shirt and trousers held up by a new pair of blue and tan striped suspenders. Millie and the two little girls, wearing their best dresses, stood with Robert, who was also looking very smart and was holding

Matthew in his arms. Georgina had asked Thomas if he would walk with her from his cottage where she had been staying since they'd arrived at Wildu Creek two days earlier.

William wished his father could be there but he was still in the south. Millie had received a letter from him only the day before: he hoped to be home for Christmas. Neither William nor Georgina wanted to wait any longer. William had sent word to Mrs Prosser with the date and place of the marriage. He had thought she might relent and come to her only daughter's wedding but there had been no reply.

Today was to be a simple affair, apart from the golden arch and the huge morning tea Millie had prepared to follow the official ceremony. They would celebrate in a few months with a meal when his father was home again.

A murmur went through the assembled group. William shifted his gaze to the path and was rewarded by the sight of Georgina on Thomas's arm. They were walking slowly towards him. Georgina's gaze locked with his and in that moment he knew everything they'd been through no longer mattered. From this day, as he knew the reverend was about to say, they would be together as man and wife always.

"Don't you look handsome?" Georgina murmured as she reached his side.

William swallowed. His tongue felt too big for his mouth. Hegarty gave a low whistle.

"What a beautiful dress," whispered Ruth.

William took Georgina's hand and swept his gaze over her. Her hair was piled on top of her head, the curls and a small sprig of purple flowers kept in place by clips, and she wore the lace dress she'd worn the night he'd proposed, which made her look as if she belonged in a palace rather than on a cattle run. "You are beautiful," he said.

"Luckily Mother sent the case of clothes I hadn't unpacked from my trip to Hawker or I might have been wearing a pair of riding trousers."

"It wouldn't have mattered." He leaned closer. "You'd still be beautiful."

"Are you ready to begin?" The reverend gave them an encouraging smile and in a very short time they were husband and wife.

William took Georgina in his arms and kissed her until they both gasped for breath and Hegarty's whistle became a loud shrill. The younger children cheered and Robert gave a loud whoop, which startled Haji so much he began to cry. Adding her laughter to the commotion, Millie ushered them inside. William wrapped an arm around Georgina and they followed the group to the large dining room that was rarely used but was decorated with wild-flowers for the wedding day. The table was covered with a white cloth and loaded with food.

"Are you expecting shearers as well, Millie?" William put his other arm around his stepmother.

"I'll pack some for you to take with you. You won't need to worry about cooking for a few days." She gave them a cheeky smile then left them to supervise the morning tea.

William was pleased to see her look so happy. Her anxious expression was banished today.

Beth and Ruth came and wanted to touch the lace of Georgina's dress. She happily obliged them, bending down to show them the layers.

"Robert and I will stay on here for a few days." Hegarty stood on William's other side, plate loaded with food already in his hand. "Clem will start back tomorrow and check cattle along the way. I've all but finished working on the wagon at Smith's Ridge, so I thought I'd stay here and help Robert with the finishing touches to the Wildu Creek one." He gave William a wink. "Once that's done we'll set off for the mines. You won't see much of us for a while."

"Thanks, Hegarty." They'd discussed the transport business extensively in the last week. Now that William was a married man it had been decided Robert and Hegarty would be the ones to set off with the wagons. In the current climate Clem and William would manage Smith's Ridge between them. William hoped once Albie felt stronger they could also find him work on the property.

Hegarty shoved one of Millie's small savoury tarts in his mouth. "These are good," he mumbled. "You'd better eat. You need to keep your strength up." He gave him a nudge.

William was grateful for the older man's help. He'd been a good friend to Joseph and now to Joseph's son. Thanks to his thoughtfulness, William and Georgina would have a few days at the Smith's Ridge house almost by themselves, with Albie off in the shearer's quarters, and Clem and Jessie likely confining themselves to their hut during the honeymoon.

Ruth and Beth had finished admiring Georgina's dress and as she stood he kissed her. "Ready to go?"

"This fellow's in a hurry to get his bride home."

Georgina's cheeks went pink as Hegarty burst into raucous laughter and belted William on the back.

Charles left his horse tethered in the trees a distance from the Smith's Ridge homestead and made his way closer on foot. Johanna had told him the day and place of Baker's wedding so he was fairly sure there would be no-one there, but he was being cautious. Someone might have stayed behind. No tell-tale smoke puffed from chimneys, and doors and gates were closed. The hens were shut in their yard, only a few horses stood patiently in the small paddock and there was no sign of the cart he knew William owned.

Feeling more confident, Charles walked up the path towards the house, past rows of vegetables, and came to a stop at the door. At one end of the verandah the space was enclosed with what he assumed was the wash house. At the other end a bed sat in the corner, a blanket folded at one end and some hessian draped from the verandah roof as a crude privacy curtain.

He lifted his hand to knock then thought better of it and pushed the door open. It scraped on the rough floor and opened into a kitchen. It was a big space with a large oven in the fireplace and a solid table and chairs. Utensils were hung above the mantle or were neatly stacked on benches. No fire burned in the grate and there was an empty ring to his footsteps on the floor.

He opened a side door. It led to a bedroom where there was evidence of male habitation. He closed the door and went into the big front room, where two more doors opened off. Once more his footsteps echoed on the bare wooden floor. He marvelled at Georgina's acceptance of this crude house after the luxury of his home in Hawker and even the much better structure and furnishings of her family home.

The first door he opened revealed a bedroom that was simply furnished with two single beds and looked unused. It was the front bedroom that drove a stab of envy through his chest. It had definitely benefited from a woman's touch.

The curtains were drawn, but the fabric was not heavy enough to block the brightness of the midday light. The double bed looked freshly made and a blue day gown hung on the hook behind the door. He slid his fingers down the silky fabric. Several items of lady's clothing — Georgina's — hung from a rail that extended along one wall, but there were no male items and only two pairs of lady's shoes sat neatly side by side below it. The third bedroom had obviously been inhabited by a man; perhaps that was William's attempt at being a gentleman.

Charles drew in a breath. The room itself had a scent he recognised. He lifted his head and inhaled deeply. Once more the pain stabbed at him. Violets.

He crossed the room in two strides and picked a small china bottle from the dresser where several little glass dishes held assorted jewellery. He put the bottle to his nose then flung out his arm. How he'd like to smash it. Georgina would rue the day she turned her back on him: Charles would make sure of it. He carefully replaced the bottle, gave the room one more cursory glance and retraced his steps.

He looked in each room again but nothing stood out to him as a likely option for sabotage. Outside, the bright sunlight assaulted his eyes. He pulled down the brim of his hat and looked around. Smith's Ridge had not been his intended destination, yet there he was. He'd paid Mrs Prosser a courtesy visit on his way back from the mine, and the poor woman had been distraught, telling him Georgina was going ahead with her foolhardy marriage to William Baker. The idea had come to him then that perhaps he could have some sweet revenge on William and Georgina, do something they would never suspect as foul play but which would cause them pain.

His inspection took him in the direction of the shearing shed and in its shadow was a wagon. Someone had obviously been working on it. Some of the wheel struts were new and the side rails had been given a coat of paint. He looked from the new timber to the grey of the old struts. Several tools were stacked beside a chopping block. Charles gave a self-satisfied smile. One of them was a saw. He slipped off his jacket and laid it on the ground under the wheel, then he picked up the saw, lowered himself to the jacket and began to work.

It didn't take him long to be content that once this wagon was loaded, the struts would eventually give way and break. The cuts he'd made were unevenly spaced, so he hoped the wood would snap in jagged lines rather than look as if they'd been cut through.

Charles dusted himself off and shook out his jacket. It would be a small victory but he felt sure only one of many barbs he would poke in William's side. He looked around. The ground was already well scattered with sawdust so he didn't think the extra he had made would be noticed. He replaced the saw and, feeling rather pleased with himself, he turned his back on the hovels of Smith's Ridge and headed back to his horse. He pulled his handkerchief from his pocket as he walked and mopped his brow.

"What are you doing there?"

The yell startled Charles. He glanced back over his shoulder and saw a man way back across the yard near the shearing shed. He was waving a rifle.

Charles ran. The thud of his heart in his chest drummed in his ears. He crossed the space to the trees where he'd left his horse and almost dropped his jacket in his haste to climb into the saddle. He galloped away expecting to hear the sound of a shot at any moment, but none came.

He looked back but there were trees behind him now. He'd been lucky the man, whoever he was, hadn't discovered him when he'd been in the house or, even worse, sawing the wagon-wheel struts.

Once he was sure there was no-one in pursuit, Charles eased his horse back to a trot and took some calming breaths. He had his own wedding to prepare for and it was to be a grand affair. Henry had wanted to keep it small but Charles had insisted on a celebration the district wouldn't forget. Even Mrs Prosser had been invited. He would show Georgina, whose own mother hadn't attended her rushed nuptials, what she had given up to become Mrs William Baker.

Thirty-six

William woke to the sweet smell of violets and the soft warmth of Georgina in his arms. Beyond the curtain there was only a gentle lightening of night to day. It was early and he'd awoken with the feeling of a man who'd slept well. He eased over to the edge of the bed and an arm wrapped around his chest.

"Where are you going?" Georgina's voice was husky from sleep.

He rolled back and kissed her nose. "To work."

She opened one eye. "But it's early."

"Clem and Albie have been good about giving us some time to ourselves but we can't stay inside forever."

Georgina pushed him back. He let her and held her in his arms as she rolled on top of him. "We've a lot of lost time to make up for, William Baker."

"We have."

"Surely we can stay in bed just a little longer this morning."

She traced a finger lazily down his cheek to his lips.

"We've already spent a lot of time in this bed."

Her eyes sparkled. "Are you complaining?"

His hands moved over her back, adjusting her body to fit snugly against his. It had only been two nights since their wedding, but he already knew every little inch of her. "No."

"That's just as well, because there's something you need to do before you leave this room." Her gaze held his and then she slowly lowered her lips to his. William returned her kiss and pressed her even closer. He closed his eyes, thoughts of the work that needed doing already banished as his body responded to her caress.

The sun was a golden ball above the ridge before William finally stepped out his back door to face the day. Georgina was beside him and they set off along the path towards Clem's hut.

Jessie was hanging clothes on the line. She smiled shyly at their approach. "Good morning."

"It's a beautiful one." Georgina smiled back and bent down to play with Haji, who was propped up in a basket at Jessie's feet.

"Is Clem here?" William asked.

"No, he's checking waterholes. I don't expect him back until this evening."

William glanced towards the horse yards. He'd only had brief conversations with his friend over the last two days. He and Jessie had kept away from the house.

"I hope he'll be home for dinner," Georgina said. "I'm cooking for all of us tonight."

"You don't have to," Jessie said.

"I insist." Georgina stood up. "William tells me I must be more sociable."

He met the cheeky look she gave him. "Is that what I said?"

"It will be lovely to have a woman's company, Jessie."

"And there are plans to be made." He ignored his wife's teasing. "We can do that over the meal."

The women discussed food and William's gaze was drawn to Albie, who was slowly making his way back from the direction of the hen house, a bowl in his hands.

William met him at the gate. Albie nodded in response to his greeting and lifted the bowl full of eggs.

"Hens are still laying well." His hands trembled.

"That's good. Sounds like the ladies are planning on some extra cooking."

Georgina joined them. "Thank you, Albie." She took the bowl he offered. "We haven't seen you since we got back. How are you feeling?"

"Better thank you, Miss ... Mrs Georgina."

She put a hand on his shaky arm. "Please call me Georgina. It's easier."

Albie lowered his gaze.

"I'm going to repair the fence beyond the shearing shed," William said. "Do you feel up to helping me, Albie?"

"I do, but first," he patted his pocket, "I've got something for you." He pulled out a roughly folded handkerchief. "While you were away there was a man here."

"Who?" William looked at Albie, mildly curious. "What did he want?"

"I don't know what he was doing." Albie shrugged. "I saw him as he was walking away from the side of the shearing shed. I called out to him and he bolted like a rabbit." Albie raised the handkerchief. "He dropped this."

Georgina gasped and took the handkerchief from Albie. "The monogram." She held it out to William.

He read the blue lettering on the white cotton. "*CW?*"

A small frown creased Georgina's brow. "Charles Wiltshire."

"The devil." William looked immediately to Jessie, who had pressed a hand to her mouth. "Don't worry, Jessie. I'm sure it would be nothing to do with you." He turned back to Georgina. "But why would he be here?"

"I don't know." She gripped his arm. "But you can be sure it would be nothing good."

"You don't have any ideas, Albie?" William asked.

"I was up the hill trying to shoot a rabbit for my dinner." Albie's shoulders drooped. "If it wasn't for this leg … I'm sorry I couldn't catch him."

"He would have been too slippery for any of us," William said.

"I've had a good look around since he was here. Don't know if anything's missing but nothing looks disturbed. Don't know what he might have been up to."

"At least you saw him and we know he was here," Georgina said. She put a hand on Jessie's arm. "He was probably simply snooping."

A prickling sensation ran across William's shoulders. Charles was spoiled, and he'd been scorned. There was no telling what he might do to exact some revenge. Once more William's gaze swept over the sheds and back to the house further down the slope. He didn't like Wiltshire having been there while they were away. "I don't trust him at all."

Clem was back by late afternoon and Georgina had just called them to wash up for dinner when the sound of horses brought them all outside. Rumbling across the yard was the Wildu Creek wagon drawn by six horses. Robert and Hegarty were riding either side of it. They both gave big waves as they approached.

"Two more for dinner, I think." William grinned at Georgina then strode out to meet the newcomers. "Welcome back. You're just in time to share our meal."

"That's good news." Hegarty lowered his big frame from his horse.

Robert leaned down to shake William's hand. "We'll see to these animals and be in."

It was a merry group that sat around the big table in the front room at Smith's Ridge that night. Georgina and Jessie had cooked a huge meal. William marvelled that even with low stores they had come up with delicious and sufficient food. It was good to be back together again, even if it meant he and Georgina would no longer have the house to themselves. Although if Hegarty and Robert journeyed to the mines with the wagons, they would rarely be home.

"Are you planning to set off soon?" William asked.

"We've only just arrived," Hegarty chuckled. "We'll try not to get in your way."

William raised his eyebrows. "I'm not trying to get rid of you. I simply want to know your plans."

"We will leave day after next," Robert said.

"That soon?" Georgina stood to gather the plates. "We shall have to do more cooking to send with you."

"Is our wagon ready?" William asked.

"I had finished it before we went to Wildu Creek," Hegarty said. "The harnesses will need some oil and we will have to decide which horses we will use to pull it, but after that there's no reason to delay. The sooner we get to the mines the sooner we make some money."

"Clem and Albie and I will manage here," William said. "In light of our news today I have a job for you, Albie, if you'll accept."

"What news?" Robert asked.

"While we were away Albie found Charles Wiltshire here."

Clem took Jessie's hand. "Why would he be here?"

William shook his head. "Albie scared him off. I hope he was simply snooping."

"Why?" Clem asked.

"We don't know, but from now on one of us will stay close to home." William turned to Albie. "And I hope you might set up camp just north of Wiltshire's mining lease, Albie. I want eyes and ears up there permanently until he gives up and leaves."

"That would be a lonely job," Georgina said.

"But an important one." He gave Albie a serious look. "I'll be relying on you."

Albie grinned. "One eye don't see so good these days, but the other's as sharp as a tack, and there's nothing wrong with my hearing."

"I can help you make a hut."

"No need. I've spent enough time with native shepherds to know how to make myself a shelter."

"I'll visit you once a week with supplies."

"Plenty of rabbits up there."

"Looks like your mind is made up to go then." William held out his hand and Albie shook it.

"It is."

Later when the others had turned in, William waited for Robert to come back inside from his check on the horses.

The younger man paused at the door and gave him a wink. "Shouldn't you be in bed?"

"I will be soon enough. I wanted to make sure this carting idea is what you want."

Robert's lips pressed together and he gave a firm nod. "I said so already. I can make a real contribution."

William gripped his brother's shoulder. "Everything you've done over the years has helped. We are a family."

"Father and Grandpa said the same before I left." Robert removed the hand and cast his serious gaze over his brother. "But this is something I can put my own mark on, be my own man, and still contribute."

"Very well, as long as you're sure."

"I'm sure and anyway you've plenty of helpers. It's a pity you have to waste their efforts on looking out for Wiltshire."

"I agree but in this case the job is what Albie needs. I hope it will aid his recovery and his sense of worth."

Robert looked William in the eye once more. "A sense of worth is very important." He inclined his head. "Good night."

The next day everyone was up early. While the previous night there had been happy voices around his dinner table, William noted the mood that day was more sombre, as everyone did their part to prepare for the various journeys ahead. Even Haji, who was normally a happy baby, grizzled to be held. Luckily Georgina was only too glad to take him from Jessie from time to time.

William planned to travel with Albie to help him make camp near Wiltshire's claim. He was loading their cart with supplies when he noticed Georgina pacing the backyard, jiggling Haji in her arms. She was singing to him softly as she walked.

"Your wife is keen to be a mother." Clem came up beside him.

"Looks that way." William lifted a bundle of wire onto the cart. He anticipated the prospect of being a father just as much.

"Jessie's upset at the news Wiltshire was here."

William repositioned his hat on his head. "I don't like the idea either."

"She's still so frightened he's going to have Haji taken away."

"I know but I don't think he'd be up here snooping around if that was his plan. He'd send the protector." William looked back at Georgina still circling the garden with Haji. "Whatever it is he's up to I don't think it involves Jessie or Haji."

"I hope you're right."

"From now on you and I will make sure one of us is never far away."

Two days later, after helping Albie to organise a basic camp, William was preparing to leave.

"Thank you for doing this job." He shook the shepherd's hand. "I know it's not very exciting, but it is important."

"And no access to liquor up here."

William drew in a breath. "It might help you to recover."

"I've got plenty of liquid." Albie waved towards the barrel of water they'd just hefted into the shade of a big rock.

"This way you won't have to go to the waterhole. Keep out of sight."

"I'm grateful to you. I feel it's my fault these fellows are here looking for diamonds."

William studied the other man's scarred face. One of his eyes was partly covered by damaged skin that had healed in a rough weal, but his good eye locked on William.

"It was me who brought that man Becker and the other bloke here." Albie shifted his weight to his good leg and rubbed at the prickles on his chin. "I shouldna done it."

"I don't understand how you knew where to take them."

"I didn't. Going on what I'd heard about your father finding a diamond—"

"The worst-kept secret." William gave a wry grin.

"Yeah well I worked out this waterhole was as good a prospect as any." Albie's face twisted into a garish grin. "They're silly buggers though. I showed them the wrong place and they gave me a pile of money." His expression became sombre again. "All gone now."

William hoped his attempt at helping the shepherd to dry out and stay that way would work.

"Anyway." Albie looked back along the creek in the direction of the waterhole. "I thought they'd look around a while and when they couldn't find the special rocks they were looking for they'd leave. No harm to anyone."

"Maybe it will take a little longer. Becker's left and Wiltshire won't want to get his hands dirty. He's got those two men working the claim. Let's hope they don't find anything interesting."

Albie nodded.

"Clem or I will be back in a week. All you have to do is keep a bit of a watch. Try not to let them know you're here but it won't matter if they figure it out. This is my land and you can camp where you like."

William waved Albie goodbye and went the long way round to where the men were working. Anger raged inside him at the sight of his waterhole completely fenced off. They both stopped their work at the sound of his horse. William swallowed his anger and went no closer. These men would only be following Wiltshire's orders. There was no point remonstrating with them. Binda and Millie's family still had the spring hidden higher up in the gorge, and he only hoped the native animals that relied on this source of water would find their way to the nearest supply. The men went back to their work. William watched them from his vantage point on the bank for a little longer then headed away. He had other work to do and he was eager to get back to Georgina. Having a wife was certainly a good reason to go home.

Thirty-seven

Charles opened the door to the main bedroom. It had been his mother's domain and he'd not been in since she'd died. Henry, though, had moved his personal effects back into this front-facing chamber. The quilt was different and there was a more masculine smell to the room but everything else was the same. Minus Laura's bed, of course, which was now in the middle bedroom.

Charles crossed to the dresser but pulled up short when he realised his mother's jewellery box was no longer in its usual place on top. He looked around. The box was nowhere to be seen. He pulled open the top drawer of the dresser that used to be his mother's. His father's handkerchiefs and socks now filled the space.

"What are you looking for?"

Charles turned at the sound of his father's voice. "Mother's jewellery." He held out his hands. "I wanted to give something to Edith for our wedding."

Henry moved to where Charles still waited by the dresser and pushed the drawer shut. "I moved it to the top of Laura's wardrobe. It will all be hers one day."

"She can have it." Charles was a little miffed at his father's tone. "I only want one thing. Edith expressed an interest in the locket that Mother always wore."

"That was your grandmother's locket."

"I know, but—"

"It's been handed down in my family for generations."

"Yes, I know." Charles spoke carefully, as if to a child. "Grandmother Harriet had it given to her when she married Grandfather, and she gave it to Mother when you were married, so it seems right that Edith should have it."

"Your mother wasn't given the locket until you were born."

Charles clenched his hands. His father was being very obstinate. "Edith is to be my wife. She will be family."

"You have a sister. Neither my father nor I had other siblings. Your mother made it quite clear Laura was to have the locket."

Charles sighed. Edith had specifically asked him for the necklace, but he didn't care enough to argue further. His mother had other, more expensive pieces. "Very well. Would you select something else for Edith then? Perhaps the pearl drop necklace or the ruby bracelet?"

"I am sure I can find her something."

"Thank you, Father. We will all have dinner together tonight, a quiet evening before the festivities begin tomorrow. It would make Edith very happy if you could present it to her then."

Charles crossed to the door.

"Have you thought any more about your living arrangements for when you return from your holiday after the wedding?" Henry's voice had a plaintive ring.

Charles looked back at his father with a tinge of annoyance. "The purchase of the employee cottage next door has gone through, as you know. I will oversee its removal and the building of a new house on my return."

Henry gave a sharp sigh. "I don't know where you think the money for this is coming from. Your transport business is the only thing in the black at the moment. The shops are barely making enough to cover costs and I have no sheep left."

"Goodness, Father, don't get yourself het up. I've said it will be a modest home. We can always build on later like you did." Charles stretched his neck and tugged at the lapels of his jacket. "Besides I am quite confident Grandmother will cover the cost of the house. She said as much when she wrote about her inability to attend the wedding. Our new house is to be her wedding gift to us."

"And where are you planning to live while all this takes place?"

"Why, here, of course. Edith and I will be perfectly comfortable until our own home is complete. I am sure Mrs Nixon will appreciate having a mistress in charge of the house again."

Henry placed a hand against the dresser as if to support himself.

"Are you feeling all right, Father?"

"Yes." Henry waved his other hand in a shooing motion. "It's been a busy day. I shall have a rest before dinner."

Charles perused his father a little longer. "Very well then, I will see you at dinner." He closed the door behind him and set off down the hall to his own room. The closer it came to the wedding the more oddly his father was acting. Charles knew he liked Edith and she was very fond of his father, so it couldn't be anything sour between them. And ever since his mother's death and then the creamery closing, his father had lost confidence in his business ability. Perhaps he was simply getting too old to manage as he had in the past. Charles would have to sit down and have a good talk with him once the wedding was over. Of course then they would be busy with Christmas. January wasn't so far away. They would talk then.

In the kitchen there was a delicious smell in the air. He gave a nod to Mrs Nixon, who was peeling potatoes at the table and chatting to Laura.

"Chars." Laura's face lit up in a smile.

"Hello. I will see you later. I must get ready for dinner. What are we having, Mrs Nixon?"

"Steamed fowl."

"Wonderful."

"Mrs Prosser has arrived. She is resting in the guest room before dinner."

"Very good. Thank you, Mrs Nixon. You seem to have every-thing in hand as usual."

Mrs Nixon gave him one of her odd little smiles as he let him-self in to his bedroom. Charles shut the door and leaned back against it for a moment. He hoped that by the time he came out she would have put Laura to bed. Tonight's dinner was for adults only and he didn't want to be the one who read Laura a story if his father didn't reappear in time.

"Edith, my dear, you look … stunning." Johanna Prosser was exuberant in her welcome as Charles led Edith into the dining room. He had already told his soon-to-be wife how beautiful she looked in her off-the-shoulder, pale yellow silk dress with leg-o-mutton sleeves.

"It's lovely to see you too, Mrs Prosser." Edith let go of Charles's arm and went to Henry, who had risen from his chair at the head of the table. She planted a kiss on his cheek. "Good evening, Father." She put a hand to her mouth. "Oh, I hope that wasn't too forward of me — but I do think of you as my father now."

Charles was pleased to see his father's lips turn up in a small smile, even though he looked a little startled.

"Of course not, my dear. I am flattered by the sentiment," Henry said.

"It's such a delightful thought," Johanna said.

"Let's sit, please." Charles tucked Edith into her place at the table and took his seat next to her. Mrs Prosser sat opposite on his father's right hand. "I have been tantalised by the delicious smells coming from the kitchen for long enough."

Mrs Prosser chuckled. "Men. You think of nothing but your stomachs. At least you will have Mrs Nixon here to continue her culinary delights, Edith. I do so miss Mrs Donovan's presence in my kitchen at Prosser's Run."

"I don't know why you stay there alone, Mrs Prosser," Edith said.

"Well, I'm not exactly alone, my dear, but where else would I go? My daughter has abandoned me." Johanna's lip trembled.

Charles flinched at her words. He didn't want to be reminded of Georgina the night before his wedding.

"Oh, dear Mrs Prosser," Edith said. "If only you were my mother. Why I would expect you to live with me."

"What a lovely sentiment." Johanna patted Henry's hand. "How lucky you are, Henry, to be gaining such a thoughtful daughter-in-law."

"How are you managing out at Prosser's Run, Johanna?"

"I am finding I'm quite busy. Mr Swan reports to me every morning and I am cooking for everyone."

"You should have a housekeeper."

"Yes, Georgina said the same, but we are so far from town. And ... well the drought is taking its toll."

"You are not alone in having to tighten your purse." Henry gave Charles a pointed look.

"You have something for Edith, don't you, Father?" Charles was keen to steer the course of the conversation away from money matters. His father was already watching every penny spent on the wedding.

"Yes." Henry turned to Edith. He reached into his trouser pocket and drew out a small velvet bag. "I thought you might like something that belonged to Catherine. I went through her jewels and found you this."

"Oh thank you, Father." Edith bounced in her seat as she reached for the bag.

Charles smiled proudly.

She tugged at the ribbon and the contents slid into her hand. He saw a small frown crease her brow. She lifted a bracelet for him to see: brightly coloured glass beads dangled from it.

"It was one of Catherine's favourites and I thought it well suited to you, my dear."

A flicker of disappointment crossed Edith's face.

"Let me help you put it on." Charles reached for the bracelet and clipped it to Edith's wrist.

She smiled and lifted her arm for the others to see.

"How pretty," Johanna said.

"Very." Edith turned to Henry. "Thank you."

Charles knew his father was doing his best but it was the least favourite of his mother's jewellery. The colours of the glass were bright and garish. Charles didn't recall her wearing it often.

He hoped Edith would be satisfied with the bracelet. She had become very demanding of late, but all that was forgotten when they were alone. In those rare opportunities she would allow him to nibble on her ears, trail kisses down her neck and even fondle her breasts. He couldn't wait for their marriage to be conducted the next day. Just thinking about what the night would bring was tantalisingly painful.

Mrs Nixon arrived at that moment with vegetable soup, and Charles concentrated on filling his stomach. Tomorrow night that would be the last thing on his mind.

Thirty-eight

February 1900

William lowered his axe and wiped the sweat from his brow. Even though it was almost dark the early February heat was punishing. He turned at the sound of horses and peered into the cloud of dust that accompanied a horse-drawn wagon with a man riding beside it. Robert waved at him as he guided the wagon to a stop at the back of the house. William laid the axe against the wood pile and reached his brother as he swung down from his horse.

"What are you doing here?"

"It's good to see you too, brother." Robert accepted William's handshake with a grin.

"It's only been a month since you were home for Christmas." William held his taller brother at arm's length. "I didn't think you'd be back for several months."

"That was the plan but I had some trouble with the wagon."

William glanced back at the wagon, which he could see was loaded with new wheels.

"This is my first load in nearly a month," Robert said. "I've spent all my time and money on repairs."

"Robert!"

They both looked around at Georgina's excited call.

"You'd better come inside. Georgina will want to feed you and you can tell us all about what's happened."

"It's so good to see you." Georgina wrapped Robert in a hug then let him go quickly. "You two wash your hands and then come inside. I want to hear all the news."

William smiled at her retreating back. Georgina was not one to fuss but she liked him to be clean when he came inside. No doubt Robert smelled worse than he did.

"How's everyone else?" Robert asked as they walked towards the wash house.

"Clem and Jessie and Haji are well. They're camped out with the cattle in the north paddock. The summer has been relentless. It's getting harder and harder to find feed and water."

"It's the same where I've been."

"Albie is managing in his role as mine watcher." William smiled as he thought of his recent trip to take his spy supplies and fresh water. "He's taken the job very seriously. Says the two fellows know he's there but he doesn't let them see him. Reckons he's got them a bit spooked."

"But they're still there?"

"Yes. Wiltshire must be paying them well."

"Work is hard to come by."

In the kitchen Georgina had already set the table. "Sit down. I've got cold rabbit pie and some fresh bread." She put the food in front of them and took her place next to William.

He said grace then turned straight to Robert. "So what happened to the wagon?"

Robert spoke through a mouthful of pie. "A wheel gave way. Simply crumpled under the weight of the load. When it tipped the main shaft broke. I'm only thankful none of the horses were injured."

"Hegarty only fixed the spokes just before you set off."

"I know. Luckily he was with me when it happened. The cart tipped right over and the load went everywhere."

"Oh, Robert." Georgina gave him a searching look. "You could have been killed. Were you hurt?"

"Only my pride and a few bumps and scratches. It took Hegarty and me all day to gather up the load again. There were logs and chains and barrels in all directions. Some of the barrels were broken, of course. With that and repairing the wagon and not being able to work for nearly a month it's been tough."

"And Hegarty?" William asked.

"Once we retrieved the goods and found space on other wagons, he continued as well. No point in both of us being laid up."

"So the wagon is fixed now?" Georgina slipped another piece of pie on Robert's plate. He had managed to down the first piece in between talking.

"Yes. Thankfully the accident happened close to Hawker. I was able to get what I needed from the blacksmith there. It's his load I'm carrying now for a farmer further south, but I thought I'd take a detour and visit you." He smiled at Georgina. "I could only bring a few supplies. Mr Garrat said my credit was good."

"You shouldn't worry about us," Georgina said. "We're managing. Not much seems to survive this drought but there are still rabbits."

"You make them taste good too." Robert scooped the last piece of pie into his mouth.

"I am concerned about the wheel," William said. "That wagon has served us faithfully for years. Perhaps the new struts Hegarty put in weren't strong enough."

"They didn't break. It was the older struts. We think they must have had wear we couldn't see."

"How do you know it won't happen again?" Georgina asked.

"I've got all new wheels." He sighed. "It will take me a while to repay the blacksmith but he was very good to me."

"Not quite what we'd hoped for," William said.

"No." Robert lifted his gaze from his empty plate. "And do you know what the worst of it was? Not long after the wagon rolled and Hegarty and I were still assessing the damage ..." Robert paused and glanced at Georgina. "Charles Wiltshire came along with one of his wagons. He didn't stop but we could hear his laugh echoing in our ears as he went past."

Georgina shook her head. "He's an ass," she murmured.

William looked to the window. It was a dark night with no moon. Georgina had the window pushed right open but there was no breeze and the room was warm. Even so a chill wriggled down his back. "Wiltshire was here while we were all at Wildu Creek for our wedding." He shifted his gaze back to Robert. "He would have had opportunity."

"As I said Charles is an ass but do you think him capable of sabotage?" Georgina asked.

William met her worried look. "I think he's capable of anything."

Robert shook his head. "But how could him being here back in October make a wheel fall off three months later?"

"I don't know. But Albie saw him near the wagon. If he did do something to the wheel struts it might take quite a while for them to wear through. He wouldn't be sure when the damage would occur."

"I can't believe it," Georgina said.

William rubbed at his jaw. "And we have no proof. Just a strong feeling."

"It is not outside his capabilities," Robert said. "I have been in and out to Hawker several times in the last month and my camp was close to the road. I've spoken to plenty of teamsters, hawkers and travellers. I've heard a lot of stories about the Wiltshires, several of them not so noble."

Georgina stood to collect their plates. "Do we have to talk about them? Surely you have other news?"

Robert raised his eyebrows and put on a pensive look. "Bicycles seem to be the popular thing these days. And not just around Hawker. One day at my camp I was passed by two shearers heading out of town."

"On bicycles?" William couldn't imagine it.

"Give me a horse any day," Georgina chuckled.

"Yes, it seems bicycles are as tricky as horses for ladys' skirts. One poor woman fell from hers outside the blacksmith shop the other day. Her skirt had caught in the chain. She was cut and bruised and the skirt ruined."

"Hmm," William said. "Any other news besides ladys' skirts?"

Robert glanced at Georgina again. "There's Mr Garrat's problems but even that's connected to the Wiltshires."

"Of course." Georgina shook her head. "Would you like some stewed apples and cream? Our poor cow is still managing to produce a little milk."

"Thank you."

"What's happened with Garrat?" William asked while Georgina served their dessert.

"He's been in court."

"Why?" Georgina asked.

"Evidently his licence is only for a cart to carry around the goods he sells. He has been using his wagon and travelling further. There is a different licence for wagons. He's had to pay a fine."

"What has that to do with the Wiltshires?" William asked.

"It was Charles Wiltshire who put in the report."

Georgina gave a soft snort and took a mouthful of her food.

"Trouble is, you know how Garrat gives so much credit and there are those who can never pay him back?"

"He's a kind and generous man," William said.

"Trying to do business next to the Wiltshires, who have always done their best to undermine him, has been bad enough but I think the fine has been a real blow for him. There's no sign of the drought letting up and people can't pay. He told the blacksmith he was thinking of closing his shop and heading south."

"So everyone would have to shop at Wiltshire's?" Georgina put her spoon down with a thump.

"And where will the natives get supplies?" Robert said. "Mr Garrat was always happy to open his door to everyone."

"There is another grocer and the general store with the saddlery," William said.

"But they don't have the same variety of goods as Mr Garrat," Georgina said.

"Or the Wiltshires." Robert grimaced. "I can see Charles rubbing his hands with glee. And that new wife of his, Edith. She's as bad as he is."

"I can't believe he married her," Georgina said. "I'm sure he would think a shop assistant beneath him."

"Well his father agrees with you, by all accounts. Evidently there's no love lost between Henry and the new Mrs Wiltshire. Mrs Garrat told me their wedding was a very grand affair and there was talk of nothing else until Christmas."

"Gave people something to take their mind off the drought, I suppose," William said.

"Money doesn't ever seem to be a problem for them," Robert said. "Charles is building a new house next door to his family home. It's not as big but you can bet it will be one day."

"His grandmother's money, no doubt," Georgina said. "He was always wheedling her support for his schemes."

"Perhaps that's how he continues to fund his mining venture."

"Oh." Georgina put her hands to her head. "Here we are back to talking about the Wiltshires again."

"How about this?" William grinned at the two faces watching him closely. "Why don't we set up our own shop?"

"In Hawker?" Robert and Georgina spoke in unison.

"No, here at Smith's Ridge."

"You wouldn't have many customers." Robert chuckled.

"Not for customers but for us. I've been thinking for some time we should set up our own store. Now that you and Hegarty have the wagons going you could bring enough supplies to last us much longer. You could do a run to Adelaide or Port Augusta. And we could have things sent up by train. We can be our own supplier."

Georgina put her head to one side. "Where would you keep all these supplies?"

"We could enlarge the cellar and build a separate room over the top of it."

"You've really been thinking seriously about this?" Robert said.

"I have."

"It will give us something to work on." Georgina put her hands on William's shoulders, leaned over and kissed his cheek.

Once more he had cause to bless the day she became his wife. Already she had helped him in so many ways. He was a lucky man.

"I think it's a good idea," she said.

"Although extending the cellar is probably not such a good idea at the moment," Robert said. "The ground will be like rock."

"We can build the room to go over the top first," William said. "It will need lining and shelving."

"Perhaps we could supply Wildu Creek as well," Georgina said.

"They could get the items from us at cost price. And even Prosser's Run."

Georgina's hands left William's shoulders as soon as he spoke. "My mother would not give up buying from the Wiltshires." Her look was grim.

"But it might be a way to bring some reconciliation."

"My mother made it quite clear she wanted nothing more to do with me. I know you want to mend things between us but there are some things that can never be repaired." Georgina gave him a sad smile. "I think I will go to bed now. You two can talk. Good night, Robert."

Once she had left the room and the door closed behind her, Robert spoke. "I saw Mrs Prosser while I was in Hawker. She looked rather sad as she wandered along the street. She was passing the time looking in shop windows."

"They are both stubborn women. I had hoped that once the dust had settled on our marriage time would repair their relationship."

"Dust." Robert slapped his thigh. "Speaking of which, did you have that storm that went through Hawker two weeks back? No-one could be outside. It was lucky I was in town and not out at my camp by the wagon."

William only half listened as Robert went on to describe the dust storm that had also swept across Smith's Ridge. It bothered him that Georgina had given up not only her inheritance to be with him but also the support of her mother. Mrs Prosser had already lost two sons and her husband. He had to think of a way to bring the two women back together.

Thirty-nine

March 1900

Edith was awoken by a warm hand sliding down her stomach and tugging up her nightdress. She opened one eye and took in the smug look on her husband's face. She bit back a sigh. His eyes weren't even open. He was probably dreaming. Charles had an insatiable appetite for her body and, while she'd quickly learned what he liked her to do best and discovered some enjoyment from their lovemaking herself, the mornings were her least favourite time for his attentions.

He rolled towards her and from the hardness pressing into her leg she knew there would be no getting away from her wifely duty that morning.

She opened her eyes wider as he slipped his tongue around her nipple and let out a gasp.

"You like that, my—"

"No, Charles, stop," she hissed. "Laura is here." She pointed towards the end of the bed, where his little sister was curled up like a cat, fast asleep.

Charles sat up. "I'm going to get a lock for our door," he growled and flung back to the bedsheet. Even though summer was behind them the weather was still too warm to warrant anything more.

"Shh!" Edith cautioned. "You are wearing no bedclothes. Don't wake her." She sucked in her lips to swallow her giggle as Charles slid from the bed to pull on his trousers. This time the usually annoying Laura had been quite useful.

"She must have had a bad dream."

"Why doesn't she go to Father's room?" he hissed.

"She probably did, but perhaps he wasn't there?"

"What do you mean wasn't there?" Charles snatched his shirt from the hook and slipped his arms into the sleeves. "Where else would he be?"

"I don't know." Edith was not yet ready to tell her husband about his father's affair with his housekeeper. That would come in useful one day. What did amuse her was that Charles was completely unaware of his father's liaison. "Sometimes he stays out late. It must be hard for him with us under his roof. How much longer do you think the house will take?"

"The builder has made slow progress in this heat, and Grandmother has not been as quick with the money as I expected."

Edith lowered her lashes and curved her lips in a pout. "It's because of me." She sniffed. "She doesn't like me."

"Of course she does, but even in Adelaide the effects of this drought have meant tightening of belts. She doesn't have as much spare money as in the past."

"I'm sure she would find it if you had married Georgina."

His eyes darkened and Edith realised she'd pushed him too far.

"Don't mention her name. It's bad enough we still have to entertain her mother from time to time."

"I'm sorry, dearest. Please don't be cross." Edith rolled to the edge of the bed and knelt forward so she could reach him. Her hands slid down his arms to his hands and she drew him to her.

"Imagine when we move to our own home. We wouldn't have to have visitors we didn't want." She brushed her lips across his, then nibbled on his ear. "There would be no-one to bother us." She trailed her fingers down his shirtfront to where it tucked into his trousers and drew slow circles. "No interruptions."

Charles closed his eyes and drew in a sharp breath. "I must pay them a visit again today. See if I can't hurry things along." He wrapped his arms around her and lifted her against him. He groaned as she wriggled her hips.

"Shh, Charles." Edith put her finger to her lips. "Put me down. I want to dress before the little miss wakes up."

Charles released her to the floor and with one last glower at his sleeping sister he left the room.

Edith pursed her lips in a smug smile. They must have their own home as soon as possible. Not that she wanted to leave this one but if she couldn't have the front bedroom, as she'd suggested to Charles, and they were to have his irritating little sister with them at every turn, she wanted a place of her own. She took her shirt and skirt from the wardrobe and turned slowly to take in the room. It was a lovely house and eventually it would be hers, but having Charles to herself in their own new house next door would do for now.

Flora was stirring something on the stove as Charles shut the door carefully behind him.

"Good morning, Mr Charles," she said. "Sleep well?"

"Yes. Is breakfast ready? I must make an early start."

"Your father is already in the dining room. I'll bring the por-ridge out now."

Charles gave a nod and made his way along the hall.

"Good morning, Father," he said as he sat on the chair furthest from the window. Even though it was early, the sun was already hot on the glass. His father preferred the curtains open, but his mother would not have been pleased to see the bright sunlight on her furnishings.

Henry glanced from over the top of the newspaper and returned to his reading.

Mrs Nixon came in with the porridge. While she was busy setting out their breakfast Henry folded his paper and put it to one side.

"Were you out last night, Father?" Charles placed several dollops of porridge in his bowl.

"No. I retired early."

"Would you like hot or cold milk, Mr Charles?" Mrs Nixon had a jug in each hand.

"Cold." Charles frowned. "But I can do it." He took the jug and looked around her to his father. "Edith and I had Laura in our bed. I thought perhaps she'd tried you first and you weren't there."

Henry coughed and cleared his throat. "I was in all night. Perhaps she had a bad dream and you were her first thought. Or Edith — a more maternal figure."

"That's all very well." Charles glanced at Mrs Nixon, who appeared to be hovering in the doorway. "Did you want something?"

"Eggs," she said. "Will either of you require eggs?"

"No, thank you," Charles said.

His father shook his head, looking a little odd. Finally, Mrs Nixon left them alone.

"Now, about Laura." Charles drew himself up. "I'm a newly married man. I can't have her bursting in whenever she pleases. I'm going to have to put a lock on the door."

"Very well."

"What?"

"Do whatever you please, Charles."

"Yes. Well I will." Charles studied his father. He looked older somehow, sad. Maybe the talk of being newly married had conjured up reminders of his own marriage. Henry was only fifty-one and quite fit. Not ready for his grave yet. "Have you thought about marrying again, Father?"

Henry had just put a spoonful of porridge in his mouth and he coughed and spluttered.

"Are you all right?"

Henry patted at his mouth with a napkin. "Yes," he croaked.

"I wondered about Mrs Prosser. She's on her own and you're—"

"I don't need you to arrange my life, thank you, Charles. I am perfectly happy with the way it is." Henry stared at him across the table. "Although it's obvious we would all be more comfortable if you were to have your own house." He placed his napkin back in his lap and picked up his spoon. "Is there any chance that might be soon?"

"You can see for yourself the house is a long way from finished." Charles resumed eating his porridge.

"Perhaps I should have a word with the builder. I did have some success keeping them on task with this house."

"I can do it, Father."

The door burst open behind them and Laura tumbled into the room, with Edith following. Laura flew into her father's arms.

"Good morning, my darling." He kissed the top of her head. "I think you've grown overnight. How old are you again?"

Laura held up her fingers. "Four."

"Is that so? I thought it was your birthday next month. Did I miss it?"

Laura giggled.

"You will be such a big girl you will be able to begin piano lessons." Henry lifted her to his hip as he stood. "You're still in your bedclothes. We'd better go and find Mrs Nixon." He crossed the room, barely acknowledging Edith as he passed.

Charles saw the sweet smile his wife gave in return. She really did her best. He thought his father would have come round by now.

Charles rose and kissed her cheek. "It seems we can have our breakfast alone." He pulled out a chair for her.

"I really don't know what I've done to make him dislike me so."

"He doesn't dislike you." Charles resumed his seat. "He's simply not used to us being married. I think having us in the house so happy together brings back memories of Mother."

"He didn't seem to mourn her for long. Did they have a very happy marriage?"

Charles thought about his parents and their separate living arrangements. Perhaps they had been happy until Laura came along.

"My mother never regained her health after she had Laura."

"But surely her weak heart was what caused her demise?"

"I suppose so." Charles recalled his life before and after his sister's arrival. "But I am certain having Laura didn't help."

"Do you think I could also have piano lessons?"

"Of course, my love. I didn't know you were interested in the piano."

"I used to play a little before ... well, once my parents died there was no opportunity."

"Then you shall resume your lessons whenever you wish."

"Did you ask him about the locket?"

Charles frowned. Edith had asked him several times to get the blasted locket. Usually when they were about to make love and he said anything to stop her talking. "There's no point, my love."

"Surely one locket is not too much to ask."

"You have the bracelet, and I will buy you a locket of your own."

"But that one is so pretty and delicate — it's a family heirloom. I think as your wife I should be the one to wear it."

"Father says Mother left her jewellery to Laura so I suspect that's why he's being—"

"Obtuse?"

"Cautious." He smiled. "Please don't fuss, Edith. I will make sure you have plenty of your own jewellery once things improve."

She sighed and poured herself some tea.

Flora came in to collect the plates.

"Will you be requiring anything more, Mrs Wiltshire?"

"No thank you, Mrs Nixon. Bread and jam is enough for me this morning."

Charles picked up the newspaper his father had been reading as Flora carried the plates to the door.

"Just a moment, Mrs Nixon." Edith said. "I'd like to discuss the evening meal."

"I haven't been to the shop yet, Mrs Wiltshire. I can let you know what we're having once I get back."

"I'll be at work."

"Don't worry then." Mrs Nixon gave a demure smile. "It will be a nice surprise for you when you get home."

Flora turned on her heel and left the room.

Charles heard the conversation but it was the click of his wife's tongue that made him look up.

"I am meant to be the mistress of this house and Flora carries on as if I am not even here."

"That's the way Flora's used to. Mother let her manage the house as she saw fit."

He smiled at his wife through gritted teeth and stood. He was tired of all these petty squabbles. "I will be gone all day. I will speak with the builder and then I have several meetings. Two of my wagons are due back in town today and I want to check on them. I could be late for dinner."

He bent to kiss her cheek and she turned suddenly and pushed her lips against his. She tasted of mulberry jam.

"I hope you won't be too tired when you return, my love," she murmured.

Charles's heart beat faster in his chest and he set off to visit the builder with a sense of urgency in his step. The sooner they had their own house the better life would be.

Forty

January 1901

The rousing sounds of the brass band reverberated around the packed crowd in the Institute Hall. The gentlemen and ladies of Hawker and districts were dressed in their finest and fanning themselves with their programs against the close heat of the hall as the band came to its closing crescendo.

The last of the clapping faded and the chatter of happy voices ensured the sudden silence didn't linger. Georgina turned to William, her pretty green eyes bright with delight.

"Wasn't that wonderful?"

"Certainly was."

"A rousing way to welcome the new year and celebrate our Federation."

William was relieved to see the happiness in her gaze. Summer had begun early after a cold dry winter. Smith's Ridge, like everywhere else, was parched and they were living a listless existence. The news that both Georgina and Jessie were pregnant had lifted their spirits, but a month before Christmas Georgina had lost her baby. It had been a terrible blow. She had stoically kept herself busy with her horses, helping with the cattle and managing the house, but they had both been saddened at their loss.

It had been William who had encouraged this trip to Hawker for the district celebrations of Federation. All around the country people were holding festivities to mark the nationhood of Australia and in Hawker a grand event had been planned. That night's concert was to be followed by a ball and then the next day would be the annual sports with athletics and equestrian events. That was the other reason he had encouraged Georgina to come. She loved her horses and tomorrow she would enjoy taking part in the activities. He had booked them a room at the guesthouse and made it into a holiday.

"Shall we go outside for some air?" William put his arm around her waist. She felt so thin beneath the fabric of her vivid green dress. "I think they want to move the seats ready for the ball."

"We've never danced together before." Georgina flashed him her cheeky smile. It made his heart glad to see it. "Are you able to dance?"

"I'm afraid I'm not much good at it." There had always been dancing at home when William was a boy, but he'd rarely bothered to make the journey to town for dances as a young man.

"Then I will have to instruct you."

"I do like it when you are forthright, Mrs Baker," he murmured in her ear as they stepped out into the night air, which was hardly cooler than that in the hall.

People stood in groups chatting and laughing. William looked around and couldn't see a soul he would call more than an acquaintance.

"Look, there's Councillor Hill and his wife, Anne." Georgina indicated a couple standing not far from them. "Do you know them?"

"Not well."

"Let's say hello."

William followed and Georgina introduced him. The two women had their heads together immediately, talking like old friends. William was reminded again of what she'd given up to marry him.

"We don't see you in town very often, Mr Baker," Councillor Hill said.

"My property keeps me busy."

"And your new wife would be such an asset." The councillor smiled. "You've made a wise choice there. Georgina has always struck me as a sensible young woman unlike ... some other women her age."

William almost thought the councillor was going to add "unlike her father".

"She's certainly been a great asset to Smith's Ridge. She has a good knowledge of cattle and horses." William spoke with pride.

"No doubt you'll be blessed with children soon." The councillor leaned a little closer. "For your sake, I hope a son. I have two delightful daughters but am never master in my own home."

"I hope I don't hear you complaining, Phillip Hill." Mrs Hill gave her husband a playful tap.

"Hello." Dr Chambers came to join them. "What a great crowd and a spectacular event." He shook their hands enthusiastically. "Good to see you young people in town for it."

There was a murmur from the group nearby and they shuffled back. William caught a glimpse of Charles, with Edith on his arm, making their way to their carriage.

"No doubt retiring to change into something grand for the ball," Anne said, craning her neck to view the departing group.

Georgina looked down at her own dress. "I hadn't thought to bring another dress."

"Don't worry." Anne flicked her program back and forth to fan her face. "I don't think there are many who are indulging in such frivolity. Anyway, you look like the belle of the ball already, Georgina. Wouldn't you agree, gentlemen?"

There were murmurs of approval and William smiled to see the pink of Georgina's cheeks deepen. She flicked him a pleading look.

"We were wondering about the new shop." He changed the subject.

"The one where Garrat's was?" Dr Chambers said.

"Yes." Georgina waved her program. "We see there's a shop among the advertisements listed here, called *Best Fit in Town*, and we didn't know the name *H Collins* beside it."

"Harvey Collins has purchased Mr Garrat's shop," Councillor Hill said. "And he has already stocked it with more merchandise. I believe he's a tailor by trade, and won't be keeping food items. Only manchester, haberdashery and ready-made clothes."

"He will also be making clothes," Mrs Hill added. "Are you staying in town for a while, Georgina? You must have a look. He has some delightful items and not at the prices of the Wiltshires."

"Young Charles Wiltshire was keen to buy Garrat's place and expand his business further," Councillor Hill said. "But Henry wouldn't be in it. I think they may have overstretched themselves of late."

"That wedding must have cost a fortune." Anne shook her head. "Quite ridiculous to spend all that money when half the district hasn't got enough to put food on the table."

"And the mines are going quiet, I hear," Dr Chambers said. "The Wiltshires had several wagons carting goods."

"I have as well and we've had to find other work," William said. "Hegarty does a regular Port Augusta run now. My brother

Robert does all sorts. Lately he has been carting wheat bags full of wattle gum."

"That's fiddly work."

"He doesn't actually prise the gum from the bark. There are plenty of families doing that. It's their only income in some places. He carts the bags to the rail."

"Goodness, it's a warm night, isn't it?" Anne was once again fanning her face with her program.

Georgina smiled. "I do hope they have some punch at the refreshment tent. I am parched."

"Let me get you ladies a drink." William made his way through the groups of people to one of the tents that had been erected to supply food and drink for the revellers.

A woman stepped back just as he approached and he bumped her arm. "I'm sorry," he said as she lifted the cup of punch she held.

"No harm done."

They both looked up at the same time.

Her mouth fell open.

"Mrs Prosser," he said.

"Yes … William Baker … isn't it?"

"It is," he replied, conscious of the eyes watching them. This was the first time he'd seen his mother-in-law in several years. She had aged considerably in that time, and there was such sadness in her eyes. William took a breath. He needed to make the most of this opportunity. Already she was looking away.

"Mrs Prosser, would you be so kind as to spare me a moment?" He hoped she would not spurn him with people nearby watching them.

She lifted her head and glanced away, then her shoulders sagged. "Very well."

"Perhaps we could stroll this way." He indicated the path from the hall towards the shops. There was some moonlight to guide them as they moved away from the lanterns that adorned the hall inside and out.

Once there was some distance between them and the nearest people he stopped and turned to her. "Mrs Prosser, I'll be quick. I know I am not the son-in-law you had hoped for but I love your daughter very much."

She sighed through pursed lips but held his gaze.

"I know you love her too and even though she's being very stubborn about it I believe she wants to see you."

"And yet she is not the one saying so." She glanced behind. "I assume my daughter is here somewhere. I didn't notice her in the crowd."

"Yes, she's here, and I believe she needs your support."

"You don't know my daughter as well as you think, Mr Baker. Georgina has made it quite clear she doesn't need me for anything."

Mrs Prosser began to turn away. He put a gentle hand on her arm and she glared at him.

"We ... well at least Georgina was having a baby, but she lost it before Christmas."

Mrs Prosser put her hand to her mouth.

"She has been so sad, and our overseer's wife is with child and I think that makes it even more difficult. It would be so good for her to have a mature woman who understands these things I don't, to help her." William's words came out in a tumbled rush. "She needs you, Mrs Prosser ... she needs her mother."

He dropped his hand. Mrs Prosser continued to stare at him.

"I have a big family," he said. "I can't imagine how hard it must be for you both to not have each other in your lives."

Still the older woman didn't speak. She shook her head and William felt the bravado he'd been holding onto slide away. In the distance he heard the sound of the dance band warming up.

He put out his arm. "I'll escort you back."

"Thank you," she said, but she didn't take the arm he offered. "I am not staying for the ball. I find these events rather lonely these days." She locked her gaze on his. "It's not easy to lose a child, Mr Baker. Both my sons are dead, of course, but I also had babies who came much too early. If Georgina would like to see me I am staying at the Temperance Hotel. I will be there until the end of the week." She turned and walked away, her head held high.

William didn't know what to feel. He had permission from his mother-in-law, but now he had to convince Georgina to swallow her pride too.

The next morning there was no time to think on arranging meetings. Tired as they were from dancing half the night, they were up early to ready the horses for the day's events. Georgina had brought Bella and a dark chestnut called Carmody, who looked half carthorse and half racehorse, and who could produce great speed. He surprised everyone, including William, by carrying Georgina first over the line in the last event of the day, which had been a kind of obstacle course with a sprint at the finish.

"Well done, clever wife," he said as they led both horses back to the yard reserved for them. Georgina had two first-place ribbons and a third.

"It's these two who are clever," she said, patting first Bella and then Carmody. Georgina's laugh cut short. "What's she doing here?"

They both stopped and the horses did the same. William looked towards the yard to see Mrs Prosser sitting on a blanket over a bundle of hay. It was where he and Georgina had shared a picnic lunch earlier in the day.

"Georgina," he cautioned. "She has come to see you. Please be civil." William watched his wife carefully, wishing he'd had time to prepare her for the meeting, but realising that might have only made things worse. Perhaps Mrs Prosser arriving unannounced was the best way forward. He reached for Bella's reins. "I'll see to the horses. You speak with your mother."

Georgina's lips pursed.

"You have lost a child, my love."

She gasped and tears instantly welled in her eyes. He felt like a monster but he knew she had to make the peace.

"You both understand that loss. Don't shut each other out any longer. There must be a way forward from here."

"William," she whispered. Tears rolled freely down her cheeks. "I can't."

He put both sets of reins in one hand and his other arm around her waist and pulled her close. "Yes you can, Georgina. I'll come with you."

He walked her forward. They were slow steps and they came to a faltering halt in front of her mother.

Johanna took one look at her daughter's grief-stricken face and held out her arms. To William's great relief, Georgina fell into them.

Forty-one

July 1901

William braced himself against the biting cold of the mid-winter morning. It had been a struggle to crawl from his swag; he'd slept little. Around him there was no other movement. The natives were under their furs in their shelters. He had slept close to the camp cooking fire, which he was sure had been the only thing to stop him freezing to death.

Yesterday he had brought supplies from the store he had finally completed at Smith's Ridge. He knew food was scarce for the remaining natives. As for everyone else, it was a difficult winter. Even the rabbits had all but disappeared.

William led his horse away as the sun turned the sky a lighter shade of grey overhead. He pushed one gloved hand into his coat pocket and led Big Red around the ridges and down the gullies. He came to the edge of a dry creek bed, where he mounted and continued on his way. He had one more stop to make before he returned home. He'd been gone over a week and longed for Georgina's arms and the comfort of their bed.

He hadn't been to the bottom waterhole for some time. He'd insisted Albie leave his post overlooking Wiltshire's claim when the winter turned so bitterly cold. Now he was so close he decided to call past himself.

He came to a halt at the sight of Binda and Jundala walking towards him leading a horse loaded with bags. Both had coats; Binda's was similar to William's but Jundala's had been made from animal skins, and her feet were bare. Binda lifted his hand in a wave as they came to a stop. William dismounted.

"Are you heading to the camp?" he said as he reached them.

"Yes. We are visiting on our way to Jundala's country."

William smiled at the grimfaced woman. "How are you, Jundala?"

"I am well."

"I hope you find your family the same."

She indicated the horse Binda had by the reins. "We have purchased some supplies from your store for them."

"Good." He was glad many could benefit from his idea. "I have spent the night with your people, Uncle Binda."

"Georgina told us your plans. We hoped our paths would cross."

"Have you checked the springs along the creek?" Jundala looked beyond him to the hills.

"All is well up there."

"What about the bottom waterhole?" Binda asked.

"I am on my way there now."

"The men are more determined miners than you thought."

"It appears so but at least they are nowhere near the true source of the original diamond. The top waterhole remains untouched."

"For now." Jundala's tone was harsh and she did not meet his look.

"I said I would not touch it and I have not. Uncle Binda's family will continue to have access." William shuffled from foot to foot. The cold seeped beneath his jacket.

Binda murmured something and Jundala glanced briefly at William. Her expression softened. She nodded.

"Let us continue." Binda reached out to shake William's hand. "Safe travels."

"And you." William watched for a while as Binda and Jundala made their way on along the edge of the creek bed. He was sorry his exuberance over the idea to channel water from the higher country had caused friction between him and Jundala. He hoped time would make it right again.

Big Red snorted and shook his head.

"Time to be on our way, fellow." William mounted and set off again.

There was no sign of life as he rounded the last bend and took in the camp sprawled from the bank to the creek bed below. He gripped the reins tighter at the sight of the fully fenced waterhole and the scattered signs of human occupation. These men had little care for the land they were camped on.

He rode closer, keeping the fence between him and the waterhole. Both man and horse lifted their heads in surprise as a chap burst from one of the tents on the bank opposite, a rifle in his hands.

"Stay where you are," he bellowed.

William stared and then the hackles rose on his neck. "Wiltshire!"

"Baker?" Charles lowered his gun then just as quickly raised it again. "What are you doing here?"

"Checking my waterhole."

"I have a legal claim to it so you can get on your way."

William glanced around. He took in the remains of the fire, the small pile of wood, the sagging second tent. There was an air of desolation beyond that of the cold day. "Where are your men?"

"That's no concern of yours."

"Not prepared to stay through the winter, I'd warrant." William looked Charles up and down. From the distance he could see his hair was dishevelled and his usually clean chin sported a beard, albeit a patchy one. "How are you enjoying tent life, Charles? Find any diamonds to keep you warm?"

"Get on your way, Baker."

William climbed down from his horse. "I might light a fire for my billy and enjoy some of my wife's cake." He stepped closer to the fence. "Your claim is on my land."

Charles thrust out his chest. "But it is my claim."

"Perhaps it won't be so easy to access before too long."

"If you're referring to your wife's reunion with her mother, that won't change anything. Johanna is happy for me to travel over her land."

"But for how much longer?"

Charles staggered down the path to the creek bed and to the edge of the waterhole. William could see his face clearly now. His skin was grey and eyes red rimmed.

"I know what you're up to Baker," Charles spat the words at him. "Trying to get your mother-in-law on side so you can take over Prosser's Run."

William shook his head. "Don't judge me by your standards, Wiltshire. I've only encouraged the reunion because a mother and daughter should be friends."

"Ha, that's what you say." Spittle dribbled over Wiltshire's lips.

A thick bank of cloud passed over the sun and the day felt colder. William glared at Charles a moment, then thought of

Georgina waiting for him at home. He mounted Big Red and rode away without a backwards look.

It was midday by the time he reached the welcome sight of home. He was chilled to the bone and looking forward to the warmth of the fire and some of Georgina's soup. They'd lived on soup that winter. Even though sometimes it was lacking in ingredients it was at least warm.

"William."

He turned back from his gate to the sight of Jessie hurrying towards him, her new baby strapped to her chest and Haji on her hip. Lines creased her brow.

"What's wrong?"

"I was about to hook up the cart." She came to a stop in front of him. "Georgina went out for a ride first thing this morning and she hasn't returned."

William's heart gave an extra thud. His first thoughts were of Charles but there had been no sign of Georgina there.

"Did she say where she was going?"

"Not really but we waved her off and she was headed north."

William turned back to Big Red.

"Wait. You must be exhausted. Come and have some bread and hot soup first." Jessie gave him a wan smile. "I'm sure she'll be all right. And you'll be better with something in your stomach."

William's stomach did indeed ache with hunger. There was sense in her words. "Thank you," he said and followed her back to her cottage.

"I'd have asked Albie to go but he went with Clem this morning." Jessie offered him a mug of delicious-smelling soup. "It's kangaroo tail. Georgina and I made it together yesterday."

William took a careful sip but it was the perfect temperature and he felt its warmth doing him good straight away. "Has she been all right while I've been gone?"

"Yes. It must be difficult for her with our Sally." Jessie's hand rested on the head of her new daughter. "But she has been happy. As cheerful as anyone could be in this frightful cold."

"That's good." They had talked about their mixed feelings of sorrow and joy when Jessie's little girl was born at the start of winter. They both longed for a child of their own but had determined that Clem and Jessie's children would fill the void in the meantime. He swallowed the last of the soup and picked up the hunk of warm bread she had cut for him.

"Take these." Jessie held out a jacket and a blanket. "Do you have the makings of tea with you?"

"Yes."

"Good. It's so cold. Georgina might enjoy a hot drink before you bring her home." Jessie gave him an encouraging smile. "I'm sure she'll be all right. Something's held her up, that's all."

In spite of Jessie's brave smile he couldn't help the worry that wormed inside him as he hurried out the door and across the yard to where Big Red waited.

The bellows of the cow filled the frosty air and made Georgina's heart race. She had helped to deliver many calves but this one was proving difficult. It had become stuck and mother and baby were in danger. The only thing for it was to pull the calf from the mother but Georgina had been trying for some time and she hadn't been strong enough to do it.

She kicked at a rock in frustration. It was certainly not what she'd planned for her morning. It had been a miserable cold winter so far and for the last few days she'd been cooped up in the house. That morning the freezing wind that had raged across the bare plains for days had finally abated and she had resolved to take Carmody for a ride. It had been a refreshing escape but the biting air had just decided her to turn for home when she had come across the struggling cow.

She stood hands on hips and shook her head. She'd brought little with her. A flask of water and a hat she'd not worn. She'd also dug around in the saddle bag and found a length of rope there from some earlier expedition; it was giving her an idea.

She lifted her gaze from the forlorn cow to her horse, and ran her hand down Carmody's stout neck. "I need your strength, boy. We will have to do this together."

She took the rope from her saddle and tied one end of it around the small leg protruding from the mother. The other end she tied to the pommel of her saddle, then she positioned herself at the back end of the cow. "Now, Carmody," she said. "Back up."

The horse lifted his head, one eye fixed on her as if he thought she were crazy. "Back up," she commanded. He took a step backwards and then another. The rope strained, the cow bellowed and the calf remained firmly where it was.

Georgina wiped hair from her eyes with the back of her hand and braced herself. "Back up," she said again.

Carmody pulled, Georgina rotated the calf, the cow contracted, and all at once the calf slithered out to land in a steaming heap at her feet. She bent to remove the rope and stepped back to let the mother take care of her newborn. The cow nudged and cleaned until it staggered up on its wobbly legs.

Georgina let out a sigh. Her breath puffed around her in a mist. The sun was hidden behind a thick bank of cloud and instead of getting warmer the day was colder than when she'd left home. A shiver went through her. She was filthy and damp.

"Georgina!"

She lifted her head at the call. Relief flooded through her at the sound of William's voice.

"Up here."

She waved as he came into view, so pleased to see him.

"Are you all right?" He was down from his horse as soon as he was close.

She moved towards him. "Of course." She waved a hand at the new family. "Had to help these two."

William wrapped her in his arms as he looked over her shoulder. "You're freezing," he said. Then he let her go and studied her at arm's length. "And you're covered in muck. Take off your jacket. I've brought a spare and a blanket."

Georgina shuddered as the cold hit her and slipped her arms gratefully into the fresh jacket he held out for her.

"I'm pleased you're here," she said. "But how did you know to come?"

He wrapped her in the blanket and held her close again. "When I got back to the homestead, Jessie was about to come looking for you. You'd been gone a while, she said. I took a guess you usually ride up to the first ridge."

Georgina shivered in his arms. In spite of the extra layers she felt chilled to the bone.

He guided her to a fallen log. "Sit here," he said. "I'm going to light a fire and make some tea to warm you before we return home."

Georgina huddled into the blanket while William worked, grateful for his presence. Carmody would have got her home, but she would have been frozen to his saddle. Further away the cow tended to her calf. Georgina's heart ached at the sight. Once more the loss of her own baby overwhelmed her. She put her head to her knees inside the blanket to hide her tears from William. Even though there would be more babies she would always hold a place in her heart for that first child who didn't live long enough inside her.

William's arm went around her and she lifted her head to see flames crackling in a little fire, the water tin nestled on the edge.

"This is the coldest winter I can remember," he said. "Once the water has warmed a little you can use some to wash your hands."

Georgina looked down at the filth plastered to her skin.

He grinned. "At least you'll be able to put your gloves back on."

Georgina nestled her head against his shoulder, so thankful for his warmth and his strength. Being with William in this country was all that mattered.

Something soft brushed her cheek.

"What's that?" William asked, batting at his own cheek.

She sat forward and looked up. He was doing the same. Georgina pulled her dirty hands from the blanket and lifted them. White flakes touched her hand then instantly became droplets.

"Snow." She looked at William, whose eyes were wide. She sprang up. The blanket fell away and she spread out her arms. "It's *snowing.*"

He was instantly beside her, wrapping them both in the blanket. "Well," he said. "I would never have believed it. Snow on Smith's Ridge."

Georgina laughed, a warm feeling inside her despite the freezing air.

Huddled together they watched as the rugged terrain around them was coated in a white layer, which quickly turned to slush.

William shook his head. "I suppose if we can't have rain we might as well have snow."

Forty-two

October 1902

Edith lowered herself to the softly padded chair in her father-in-law's sitting room, closed her eyes and let out a long sigh. It was so much cooler there than in her little house next door. The baby moved inside her and she shifted in the chair to find a comfortable position.

Why she had ever thought it a good idea to have her own house? The cottage had never compared to the Wiltshire home. Charles had not been able to cajole any further money from his grandmother and with the downturn of their finances it had never been properly finished or furnished. If they entertained guests Edith always had to ask Henry's permission to hold the dinner in his house, and then there was Mrs Nixon to deal with. A vision of the housekeeper's sanctimonious look had Edith digging her fingernails into the padded arms of the chair.

How Edith would like to be rid of the woman, but she knew it would be no easy task. Henry wouldn't allow it, of course, and Charles thought Mrs Nixon a dependable help for his sister and father. If only Charles knew the extent of Mrs Nixon's help to his father. Ever watchful, Edith suspected the liaison continued. Sometimes it was a look, a touch more than accidental. She couldn't believe Charles had lived in that house most of his life and not known.

She shifted again in the chair. Carrying a child was really the most hideous of conditions, and she longed for it to be over. The heat was already oppressive and it was only spring. Honestly, she was too irritated to care one way or another what Henry or even Flora Nixon did at the moment.

She pushed up from her chair and walked restlessly around the room. On the mantle was a portrait of Henry and Catherine holding Charles as a baby. Edith had looked at the photograph before, but today the sight of the locket around Catherine's neck added to her frustration. Why couldn't Henry give it to her? It seemed ridiculous to keep all Catherine's jewellery hidden away for one spoiled little girl. Laura was too young to wear it and Edith was sure that by the time she was old enough she probably wouldn't appreciate it.

Edith stared at the photo a moment longer then replaced the frame and began to pace the room again. She stopped. A bold idea sprang into her head. Laura's room was opposite the sitting room. She would not be denied what should be hers. Edith went to the door, poked her head into the hall and listened.

She knew Flora had walked Laura to school and she had taken her shopping basket. There was no sound to indicate she had returned. Edith crossed the hall and let herself into the little girl's room, closing the door carefully behind her.

Charles had said his mother's jewellery was in a wooden box put away in Laura's room. Edith looked around. The room had only a few pieces of furniture: a small chest of drawers beside the bed, a trunk under the window and a wardrobe along one wall.

She went to the wardrobe first, opened the doors and reached to the top shelf. It would be too high for Laura. There were several items of folded clothing, which Edith slid out and placed on the bed. Several pairs of gloves and a drawstring purse sat on top of a soft pink dress, a beaded jacket and a velvet wrap. Edith assumed they had been Catherine's.

Tucked in the space at the back of the shelf was a polished wooden box. She took it eagerly from its hiding place and sat on the edge of the bed with it resting on her knees. It was quite heavy, so she was impatient to see what else might be in it. To her dismay she noticed it had a lock. She tried the lid but it wouldn't open. She lifted the box and looked underneath and all around.

She clicked her tongue, set the box aside and stood up. Where might the key be? Dolls lined the mantle surrounding a single portrait of Catherine. Edith picked up the frame and looked all over but no key was hidden there. She turned slowly to take in the room. Her gaze fell on the bag. Quickly she scooped it up and tugged it open. Inside was a neatly folded handkerchief. Edith felt for it and immediately she smiled. There was something inside the handkerchief. She opened it and there was a small key. It fitted the lock.

The door pushed open behind her and Edith swung around. "Good heavens, Mrs Nixon, you scared me half to death."

"I'm sorry, Mrs Wiltshire, I didn't know you were in here." Mrs Nixon looked down at the box. "Can I help you with something?"

"There was no-one home when I came in. I was looking for something special to wear with the dress I've got for the baby's christening. I thought Mrs Wiltshire would have liked it if I wore something of hers."

"My, you are thinking ahead." Mrs Nixon's expression was unreadable.

"I remembered Charles said his mother's jewellery box was kept here."

Mrs Nixon came further into the room, put down the bucket and broom she was carrying and took the box from Edith's hands.

"Mr Henry is only in Adelaide for a week. I am sure there will be plenty of time for you to ask him when he returns. Now I really must get on," she said. "With Miss Laura at school and Mr Henry away I planned to do some spring cleaning."

"It has been so hot." Edith put a hand to her stomach, looking for some sympathy. "It's so much cooler in the big house."

Flora gave her that expression that made her feel the woman could see right through her. Edith knew she was wasting her pout on Mrs Nixon. She fixed the housekeeper with a steely glare. "And then you come sneaking in, giving me such a fright. How dare you? It's not good for me in my condition."

Flora returned the box to the wardrobe shelf. "I'm sure you'll be all right, Mrs Wiltshire. You always seem to land on your feet." She smiled and began to refold the clothing that had slipped across the bed.

Edith gaped at her. "What do you mean by that remark?"

Flora paused, the velvet wrap in her hands. "Things have a habit of going your way."

"Is that so?" Edith drew herself up, outrage at the housekeeper's words gnawing deep within her. She would have no more of this woman's disrespectful talk. "And what about you, Mrs Nixon, or perhaps you would prefer you were also Mrs Wiltshire."

Flora was lifting the clothes to the shelf. Edith saw her falter then push the clothes in. She shut the wardrobe door and turned.

"I know about your sordid affair with my father-in-law."

Flora's eyes closed briefly then she fixed her gaze on Edith. "There has never been anything sordid about it."

"Don't take that tone with me, you deceitful woman. You were in your master's bed when your mistress was still alive."

Flora's shoulders sagged.

"Poor Mrs Wiltshire," Edith tutted, sure she had her victim firmly in her clutches.

"You know nothing about it," Flora snapped.

"Oh, but I do. Henry told me everything. It's amazing what he was prepared to do in order to keep you here."

Flora frowned.

"Yes, your continued employment here has been in my hands and now … well now I realise you have your sights set on marrying Henry and having his wife's jewellery and her house for yourself. Why I even imagine you see yourself as Laura's mother." Edith lifted her head and smiled as Flora paled. "I see that I'm right."

"You are not." Flora's chin lifted and she looked Edith in the eye. "You have such a terrible twisted mind, you would not understand true love."

"Indeed," Edith huffed. "I love Charles. I am not his mistress but his wife and it is my duty to protect the family name." She drew herself up, turned on her heel and strode from the room, a smug smile on her face. She was quite sure Flora Nixon would soon be gone.

Charles closed the back door of the shop and set off along the lane. He did hope Edith was in a better frame of mind than when he'd left home that morning. His initial delight at the idea of becoming a father had dissipated as her time advanced. She was less and less interested in pleasuring him and it had been weeks since he'd done more than kiss her cheek.

Charles turned from the lane to cross the road. A cart drawn by two horses rolled past, coating him in dust. He hissed and brushed

at his jacket. He crossed behind the cart and had to jump out of
the way as a blasted bicycle careered past. Once across the road, he
strode up the path towards home.

What a week it had been. First the fellow he'd installed at the
mine had come back claiming the place was haunted and saying
he wouldn't work there. Charles had found another to replace
him but had wasted days taking the new worker there and showing him what to do. Henry had gone to Adelaide to visit Grandmother and left him with several appointments, none of which
had proved very lucrative, and then this afternoon he found the
damned Bakers had stolen a big transport contract from under
his nose. He blamed his father. If Charles hadn't been conducting
Henry's business, he would have had more time to follow up his
own. Now he would have to let go one of his drivers.

The drought that had plagued them for several years was showing no signs of letting up and was in fact affecting the whole
country. Finances were stretched and there was little work coming in.

Charles stomped along the path past his father's house and up to
his own front door. He tugged at his collar, which was too tight
in the heat, and let himself inside. His feet echoed on the polished
wood of the passage. They had no money for floor coverings yet.

"Edith, I'm home." He listened. Had he heard a small sob? He
turned his head to the left, which was the direction of their small
sitting room. "Edith?"

He went in to find his wife collapsed in a chair, her eyes closed,
a handkerchief pressed to her mouth and her other hand on her
stomach. He strode to her side and kneeled down. "Edith, my
dear, what is it? Are you unwell?"

She opened her eyes, which were red from crying.

"Oh Charles," she said. "I am so glad you are home. I have …
I have some terrible news."

"What is it?" He looked fearfully at the swelling under her hand. "Is something wrong with the child?"

"Oh, no. The baby is perfectly fine. I've just had a shock, that's all."

"Dear Edith, please tell me." Charles was finding his knees beginning to ache on the solid wooden floor.

"It's Mrs Nixon."

Charles sighed. "What has she done now?" Sometimes Edith could get upset over small interferences by his father's housekeeper.

"Prepare yourself, Charles. I have discovered the most hideous thing." Edith drew in a deep breath. She dropped her handkerchief and clutched his hand. "Mrs Nixon and ... and your father are having a ... a *liaison*."

"What?" Charles scratched at his head. "I'm sure that can't be true."

Edith's eyes flashed. "I'm your wife, Charles, do you doubt my word?"

"Of course not, but how can you know this?"

"I have wondered about it for some time. There are things a woman notices that men don't. Last week I heard them together."

"She is the housekeeper, Edith."

"What I heard was more than that. I went early to the big house to see if there was any milk for your breakfast as I had run out. The kitchen was empty and I heard voices." Edith patted at her cheek and drew a breath. "Soft giggling sounds and words that were rather ... intimate. They came from your father's bedroom. I am a married woman and I have no doubt about what was happening in there. I waited in the kitchen with the door ajar. I saw Mrs Nixon coming out of your father's bedroom. She was still buttoning her shirt. I didn't let her know I was there of course. I felt so embarrassed. I came straight back home."

"I can't believe it," he gasped. Mrs Nixon had been the one constant in his life. The one who had entertained him, read him stories, taken him to school, tucked him in at night. His mother had often been unwell and his father busy with work, but Mrs Nixon had always been there for him.

"I'm sorry, Charles, but it's true. Today I went to the big house to take some respite from the heat. I was feeling uncomfortable and it's so much cooler there. I caught Mrs Nixon with your mother's jewellery box. She was angry with me for discovering her. I was terrified but I confronted her. She told me she'd been your father's mistress. She was gloating about it." Edith stopped and clutched his hand tighter. "You must brace yourself, Charles. She has been your father's mistress for a long time — since well before your mother died."

Charles felt as if the wind had been knocked from him. Mrs Nixon and his father were lovers. It did not bear thinking of.

"More than that, Charles, she intends to marry him. She sees herself as his wife, Laura's mother and mistress of the big house." Edith squeezed his hand again. "She wants to take what is rightfully yours."

Rage filled Charles as the air flooded back into his lungs. He grasped the arm of the chair and pulled himself upright.

"It's madness." He paced the small room then stopped in front of Edith. "You're sure? There can be no way you've mixed this up, misunderstood?"

Edith struggled up from her chair. "Charles, I can't believe you would think I would spread gossip. If you don't believe me, ask Mrs Nixon. She was only too happy to tell me her sordid story."

Charles thumped his fist into his palm. "Wait until Father comes home. I'll have this out with him."

"I don't think we can wait, Charles."

He frowned at Edith. "Why?"

"Imagine the scandal if people found out. I can't believe it's not been discovered before this. I think Flora has become more brazen with your mother gone and now with us out of the house."

Charles shook his head.

"Think of your sister, Charles. Laura is older now. I can only hope they are discreet when no-one else is there, but what if Laura was exposed to their ... being together."

"You're right. I should talk to Mrs Nixon. Tell her it must stop."

"Do you think that will work? They've been lovers a long time and they are together in that house."

"What do you suggest?"

"You must send Mrs Nixon away before your father comes home. She has children. We can tell him one of them needs her and she's decided to live with them."

"Father needs a housekeeper."

"It's an expense we can do without. If we lived in the big house I could manage it."

"But my dear Edith. You will be busy with a new baby soon."

"I can get someone in to do some of the heavy work. It would be much cheaper than a housekeeper. We could rent this house out. It would more than cover the cost." She took both of his hands in hers. "Think of it, Charles. Your father's house has plenty of room. If Mrs Nixon wasn't there we could use her quarters and the guest room as our own." She pulled him closer so that her body pressed to his. "We would still have our privacy, but be able to use the rest of the house when we needed."

Charles wrapped his arms around her and she nestled closer. She trailed a finger down his cheek and over his lips. He shuddered and bit back a groan. "Edith. What would I do without you?"

She gave him one of her coy smiles. "You look very tired, Charles. It's been such an awful day. Why don't you lie down and

I will bring you a cool drink? We could have a rest together." She walked her fingers down the front of his shirt. "Dinner can be eaten later."

Charles drew her too him and pressed his lips to hers. "Don't take too long, my love."

As the last light faded beyond the curtain, Charles nestled back onto the mattress a happy man. He watched as Edith lit the lamp and then slipped her loose house dress back around her. She sat back on the bed beside him.

"I shall make your dinner now."

He put a hand to her breast. "I find I am quite ravenous."

She leaned towards him; the fabric tied loosely across her breasts fell open and he slipped his hand inside. He nuzzled his head against her.

"I think I should be the one to send Mrs Nixon on her way," Edith said.

"Do you, my love?" He was barely listening, enjoying the feel of her soft flesh.

"She will probably only plead and beg if you do it." She leaned down to trail her lips across his cheek to his ear. "You have so much to do, Charles. Let me take this responsibility for you." She pushed him back onto the pillow and pressed her breasts to his bare chest.

Charles closed his eyes and sighed. "Thank you, Edith."

Forty-three

Henry dragged himself up the path to his front door. He looked to the window but no cheery face was there to welcome him. Flora knew he would be home this evening. She usually allowed Laura to stay up and watch for him. He felt a pang of disappointment.

He was tired and had left his travel case at the shop rather than have to lug it home. Under his arm was a parcel for Laura: a new dress from her grandmother. He sighed at the thought of Harriet. His Adelaide visit had been a difficult one. Placating creditors was bad enough but his mother had been demanding, and then almost begged him to stay. Her eyesight was so poor Miss Wicksteed managed most things in the shop for her now and even helped her to dress each morning, but her mind was as sharp as ever. Henry had suggested his mother should sell her business and retire to a little house by the sea, but she would have none of it.

The curtain twitched as he reached the verandah and he looked expectantly at the window only to be disappointed by a brief glimpse of Edith's silhouette. He did hope Edith and Charles weren't expecting to join him for dinner. He wasn't in the mood for their company. A simple meal with Flora in the kitchen would be better.

He went inside and felt a pang of disappointment at the sight of Charles standing in the dining-room doorway.

"Good evening, Father. I hope your journey to Adelaide was successful."

"Moderately." Henry glanced down the hall.

"Laura is in bed." Charles stepped back. "Edith and I have been waiting for you to dine with us."

Henry had a glimpse of Edith's straight back seated at the table. "I'm very tired, Charles."

"Edith has prepared a special dinner for us."

Henry sighed. "Very well. I'll go and wash first." He continued down the hall. He stopped at Laura's closed door and opened it. A lamp still glowed on the small table beside her bed. He crossed the room and looked down at his sleeping daughter. Her nose was red and her face damp with tears, but she was sound asleep. He bent to kiss her and tasted the salt on her pink cheek. He wondered what had upset her. He placed the packet at the end of her bed and tiptoed from the room.

The kitchen was empty. He assumed Edith had given Flora the night off. He went to the back door on his way to the bathroom and looked out across the courtyard. No light shone from her window. Perhaps she was out visiting. Henry sighed and resigned himself to dinner with his pompous son and his arrogant daughter-in-law.

In the dining room he kissed the cheek Edith offered and took his place at the head of the table. In front of him was a serve of some kind of meat in a glutinous splodge.

"I've made jellied fowl to begin." Edith smiled broadly.

Henry said grace and picked up his fork. Charles was already devouring his. Henry poked at the wobbly concoction before putting a small forkful into his mouth. Rather than tasting bad there was hardly any taste at all. He swallowed, grateful it was only a small serve.

"Have you given Mrs Nixon the night off?" he asked.

Charles and Edith glanced at each other across the table.

Charles put down his fork, his plate already empty. "Mrs Nixon has left our employ, Father."

"What?" Henry turned to Edith, but her eyes were lowered. "Why would she leave?"

"You remember her daughter, Martha?" Charles said. "She was in need of her mother's help."

Henry frowned. Flora had rarely mentioned her children once they left home, though he knew she had sometimes sent them money. Her husband had died many years ago and other than telling Henry about that, she discussed nothing of her own personal life.

Henry looked back at his son. "Why did Martha suddenly need her mother?"

"Flora didn't say why and I didn't ask. She was in a hurry to go. I paid her the rest of the month's wages and—"

Henry slammed his hand on the table, making the cutlery and Edith jump. "Where has she gone?"

"Calm down, Father." Charles frowned at him. "She didn't give me an address. It was her decision. There was little Edith or I could do about it."

"Perhaps she'll send you a letter when she's settled." Edith's words were like icicles in the warm room.

Henry met her gaze and he knew straight away she had somehow been complicit in this sudden departure. His heart sank. What had she done to his dear Flora to make her disappear without a word?

"You don't need to worry, Father," Charles said. "Edith will run the house with some help from the lady across the road, Mrs Coleman. It's quite silly us maintaining two houses when there's more than enough room for all of us here. We are going to move into the rooms at the back of the house — Mrs Nixon's rooms and the guest room — so we won't be in your way."

"What if I have guests? Johanna uses the guest room."

"You can always use my old room, but you haven't had guests to stay in a long time in any case. Mrs Prosser stays at the Temperance Hotel." Charles sat back and clasped his hands together over his broad chest. "Our household finances will be improved without Mrs Nixon's wage and we can rent out our house."

"And you won't be alone any more, Father." Edith gave him such a sweet smile he could almost have believed it was genuine.

"I wasn't alone before. I have Laura."

"Of course but—"

"She needs someone to look after her."

"Edith will do that." Charles inclined his head towards his wife across the table. "Laura's six years old now and hardly needs a nursemaid. Mrs Nixon did spoil her somewhat."

Henry lifted his napkin, folded it carefully and laid it across his unfinished dinner. "Well, you appear to have everything worked out. Thank you for the meal, Edith."

"That was just the starter. I have liver fritters for the next course and then custard tart."

Henry stood. "I am too tired to be good company. I will retire and leave you to enjoy the food."

Henry closed the door behind him. Once in his own bedroom he shut that door too. The lamp he had lit earlier still shone brightly. He closed his eyes and took a long slow breath. His head was pounding from the task of trying to control his anger. He was sure Edith had blackmailed Flora as she had him, but Charles was so besotted by the woman. Henry couldn't be sure how much his son knew. Was he aware of Henry's relationship with Flora, and had conspired to send her away, or had Edith simply used her hold over him to get what she wanted?

Regardless, Henry was trapped. He couldn't speak out for fear of exposing his second life — and he had dear Laura to consider.

He'd be damned if he was going to let Edith poison his daughter's sweet nature.

Henry sank to the edge of his bed and put his head in his hands. There were so many financial problems at the moment. Charles was too caught up in his own schemes to see the overall extent of their combined debt. And now he was to face evenings without the company of his dear Flora. How he would miss her listening ear, her gentle reassurance and her warm embrace.

A drop fell to his trouser leg and then another. Henry began to sob. He was more heartbroken than he'd felt when Catherine died. In many ways she had been his housekeeper and Flora his wife.

His door opened and a little face peeped around. "Papa?"

Henry wiped his eyes. "I am here, Laura, my angel."

The little girl ran into his arms. She kissed his cheeks then touched them gently with her fingers, her gaze searching his. "Why are you crying, Papa?"

"I was missing you, my angel, but now you're here, I'm happy." He pulled his face into a smile.

"I thought you might be sad because Flora has left."

"Yes, that is sad."

"Did you send her away, Papa?"

"No, Laura. She had to go and look after her own family."

"But we are her family."

"Yes we are, but she has children of her own who need her now."

"Flora was my dearest friend, Papa. I shall miss her very much." She tilted her head and looked earnestly up at him. Tears welled in her eyes.

One trickled down her cheek and Henry took out his handkerchief and wiped it away. "You remember when your mama died and you had to be very brave?"

Laura chewed her lip and nodded.

"You must do the same now. Like your mama, Flora will always be in your heart and you in hers."

Laura looked up at him with such trust it brought tears to his own eyes. He blinked them away. "Can you be brave, my angel?"

"Yes," she whispered.

A door opened beyond the bedroom and Edith could be heard walking down the hall. Laura slipped from his lap, closed the door and came back to sit beside him. She glanced to the door then back at Henry.

"Flora told me a secret, Papa. She said I was only to share it with you."

Henry grasped Laura's hands in his, hoping there was some message, some way he could contact Flora.

"She said I was a lucky girl because my mama had left me some lovely jewellery in a special box. She was worried someone might want to take it so she hid it. She said the only person I was allowed to tell was you, Papa, so you could keep it safe."

Henry sighed. He really didn't care about Catherine's blasted trinkets but Flora was right. They were meant for Laura and no doubt Edith would want to get her grasping hands on them.

Laura pulled him closer so she could whisper in his ear. "They are under your bed. Flora said you would find a safe place for them until I am old enough to wear them."

Henry patted the soft hair on her head. "Let's get them out now."

They both got down on their knees and Henry dragged out the box. They sat on the floor, their backs against the bed, and looked at the box. The key was in the lock. Henry turned it eagerly, hoping Flora would have put a note inside for him. He lifted the lid and rummaged through the pieces. He sighed. There was no note.

"This is pretty." Laura had picked up a cameo brooch. "Mama wore it at her neck."

"Yes, but not suitable for you yet." Henry looked at Laura admiring the brooch then back at the box. He rummaged again until his fingers found the filigree heart-shaped locket. He lifted it from the box and held it to the light. It was an intricate and pretty piece of jewellery, with the letter *H* shaped into the front.

"That's Mama's locket."

"Yes," Henry said. "And before that it was my mother's and before that my grandmother's. Now it's your turn, Laura." He lifted the chain over her head. "You're old enough to take care of it, aren't you?"

"Oh yes, Papa." Laura's eyes shone as she looked up at him. "I will look after it. Thank you. Now Mama's heart is close to mine."

She pressed the locket to her chest and once more Henry blinked back the tears. He put his arm around his daughter and held her close. At least he'd had one small victory. If he made this gifting official it would be difficult for Edith to claim the necklace. He had denied her the piece of jewellery that she so badly wanted.

Forty-four

April 1903

Charles turned back from seeing the customers out of the shop and looked down at the baby in his arms. Leonard Charles Wiltshire had been born in the extreme heat of January and yet he had thrived. Charles looked down at the perfect little pixie face and wondered once more how such a small scrap of flesh could make such a big change to their lives. He had a brief image of his mother holding baby Laura the first time he had seen his sister. His mother had been totally besotted and Laura had been thoroughly spoiled as a result. He would have none of that nonsense for his son. The baby was strong and healthy and Edith was a fine mother without fussing: that was what was necessary for a child.

"I've finished instructing Miss Fisher now, Charles. Time for Leonard and I to return home. He must be back in his cradle by ten o'clock."

Charles handed over his son and watched as Edith tucked him back into the perambulator. He kissed the cheek she offered.

Edith adjusted her hat. "I will see you at midday for luncheon."

"I'm afraid there has been a change of plan. I must ride out to the diamond mine. My deliveryman tells me the fellow wants to leave. I must go and convince him to stay."

"Have you finished unpacking all those boxes, Miss Fisher?" Edith's tone was sharp.

Charles turned to see their new shop assistant at the end of the counter.

"Not yet, Mrs Wiltshire."

"Then set to it." Edith clapped her hands. "We can't sell it if it's not out of the box." She drew Charles aside and lowered her voice. "You haven't forgotten Leonard's christening is on Sunday."

"Of course not." Charles could hardly forget the party that had been in the planning since before his son's birth. "I will be back by the weekend."

"I really think it's time you gave up on that mine. It drains money and your time and we've had not one sign it's worth pursuing."

Charles inhaled deeply. "There are diamonds there, Edith. I am sure of it. We are so close to finding them."

She gave him an indulgent look. "Very well, but please don't be away too long. There is so much to arrange. I had thought that postponing the christening until April might mean slightly cooler weather but the heat hasn't let up. I don't know how I am going to keep the food cool. And just this morning your father has decided we should also have a cake for Laura's birthday. This party is for our son, not your sister, Charles. You really must talk to him about it."

"When I get back, Edith." He cupped her elbow in his hand and guided her back to the perambulator. It was a large contraption they'd ordered from England, and was Edith's pride and joy. "In the meantime, you and Mrs Coleman will manage, I am sure, and I promise I will be back in time to help."

It was late afternoon by the time Charles and his horse and cart approached the waterhole where his employee, Barnes, was working the claim. It had been a long hot drive. Charles was covered in dust, tired and hungry.

Barnes was propped against a tree with his feet in a bucket of water when Charles brought his horse and cart to a stop behind the tents. He called a greeting but didn't get up.

"I've brought you some supplies."

"Your man's only been here yesterday."

"These are extra supplies." Charles tossed back the canvas from the cart and lifted a bottle of whisky into the air.

This time Barnes did get up. "That's very sociable of you, Mr Wiltshire." He hobbled across the rocky ground on his bare feet and took the bottle Charles offered. The stopper was out before Charles could blink. Barnes sniffed the bottle then took a swig. "Ah!" He wiped his mouth with the back of his dirty sleeve. "That goes a long way to making a man feel better."

"You know liquor was not part of the deal here but seeing you have been so loyal I thought I should reward you."

"And get me to stay longer." Barnes gave a throaty chuckle, took another swig and pushed the stopper back in. The smile left his face. "Baker's been back here."

Barnes waved towards the waterhole in the creek bed below and Charles saw what he hadn't noticed before. The fence that had circled the waterhole and reached back to the bank on their side of the creek had been moved. It now cut through the middle of the dwindling water supply.

"Who did that?"

"Baker and his offsider, an older man, big with shoulders like an ox. Came up here last week. Told me their cattle needed some of the water. They shifted the fence and before they left the big man threatened me. Said he'd come back and break every bone in my body if I shifted that fence." Barnes gripped the bottle tighter. "I believe he is capable."

"He was just trying to frighten you." Charles snorted. "Looks like he succeeded."

"You don't pay me enough money to risk a beating."

"Baker wouldn't let the man hurt you. He's not a fighter. Prefers the easy path, like sneaking around doing things behind my back." Charles spoke brashly but he knew Baker was not a sneak, and was capable of violence. He remembered the force of the punch Baker had thrown. Charles turned back to the cart. "I've brought you some extra items to make your life here more comfortable."

Barnes shook his head. "In this heat there's nothing can make a man comfortable."

"I've brought a bigger tent, with a proper bed and a mattress."

Barnes waved the bottle he still clutched. "What about this stuff?"

"I'll make sure there's a bottle in your regular supplies." Charles glared at him. "As long as you continue to work the claim properly."

Barnes waved at the pile of rocks beside the bucket he'd been soaking his feet in. "I'm doing exactly as you showed me but I haven't found anything that looks like a diamond. I've put some aside that look promising just in case, but I think they're just rocks."

"Show me."

Barnes waved to the table under the shade of the large gum. "Help yourself." He pulled the stopper from the bottle and took another swig. "I've knocked off for the day."

Charles snatched the bottle from the impudent man. "Not until you've unloaded the wagon." He held out his hand for the stopper, which Barnes reluctantly handed over.

Tucking the bottle under his arm, Charles left his grumbling employee and went to inspect the rocks. He picked one up that had an almost octagonal shape, but he doubted it was a diamond. He slipped it into the pouch he carried along with a couple of other possibilities. Becker had given him the name of a man in Adelaide who would check them. He shoved the pouch back in his pocket, frustrated by the lack of any progress after all this time. He scrambled down the bank, following the path worn in by the men who had worked for him there.

Down in the creek bed were the scrapings and diggings of years looking for diamonds with no result. He kicked at the rubble at his feet. Perhaps Edith was right and he should give it up — but he'd spent so much money already and the diamonds had to be there. He kicked the ground harder in frustration.

The bellow of a cow drew his gaze back to the waterhole. A large black bull looked at him from across the water. Two cows were also making their way across the sandy creek bed to the water's edge.

Damn Baker and his cattle. The waterhole had diminished considerably and these cattle would only make it worse. Water was of the utmost importance to his claim. No searching for diamonds could be done without it. He could get Barnes to shift the fence but no doubt Baker would just move it back again. He needed a more permanent solution to his problem. Charles put his hands on his hips and glared at the beasts, their heads lowered, drinking. He needed to get rid of those cattle.

Charles was relieved to see there was no sign of life at Prosser's Run. The men must be out on the property, and Johanna would no doubt be on her way to town to attend Leonard's christening. He was pleased his father continued to include Johanna in family events, even if she was a little cool with Charles and Edith since her reconciliation with Georgina. Charles understood she still hadn't come to terms with William as her son-in-law and one never knew when that advantage might prove useful.

He drove his horse and cart to the sheds beyond the house. The second smaller shed was his goal. He was sure it would contain what he was looking for.

It was an hour later when he had finally loaded the last barrel onto his cart. He could have done with help from one of the Prosser shepherds, but it was better that no-one knew he'd been there.

The heat of the sun pounded down and he lifted his hat to mop his brow.

"Good heavens, Charles, it's you."

Charles turned, alarmed by Johanna Prosser's arrival.

"I thought Swan or one of the men must have come back early," she said.

He glanced back at his cart, where the barrels hid the bottle he had stowed first. "You surprised me, Mrs Prosser. I didn't know you were home or I would have come to speak with you first." He waved a hand towards the barrels then stepped away from the cart to the post he'd hung his jacket over, drawing her attention with him. "I've borrowed some barrels and filled them with water. My man at the claim is complaining about the water quality there. The level is getting low and he must share it with Baker's cattle."

"Stock need water, Charles, or they die."

Charles was taken aback by her directness. "Yes ... well ... I have my mining claim there so ... I'll replace your barrels next time I come this way." He stopped. Johanna was studying him closely, her gaze so direct he was squirming inside. "I thought you would be in Hawker already." He changed the subject. "You usually have several days in town when you go."

"I've been needed here." She looked away towards the south. "The men have been shifting the remaining cattle, trying to find them food and water. We don't have a lot of stock left. The conditions since summer have been the worst we've experienced."

She turned back to him and he noticed the wisps of hair that had drifted from under her hat were grey. Her face had also aged since he'd seen her last.

"All the more reason to come to town for a party."

Johanna turned back to him. Her gaze a mixture of sadness and something else — annoyance perhaps.

"Not this time, Charles. I hope young Leonard is doing well."

"He is. Edith is a wonderful mother."

"Of course." She adjusted the brim of her broad hat. "It's very warm again today. The heat is relentless. Can I offer you some refreshment before you leave?"

"No, thank you, Mrs Prosser. I have to get this water to my man and then return to Hawker. Still things to prepare for the christening."

"Very well. Please give my best to your father."

"I will." Charles returned to his cart and climbed onto the seat, waved and set off.

He felt a prickle down his neck and glanced back over his shoulder to see that, in spite of the warm day, Johanna was still standing in the full sun where he'd left her, watching him drive away.

Forty-five

Two wagons, several horses and a crowd of people gathered outside the homestead at Smith's Ridge in the fresh air of early morning. The sun was spreading a pink light across the cloudy sky and a splash of screeching colour wheeled overhead as a flock of galahs took flight from the trees along the dry creek bed. There was an almost festive air to the group, but the occasion wasn't exactly a happy one.

All of the Bakers were present except for Thomas, who had stayed back at Wildu Creek, and Robert, who was away carting. Ruth and Matthew played with Clem's boy, Haji, and Beth held his daughter, Sally. The women had loaded Hegarty's spare horse with so much food he threatened to take offence, saying they must think he did nothing but eat.

Joseph stood back as Clem and William took a turn at shaking Hegarty's hand. Finally, the big man was standing in front of him. Instead of offering his hand Joseph wrapped his arms around his giant of a friend.

"I'm sorry you have to leave, Hegarty." Joseph let him go and looked into the laughing eyes of the man who had helped him so many times since their meeting on the goldfields at Teetulpa, and through their years as friends at Wildu Creek and Smith's Ridge. "You've become part of the family."

"This is the longest I've ever stayed anywhere. It's time for me to move on." Hegarty gripped his shoulder. "You've got plenty of helpers and there's another goldfield calling."

Joseph was going to miss his friend. Even though Hegarty had shifted to Smith's Ridge and for the last year he'd been on the road carting goods with their wagon, they still caught up from time to time. If only the seasons weren't so bad he might have stayed instead of following the lure of another gold mine. But he was right. There were plenty of people on both properties and little work for them to do. The drought had sucked the life out of almost everything.

"Travel well, my friend," Joseph said.

"And you." Hegarty swung up into the saddle. He waved to them all then moved his horse closer to where William stood with his arm around Georgina. "You look after my share of that stallion, lass."

"I will." Georgina laughed and Hegarty urged his horse away, towing the heavily loaded packhorse behind.

"Now, I suppose we have to load another horse," Millie said as Hegarty disappeared among the trees. She looked at Joseph and frowned. "Are you still going with William to see this waterhole?"

"Yes. Imagine how terrible it will be for you to have two days of uninterrupted talking with Georgina and Jessie."

Matthew and Haji ran past screeching like galahs. Millie's hands went to her hips. "Does that mean you are taking the children with you?"

Joseph grinned, pleased to see some spark back in her look. "Not this time." He glanced towards the store his son had built against the side of a low hill. William was there, adding some final supplies to the cart they'd already loaded. Joseph was going to accompany him to take the supplies to his shepherd, Albie, who camped near the waterhole. "I'd better help."

She raised her eyebrows but a smile played on her lips as he turned away.

Joseph had brought his family to Smith's Ridge to break the monotony. It had also been a chance to farewell Hegarty and spend some time with William and Georgina. Millie had been more relaxed in the last few days than he'd seen her in a long time. She had never been able to shake the terror of having her children stolen, and always stayed close to home. It had been years since she'd made the trip to Hawker. She was still the happy woman he had married but not as carefree as she had once been. Of course the drought had eroded the optimism of everyone, except for Thomas, who still greeted each day with a spring in his not-so-quick step.

William was rolling a barrel towards the cart and Joseph reached him just in time to help trundle it up the planks.

"Why are you taking barrelled water from your precious supply?" Joseph asked. "Is the waterhole so bad he can't use it?"

"We're careful. Our tanks aren't too low yet. I've always supplied Albie's water so he can keep a watch but not have to actually use the waterhole. And now we've shifted the cattle back and the waterhole is getting low, it's better I take him his own supply."

William went into the shed and came out with a bag of flour.

"Stockpiling your own supplies was a good idea." Joseph peered inside the structure and waited for his eyes to adjust to the gloom after the bright sunshine outside. It was a good solid shed with lined sides and a ceiling stuffed with hay. Shelves covered every wall except for a space in the back, where a door opened into the cellar. It was small but serviceable and had kept William, Clem and sometimes Robert busy during the winter digging into the hillside. "At least Millie can come to a shop, albeit a basic one."

"She still won't go into Hawker?"

Joseph shook his head.

"Neither will Jessie."

"I can't even take the children. People must think I'm ashamed of my own flesh and blood. They're never seen with me beyond Smith's Ridge."

"Perhaps once they're older ..."

"Town will be a foreign land to them." Joseph looked back to where the women were chatting at William's back fence, the children playing happily nearby. Georgina was holding baby Sally. "No sign of a child for you yet, son."

William gave his father a wry grin. "It seems creating children is not as easy for us as it has been for you, Father."

Joseph clapped him on the back and laughed. "Patience! Your time will come, I am sure."

The last of the supplies were loaded and the pies and cakes from the women carefully stowed, and the two men were soon waving goodbye. The children ran behind the cart for a short distance until the horses picked up speed. The homestead was lost from view behind the trees, along with the sound of the rabble of children.

Joseph and William rode in companionable silence, each deep in his own thoughts. They made good time. Joseph stared up at the ridges stretching above them, where the trees and foliage formed jagged dark green lines in the russet rocks. The two men and horses skirted the bottom of the barren hills until they reached a track winding along a gully. William came to a halt. They were still some distance from the waterhole.

"I take the cart up around the back way to where Albie is camped," William said. "That way the track's not obvious." He left the horse and cart a little way up the track then rode on with Joseph towards the waterhole.

As they crested the bank Joseph was both dismayed at the fence that crossed the waterhole securing the deepest section on the side of the claim, and astonished to see how extensive the fossicking camp was. There were three tents, one quite a bit bigger than the others. Two barrels and a table and chairs sat in the shade of a giant gum. There was also a small yard with two horses.

Joseph gave a low whistle. "This is much more substantial than my little home when I mined at Teetulpa. We only had—"

"What the *devil*?" William's curse cut him off.

Joseph glanced at his son and then in the direction he was looking, along the dry creek bed below the waterhole.

William urged his horse down the bank and Joseph followed to where a man was crouched over a dead cow. Beyond him was a young bull, also dead. The sound of horses brought the man to his feet.

"What are you doing?" William's horse had barely stopped before he was sliding from the saddle. "You can't butcher my cattle."

Joseph dismounted right behind him.

"The cow was already dead," the fellow said. He held a large knife and there were signs he'd been attempting to cut off the hindquarters of the animal.

"Who are you?" Joseph asked as his son bent to inspect the cow.

"Barnes. I work the claim over there." He jerked his head over his shoulder.

"Look at this, Father."

Joseph moved around the man to where his son leaned over the head of the cow. The animal's eyes were bulging, and some kind of frothy liquid coated its swollen lips. Joseph turned to study the rest of the beast then he turned back to Barnes. "I don't think you'd be wise to eat this animal."

"I told you I didn't kill it," Barnes growled. "Just noticed it this morning. Wasn't going to waste fresh meat."

"Not so fresh." Joseph gripped William's shoulder. "I'd say this cow has been poisoned."

Barnes staggered back. He brushed his spare hand down his trouser leg and stared at the cow. "Poisoned?"

William stood. "That's what I thought, but how?" He strode to the other animal. "Looks like it died in the same way."

"Perhaps some kind of vegetation it discovered."

"You can see there's not much around and what there is has always fed my cattle."

There was a bellow behind them and the black bull with a cow following lumbered slowly along towards the waterhole.

Joseph looked at the animal at his feet then back at the waterhole. "It's the water, William!"

William set off running to his horse before Joseph could say any more. He leaped onto Big Red and shouted at the animals as the bull lowered its head to the water. The cow skittered away from the man and horse but the bull lifted his gaze only a moment and then began to drink.

Joseph watched, helpless, as his son's last remaining bull quenched his thirst then finally gave in to William's urging and moved away, slowly following the cow back up the creek. Once the animals were out of sight William turned his horse and came back to where Joseph waited with Barnes.

Joseph could see the despair on his son's face as he climbed down from his horse. "He might be all right. Whatever it was may have been limited to one patch. Or perhaps it's not the water at all."

William marched up to Barnes. "Has anyone else been here?"

The man shook his head but Joseph could tell by the way he wouldn't meet William's look that he was lying.

"Do you drink this water?" Joseph asked.

Barnes glanced warily from William to Joseph. "Not since the cattle have come back. I get fresh water in barrels with my supplies."

"I've never seen barrels here before," William said.

Barnes looked at him directly this time. "The supply has never been this low before."

"We'll have to fence off that waterhole," Joseph said.

"There's no water anywhere else." William rounded on him. "At least none that's accessible to cattle."

Joseph saw Barnes shift his head slightly and give William a searching look.

"What's to be done?" Joseph said.

"I've got work to do." Barnes turned on his heel and set off back across the creek and over the fence to the claim.

"I'm going to follow that bull," William said. "See if he drops like these poor creatures."

"Let me do that," Joseph said. He glanced to where Barnes was already climbing up the bank on the other side. "You go back for the cart. Take the supplies to Albie. He might have some ideas about the poison. Then we'd better meet back here and drag these two to higher ground."

"Just in case it rains?" William said.

Father and son laughed, but it was a hollow sound.

William urged Big Red along the bank, skirting the edge of the creek. Anger burned within him. When he'd told Albie about the poisoned cattle, the shepherd had been quick to tell him he'd seen Wiltshire at the waterhole just the day before. William had climbed straight back on his horse. Now he urged Big Red down the bank and directly to where Barnes was shovelling rocks into his bucket. William slid from the saddle, leaving his horse untethered, and stormed at Barnes.

"What did Wiltshire put in the water?"

Barnes inched backwards a little. "I haven't seen Wiltshire."

"Liar. He was here yesterday." William pushed his face closer. "What did he put in the water?"

"How would I know what Wiltshire does? I'm employed to work this claim, not be his mate."

"Tell me what he did when he was here."

"He brought me some supplies."

"Did he go near the waterhole?" William saw the sideways look Barnes gave. "What did he put in it?"

"I didn't see anything."

William growled in frustration. He glanced around the camp and his gaze stopped at the mug on top of the water barrel. He marched over, snatched it up and made his way to the waterhole where he scooped in some water.

Barnes frowned as William stepped back up to him and pushed the mug at him.

"Take a drink."

"No."

"This water's fresh from a spring." William lifted the mug to the man's lips. "Take a drink."

Barnes turned his head away. "No. Wiltshire said not to."

William splashed some water at Barnes. The man gave a yelp and recoiled.

"William, what are you doing?" Joseph was striding towards them from the other side of the fence.

"Barnes is showing me this water is safe to drink." William glared at the prospector, who took another step back.

He lowered his gaze as both Baker men stared at him. "Look, I don't know anything." He pulled a dirty handkerchief from his pocket and mopped his face. "Wiltshire did go to the waterhole over the fence when he came back, but I didn't see him do anything. I was too busy unloading the barrels of water he gave me. All he said was I was to use them for drinking from now on because the cattle would foul the water."

"Came back from where?" William asked.

"I don't know. He brought me some supplies, then, when he saw you'd shifted the fence, he was gone for half the day. When he came back he had two barrels of water. He told me to unload them. I did it on my own while he went off. When I was done he told me to only drink from the barrels and he left."

William wanted to shake the man. "You must have seen him do something."

Barnes shook his head. "That's all I'm saying."

"Let him be, son," Joseph said. "He's not the one responsible."

Barnes hurried back to his tent. William shook his head and dropped the mug. He watched the last of the water soak into the sandy soil.

"The bull's all right." Joseph spoke calmly. "Whatever it was hasn't affected him."

William shot one last glance in Barnes's direction, then he turned and walked with his father to where Big Red waited.

"It had to be poison," William said. "Either it wasn't very much and those two were unlucky enough to drink the affected water soon after, or perhaps the size of the waterhole and the fresh water entering from the spring has dissipated it."

"Thank the Lord the natives don't come here."

"And that Albie has his own supply." William surveyed the camp. "Barnes said Wiltshire came with supplies but when he saw the cattle he went off somewhere and brought back water in barrels. I can't believe he would have a sudden concern for his employee's health. It's only a few cattle and over here the water-hole is deeper where the spring feeds it."

"What are you thinking?"

"Wiltshire was gone for about half a day. Then he came back with the barrels. The only place he could get to and back from here would be Prosser's Run."

"You think that's where he went?"

"It's possible. Swan told Hegarty they made poisoned water traps for rabbits. It was back when we all still had grass."

"I'm glad we didn't do that."

William remembered the discussion they'd had. Joseph had been so against poisoning the fenced artificial waterholes they'd had to resort to other methods of depleting the rabbits.

"There could well be some poison still kept at Prosser's Run." William glanced away as a movement over Joseph's shoulder caught his eye. Another cow was making its way to the waterhole. Damned Wiltshire. If he'd poisoned the waterhole he'd really gone too far. "Do you mind staying here a little longer, Father?"

Joseph frowned. "What are you going to do?"

"I'm going to Prosser's Run. See if I can find any answers there."

"You won't make it back here before dark."

"We'd planned to camp anyway. You stay here somewhere close to the waterhole. Make sure the remaining stock stay healthy. I'll be back by morning." William looked in the direction of the tents. "And it won't hurt for Barnes to know we're watching."

Forty-six

William approached the sprawling Prosser's Run homestead with caution. The sun was a low orange glow casting long shadows of filtered light across the landscape by the time he got close. He hoped his mother-in-law would be home. He was not in the mood to trade insults with Swan.

There was little more than a breeze to ruffle the gums that dotted the front fence line of the house yard. Inside the fence the house sprawled low and wide with its verandahs stretching all the way around the outside. He'd only ever been as far as the kitchen, but William knew it was several rooms bigger than the house at Smith's Ridge.

The lowering sun bathed the house in a golden glow, turning the stone walls to copper and honey. He was disappointed no smoke puffed from any of the chimneys. Perhaps Mrs Prosser wasn't at home. He followed the house fence towards the buildings beyond and the sound of an axe echoed back at him.

He rode on past the house and in the fading light he could see Johanna bent over a log. She lifted her head at the sound of his approach and put a hand up to shield her eyes.

"William?" Her look of surprise turned to worry. "What are you doing here?"

He climbed down from his horse. He hadn't seen his mother-in-law since the Federation celebrations. Georgina had of course, but he was stunned to see how much older again Johanna looked.

"Is it Georgina?"

"She's perfectly well." William gripped Big Red's reins tightly. All the way there, he'd mulled over how to approach his mother-in-law on the topic of Charles Wiltshire. Now he wasn't sure.

Johanna turned back to her axe.

"Let me do that." He let go the reins and stepped forward.

Johanna sighed and allowed him to take the axe. "Swan hasn't had time to cut me more wood and I've run out."

"Where is Swan?"

"He and the men are off shifting the cattle. They're not here often these days." Johanna swayed.

William shot out a hand to support her. "Are you ill?"

She shook her head. "We've so little feed and water and only a few cattle left. Money is tight. I'm tired and I don't sleep well, but I'm not ill." She straightened and eased from his grasp. "No different from most bush people, I suspect. This drought is going to keep squeezing until our stock are all dead and we're turned lifeless with them."

William was surprised at her defeated air. Johanna Prosser had always struck him as a survivor. "You are too much on your own. I wish you would come and stay with us for a while at Smith's Ridge."

Johanna gave a soft snort. "Georgina said the same the last time she was here but I wouldn't be comfortable there. And who would look after Prosser's Run?"

The Mrs Prosser he knew had returned.

She stooped to collect the box she had partly filled with wood. "I'll take this in and get the fire going, make up a pot of tea." She gave him a steady look. "Then you can tell me why you've come."

William nodded. She walked back to the house and he set to the task of chopping the wood.

The night was dark by the time William had finished a decent stockpile and seen to his horse. There were few clouds, only a sliver of moon, and a drop in the temperature that chilled his skin beneath his damp shirt. Arms loaded with more wood, he made his way carefully towards the lamp Johanna must have set at the back door. She showed him the wood box and where to wash. By the time he joined her inside there was a meal on the table and two places set.

"You were a long time out there chopping." She gave him a tight smile. "Thank you." She waved towards the second setting. "I thought you might be hungry."

William's stomach rumbled at the sight of the beef and potatoes she had served. "Very." He grinned and took his place. He bowed his head as she said grace and watched her pour a mug of tea for him and a delicate teacup full for herself.

"Ellis never liked a cup for his tea. Said a man needed a decent stomach-full, not two sips."

William took the napkin she had placed beside his plate.

"Do eat," she said and picked up the knife to slice some bread. "I'm sorry it's not much. I wasn't expecting company."

He had already downed two mouthfuls. "I'm grateful. It's been a long time since breakfast."

They ate in silence, the crackle of the fire and the flutter of moths against the glass the only sounds.

"How is my daughter?"

"Very well. She spends a lot of time working the horses."

"That's good," she said and they lapsed back into silence.

William could not think of any common ground between them. When he'd finished, she offered him more meat. He accepted it between two layers of her fresh bread.

"Perhaps you'd better tell me why you've come." Johanna sat her cutlery neatly across her partly finished meal and studied him. "I am assuming it's not a social call."

William washed down his mouthful of food with some of the tea. He opened his mouth, closed it again and took a breath.

"Best just spit out whatever's bothering you," she said.

"I believe — I'm not sure — but perhaps Charles Wiltshire paid a visit here yesterday."

She inclined her head slightly, watching him.

"After he returned to my waterhole, where he has his mining claim, and before I arrived today, two of my cattle died. I think they were poisoned."

Johanna frowned.

"I came to ask if he got that poison from you."

She gasped. "I know I haven't treated you well in the past but I hope you wouldn't think so badly of me that I would be a party to such a terrible deed."

William shook his head quickly. "I'm not accusing you of giving it to him, I simply wondered if he might have obtained the poison at Prosser's Run."

"I didn't know he was here until he'd already filled and loaded two barrels of water. I did think he was acting rather strangely." She sniffed. "Usually he wants to spend his time trying to charm me, but there was none of that yesterday. He was anxious to be on his way. After he left I went to the buildings where he'd had his cart. We keep spare barrels in the big stone shed." A strange look crossed Johanna's face and she put a hand to her cheek. "And the smaller building right next to it is the place where Swan stores the poison."

William pushed back in his chair. "Mind if I take a look?"

"You won't see too much out there tonight even with a lantern. Can you stay? We can have a look at first light. Swan could even be back by then. He will know if anything is missing."

William studied Johanna. Her stance was stiff, her look said she did not care whether or not he stayed, but William thought otherwise. His mother-in-law was lonely and in spite of the truce between her and Georgina there was still much to be done to mend the rift that marriage to William had caused.

"Thank you," he said.

When he finally went to sleep in the strange bed with sheets that smelled of camphor William slept so heavily it took him a moment to work out where he was when he first opened his eyes the next morning. The room was dark and the dull glow of early light came from behind a curtain, which was in the wrong position. Then he remembered he was at Prosser's Run. He rose immediately and drew back the curtain. He had slept late. There was already enough light for him to investigate the outer buildings. He pulled on his clothes and made his way along the hall, through the sitting room and into the kitchen. Johanna was already there. She was pouring hot water into the teapot as he entered.

"Just in time." She gave him a tentative smile. "Did you sleep well?"

"Very." He didn't sit where she'd set his place at the table.

"It's crisp outside this morning." She poured tea into a mug. "You will need something warm inside you before we go to the outbuildings."

He took the mug she offered. The kitchen was warm but the late April mornings were cool first thing. He hadn't drunk too much of the tea before his anxiety to head out infected his hostess.

Johanna pulled on a coat and he followed her outside to retrieve his boots.

They retraced the steps they'd both taken yesterday to the woodpile, where Johanna nodded thoughtfully at the large stack of logs he'd cut. Big Red nickered from the yard nearby as they crossed to the first of the stone buildings. William paused in front. It was a huge structure with high walls and strong wooden rafters supporting a tin roof. It had two doors that stretched almost the height of the wall. One was locked open. The building could house wagons, bags of grain, even horses or cattle if necessary, but today there was only a wagon, Johanna's compact sprung cart and a stack of empty barrels inside.

Johanna dragged open the door to the second smaller shed before William had caught her up. The weak early-morning light filtered in around them as they stepped inside.

"Swan knows what's kept here better than I but he wasn't here the day Charles came."

The musty smell from the dirt floor dissipated as the cooler outside air flowed in. Shelves lined one wall and William followed Johanna to inspect them.

"There," she said almost straight away. Lined up along the top shelf were several jars and bottles, and in the middle there was a space.

William stretched up just high enough to see the round mark imprinted in the dust where something had recently stood. He felt his anger returning, spreading its burning tendrils inside him. "Something has been newly removed from here."

"The bottle of poison. It was clearly labelled. We've had no use for it for at least a year." Johanna shook her head in tiny movements, her mouth slightly open. "And you think he used it to poison your cattle?"

William looked her steadily in the eye, his hands closed into fists at his sides. "I would stake my life on it, but I have no real evidence."

She sagged as if the wind had gone from her. "I've been such a fool. I realise now I thought more about the Wiltshires' standing in the community than I thought about the people they are. Ever since Charles married his shop assistant I've seen another side to him. I know he can be forceful and ostentatious but ..." She gripped William's arm. "Do you really think he is capable of poisoning stock and putting people's lives at risk? I know it's out of the way, but what if one of your stockmen or mine had stopped to drink at that waterhole?"

"Or the natives who live in the hills."

Her hand fell back to her side. "It's too terrible to contemplate."

"I must get back. My father is camped at the waterhole keeping a watch on the cattle." William had made up his mind he would ride to Hawker to have this out with Wiltshire. Even though he had no solid proof, he was sure he was right about the poisoning.

"Of course. Will you go to see Charles?"

"Yes."

Johanna's shoulders drooped. She looked suddenly very old and small. William thought about the big empty house and the table, a place set for his breakfast. Then just as quickly she drew herself up, determination on her face.

"I will get you some food while you saddle your horse."

"Thank you."

"And William." She looked him up and down. "Perhaps a change of clothes."

In a brand-new shirt and trousers, once meant for Georgina's brother, Rufus, William made it back to the waterhole in good time. Clouds kept the mid-morning sun from becoming too fierce. They even looked as if they could contain rain but William had seen that look too often over the last few years, and only little or none at all had eventuated.

He skirted around the claim to the vantage point above the waterhole on the other side of the creek, where his father was putting out his small fire.

"How did you get on?" Joseph asked as William climbed down from his horse.

"Charles was definitely at Prosser's Run. Mrs Prosser said he was acting strangely and I saw the place where the poison bottle had stood gathering dust until very recently. Still she didn't actually see him with the bottle."

"Have a look there." Joseph pointed behind him to a log just beyond his fire. A small calico bag rested against it.

William picked up the bag, feeling a solid shape through the fabric. He peered inside. A dark cork was wedged into the top of a brown glass bottle. He slowly shifted his gaze back to his father. "Where did you find this?"

"It was stuffed inside that hollow log. The very log I sat on last night to eat my food. I only noticed it this morning when I dropped my mug. I bent down to retrieve it and saw the end of the bottle just inside the hollow."

William lifted the bottle from the bag and read the label. *Rabbit poison* was clearly marked on the side.

"There's still some left," Joseph said. "Not a good sign."

William tilted the dark brown bottle to see there was indeed some liquid still inside. "So he was planning to come back and try again."

"Perhaps." Joseph shrugged his shoulders.

The bellow of a cow made William turn and look down at the waterhole. This time there were three thin-looking cattle heading towards the water. He sucked in a breath.

"They'll be all right," Joseph said. "I've watched several drink — some yesterday and some early this morning. They don't seem to be bothered. I think the poison has been diluted by the large expanse of water. Those first two were probably unlucky to drink not long after it was added."

William slipped the bottle back into the bag. "Can you take the cart back to the homestead?"

"Where are you going?"

William stashed the bag with its grim contents into his saddle bag. "To Hawker."

Forty-seven

Henry sat in a chair tucked to one side of his sitting room and watched the milling group of people drinking his wine and eating his food. They were mostly friends of Charles and Edith. Not that the house was overflowing with guests. Thankfully for his purse the christening was a much smaller affair than their wedding.

Few of Henry's old friends were there, having found some other event or work that meant they could decline the invitation to Leonard's christening. Councillor Hill and his wife were there but with only one of their daughters. The eldest had married and now lived in Adelaide. The Buttons were there of course, they could always be relied upon, but the Taylors were in Port Augusta, where Sydney had recently accepted the stationmaster's role, and they had yet to meet this replacement.

Henry took a bite of the savoury puff he held in his hand. It had gone cold and wasn't as nice as those Flora used to make. He drew in a breath; the pain of Flora's loss still ached inside him. He had tried every avenue he could to track her down. Unbeknown to Charles he'd even hired a chap in Adelaide to do some searching for him, but it had cost him a handsome packet with no return. Henry had resigned himself to a lonely existence.

A burst of children's laughter drifted through the open window, Laura's giggles soft and sweet among it. The few children who had come along had been relegated to the side verandah. Henry was thankful he had his dear daughter, who brought sunshine to his life and was always happy. Even when Edith was reprimanding her, Laura kept her good humour.

"Leonard is off to his bed now, everyone."

Henry shifted his gaze to his son, who was posturing proudly in the centre of the room with Edith beside him, holding the baby. The christening gown had been replaced by a new outfit: something not quite as frilly this time. Leonard had been christened in the gown worn by his father and his Aunty Laura but Edith had insisted on something new for afterwards.

There were best wishes and soft calls from those gathered as Charles guided his wife from the room. Henry glimpsed movement at the window and saw Laura peering in. At least the weather was pleasant enough to be outside. A sunny autumn day with a gentle breeze rather than the burst of hot days they'd had all week. The voices in the room grew louder again. Henry sighed. He hoped the party wouldn't drag on too long.

Leonard's tiny face was red, his eyes squeezed tightly shut as he drew breath and then began to cry. Edith was bent over his cradle making tutting noises.

"What's wrong with him?" Charles asked. He had rarely seen his son so upset.

"Too much fussing." Edith stood back and Leonard continued to bellow, his arms and legs flailing and disturbing the blanket she had tucked around him. "Mrs Button and Mrs Hill both insisted on taking him from his perambulator and holding him. His routine is out of kilter."

Charles winced as Leonard's wails grew louder. "What are we to do?"

"He will cry himself out." Edith took her hand from the cradle. "One of the good things about living in these cramped quarters is he can't be heard from the house."

Charles looked down at his distressed son and longed to pick him up, but he knew that would make Edith cross. She insisted too much holding would spoil the child.

"Oh for goodness sake, I shall have to feed him." Edith lowered herself to her chair and began to unbutton her shirt. "All that yelling has made my milk flow. Pass him to me, Charles."

Charles did as he was bid and felt instant relief as his son's cries ceased at his wife's breast. He moved away. The sight of his son suckling turned his stomach, though he would never admit as much to Edith.

She exhaled sharply. "I shall be a while now. You go back to our guests. I will be there as soon as I can."

"Very well." Relieved that all was settled, Charles let himself out into the courtyard and made his way towards the back door of the house. Footsteps crunched on the gravel path from the garden, and Charles turned, thinking one of his guests was outside. The smile dropped from his face.

"William Baker," he snarled. "What are you doing here?"

"Your sister told me I might find you here."

William came no closer, standing in the sunshine with his hat firmly on his head, shading his face, and his shirt so white it made Charles crinkle his eyes up to look at him.

"What do you want?"

"I see you have a big tank here, Charles. Still plenty of water in it for your family?"

"Enough." Charles watched William take two steps forward so he was under the tin roof of the courtyard. "Why are you here?"

"I thought I'd return the favour you did for me." William held up a calico bag, his hand gripping whatever was inside it.

"What game are you playing?"

William's features hardened. "I don't think it's a game," he growled and tugged a bottle from the bag.

Charles felt his knees weaken at the sight. He glanced in the direction of the big stone tank that collected all the water from the roof and was their household supply. "What have you done, Baker?"

"Given you a taste of your own medicine." William waggled the bottle at him.

"You wouldn't." Charles gasped. He felt sick. "You haven't."

William's face contorted into a malevolent grin. "Of course not. I'm not like you, Charles, but it was worth pretending — just to see the look on your face." William jerked his head in the direction of the house. "Have you got the constable in there at your party? He should be interested in what you're capable of."

Charles watched William swagger three steps closer. The shock of seeing him with the poison had thrown him for a minute but now he regained his composure. "He is not, but perhaps I had better send for him."

William raised his eyebrows.

"You've come to my house and threatened to poison our water supply."

"In front of a witness."

Charles turned at the sound of his father's voice behind him.

Henry stepped closer. "How dare you, Baker, come here and threaten my family?"

"Your son poisoned the only water my stock had to drink. I've lost two beasts, maybe more."

"Don't listen to him, Father." Charles was glad Henry had defended him. Sometimes of late it appeared they were on opposite sides. "Why would I poison the very water needed for my claim?"

"You can still use the water for your claim. It's just not drinkable. Luckily you supplied your man with separate water."

Charles jabbed his finger in the air in front of William's nose. "Because your cattle were fouling it; that's probably what killed them."

William pushed the bottle close to Charles. "This is what killed them."

"How would that get in the water?" Henry said. "You're just like your father, always looking for something to blame for your ills other than your poor management."

William was close enough for Charles to see a vein throbbing on his neck and anger deepening the red of his cheeks. He allowed his lips to turn up in a smile. "I can't see how you can blame me. I have no access to poison."

"You're a liar and a murderer, Wiltshire." William grabbed a handful of his jacket, but Charles shrugged him off.

"That is enough." This time it was Edith's sharp voice that surprised them. She carefully closed the door to the quarters behind her. "I have a sleeping baby here and guests inside."

William stepped back and removed his hat. "My apologies, Mrs Wiltshire."

Edith looked down her pointy nose at him. "I think you should leave."

"I was about to." He pushed his hat back on his head and glowered at Charles. "I am on my way to see the constable."

Charles leaned forward. He would have liked to have had a swing at Baker but his father put a hand on his arm.

"Let him go, Charles. He can't prove something that didn't happen." His father gave him a thoughtful look. "Can he?"

Charles glared as Baker turned and walked away around the building. "Of course not." He shook his head, glad he hadn't told his father everything about his recent trip to the claim.

"My goodness that man is so aggressive. Are you all right, Charles?" Edith crossed the courtyard and patted his necktie into place.

"Of course." Charles didn't think there was any proof he had administered the poison. He'd been careful not to let Barnes see him. It was unfortunate Baker had found the bottle though. "Baker could make such a fuss that the constable might feel he should investigate, that's all. Then I will be obliged to answer questions. It is not good for our reputation, even if there is no substance to Baker's story."

"We will deal with that if it happens," Henry said.

"He can try to see the constable but he'll be waiting a while." Edith had a smug look on her face. "I invited Constable Brown to the christening, but he has been called away to Hergott Springs. That's a long journey north. I don't imagine he'll be back for a week, could be two or three. Mr Baker will run out of huff and puff before that."

"I do wonder if it's not time to let that claim go," Henry said. "In these times we should be tightening our belts."

"I agree with your father, Charles." Edith nodded and Charles noted the stunned look on his father's face.

"We will discuss it later," Charles said. It was unlike Henry and Edith to agree but he was sure he could convince them to keep up the search for diamonds, just as he was sure the elusive rocks would soon be found.

Charles patted the hand Edith slipped through his arm and he was pleased to see his father take the other hand she offered. They made a good team, the Wiltshires.

"Let's return to our guests," Edith said and propelled them forward.

William couldn't believe what he was reading. The sign on the police-station door said the officer was away for possibly a month and any urgent business would have to be taken up with the police at Quorn. He shook his head. The next nearest policeman had been at Cradock but that office was permanently closed now, and he certainly wasn't going to ride to Quorn. The bottle of poison was still clutched firmly in his hand, but he had nowhere to go with it. He paced the path in front of the station. Charles Wiltshire always wormed his way out of danger. William stopped as he noticed a couple watching him. Had he been muttering out loud? He dipped his hat and they continued on their way.

At least there was one thing Wiltshire had missed out on. William's love for Georgina and hers for him had ruined any plans for a Prosser — Wiltshire dynasty. Thinking of his wife softened William's anger. She would be worried about him by now. Joseph would be back at Smith's Ridge, telling them all that had happened. And she would be watching for William's return.

He retraced his steps to his horse and led him back along the road towards the shop that had replaced Garrat's. 'Best Fit in Town' was sure to have something for him to take home as a gift for Georgina — then his trip to Hawker wouldn't have been a total waste of time.

The next morning he was on his way early after a restless night in his swag. Except for the yellow where the sun was rising, the cloudless blue sky was edged in every direction with a soft pink. Birds chattered around him in the trees. He was following the track along a dry creek bed dotted with the brown and white trunks of the gum trees, their foliage varying in colour from dusty green to silvery grey, affording him some shade. Beneath Big Red's hooves the crisp and brittle leaves and bark crunched with every step, and ahead of him in the east, the hills and ridges of Smith's Ridge glowed orange and brown.

His land was in the grip of a drought being felt across the new nation of Australia. The newspaper he had purchased in Hawker had been dismal reading, but he had brought it with him for the others to peruse anyway, and after that it would make a good lining for drawers, or shoes with holes, or gaps in windows.

He pulled Big Red up at the first glimpse of the house. There would be a barrage of questions and he wasn't looking forward to telling them he had failed to bring Charles Wiltshire to justice. With a heavy heart William squeezed his legs and his faithful horse continued on. He hoped Georgina wouldn't think him silly, but he hadn't known what to choose in Mr Collins's shop. He had finally decided on a length of emerald green ribbon. It was velvet ribbon this time, and he hoped she would find some useful purpose for it.

Forty-eight

May 1903

Georgina cast her gaze to the dark clouds on the western horizon then back to the track to her front door. The trees close to the house were tossing in the gusting wind and the temperature had dropped. The end of autumn had brought them bitterly cold weather but no rain. She pulled her shawl closer.

There had been no wind and no grey clouds when William had set off in the cart at first light to collect Johanna from Prosser's Run. Georgina was hanging out the washing when she had noticed the sky was turning a murky grey, clouds were banking to the west and a stiff breeze made the bedsheets flap on the line. By mid-afternoon it had been a struggle to bring them in again and the strengthening wind was full of dust. She'd shut up the chickens and brought the horses into the yard close to the house.

Now she let herself back inside and added more wood to the fire in the front room and the one in the kitchen. She checked the shepherd's pie then glanced around her tidy kitchen. There was nothing more to be done until they arrived.

Unable to settle, she moved through the house once more, glancing into each room. This would be the first time her mother would visit her at Smith's Ridge. Now the bad weather added to her unrest. She wished she hadn't admitted to William she was with child again; then she would have ridden with him to collect her mother. Instead he had insisted she stay home. She had only told him about the baby the day before because she knew he would see her rounded stomach for himself soon enough. This baby was well past the time she had lost the first and she allowed herself to breathe and to imagine it would grow strong and be born safely.

At least now William knew she could also tell her mother and Jessie and Clem when they returned from checking the cattle and taking supplies to Albie. In the room she had prepared for her mother Georgina tugged at a corner of the quilt and ran her hand over it, smoothing away imaginary wrinkles. She hoped Johanna would be comfortable.

Her mother's message, brought by one of the Prosser's Run shepherds, had frightened her. Johanna had been weakened by a bout of coughing sickness and must have been feeling terrible indeed to send for her daughter. Georgina had wanted to jump on her horse and ride straight over but William had stopped her. He had insisted they look after her mother at Smith's Ridge where he could keep an eye on both of them.

In their bedroom she smiled at the hat she had decorated with the beautiful velvet ribbon from Hawker. It was a wide straw hat, very plain, and the ribbon brightened it considerably. Over a month had passed since William's angry dash to make a report to the police about the poisoning of their cattle. He had returned annoyed and a little embarrassed that he had been unable to expose Charles Wiltshire's treachery.

She startled at a loud clatter on the roof: probably a branch from a tree. From the bedroom window she could see the wind was much stronger. Fear wormed inside her and then a rush of relief replaced it as she saw their horse and cart emerge from the trees and career towards the back of the house.

Georgina hurried outside. Her mother was wrapped like a parcel in blankets perched on the seat next to William.

He slid down from the cart and gripped Georgina's arms. "We must get her inside quickly. We're in for a big storm. I hope Clem has found somewhere safe for Jessie and the children."

Georgina glanced west, where the sky was now black. A flash lightened the dark and then was gone. She hurried around to where William was lifting Johanna down.

"I'll carry her," he said.

"You will not," came a muffled response. "You have enough to do. Georgina will get me inside."

Georgina put an arm around her mother. William hesitated a moment, watching them.

"You go." Georgina had to shout against the noise of the wind.

He turned quickly and led the horse and cart away while she guided her mother inside. The first rumble of thunder echoed in the distance as she closed the back door on the storm.

Johanna shrugged out of all but one of the blankets, and coughed several times then looked around. "The last time I was here was not a very happy day. Sad that William lost his mother so young."

"That was a long time ago, Mother." Georgina drew out a chair. She was shaken by her mother's frail appearance. Johanna appeared to have withered even since Georgina had visited her last. "Sit here by the fire. I wish I'd known earlier you were so unwell. How have you managed on your own?"

"Swan sent one of the shepherds to stay back at the homestead. He was a reasonable cook and made a good cup of tea." Johanna looked pointedly at the pot on the table and began to cough again.

Georgina took the steaming kettle from the stove and made the tea while her mother regained her breath.

"A hawker came by a few weeks ago," Johanna said. "I made him afternoon tea and bought some gloves from him. Poor man had a terrible cough. I am sure that's how I came to get it."

Georgina poured the tea. Wind howled around the house and another growl of thunder rumbled closer. She glanced to the window where darkness had come early, and hoped William would be back inside soon.

"I do pray this storm isn't an empty promise." Johanna gripped her cup in two hands.

"Thank goodness you're here with us, Mother."

"I wouldn't have been, only William said you were not well yourself and he had to bring me here so he could look after us both." Johanna's steady gaze locked on Georgina. "You look well enough to me."

"William is being a little ... over protective." Georgina smiled. "I am with child."

Johanna put down her cup and reached across the table for Georgina's hands. "That is wonderful news." She started to cough again.

A clatter sounded from overhead and grew louder. They both looked up.

"*Rain*," Georgina said. She held her breath waiting for the sound to fade as it so often had in the last few years, but instead the sound grew heavier and settled to a steady thrumming on the roof.

The back door slammed open, making both women jump.

"Sorry." William heaved the door shut against the wind. When he turned back he was drenched but his face was lit with a huge smile.

It rained steadily for two days. Several pots had to be deployed to catch drops from leaks they didn't know they had. The creeks roared to life and the ground, parched for so long, soaked in the water and became sodden. By the second day the paths to the chicken house and milking shed were indistinguishable from the rest of the yard. It was a slippery walk and William worried about Georgina maintaining her balance and holding the bucket of milk. With little else to do until the rain stopped he went with her.

"I hope Jessie and the children are all right," she said as she tried to find the best place to scatter the scraps for the chickens.

William turned his face to the sky. The rain had eased momentarily but they could see there was more coming. "There's a creek between us and them and with this much water and the earth baked so hard there's bound to be water flowing everywhere. He couldn't risk trying to come home. I'm guessing he's teamed up with Albie, who knows those hills well. I'm sure they'll be safe." He wondered briefly about Barnes at the claim and hoped the man had had the good sense to seek higher ground.

"I'm glad you got Mother here in time," Georgina said. "Being housebound has given us plenty of time to talk."

William turned back from the cow he was tethering. Every night Georgina would tell him about her attempts to get her mother to stay with them. He was not so keen on the idea but kept his own counsel on that.

"Mother has decided she wants to move in to Hawker. She's not going to sell Prosser's Run. Oh William, I'm so relieved. I'm sure she will pass it on to us eventually." She put a hand to her stomach. "For our child."

"Is she leaving Swan in charge?"

"Yes, but she wants him to confer with us." Georgina's eyes sparkled. "We will be the managers on Mother's behalf."

"We have our work cut out here at Smith's Ridge."

"I know, but we can get more help. Now that we've had good rain we can restock. Mother has been very thrifty, and so have you. We've money between us to make this land prosper again."

"Georgina Baker, you are a task master."

She reached out a hand to him. "You want this too, William. We both love this country."

He took her hand then pulled her into his arms. Over her shoulder he took in the grey day as another shower clattered on the tin roof of the cowshed. "It will be a challenge," he murmured into her soft curls. But one he would readily accept.

The rain continued on and off for over a week until finally they awoke one morning to weak sunshine. The small torrent that had forged its way across the space between their house and Clem's cottage had reduced to a trickle and the roar of water in the creek below the house had eased. William rode out from the homestead finding new waterways cut into the earth, rushing and carrying everything in their path from small branches to giant logs. He delighted in the fresh smell of the earth and bush and the sight of the deeper green of the leaves washed clean of years of dust. He visited the most likely place for Clem to cross back over the creek but there was no sign of him.

Georgina was growing more and more anxious for the young family. Johanna had recovered during their enforced period of being confined to the house and she was worried about Prosser's Run.

"Swan will have everything in hand there," William said. "I'm going to see if I can cross the creek and look for Clem."

Georgina gave him a worried glance.

"He's got the cart and it won't be easy for him to get back. I'll take them some supplies, see how they are," William reassured her.

He came across them not long after he traversed the creek. Clem was riding beside his family in the cart — he'd rigged a canvas cover over it — and Albie was bringing up the rear. They all looked surprisingly well. Haji waved at him from under a corner of the canvas and then it lifted further and he could see Jessie holding the baby. They all dismounted and started on some morning tea while they caught up.

"Albie came and got us at the first sign of the storm," Clem said. "The natives had moved to some caves near their camp and they let us share their space."

"We had plenty of supplies," Albie said. "It was fair trade."

"We would have tried to make it back sooner." Clem's face had taken on a grim look. "Only we thought we should check to see if Barnes was all right." He glanced back towards the small fire they'd lit for Jessie to boil water for some tea. Haji was busy scouting for more sticks dry enough to put on it.

"The claim was completely washed away." Albie took over the story. "The bank where his camp had been was gone, and no sign of him ever being there. The horses were gone too, so we hoped he'd got away in time. We had accounted for the cattle except for the black bull, so we continued downstream a short way. We found the bull scratching himself against the roots of a tree and …" Albie glanced towards the family at the fire and lowered his voice. "We found Barnes. He was dead. His body was wedged in the fork of a tree."

"We buried him there," Clem said.

William was sorry. He wanted the claim gone from his property but he had wished Barnes no ill.

"Come and have your tea," Jessie called.

They all took the warm mugs gratefully.

"I hope we can make it home tonight," she said. "It will be so good to have a proper roof over our heads again."

Haji dashed past with a stick in his hand and boots and trouser legs covered in mud, playing some imaginary game.

"And at last enough water for a decent bath," Jessie added with a chuckle and slipped her arm around Clem.

All of William's remaining cattle had survived, but gradually they heard from other neighbours and later the mailman of not such happy results. A man had been swept off his horse in a swollen creek, some shops in Hawker had lost their roofs and houses and shops close to the creek in Cradock were flooded. It was not only the towns that suffered from the raging storm. There was widespread damage to fences and properties. From those who had sheep and had managed to keep them alive through the drought came stories of many of the poor animals washed away and drowned. At Wildu Creek Joseph had put his remaining mob in sheds and yards and kept them safe, and the report from Prosser's Run was they had lost only one of their few remaining cattle in the bulging creeks.

From drought to flood their lives were still tenuous, but for William at Smith's Ridge there was cause for optimism. They still had a cold — and hopefully continuing wet — winter to face, but there would be a new baby at the end of it and that was something to be thankful for.

Forty-nine

June 1903

It was a chilly winter morning when William and Georgina set off in the cart to return Johanna to Prosser's Run. The two women would stay there and sort out the house while William went on to Hawker to find a suitable residence for his mother-in-law.

Most of the tracks had been washed away and he chose to take the cart over the lower plains where the creek beds were wider and easier to cross. They reached the boundary between the two properties by mid-morning and stopped to stretch their legs and take some water.

"You will be pleased to see your house again, Mrs Prosser." William smiled. She had asked him to call her Johanna but he couldn't bring himself to do it.

"Yes, but I will be saying goodbye to it. The time has come for the next generation to take it on." She looked at William. "You should move to Prosser's Run once I'm settled in town."

"There is nothing wrong with where we live at Smith's Ridge. My parents raised four children in that house."

"I know that, but the homestead at Prosser's Run is bigger and it's too good to let someone like Swan live in it. You have family, too, who would appreciate your house. Jessie and Clem's cottage is very basic."

William glanced at Georgina, but she wouldn't look at him. Did she agree with her mother? "What do you think?" he asked.

Georgina lifted her shoulders. "I think I am happy wherever you are."

Johanna gave a wry smile. "Think on it, is all I ask." She turned back to the cart. "Now we should get moving. By the look of this fence there will be work to be done and Swan needs firm directions. I only hope there is no damage to the buildings at home."

Two days later after a thorough inspection of the homestead and outbuildings at Prosser's Run, where nothing more than a water leak in the wash-house window and some loose iron on the big shed was evident, William arrived in Hawker. There had already been a big clean-up around town, judging by the piles of debris arranged here and there along the sides of the roads. The cabinetmaker was on his roof hammering and the chemist had a *closed for repairs* sign but most of the other shops were open. He noted one side of Wiltshire's shop was also closed for repairs. It was the older part of the building and had obviously not stood up to the ravages of the storm.

William was not proud that he was glad the Wiltshires had to deal with damages. Over the years they had caused trouble for many people. He had not given the poisoning of his cattle a thought since the rain had come, but it rankled now to think he'd let Charles get away with such an act. However, Georgina had only agreed to stay back at Prosser's Run if he promised not to cause trouble. William had to be satisfied that the loss of his claim was repayment of Wiltshire's debt.

The business William was seeking was housed in the building alongside Wiltshire's. He came to a stop in front of the auctioneer's office and looked up and down the street. People hurried back and forth on foot, in carts or on horseback, most with thick jackets to keep out the cold. Even though the sun shone the wind still chilled to the bone. It was good to see Hawker busy. The storm had done some damage, but it had also brought confidence for the future. And in Mr Reed's office it looked to be business as usual. William could see the glow of a fire through the window. It would be warm inside and he hoped Mr Reed would know of a suitable house for Mrs Prosser.

The Wiltshires were unaware of William's presence in town. They were at home. Henry had called a meeting and since the damage in his office was considerable he had been doing all his work from the dining room. Henry had wanted to meet with Charles alone but Edith had delivered their tea to the dining room and once her tray was empty she had put it aside and taken a seat at the table. No doubt Laura had been commandeered to look after Leonard. Not that the dear girl minded — she adored her little nephew — but Henry didn't like the way Edith treated her as a house help rather than a sister-in-law.

"What's this about, Father?" Charles said.

"I've been taking stock of our assets." Henry glanced down at the papers spread in front of him then back at Charles. "It seems this house is the only thing we own outright."

"And the shop."

"We're still paying the bank for the extensions and the large verandah, and we will need to borrow more to fix the damage."

"What about the insurance?" Edith said. "Surely that will cover it."

Henry fixed his gaze on Charles, who wouldn't return his look.

"What about the insurance, Charles?" he said.

"I only delayed paying it for a short time."

Henry picked up the letter he'd received from the insurance company. "It seems we haven't paid our dues for over a year."

"What?" Edith turned to Charles. "Why didn't you pay?"

"There have been several drains on our finances in recent times. You always want the best, Edith."

"Don't you blame me. You know I wouldn't have asked if there was not enough money."

Henry sighed as they bickered beside him. He thought sadly of his original shop, which had also been his home. He had been so proud of his achievements, but now the ceiling over the door between the older shop and the rooms at the back had given way in the storm and the shop was flooded.

"What about our house?" Edith cut into his thoughts. "That's bringing in a return."

"The rent doesn't pay what we owe on that either." Henry looked from one to the other. "It ended up costing far more than my mother's contribution and we still have no money to finish it."

Once more Edith turned to her husband. "I thought you paid off that loan with your transport business."

Henry noticed his son didn't look at her but stared straight ahead, his chin jutted forward. "I needed the money for other things."

"Yes, let's discuss those other things." Once again Henry looked down at his papers. "The mining claim has been an ongoing drain on our finances." He looked back at Charles. "For no return."

"Well, that's gone now," Edith said in her most clipped tone. "We won't be going back to stake it out again, will we, Charles?"

Charles remained silent.

"I should hope not," Henry snapped. "A man lost his life."

"Charles has given some money and supplies to his wife."

"That should be some comfort to her." Henry couldn't help the sarcasm that dripped from his words. "As well as being another cost to us."

"I didn't know Barnes even had a wife," Charles growled.

Henry raised his eyebrows but said no more on the subject of his son's ridiculous obsession with diamonds. "And your transport endeavours? I don't have access to your figures there either."

Charles thumped the table and stood up. "Don't play this game with me, Father. I don't have access to your farming figures. We have always diversified and not tied our various business interests together."

"You have farms?" Edith frowned at Henry.

"Not any more, as Charles well knows. I sold them off during the drought. The pittance I got for them has not gone far." Henry waved at the chair his son had vacated. "Resume your seat, Charles, and tell me about the state of your transport business. It may be the only thing to ensure our survival."

Charles sat heavily and clasped his hands in front of him. "One of the wagons was caught in a wash away when the rains came. The driver only reached Hawker yesterday. The load of bagged grain is ruined. I haven't heard from the second man. He was doing a run to the north and hasn't returned as yet." Charles glared at Henry. "You know that it's been difficult to get as much carrying work since most of the mines petered out again. I sold off the bullock wagon I had. There were for a time plenty of wagons and not enough loads to keep them all busy."

"At least the drought is over." Edith put a hand on her husband's shoulder. "Things should improve; we shall just have to tighten our belts."

"We most definitely shall." Henry wanted to shake his head at her but he kept his manner calm. Baker's unexpected visit during the christening had brought him closer again to Charles — it was an uneasy alliance and one Henry thought it important to maintain. It had shocked him to discover the insurance hadn't been paid but they would just have to make the best of it if they were to put these dark days behind them and rebuild their empire. Henry needed Charles and therefore Edith. They could look after themselves, but he was not getting any younger, and he had Laura to provide for. At least his house was debt free. All of their loans were against the business.

Charles straightened. "I shall go and visit Grandmother."

"Good heavens, Charles." Henry was really struggling now to remain composed. "Times have been difficult across the country. There are few places that haven't been affected by this drought. Your grandmother has suffered too and now that she can barely see she has little input into her business. You must allow her to put aside some money for her final years."

"We can let Miss Fisher go."

Charles and Henry both turned to Edith.

"It will be some time before the old shop will be able to open. I can help Mr Hemming."

"But you have Leonard," Charles said.

"I can take Leonard with me. He can sleep in the storeroom or perhaps in the afternoons Laura and Mrs Coleman could watch him. That would be a saving." She nodded her head emphatically.

"It would indeed, my dear." Charles stood and looked at Henry. "We will get out of this, Father, you will see. But I should return to the shop now and continue sifting through what is salvageable and what is not." Charles kissed his wife and left.

Edith gathered their only partly drunk cups of tea. Henry settled back in his chair and looked along the length of his fine mahogany table. This house was still grand in spite of their current financial troubles and for the first time in years he felt as if he were in charge again. The loss of Flora had set him back but he had survived it. Regular trips to Adelaide to visit his mother allowed him other discreet outlets for his physical needs.

Henry ran his fingers over the bump in the table's edge, where years ago his half-brother had gouged his initials in the expensive wood. He'd survived Jack Aldridge's attempts to take what he had built up and he would survive this current setback. He did feel a little sorry for Miss Fisher, however; her wage helped her care for her ageing father. As Edith had said, it was a start in clawing back from their financial difficulties but he would be sad to let Miss Fisher go. He'd grown quite fond of her pretty face in his shop.

William folded the papers Mr Reed had given him and stepped out of the warm office. He buttoned his outer coat tight against the sudden cold. Mrs Prosser had been clear about the kind of residence she wanted, and he thought she would be well pleased with the house he had chosen. It was only one street back from the shops and, while not huge, was still a good size with a lovely garden that had already sprung back to life since the rain. Mr Reed had given him a sketch of the house to show her.

William was knocked sideways by a man hurrying past. An elbow had caught him in the ribs and had he not caught hold of the verandah post he would have toppled onto the road.

"I'm very sorry."

The hairs on the back of William's neck prickled at the voice. He straightened himself and looked directly into the face of the man who had knocked him. Charles Wiltshire stood in front of him, feet planted, arms crossed. William could tell by Wiltshire's smug smile that the knock had been no accident. He felt his old anger stir.

"Well, well, Baker." Charles's grin grew wider. "I didn't realise it was you."

"Very clumsy of you." William kept his voice even.

Now, as the winter evening closed in, the street was deserted except for one horse and buggy at the front of Wiltshire's shop. Somewhere nearby a bell tinkled. Neither man looked away.

"What's brought the native lover to town?" Charles postured. "I thought you were self-sufficient in your little hills paradise."

"I'm doing business for my mother-in-law. Not that it's any concern of yours."

"Ah, yes. Mrs Prosser. Such a needy woman. We were glad when you married her daughter. Took them off our hands."

A woman gasped.

"Charles!" Henry Wiltshire's scolding tone distracted them from each other.

Henry was standing outside his shop; he carried several parcels and beside him was Mrs Hill, who had a face that looked as if she'd swallowed a sour lemon.

"Good evening, Mrs Hill. I was just saying it's a son-in-law's duty to look after his wife's mother. I only wish my dear Edith's mother were still alive so I could have the honour."

Henry glowered at his son and turned away to help Mrs Hill into her buggy.

William shook his head. "Lying comes so naturally to you, Wiltshire. You no longer know the difference between reality and your fabrications."

Behind him Henry called goodbye and the horse and buggy set off down the road.

"I know what I want and I go for it." Charles lifted his chin and smirked.

"Like your search for diamonds. How many of those did you find?"

The smirk disappeared and Wiltshire's eyes narrowed. "I know they're there. Once the creek goes down I will keep looking."

This time William smirked. "You won't find anything."

"I don't care how long it takes, Baker, I will keep that claim alive."

"I still have that bottle you used to poison my cattle."

Charles lurched at William and grabbed him by his coat. His blotchy red face was only inches from William's. "Don't you dare threaten me, Baker."

"Charles, that's enough." Henry had come closer. "I will not have you making a scene in the street like a common man."

Both men ignored him, their angry looks locked on each other.

"It's not a threat, it's a surety, Wiltshire. One day you'll get what you deserve. It might not be from me." William stared hard into the other man's eyes. "But you will get it." He brought his hands up swiftly and shoved Charles hard in the chest so that his grip was wrenched from William's coat, then spun on his heel and strode away. He hadn't exactly broken his promise to Georgina. Trouble had found him and he hadn't been prepared to walk away without shutting it back in its box.

Fifty

April 1904

"Isn't it marvellous to have so many people at Prosser's Run again?" Johanna looked up from the contented face of her granddaughter, who was nestled in her arms fast asleep.

Georgina paused from piling dainty cakes onto plates and listened to the voices and laughter coming from the sitting room. "It is, Mother, yes." She bent to gently touch her precious daughter's cheek then returned to arranging the cakes.

"I love it when we are all together." Millie lifted a large fruit-cake from a wooden box. It had little sprigs of white flowers on top, and a white ribbon circled the outside of the cake.

"Oh, Millie." Georgina hugged her mother-in-law. "That looks so pretty. Thank you for making it."

"And I am sure it will taste divine too." Beth smiled. "Mother's cakes always do."

"Will two jugs of lemonade be enough, Georgina?" Ruth hovered beside a tray with jugs and glasses already loaded. She was an eager helper like her sister.

"Yes, Ruth, thank you."

"What's going on in here?" William strolled into the kitchen then stopped and clutched his stomach. "Not more food."

"The christening of your daughter is a special occasion." Millie placed the cake on the large china plate and turned to William. "There has to be food."

"She was christened six months ago. Look at the size of her now."

"The belated celebration of her christening then, now that we are all finally together." Millie lifted the plate. "Shall I take this through to the dining room, Georgina?"

"Yes. Once the kettle has boiled we'll gather everyone in there." Georgina kissed her husband's cheek. "I'm sure you'll find room for sweets."

William groaned as Millie passed him. "If I must." He walked to his mother-in-law and bent down to look at his daughter. "Grandpa was wondering where Eleanor was. I think he'd like a cuddle."

"Of course." Johanna passed the sleeping baby into his arms.

"I'll take these cakes into the dining room." Beth lifted two of the laden dishes.

"I'll help then come back for the lemonade." Ruth lifted another plate.

"Thank you." Georgina watched as her husband and her sisters-in-law left, all with hands full.

"You're so lucky to have married into a big family." Johanna stood and began to stack cups and saucers onto a tray.

"You are a part of the family too, Mother. For better or for worse."

"It was a good idea to hold this party now."

"Well no-one could come to Hawker for the church christening, except for you of course. Christmas was too hot to travel so it has worked out rather well we could all be together now. At least it's cooler. Even Robert managed to make it between runs."

"The church christening was busy with the congregation."

"Of course, and I thought it so sweet that Laura Wiltshire wanted to come with you."

"She's a dear. She's only just turned eight, you know, but she calls on me sometimes. I think she gets rather made use of in her brother's household."

"That would not be a surprise." Georgina lifted the steaming kettle from the fire and poured the water into the large teapot.

"It's probably also not a surprise to learn there is some ill feeling building towards the Wiltshires in Hawker."

"Really? What's Mr Wiltshire done?"

"I don't think it's Henry so much — he spends quite a bit of time in Adelaide these days."

Georgina put a pile of dainty napkins on the tea tray. "So it's more about Charles."

"Mrs Hill has taken rather a dislike to him."

"I don't think she's ever forgiven Charles for not marrying one of her daughters."

"Possibly, but she says he is rather two-faced and she rarely shops at Wiltshire's any more. Some of her friends are following in keeping away. Edith is not well liked either. She puts on a lot of airs and graces for someone who started as a shop girl."

"Oh dear." Georgina couldn't help the smug grin on her face. "Poor Charles."

Thomas sat back in his chair at the head of the table, his stomach heavy after a piece of Millie's fruitcake and two of Johanna Prosser's cream cakes. He had developed quite a sweet tooth in the last few years and the women loved to encourage him. He could hear their voices now, busy in the kitchen cleaning up after the marvellous luncheon they'd all enjoyed, and no doubt planning what they would bring out for supper in only a few hours' time.

Beth had taken her two younger siblings off to inspect Georgina's horses, so only the four men remained at the table. It being such a rare occurrence to have all the Bakers together and not working, they were making the most of the late afternoon, sitting and talking.

Joseph produced a bottle of whisky and William found glasses. Thomas declined the drink, he'd never had much of a taste for it, but Robert joined his father and brother and they all relaxed back into their chairs.

"How are you finding fatherhood, William?" Joseph looked at his son over the top of his glass with a proud smile.

"Now I know why you had so many children, Father." William smirked back. "It is certainly a great joy."

"Life's greatest," Thomas agreed.

"You're always a soft touch when it comes to babies, Father. Look at how many grandchildren and great-grandchildren you have. My sister has certainly done her part."

Thomas smiled. "Ellen's latest letter is all about her new grandchildren. Both Isabelle and Charlotte are wonderful mothers."

"Of course," Joseph said.

"And dear Violet and Esther with their growing families." Thomas thought lovingly of Joseph's daughters, who he and Lizzie had helped to raise after their mother's death.

"Esther wanted to come." Robert shifted in his chair and Thomas turned his gaze to his grandson. "I stayed overnight with her recently on my last trip north. They are mustering at the moment and she couldn't get away."

"How are you finding the transport business, Robert?"

Thomas noticed his grandson look to his father and brother before he spoke. "I have more than enough work and I enjoy it."

"You don't find it lonely?"

"Not at all. As I said I stayed with Esther just last week and I see Violet when I go to Adelaide, and sometimes Aunt Ellen on the times I head south-east. Along the way there are always other teamsters, carriers and travellers. I find it interesting to meet such a cross-section of people."

"Well, that is good." Thomas hadn't thought about the life Robert led as being social.

"And you know there is always room for you at home if you ever tire of it." Joseph leaned forward and held Robert's gaze.

"I know, Father."

"There's miles of fencing to be done." William drained his glass. "I am grateful for the help of the local natives but now that we're rebuilding our stock I think I will have to employ another permanent stockman to work between here and Smith's Ridge."

"I wish fences would keep out rabbits and wild dogs." Joseph refilled his glass.

Thomas noticed both Robert and William declined a second, and he was quietly thankful. Too much drink could ruin lives. He'd seen enough of that in his time.

"We have trouble with them here as well," William said. "The dogs not so much as they don't seem to bother the cattle, but the rabbits can mow through the new grass."

"You won't use poison?" Robert asked.

"No." William's reply was emphatic. "I want none of that on my land."

"We've discussed it," Joseph said. "We will find other ways to keep the vermin out."

"There's always rabbit pie." Robert chuckled.

William groaned. "You and your rabbit pie. Always thinking of your stomach."

"How are you gentlemen faring in here?"

They all looked up as Johanna came in, carrying a plate piled high with biscuits. "I wonder would anyone like to try one of my burned-butter biscuits."

There was a chorus of groans. Johanna stopped, her eyebrows raised.

Thomas chuckled. "I'm sure no offence was meant, Johanna. It's simply that our stomachs are still full from the magnificent lunch we enjoyed." He leaned across to look at the plate a little closer. "However I am sure I might have a small space to accommodate one of those delicious biscuits."

This time the chorus was of laughter and Thomas noted he wasn't the only one to take one of the offered delicacies.

Georgina and Millie joined them, one carrying the teapot and the other a tray of clean cups. When everyone had a fresh cup of tea Joseph raised his glass of whisky.

"Let us drink a toast to the newest member of the Baker clan, my beautiful granddaughter, Eleanor."

"To Eleanor," echoed around the room.

Thomas smiled as William kissed his wife's cheek. They made a fine young couple and Eleanor was a bonny baby. He silently wished them many more children, but he of all people knew that was not always easy.

Fifty-one

September 1907

It was dark by the time the little steam motor coach began to slow for its arrival at the Hawker railway station. Georgina was thankful Eleanor had finally given in to sleep but now the little girl was a heavy weight in her arms. This final stage of their journey had at least been comfortable in the more spacious first-class section with its armrests and a seat by the window. This had been their first ride in the quaint little engine, which at first sight Eleanor, through the wide eyes of a four-year-old, had declared looked like a toy. Regardless of its size Georgina had been pleased to see it waiting when she alighted from the Adelaide train at Quorn. It meant they could travel on to Hawker without an overnight stay as they had done on the journey to Adelaide the week before.

As the coach rolled to a stop Georgina was glad to see William standing among those waiting on the platform. He had his hands in his coat pockets and was stomping from foot to foot. The night air of September in Hawker could be very cold. Georgina knew she would be glad of her thick coat. She waved and pointed to

Eleanor. He stood to one side waiting for the last passenger to step off then came to help her.

He kissed her, his lips cold against hers. "Good holiday?" he murmured.

"It was, but I'm glad to be almost home."

"Any other news?"

"We'll talk later," she said, aware that the porter was hovering nearby.

William scooped his daughter into his arms and kissed one rosy cheek. Eleanor nestled against his chest and remained fast asleep.

Georgina felt drained. The trip to Adelaide hadn't been all holiday. The new Hawker doctor had referred her to a specialist as she had lost two more babies since Eleanor's birth. The poor little things only grew inside her a few months, and then they were gone. The specialist hadn't been much help, unfortunately. She looked up at her handsome husband and wished she could be scooped up safely into his arms like their daughter.

"I've got your bag, Mrs Baker." The helpful porter had lifted down her small case from the rack above.

"Thank you." She rose and followed her husband from the coach.

Georgina climbed into the waiting carriage, with its roof to protect them from the variable weather. "It's late," she said as William handed Eleanor back to her. He tucked a blanket around them both for the journey to her mother's house.

"I've come straight here from Prosser's Run. I didn't have time to stop and see your mother. I assume she will be in bed."

Georgina rested her head against his shoulder and closed her eyes as he urged the horse into motion. She longed for bed herself.

"Well, well." William's tone made her look up.

Her mother's house appeared to have a light shining from every window.

Johanna hugged her and supervised them putting Eleanor to bed.

"I have a pot of tea ready and some vegetable tart," she said. "You never eat well on the train."

William brought their bags inside. The house had three bedrooms and the middle one was reserved for William and Georgina. She removed her coat and looked longingly at the bed before she joined her mother and her husband in the dining end of the large front room. A fire burned cheerfully in the grate and Georgina held her hands towards it before she sat.

"Sit down and eat."

Georgina did as her mother bade even though she didn't feel the slightest bit hungry. William on the other hand was obviously glad his mother-in-law had provided supper, judging by the size of the slice he was devouring.

"How was Adelaide?" Johanna asked.

"Busy. We went to the art gallery and the museum." She inclined her head towards William. "Eleanor was astounded by some of the exhibits. I wish you had been there to hear her."

"And your appointment?"

They all stopped at her mother's question. It was William who broke the silence by taking her hand. "What did the doctor say, Georgina?"

She sighed. "Nothing new to report, I'm afraid. He puts it down to some kind of internal problem and, because I carried Eleanor to almost the full confinement, he seems confident I will do so again."

"Then that's good news." Johanna gave her an encouraging smile.

William squeezed her hand. "We have Eleanor."

"Yes and that young lady is enough to keep everyone busy." Johanna slid another piece of tart onto William's empty plate.

"She is so like you, Georgina." She leaned into the table. "Now I've had some terrible news."

"What is it?" Georgina was glad to no longer be the centre of attention.

"Henry Wiltshire is dead."

"Oh! That is sad news," Georgina said. "He was such a help to us after Father died; whatever else happened with the Wiltshires I'll always be grateful for that."

William took up his mug of tea. "How did he die?"

"He was in Adelaide visiting his mother and caught a terrible cough."

Georgina felt a stab of fear. "There were reports of people with influenza while I was there. I hope I haven't exposed Eleanor to it."

William gave her a reassuring look. "She's young and strong."

"She's all we have."

William's face creased with concern. "And we have each other. We cannot see the future, Georgina. We must take each day as it comes."

"And how lucky are you to have married such a sensible man?" Johanna gathered their plates. "When I reflect on who you could have married." She shook her head. "Well, it just doesn't bear thinking about." She carried the plates to the bench, tutting as she went.

William stood, a grin on his face. "Time for bed, I think." He bent and kissed Georgina's cheek. "I won't be long."

She watched him leave the room and then her mother as she put more wood on the fire. They were both right. She was the luckiest woman alive. She had a loving husband and a beautiful daughter.

Johanna returned to sit beside her and reached for her hand. "How are you really, Georgina?"

Immediately the optimism left her and tears filled her eyes. She drew in a sharp breath. "It's ironic, isn't it, Mother? Once I had no interest in children and now … when it seems I am to be denied them, I long for nothing else."

"Circumstances change us all. I have had to change my ideas considerably in recent years."

Georgina took in the wry look on her mother's face.

"Here you are married to William Baker, who it turns out is a worthy husband and, as he so wisely said, you have Eleanor. If she is to be your only child then so be it. Perhaps you need to forget about having babies and occupy your thoughts otherwise." Johanna raised her hand to cup Georgina's cheek. "Having an only daughter is a wonderful thing. She will bring you such joy."

"Oh, Mother."

They collapsed into each other's arms. Johanna's hug was firm and when they finally drew apart her eyes were damp. "I think it's time we all turned in." She stood.

"You go." Georgina gave her a brave smile. "I'll turn out the lamps."

Johanna kissed her cheek and left.

Georgina pondered her mother's words. Her world had become centred on having babies and it wasn't healthy. She had to find another motivation in her life. It was time she took up interest again in their cattle, and turned some of her focus back to her horses. She had neglected them since Eleanor's birth. The seasons had been good since the drought and the Lord knew they had plenty of space across three properties. She smiled and felt the weight of the worry that had plagued her for months ease just a little.

Charles slammed the front door behind him. His steps were heavy along the hall in spite of the thick run of carpet beneath his boots.

"Edith," he called.

She appeared in the kitchen doorway. "Good heavens, Charles, please stop your noise; I've just put Victoria down for her sleep." She studied him closely as he came to a stop in front of her. "Whatever is the matter? I wasn't expecting you back until tomorrow. Is your grandmother all right?"

"Grandmother is in perfect health, apart from her eyes and her sore hip. It's Father who's ruined us."

Edith glanced at the back door. "Lower your voice. What do you mean ruined us? You were going to conduct a simple funeral."

"Oh yes, yes. That's all done. It's his will. He had one drawn up by a solicitor in Adelaide."

"Come and sit down, Charles, and tell me what has upset you so."

Charles followed her into the kitchen, where she had obviously been cooking, judging by the mess everywhere.

"Where's Leonard?" he asked.

"Laura is with him. They are in the backyard. I had to tell her about your father's death, Charles. Word has got about. It wouldn't do for her to have heard the news from elsewhere."

A fresh wave of anger swept over him. He had been engulfed by it ever since his father's snooty solicitor had read the will to him three days earlier. "Laura is what this is all about." He tugged the envelope from his jacket pocket and spread his father's will on the table before him. "Father has left the house and mother's jewellery to Laura."

"What?" Edith's sharp look faded and she slumped onto a chair. "What about the shop?"

"That's ours, of course, along with all its debts." Charles gripped his head in his hands. "I can't believe Father would do this to me. We still haven't recovered our losses from the drought and then the storm. Grandmother has offered to have Laura live with her and the executor wants to know what's to be done about the house." He looked imploringly at Edith. "I don't know what to do."

Edith began to pace. "We must think on it."

"We don't have long. Grandmother wants an answer and so does the executor."

"We have to stay here."

"How, Edith?" he growled. "We've sold the cottage next door for a pittance. We have two children. Are you planning on pitching a tent?"

Edith drew herself up. Her eyes blazed. "You are distraught, Charles, so I will overlook your sarcastic manner. Of course I'm not suggesting we live in a tent or any other such ridiculous place. By here I mean this house which provides a perfectly fine roof over our heads."

"I've just told you, Edith, it is not ours."

"I am assuming your father at least made you Laura's legal guardian, and you must act on her behalf."

"Yes, but he's tied it up tightly so that I cannot take the house from her."

"You don't need to. Not for some years anyway." Edith rose, came to stand beside him, and rested one hand on his shoulder. "Did you imagine she would live here on her own?"

Charles's jaw fell open.

Edith leaned closer, her words soft in his ear. "She's a child, Charles. She's only eleven. As her guardian you are entitled to live in the house to look after her."

"Of course. The executor only expects an annual report on the state of the house if we decide to stay." He threw his arms around Edith and pulled her onto his lap. "You are so clever, my love."

"She's too young to understand." Edith kissed his cheek. "If we don't tell her she won't even know the house is hers."

Charles tensed as he remembered his grandmother's letter. "What about Grandmother's offer? I assume if we won't go to Adelaide, she plans to groom Laura to take over her business."

"We can't let Laura leave, Charles. If Harriet gets her in her clutches she could turn Laura against us and even encourage her to sell the house."

"Grandmother did not attend the reading of Father's will, and asked nothing about it. She's left everything for me to deal with — but in the case of her offer what are we to do? She will expect an answer."

Edith's face took on the sharp look she got when she was planning something. "Don't give Laura the letter."

"I must."

"No, Charles. You can simply tell Laura a modified version of the contents."

He frowned. "I don't follow."

Edith tutted. "We will tell her together. I will take the lead. And you must burn that letter. Your grandmother doesn't correspond often now, what with her eyesight, and when she does send a letter it's addressed to you. We simply vet any correspondence she sends and if we word Laura's reply carefully I think we can keep her satisfied that Laura wishes to remain in Hawker."

"You may be right."

"Of course I'm right."

"Very well." Charles slid one hand around to cup her breast. He had been away nearly two weeks and he'd missed his wife. "You are such a good woman, Edith."

She smiled. "And now I have my own news to impart. We are to have another child."

"Edith, my love, that is splendid news." Charles was proud of his two healthy children. Leonard was four and little Victoria two already. Another baby would certainly strengthen the Wiltshire line. "Perhaps another boy this time?"

"We shall see."

He trailed kisses down her neck. "Since Victoria is sleeping and Laura has Leonard outside, I think we should retire to our bed for a rest."

"Just a short one. I must prepare dinner."

He set Edith on her feet. She took him by the hand and gave him one of those provocative smiles that always sent his blood racing. Instead of leading him to the back of the house, she took him towards the hall.

"While you were away I took the liberty of moving our things into the front bedroom." She gave a throaty chuckle. "No more living in the servants' quarters for us."

"Come and sit at the kitchen table, Laura." Edith's tone was almost kindly.

Laura swallowed her sigh. She had finished tidying the kitchen. The little ones were in bed and usually Edith and Charles preferred the evenings to themselves. She didn't mind being alone, especially since Edith had told her about her dear papa's death. Laura was so sad, but she tried not to show it during the day. Edith had said they all missed Father, and little Leonard would be distraught — she was not to mention it. So Laura swallowed her sorrow and it was only when she slipped into bed and turned off the lamp that she allowed her grief to engulf her.

"What is it?" she asked. Edith had already taken a seat beside some paper, pen and ink. Charles paced up and back behind her.

"Your grandmother asked me to tell you she'd like you to come and live with her." Charles made it sound as if that was a terrible thing, but Laura loved her grandmother Harriet.

Edith smiled at her and patted the seat beside her. "Sit down, dear."

Laura's stomach squirmed. She did as she was asked but Edith was acting just as she had when she'd imparted the news of Papa's death.

"Why don't you sit as well, Charles? We feel uncomfortable with you strutting beside us." Edith gave Laura a conspiratorial smile. "The thing is, Laura, we are your legal guardians, and we are also your closest family. Of course we want you to do whatever you think best, but we would miss you terribly if you went to live in Adelaide."

Laura chewed her lip. "What do you think, Charles?" She looked to her big brother, as she'd always done.

He took one of her hands in his big hands, his face serious. "I am a little concerned that Grandmother would rely very heavily on you. She has Miss Wicksteed, but you are her flesh and blood. She might become rather demanding as she gets older and you are too young to be burdened with the care of an old woman." He sighed. "Of course you must go if that's what you want, but we've just lost our dear father. I would be so sad if you were to go too."

"As would I," Edith added. "And Leonard and Victoria would be heartbroken."

Laura looked from one to the other. She didn't think herself capable of any more sadness. It would be a big change to move to her grandmother's, and she did love her niece and nephew very much. Spending time with them brought her such joy. Edith could be demanding, and Charles was often moody, but they were her family.

She smiled at him now. "I would rather stay here."

"Oh that's wonderful." Edith hugged her. It was such an unusual event it disconcerted Laura.

"Why don't you write to Grandmother now?" Charles slid the blank piece of writing paper in front of her.

"I can help you with the wording if you like." Edith let her go.

"Thank you." Laura smiled from one to the other. They were almost treating her like a grown up. It would be better to stay here within the arms of her family. She dipped the pen in the ink and began to write: *Dear Grandmother ...*

Fifty-two

April 1910

The sun was shining on a perfect autumn day outside and both Charles and Malachi Hemming were busy serving inside. Charles couldn't be sure why he'd received a sudden influx of customers in the late afternoon but he was more than happy to take their money. Perhaps it was the cooler April weather after the heat of March, which had seemed more like summer, or perhaps some were keen to inspect the work being done to restore the older part of the shop. Whatever the reason they were getting first look at the new stock — stock he'd had to outlay money up front for. His credit was still not good with his suppliers. At least these people would help spread the word that Wiltshire's Emporium was returning to its glory days.

He smiled pleasantly at Mrs Edwards from the drapery along the street. She had purchased a new wooden tea caddy that had just arrived. He wondered if he would see her back again once the older part of the shop reopened the following week. Wiltshire's Emporium would provide much more than the Edwards' small drapery. In the refurbished shop, where once he had sold groceries — and still would if Edith had had her way — he was creating a space purely for ladies' fashion.

He had employed a pretty local girl to take care of the counter. Ladies liked to see how they imagined they would look in a hat or a jacket, rather than the reality. He'd also employed a part-time dressmaker, who would work from what had been his father's office. With all the ready-made fashion he was stocking, ladies needed clothing altered to obtain the perfect fit, and he would have someone on hand to do so. Laura would have been a much cheaper alternative, and at fourteen she showed great dexterity as a seamstress after several visits to her grandmother's over the years, but she was also very good with the children and with three young ones and little household help Edith needed her at home.

As it drew closer to closing time the customers dispersed. Charles left Mr Hemming tending to the butcher's wife, lifted the temporary curtain that had been hung between the two shops and let himself into the older section. They had to wait for the carpenter to finish the new front wall and then the glazier to install the windows before they could unpack the new stock and set out their displays.

Charles inspected the work, which had been encased with hessian bags on the outside so no-one would see the new showcase windows until the opening. It had been difficult to get a carpenter and then he'd had to pay the man up front. He still wondered whether they wouldn't have been better to cut their losses and start afresh in Adelaide. It was taking longer than he had hoped to rebuild his reputation in the Hawker community.

The big drawcard would be the new buggy he would park at the front of the shop. It had four wheels, a padded leather seat and a shade that could be raised or lowered depending on the weather, and it would be available for hire. Charles had never gone back into wagon transport, and he no longer needed a cart for deliveries, so he had sold it and upgraded to the buggy. The old horse had also been sold and a fine new mare purchased: a horse with a quiet steady temperament, according to her previous owner. He hadn't told Edith about that yet. She knew he had sold the horse and cart but not that he'd purchased the buggy and a new horse. They were being delivered to the stables at the house the next morning. He hoped she'd had a good day.

Charles collected his hat, said good evening to Mr Hemming and made his way home. On his walk up the side of the house he was met by the less-than-dulcet tones of his wife singing a hymn, obviously to her own accompaniment, judging by the odd misplayed note of the piano.

The noise from the backyard almost drowned that of the piano. The baby was screaming in Laura's arms, Victoria was standing by the back door crying and Leonard was yelling from his position in the fork of the lemon tree.

"What is going on here?"

They all stopped their noise except for two-year-old Grace, who continued to air her lungs. He took her from Laura and jiggled her on his hip.

"Father," Leonard and Victoria called at once.

"Laura won't let us in the house." Leonard's voice had an indignant tone.

Charles noticed several lemons scattered around the yard and a rip down the back of his son's shirt.

He looked at his younger sister. "Laura?"

She simply smiled and picked up Victoria, who was still snivelling. "It's all right, Vicky. Your papa is home now."

The little girl put her head on Laura's shoulder and clutched the locket his sister never removed.

"What's wrong with them?" Charles couldn't seem to soothe his youngest daughter, and Victoria's face was blotchy from crying too. "Why won't you let them inside?"

"They're fine really." Laura wiped Victoria's face with the edge of her apron. "Edith asked me to bring them outside while she practised her hymns for church on Sunday."

"We've been out here for ages," Leonard said.

"Leo's getting hungry," Laura said.

"So am I." Victoria made a loud wailing noise.

"Shh, Vicky," Laura soothed. "Your papa will let us inside, and if you're very quiet and don't disturb your mama I will make you all some dinner."

"Why haven't you done it earlier if food is all they want?"

Laura gave Charles a small smile. "The door is locked," she murmured.

Charles sucked in a breath and withdrew his key from his pocket. "All right, everyone inside."

There was an uproar of cheers.

"Stop." He rounded on them. "You must do as your Aunt Laura says and sit quietly while she prepares you food."

They followed him inside. He slid Grace into her high chair and she immediately began to cry again.

"Here you are, Gracie." Laura gave her a piece of buttered crust.

"Can I have some?" Victoria whined.

"Me too," Leonard added.

"Vicky, Leo, where are your manners?"

Laura chuckled as they chorused, "Please."

Charles let himself into the hall and shut the door again behind him. He didn't blame his wife at all for needing some time to herself. Their three children were very busy.

He sighed as the sounds of the piano reverberated out into the hall. A short time of peace and quiet in his own home was all he wanted. He would never say as much to Edith, but his sister was a much better pianist, with an angelic voice. As he crept past the sitting-room door the noise stopped.

"Is that you, Charles?"

He sighed and stepped in to see her.

"Good heavens, is it that time already? I've hardly had a moment to practise." She closed the piano and slid her music under the lid of the stool. "I'd better see to the children. Laura lets them run wild."

Charles crossed to his drinks table. "Laura is feeding them as we speak." He lifted the decanter of sherry. "Why don't you join me for a drink before you go? We don't often get the chance to enjoy a quiet tipple together."

Edith smiled. "What a lovely idea."

"If we have two, Laura may even have put the children to bed and we can eat our meal in peace as well."

Edith took the glass he offered and sat. Charles waited until her second glass was nearly empty before he broached the subject of the new horse and buggy. He had no trouble convincing her it was a good idea and she didn't ask where the money had come from.

When finally she left to check on the children he poured himself a third and settled back into his chair. Charles smiled to himself as he swirled the amber liquid in the dainty crystal glass. He had worked out a while ago that a few glasses of sherry smoothed out some of Edith's pointier edges.

"Will you come with me tomorrow afternoon to the reopening of the Wiltshires' shop?"

Georgina looked up from her needlepoint, surprised by her mother's proposal. "I really can't be bothered, Mother. I've long since given away any thought about what Charles Wiltshire does."

"I care little either, but it's always interesting to see what scheme he's going to come up with next. I don't know where he gets the money." Johanna shook her head. "He must have bled his poor grandmother dry by now."

Georgina had come to town to purchase a new saddle and do business at the bank. She had brought Eleanor with her for a visit to her grandmother's, and now, with the little girl tucked up in bed, the two women sat in Johanna's sitting room. It had been a pleasant enough day but they were both grateful for the fire after dinner.

"I am enjoying this needlework." Georgina decided to change the subject. "I haven't done any for years."

"I've got a simple design ready for Eleanor to try in the morning while you're out."

"She'll love that."

"I'm sure she'd love the shop opening as well. There's to be a singer and sweets for the children and a grand unveiling of the new windows at two o'clock."

Georgina said nothing but continued with her stitching.

"Charles Wiltshire spares no expense," Johanna continued.

"A trait that has got him into trouble before."

"There are several tradespeople who won't do business with him, and Mrs Hill has encouraged friends to stay away."

Georgina looked at her mother and raised her eyebrows.

"I keep my ears open." Johanna adjusted her needlework on her lap but didn't resume sewing. "He really should take more care. He has a wife, a sister and three children dependent upon him."

"Now that is one small thing I do envy him." Georgina cast her gaze away towards the fire. Since her trip to the doctor in Adelaide she had lost another baby, and each time it happened it was as if a little piece of her were lost too.

"Rubbish, Georgina. Have you seen those children? They're as plain as plain can be, and quite unruly at times. Poor Laura is simply an unpaid nanny but she's so good with them."

"She still takes tea with you?"

"On occasion." Johanna leaned closer. "You have been blessed with Eleanor. She's as beautiful as you, and such a mild-tempered child."

Georgina smiled. "You don't think you may be a little biased there, Mother?"

"Perhaps." She settled back in her chair, her needlework forgotten. "You are happy living at Prosser's Run, aren't you?"

"Of course."

"And William?"

"It's worked out well, as you suggested it would. Jessie loves the house at Smith's Ridge and William is grateful to have Clem overseeing there. Robert may decide to settle there if he ever gives up his carting business, but in the meantime we're happy Clem and Jessie are there." She looked at her mother. "Swan's gone."

"I didn't think he would last."

They were both silent a moment.

"How are William's family at Wildu Creek? I never see them in town."

"Joseph comes sometimes but Millie won't, even now the children are grown. The girls have come once or twice and Matthew accompanies Joseph everywhere else but never here."

"Such a pity. They're delightful young people. How will they learn to mix with others?"

"Millie spends more time with her own family in the hills now. William says she all but shunned them when she was younger, but now she wants her children to understand more of their culture."

"I can understand that. I wanted to take you back to England, remember."

"I don't think it's quite the same."

"Why not? When you become a mother you want your children to know where they came from."

"Eleanor won't have to travel halfway across the world to know that."

Johanna gazed at the fire. "I'm sorry I was unkind about Joseph's marriage to Millie. She's a good woman. She must be so strong to have made the choices she has. I really enjoyed our Christmas all together last year. It was wonderful to see the house at Prosser's Run full of people again."

Once more they lapsed into silence. Georgina recalled her days in England and how different life was there. She wondered what Millie's children thought of their Aboriginal family. Beth and Ruth came to stay at Prosser's Run from time to time: they were both well spoken, rather shy but keen horsewomen. They rode out together when they came and she enjoyed their company.

"I had planned to go back to stay, you know."

Johanna's comment startled Georgina from her thoughts. "Where? To England?"

Her mother nodded.

"When?"

"You married William against my wishes. I felt as if my whole family were lost to me. The only ones I had left were in England."

"You wouldn't have gone back to live with Aunt Anne and Uncle Winston?"

"Look at your face." Johanna laughed.

"Anyway, they're both gone now, Mother. You would have been on your own all the way across the world."

"I am thankful you and I have reconciled." Johanna's face was remorseful. "I made a mistake. William is a fine husband and if you are only blessed with one child look at the wider family you have married into." Johanna smiled. "There are so many of them."

Georgina thought of her extended family and chuckled. "You're right about that, Mother."

Fifty-three

November 1912

Johannes Becker paused at the gate outside the big house. All the windows were open and the most beautiful sounds drifted out to him. Someone was playing the piano and singing. He looked up and down the street. It was the only house of such grand size and had to be the one he'd been directed to. He stepped through the gate that hung by one hinge against the fence and made his way along the lavender-lined path around a cherub to the front door.

He lifted the brass knocker and paused, not wanting to interrupt what must be an angel singing. A horse clopped past on the road behind him. Not wanting to appear as if he were loitering, Johannes rapped the knocker sharply two times. The music stopped. There was no further sound from beyond the solid wooden door, then suddenly it opened. Standing before him was indeed an angel. A beautiful girl dressed in a soft white shirt tucked in to a deep blue skirt. Her dark brown hair fell to her shoulders and the locks that were pulled back from her face were tied with a blue bow that matched her skirt. A pair of grey eyes studied him.

"Good morning," she said in the same lilting tones as the singer. It was she.

She put her head to one side. "Can I help you?" The exquisite heart-shaped locket on a chain around her neck slipped sideways across her shirt.

"Charles Wiltshire." Johannes cleared his throat. He was twenty-one, but the words had come out in the squeaky tones of his pubescent years. "I was told he lived here."

"Yes, he does." She looked at him expectantly.

Johannes swept off his hat. "I am Johannes Becker. Mr Wiltshire is expecting me."

A puzzled frown creased her face. "Today?"

"Not exactly. I wasn't sure how soon I would arrive. I have ridden from Adelaide. I sent Mr Wiltshire a telegram a week ago."

"Oh, I see." Her smile returned. "I am Laura Wiltshire. Would you like to come in and wait? I can make you some refreshments."

She stepped back from the door and Johannes entered. The house was suddenly cool after the warmth of the sunny day outside.

"This way, Mr Becker."

She led him along a hall to a large sitting room. Against one wall was the piano, the lid still up and music sheets propped on the stand. Laura crossed to it, put away the music and closed the lid. He knew he was staring but her every movement was so graceful and her smile so sweet he couldn't help himself. Charles was an older man. Surely she was too young to be his wife. Perhaps his daughter?

"Please make yourself comfortable, Mr Becker." She held out one slender hand towards the chairs. "My brother and his family are at a Sunday School presentation. They shouldn't be long."

Johannes lowered himself to one of the brocade-covered chairs. The stuffing was soft and he sank lower than expected, falling the last few inches.

"I'm sorry." She grinned. "Our furniture has taken some poundings these last few years. Would you prefer a straight-backed chair?

"No, no. I am quite comfortable here, thank you ... Miss Wiltshire?"

"I am. Now can I make you some tea? I baked biscuits for the Sunday School gathering first thing this morning, and have kept a few back."

"Thank you."

While she was gone he made himself more comfortable in the chair and took in the room. The furnishings were indeed showing signs of wear and the curtains fading, but there was no mistaking the quality. Charles Wiltshire's house was certainly one of the best in the small Hawker settlement. Johannes wondered once again about the man his uncle Heinrich had staked his diamond claim with. No word had ever come from Australia: Johannes didn't know if that meant there were no diamonds or Wiltshire had kept the find to himself.

Laura returned with a tray of tea things and a dainty plate of biscuits. She set them out on the small table beside him. There was only one cup.

"Won't you join me?" He wanted to spend more time in the company of the delightful Laura Wiltshire.

"I'm sorry, Mr Becker. The baby is stirring and I must see to her. I shall return in a short while." She gave him a radiant smile. "Enjoy your tea."

Johannes sagged in his chair. Baby? Surely not her own? She had agreed that she was *Miss* Wiltshire. Noisy chatter and footsteps crunching over the gravel path outside distracted him. He could hear doors opening and closing and more voices from the back of the house, then a door shut, muffling the sounds, followed by a heavy tread along the hall runner.

Johannes struggled to his feet as a tall portly man appeared in the sitting-room doorway. The man paused and looked around before his gaze fell on Johannes again.

"My sister said Mr Becker was waiting for me."

"That is correct." Johannes crossed the room and extended his hand. "I am Johannes Becker, Heinrich's nephew."

"Your telegram simply said Becker. I assumed ..." Charles looked past him. "I see Laura has brought you some refreshments. I will join you and you can tell me why you are here. Please sit down." Charles crossed to a padded seat with an upright wooden back. "How is your uncle?"

"Uncle Heinrich was killed during the war."

"I'm so sorry for your loss. Heinrich was a fine man."

"I liked him, though I was very young when he died." Johannes studied Wiltshire closely. He had no idea about the man's character, but his lack of eye contact made Johannes uneasy. "When I came across papers about a diamond claim in Australia, I decided to travel and see for myself the country he thought so much like our own. It is a pilgrimage, of sorts."

"I'm glad you've come. I did wonder why I hadn't heard from Heinrich since he returned to South Africa."

"And the claim?"

"We had no luck there, I'm afraid. After your uncle left I continued to work it for several years with little sign of anything remotely like a diamond. Then a terrible storm washed away all the work we'd done. I go back regularly and spend a week there, but I'm afraid I've found nothing."

"I've come all this way, Mr Wiltshire." Johannes looked the man squarely in the eye. "You can understand my yearning to see the place my uncle spent some time working for myself."

"Of course — I can take you there, but I will not be free to do so for a few days. How long are you staying, Mr Becker?"

"I don't have a return date yet."

Light footsteps sounded from the hall. Johannes turned expectantly but was disappointed that an older woman appeared in the doorway, and not the delightful Laura. She carried a tray with more tea things. He struggled out of the sagging chair.

"This is Mr Becker, Edith. Mr Becker, my wife."

"I am pleased to meet you, Mrs Wiltshire."

The polite curve of Mrs Wiltshire's lips did little to relieve her sour look. She raised one eyebrow. "Mr Becker?"

"This is Heinrich's nephew, my dear, Johannes Becker."

"I see." The woman gave a perfunctory nod and crossed the room to unload her tray. "Would you like more tea, Mr Becker?"

"No, thank you. I shall finish this then go in search of accommodation."

"Why, you should stay with us, Mr Becker," Charles said. "We have rooms at the back that were once the housekeeper's."

The offer appeared genuine, but Johannes noticed Mrs Wiltshire's shoulders stiffen.

Charles went on. "I was very fond of your uncle and I would like to extend to you our hospitality. I am sure you would find it most comfortable here as our guest." He turned to his wife. "Wouldn't he, Edith?"

"We are a busy household here, Mr Becker — we have four children — but the quarters are quite separate." She crossed back to the door. "I shall get Laura to prepare them for you."

"Thank you," Johannes said, but she was already gone. He wouldn't have accepted Wiltshire's offer but the thought of perhaps getting to see Laura again and spend some time with her was paramount in his mind.

Laura hefted the washing basket to her hip and turned to make her way across the courtyard. As she did the door to Flora's old rooms opened, and Johannes stepped out. He hurried towards her.

"Let me take that for you," he said and had it before she could protest. Not that she minded having an excuse to walk beside him. Johannes Becker was the most handsome man she had ever met, and her heart beat faster at the sight of him. He had ginger hair cut short, and a neat beard and moustache that hid much of the pale skin of his face. When he smiled at her his blue eyes sparkled with a look that seemed to be for her only, even though they were rarely alone. He had been staying with them for four days now and she felt anxious at the thought that tomorrow Charles was taking him to visit the diamond claim, and then he would most likely return to South Africa. Already she couldn't abide the thought of not being able to see him again.

"How are you finding our little town, Johannes?" She felt a small thrill that he insisted she use his first name and she loved the way her name sounded so different when he spoke it.

"I like it here. It is different to my home in South Africa and yet some things are the same. I can see what attracted Uncle Heinrich here." He smiled as she opened the back door to the house. "I am looking forward to visiting the claim tomorrow."

The last of his words were drowned by the crying of baby Emma. Johannes cast a look at the cradle in the corner of the kitchen, where four-year-old Grace was trying valiantly to soothe her baby sister. The door to the hall was closed, and Laura swallowed a small flutter of irritation — no doubt Edith was resting or playing piano. Laura loved her sister-in-law as it was her duty to do, but sometimes Edith was rather selfish when it came to her children.

"Thank you for helping, Gracie." Laura scooped the baby from the cradle and cuddled the dear little mite close. Such a pity her own mother didn't do more of it. Laura's arms were always full of children and Edith's rarely. "There, there, Emmie." When she turned Johannes had placed the basket of washing on the table and was standing watching her. She lowered her own gaze at the adoration she saw in his.

"You are so good with the children, Laura. A natural mother."

Emma nestled into Laura's shoulder and she took Grace's hand. "It's certainly easier when the older two are at school."

"Can I have a biscuit, please?"

She looked down at the little girl pulling on her hand. "Of course, Gracie." She smiled at Johannes. "Perhaps Mr Becker would like to join us for morning tea."

Gracie ran to him and began tugging on his hand. "Yes, sit with us, Mr Becker." The children were as taken with Johannes as Laura was.

"Very well," he said. "I shall help. I will put the kettle on and you ladies can sit."

Grace giggled in delight at being called a lady. Laura sat and felt a small rush of relief. She had been up at first light to get breakfast for everyone and then had washed several of her brother's shirts and some of Leonard's. Then she had baked a pie for lunch and some biscuits. Grace had helped her with those. Laura was always so busy with household chores. Thankfully Mrs Coleman still did some of the heavy cleaning, and at least Edith had made the beds today. Often she only made her own in the big front bedroom. Laura rarely went in there.

Johannes lifted the teapot and took down the wooden tea caddy. Laura felt herself relaxing even more. It was so pleasant to be waited on and even better to bask in the sunshine of Johannes's attentiveness.

That was how they were, seated around the kitchen table, chatting easily together, Johannes with Grace on his knee and Laura nursing the baby, when Edith came in.

"Good heavens, what is going on here?"

Grace bounced up. "We are having a tea party, Mother."

"So I can see." Edith reached for the now sleeping baby. "I've told you not to keep picking her up, Laura. She will never learn to sleep in her own bed."

Laura's shoulder was cool after the warmth of the baby against her. She felt sad for dear little Emma, who was only three months old. She determined if she ever had her own babies she would cuddle them whenever she wished.

"Have you finished all your jobs, Laura?"

Before Laura could reply, Johannes got to his feet. "It's my fault if she hasn't, Mrs Wiltshire. I was in need of a cup of tea. I asked Laura to join me."

"And me," piped Grace.

"Yes, well we are busy, as you can see, Mr Becker. Perhaps you could pay a visit to my husband at the shop."

Laura was embarrassed by Edith's tone.

"I have some tasks of my own to complete." Johannes turned to Laura and gave her the most wonderful smile. "I shall see you all at dinner this evening."

She followed his progress to the door, wishing with all her might she was walking out with him instead of remaining there.

"Laura." Edith's voice was especially high pitched, which meant she was annoyed about something. "There are still dishes to be done. Grace, you are to leave Laura to get on with her work. You can come up to the sitting room with me while I practise piano."

Edith bustled from the room, dragging Grace with her. There was a tiny sigh from the cradle; Laura glanced in but Emma remained asleep. The sounds of the piano drifted from the hall and Laura winced as Edith began to sing. Quietly she closed the door to the hall then retied her apron. She sang softly to herself as she worked, picturing Johannes's handsome face.

Edith turned out the bedside lamp and Charles snuggled against her, but she remained rigid in his arms.

"I tell you, Charles, we must be vigilant. Your sister must be chaperoned."

He sighed and rolled away onto his back. He could tell he would get no interest from Edith tonight. She had been going on about Laura ever since they retired to their bedroom.

"She usually has at least one child with her, often all four." He still thought of Laura as a little girl too.

"Laura is well on her way to seventeen, and more than old enough to draw the attention of men." Edith turned her face to him. "You should have seen the way Johannes was looking at her across the table when I came into the kitchen today."

"He will be gone soon. We will go to the claim tomorrow and then he will no doubt set off for Adelaide."

"There will be others. Laura doesn't know this house is hers, but if she marries she will need somewhere to live — who knows what might come out?"

"Her husband can provide for her. When or if it happens."

"This house is hers, Charles," Edith hissed. "What if she learns the truth?"

"Don't worry, Edith." He reached for her again but she inched away. "I can handle my sister."

"Very well. Good night." Edith turned her back to him.

Charles ground his teeth. Edith had been less agreeable since the last baby. She pestered him for a full-time housekeeper but Laura cost them nothing and was easily managed. He would have to think of some other way to sweeten up his wife.

Fifty-four

The two men on horseback crested the hill and paused at the sight before them. A wide creek bed with signs of recent erosion spread out in front of them. Further up it disappeared into a narrow gully crowded with rocks and trees, and downstream it spread out even wider. Large gum trees dotted its sandy soil. Down the middle a deeper section still ran with water from a larger pool just below them.

It was a pleasant day in late spring, sunny and warm with few clouds in the sky. Everywhere the browns and reds of the rock and soil contrasted with the greys and greens of grass and foliage. Johannes thought it magnificent country.

Charles pointed towards the waterhole. "From that section there back to this bank that has been washed away below us was the claim. I have let the claim lapse. It was wasted money paying the rent and employing someone to work it for no return." Charles looked over his shoulder. "Although I have come here on the quiet and searched a few times since."

"So you still found nothing even after the creek flooded?"

Charles shook his head. "Since the big rain several years ago there have been others. This creek has been flowing almost continuously, although not to the extent it did with the big storm we had in 1903." Charles cast his arm in a wide arc. "You see how wide it can be when there's been a lot of rain."

Johannes walked his horse on and down an embankment to the sandy creek floor. He got down from his horse and looked around. "It could have been washed from further upstream or come out of the ground right here. There's no way of knowing. Any chance I could take a look at the diamond that was found?"

"None." Charles shook his head emphatically. "Joseph Baker, who found it, is despicable and irrational. You would have no luck with him. In fact, I expect he would have you forcibly removed from his property. This area where the claim was has proved difficult enough to access. It is on land leased by Baker's son, William, who is very like his father. Best to keep away from them."

Johannes scuffed at some pebbles with the toe of his boot.

"How long do you wish to remain here?" Charles hadn't dismounted. "I would like to be home before dark."

"You go if you wish. I would like to stay a night or two and have a bit more of a look around."

Charles frowned down at him. "There's nowhere to sleep."

"The weather is clear and I have my swag." Johannes patted his saddle bag. "I managed very well with it on the journey from Adelaide. And Laura has very kindly packed me some provisions."

"I see." Charles lifted his chin. "I expect you will be leaving for Adelaide once you have finished here."

"Not yet." Johannes looked up at Charles, whose face was in the shadow of his hat. "I plan to stay in Hawker for a while. Mr Reynolds the builder could have work for me." Johannes had spent the last few days looking for employment — anything that would enable him to stay longer. He planned to court Laura Wiltshire, but he didn't think now was the right time to broach that subject with her brother.

"Is that so?" Charles's horse shifted its weight and did a side step. "If you stay on in Hawker I'm afraid we would no longer be able to offer you board, Johannes."

"Of course not. I appreciate your generosity in putting me up for this long. I have already made enquiries and arranged lodgings for when I return to town. I'll collect the rest of my things then."

Charles removed his hat to wipe his brow.

Johannes said, "I will be perfectly fine here on my own. You return to your family and I will follow in a few days."

"Very well." Charles gazed at him a little longer then pressed his hat back to his head. "I will see you in Hawker."

Johannes watched for a moment as Charles rode away and then he cast his gaze around for somewhere suitable to make a fire and spread his bedroll. He was looking forward to fossicking for diamonds in this creek bed: at least he would have something to keep his mind occupied. Staying at the Wiltshires' he had found it difficult to think of anything but Laura.

The strain on the wire was just right, and William was about to twist it into place when a call distracted him. The pliers slipped from the end and the fence sagged. "Damnation," he muttered.

He looked up to see a man approaching on horseback. William waved. He had been expecting help to arrive that day and was grateful it was Clem who had come and not the stockman they had employed to live at Smith's Ridge. The new man was excellent with stock but not so handy at fencing.

Robert walked closer as Clem climbed from his horse and the brothers took turns to shake Clem's hand.

"Good to see you," William said. "We are in need of help if we are ever to finish this vermin-proof fence."

They all looked to where Robert had been knocking posts into the ground. Beyond the one he'd just put in the land stretched on for miles.

"Stop complaining." Robert gave his shoulder a playful push. "At least the cost of the wire has been subsidised by the government."

"A help for our pockets, I agree," William said. "But we may be old men before we finish the job."

"Speaking of old men," Clem said. "Your grandpa had a fall a week or so ago."

William's heart lurched. His grandfather had turned eighty-six and, while still quick of mind, he had looked rather frail the last time he saw him. "Is he all right?"

"Matthew came over from Wildu Creek and spent a couple of nights. He told us about it. Said Thomas was shaken up and a bit bruised but no major harm done. He was carrying an armload of wood in."

"I thought he'd moved into the big house with Father and Millie," Robert said.

"He has. He was getting the wood for Millie."

"He shouldn't be carrying wood," William growled. "There are any number of younger, more able bodies at Wildu Creek."

"Everyone was busy. Matthew said he likes to feel useful."

William shook his head. He could imagine his grandfather looking for jobs to do. He wasn't one to lie around.

"There's something else." Clem jerked his thumb back over his shoulder. "I always come the back way past the claim. There's a bloke there. Set up a small camp."

William looked in the direction of the claim. In spite of Wiltshire's threat, Charles had hardly been there since Barnes was washed away. Each time he pegged it out and left, William removed the pegs. "Don't tell me Wiltshire has employed some-one to work it again after all this time?"

"I don't think so," Clem said. "The chap was very friendly. Gave me a big wave. He was walking back from the direction of the narrow gorge upstream and there was no sign of a tent. Just a small campfire and his horse."

"And it's not Wiltshire?"

"No." Clem chuckled. "Too good-looking for Wiltshire. I got a gander at the fellow. Much younger, good build, fair of skin. And as I said, friendly."

William and Robert glanced at each other.

"I think I'll investigate further," William said. "Can you take over here, Clem? I shouldn't be too long. I'll just see what the fel-low is up to. After all, he is on our land."

William crested the rise and looked down on the creek, which was much wider now than it had been before the big rain of 1903. Sure enough there was a chap on his haunches close to the edge of the big waterhole. He appeared to be sifting through the sand with his bare hands.

On higher ground against a natural cliff were a horse and a campfire.

William dismounted, tethered his own horse and made his way down the rough escarpment. At the sound of his boots on the gravel the man looked up and scrambled to his feet.

Before William reached him the other man's face lit in a wide smile and he stretched out his hand.

"Hello," he said. "I am Johannes Becker."

William hesitated. Becker had been the name on Wiltshire's claim.

"My uncle had a claim here. I was curious when I heard about it and have travelled from South Africa to see it."

William shook the hand the smiling fellow still offered.

"William Baker."

"Ah. This magnificent country is yours."

"That's right. You're on Smith's Ridge. Your uncle's claim is only this area here." William indicated a large arc with his hand.

"Not my uncle's any longer. He died during the Boer War."

"I'm sorry."

Becker glanced away. "So this is where the original diamond was found?"

William remained silent. He didn't want to have a discussion with Becker that might encourage him in any way to stay.

Becker looked back. "I mean you no harm, Mr Baker. I simply wanted to see for myself this place my uncle spoke so highly of. I gather from Mr Wiltshire a lot of searching has been done here without any result." His clear blue eyes focused firmly on William. "The original diamond must have been one of those lucky finds. The earth is retaining her riches."

"The only riches here is that water over there." William waved towards the creek behind Becker. "Without it nothing else happens."

Becker nodded.

As if on cue a cow ambled down to the creek and then another.

"They're fine beasts," Becker said. "I spent the night here. Quite a few came down to drink in the late afternoon yesterday."

William glanced at his cattle. "They are well filled out now. We've had another year of good rainfall. They have plenty of feed." It had taken several years and the last of their money but they had restocked all three properties. Wildu Creek was predominantly sheep and the other two properties cattle but there was some movement between them. "Trouble is the rabbits and the wild dogs, and now we have foxes. They don't bother the cattle so much but my father stocks sheep. We're building a vermin-proof fence at the moment around a paddock we will run some of his lambs in to fatten them up for sale."

"Nearby?"

Once more William remained silent.

Becker gave a wry smile. "I am interested in what's happening in the area, that's all. I'm planning to stay in Hawker for a while. The builder, Mr Reynolds, said he might have some work for me."

William scratched his chin. Something about the fellow's manner made him hard to dislike. "I'm in need of help here, if it's work you're after." The offer was out before he'd had time to think about it.

Becker's face glowed. "I'm not afraid of work, Mr Baker."

"Well, pack up and come with me. We could use another pair of hands to build this fence."

Fifty-five

William climbed down from his horse and listened. It was a warm day with only a slight breeze barely disturbing the leaves of the thick bush around him. A shiver ran down his spine in spite of the warmth. It was quiet, almost too quiet. The native camp was only just beyond the outcrop of rounded boulders ahead. Usually there was some sound or a waft of smoke to mark their presence, but today he could hear nothing. No chatter of women or laughter of children. Perhaps the men were out on a hunt, but it was unusual for no-one to be around. The families had dwindled over the years, but William continued to visit every two months with supplies, and find work for the men who wanted it.

He moved on around the rocky outcrop, leading his horse and the two donkeys Robert had brought home from one of his trips north. Past the rocks and through the straggly patch of trees he caught a glimpse of the camp. William pressed on and then once more came to a stop. The camp was indeed deserted — not only that, but in a state of disorder. He had last been there in the heat of February and the camp had been busy, but now the shelters

505

were falling down and the fires were destroyed. The group could simply have moved on to their autumn camp, but they hadn't done that for many years.

He wandered in the remains and a sense of sadness overwhelmed him. Yardu's bequest to look out for his people was a burden, but one he did his best to carry. What was he to do now? Had they moved on permanently or would they return? He sat for a moment in the shade contemplating. He couldn't leave the supplies: they would be ruined in a short time.

"Cooee."

William was surprised by the call that echoed from down the ridge. He stood and headed in that direction as another call followed. Then to his amazement Millie and Matthew emerged from the track below.

"What are you doing here?" he asked as he hugged his stepmother. She felt thin in his arms and her face was creased with lines, but her smile was warm. Matthew shook his hand heartily.

"We were at Smith's Ridge," Millie said. "Jessie told us you had just left with supplies for the camp." She glanced around, the smile disappearing from her face. "They've gone, William."

"We thought we should come and tell you," Matthew added. "We left the cart at the bottom of the hill and walked up."

William raised his eyebrows. That would be quite a hike. No wonder Millie looked a bit weary.

"I haven't been up here since last year." She was still glancing around the deserted camp. "Binda was here a few weeks ago." She turned her gaze on William and he could see the sorrow in her eyes. "They've moved to the reserve."

William blew out a breath. "They will be safe there."

Millie continued to stare at him. She always had the uncanny knack of being able to tell what he was thinking. "Safe or no longer your problem?"

William gaped at her. Millie knew he'd done his best to care for her people.

Matthew shifted behind her. He lowered his head and shoved his hands in his pockets.

She sighed and her shoulders drooped. "I'm sorry, William. That was unfair of me. I'm the one who's let them down. They were my family." Once more she cast her gaze around the camp. "It's only since my own children questioned their heritage that I realised what I had left behind."

"You haven't let them down, Mum. You didn't make the senseless rules." Matthew put a hand on her shoulder. "And the reserve's not far."

"You can still keep in touch," William said. "Spend time with them."

"I won't go there. I can't bear to see them like that."

"But you have been happy living as we do." William looked earnestly at Millie. Surely she had.

"I like the life I have, William, but I had a choice." Millie drew herself up again and Matthew's hand dropped away. "I love your father and all of you children and I'm happy living in a house and wearing clothes, but they won't be." She shook her head. "I am frightened this will be the end for them."

"They could have stayed here." William felt her sorrow.

Once more she shook her head. "Not for much longer. Since the new Aborigines Act more and more of our people are being moved to missions and reserves." She looked at her son. "Thank goodness my children are all grown now, or they still could have been forced to move."

"What should I do?" William looked imploringly at the woman who had raised him after his own mother's death and loved and cared for him as she had all her children.

She took a deep breath. "There is nothing you can do."

The finality of her words lodged heavily in William's heart. The day went grey and he looked up to see a heavy bank of clouds blocking the sun, which was already low in the sky. He had planned to stay the night there but now it would be too lonely.

"We're going to camp down by the cart tonight." Matthew glanced at his mother. "Too much sadness here now."

"I'll stay with you," William said. "I'll have to return the supplies to the store at Smith's Ridge. We can travel back together tomorrow."

William collected his horse and Matthew led the donkeys. At the top of the ridge Millie turned and looked one last time in the direction of the camp, and then walked stiffly ahead of them, following the rough track down the hill.

They made it back to Smith's Ridge in the late afternoon of the next day. Jessie sensed their sombre mood. She didn't ask questions but simply invited them in.

"The kettle has just boiled." She smiled and took Millie's arm. "I'll make tea."

William was grateful to the younger woman for her good sense. "I'll see to these stores and the animals before I come in."

"I'll help."

William gave Matthew a grateful nod. The emotions of the last two days had left them all tired.

The two of them worked well together and they made their way back to the house as the sun was lowering in the sky. A horse snorted and they both stopped at the sound of hooves. William's spirits lifted as a team made its way along the track towards them guided by a man on a horse. It was Robert. He raised his arm, giving them a quick wave.

"It's good to see you," William said. "I thought you'd still be a few weeks away."

"I had a quick journey both ways." Robert grinned. "No hold-ups."

"Where is the windmill we've all been waiting for?" Matthew asked.

"Still in pieces on the wagon," Robert said. "I thought there was little point in bringing it to the homestead, since it's being installed on the plain."

"I agree." Smith's Ridge was the driest of the three properties and it had been decided it would be the place to erect their first windmill. They would have underground water for stock, and not have to rely so much on the creeks. If the first was successful they planned to order more.

Clem arrived home and they all helped to see to the horses before Jessie called them in for supper. While the four men washed their hands and removed their boots William explained about the trip to the native camp.

"What about Rex?" Robert asked.

"He's was still working at Prosser's Run when I left," William said. "I don't know if he'll stay on."

"He's a good bloke."

"He is and he knows cattle work. I hope he'll want to stay."

"Food's getting cold while you all natter out here." Millie stood in the doorway.

Robert was the first to move. Millie held her arms open and gave him a hug. "It's good to see you," she mumbled into his big shoulder.

Inside the front room was cosy with a fire and several lamps lit. The children were already at the table and the men joined them while the women brought in the food.

Once they were seated and grace had been said they started their meal in silence. The mood was still sombre but William was hungry. The mutton stew was warm and flavoursome.

Millie looked across the table at Robert who was also tucking in heartily.

"Tell me about this windmill," she said.

Robert put down his spoon. "It will be a huge tower."

"Who will build it?" Matthew asked.

"I got the instructions from the bloke who made it. It will need all of us to work on erecting it."

"I'm keen," Clem said.

"And me," Matthew added.

It was decided they would meet in a week at the windmill site and when Jessie and the children heard about it they wanted to go too.

"We can camp there," Haji declared, his face full of excitement.

"Why not?" William ruffled the boy's hair. He had just had his fourteenth birthday and had his father's shorter build. He was already proving to be a good stockman.

"We're coming too." Twelve-year-old Sally put her arm around her younger sister.

"Looks like it's to be a family affair." William chuckled. The faces around the table reflected his enthusiasm and he was pleased to see that included Millie.

When they gathered a week later at the site they were a big group. Millie had returned to Wildu Creek, but Matthew had stayed behind to help. Robert was there, and Clem with his family, and Georgina and Eleanor wouldn't be left behind once they heard about it. Eleanor loved any chance she had to play with Clem's girls.

The men helped set up the camp then left the women and girls to finish it while they inspected what was to be done.

"You're the one who knows what to do, Robert," William said. "We shall rely on you to direct us."

The men laboured each day while the women made sure everyone was fed and took the children for long walks. Matthew had a mouth organ, which he played as they sat around the campfire each night. They had survived some tough times and William was thankful for this rare opportunity to be together, working and playing.

The children were in bed early on the last night but the adults were reluctant to turn in. It would be their last chance to enjoy each other's company for some time. Matthew put away his mouth organ as mugs of tea were handed around.

"Johannes would have enjoyed this," Georgina said as she settled on the ground beside William.

"We haven't seen him out our way for a while," Jessie said.

"Nor at Prosser's Run," Georgina said.

"Now he's got permanent work I expect he's too busy with that and courting the pretty Laura Wiltshire to have time for us," William said. Johannes had ended up working for them for a few months, and had endeared himself to everyone during that time.

"She seems a nice young woman," Jessie said.

"Hard to believe she's Charles's sister, isn't it?" William said and noticed Jessie's face still darkened at the mention of Wiltshire's name.

"She's more like her mother," Georgina said. "And she was raised by Mrs Nixon, who was the Wiltshires' housekeeper. She was a sensible and kindly woman."

"I spoke to Johannes a month ago in Hawker," Robert said. "I think he was working up to asking Laura to marry him."

William raised his eyebrows. "I wonder what the high and mighty Charles Wiltshire will think about that. I like Johannes, which is a good reason for Charles not to."

"And I'm afraid Charles is rather a snob," Georgina said. "Johannes is a labourer. I am sure Charles would hope to marry her to someone with money." She smirked at Robert.

"Laura Wiltshire's far too young for me."

"No meddling, Georgina," William said. Besides, he had an idea Robert had met a young woman in Quorn. Robert hadn't said as much but most of his trips south took him that way, whether he needed to go through Quorn or not.

"I'm going to turn in." Robert lumbered to his feet and the others followed.

"It's such a beautiful night," Georgina said as William helped her up. She looked to the starry sky and the firelight reflected on her face, highlighting her smile.

"Let's go for a walk before we go to our swags," William suggested. They were both so busy they rarely had special moments like this to themselves.

She threaded her arm through his and they set off together. Away from the campfire their eyes adjusted to the darkness and between the moon and the stars there was plenty of light. They walked in silence for a while and when Georgina broke it her words astounded him.

"It would be good if Robert married. He might produce a son to inherit all this."

"Good heavens, Georgina, you of all people know we don't need a son to take this on. Look what you've done with Prosser's Run."

"With your help." She leaned her head against his shoulder.

"We've done it together. Surely you wouldn't want our daughter removed from her own property?" Even as he said it he recalled the empty camp in the hills and sadness swept over him. "With all that's happened with the windmill I forgot to tell you the natives have left the camp for the reserve."

"I'm glad."

He was surprised by her response. "Why?"

"Don't you think they'll be much better off there than camped in the hills? They'll receive food and have proper homes."

William remained silent. He wasn't so sure.

"Well, if Robert won't produce any children I'll have to see about a wife for Matthew."

He shook his head at her. Obviously his wife wasn't giving up on the idea of a male heir for the Bakers.

"Who's to say we won't have another child?" he said. "Perhaps a son this time."

He felt Georgina stiffen within the circle of his arm and immediately wished he hadn't spoken.

"Perhaps," she murmured.

They didn't talk about another child any more, though it was an unspoken wish between them. They both knew how lucky they were to have Eleanor, but they couldn't help their longing for more children. William didn't like to see his wife suffer any more losses. Each little baby lost had been so hard on her. Yet he knew that even though Georgina filled her days with Eleanor and the horses and working alongside him, there was still a hole in her heart none of that could fill.

They went on together under the blanket of a million stars. William looked up at the brilliant display and knew he would wish on every one of them if it would bring Georgina the son she longed for.

Fifty-six

Johannes approached the Wiltshires' front door with trepidation, and yet with a spring in his step. It was a glorious April — and it was Laura's seventeenth birthday. Today he was going to ask her to marry him. He felt sure she would say yes. His trepidation was over her brother's likely reaction when Johannes asked for her hand.

The curtains at the dining-room window fluttered. He grinned. He knew Laura would be watching for him. Before he reached the door it flew open and there she was, his angel, smiling back at him with the same excitement as his in her look. He brought forward the hand behind his back and showed her a bunch of flowers he'd managed to cajole from his landlady.

"Happy birthday."

She took them from him and put them to her nose. "Thank you, Johannes. They're so pretty." She glanced behind her, pulled the door to and before he knew what she was doing she had planted a kiss firmly on his lips. He was stunned but then wanted her to do it again. They had contrived stolen moments alone on several occasions and he had held her in his arms and kissed her but she had never offered him her lips in this way. He grabbed her hand, tugged her to the space beside the door and kissed her back. She tasted sweet and smelled of lavender.

There was a thud from somewhere inside. "Is there someone at the door, Laura?"

He stepped back quickly at the sound of Edith's querulous voice, then smiled as Laura pouted her lips in an exact imitation of her sister-in-law. Laura put her head to the door. "Johannes has called to wish me happy birthday."

The door swung back and Edith glared at him. "That's very kind of you, Mr Becker, but Laura has jobs to do."

"Even on her birthday?" Johannes was being bold, but he felt someone had to stand up for Laura.

Laura smiled sweetly at Edith. "We have time to have a cup of tea and some of that cake I made, don't we? I'll finish doing the dusting later."

"Your brother is working in the sitting room and you know he doesn't like to be disturbed. He has much on his mind."

"We'll take our tea in the kitchen."

"Actually I did want to speak with your husband, Mrs Wiltshire. How fortuitous that he is at home." Johannes gave her his most charming smile. He had already called at the shop to see if he could speak to Charles but Mr Hemming had told him Mr Wiltshire was working at home this morning.

"I'll let him know you're here."

Laura spoke before Edith could then disappeared down the hall.

"You'd better come in, Mr Becker."

Johannes removed his hat as she stepped back to allow him to pass. Edith closed the door firmly behind him. It was dark in the hall after the bright sunlight outside. Ahead of them Laura backed out of the sitting-room door.

"My brother would be happy to see you now, Johannes." Laura gave him an encouraging smile. "Edith and I will prepare the morning tea so come into the kitchen when you are finished."

"You can prepare the morning tea," Edith snapped. "I will accompany Mr Becker to the sitting room."

"Very well, Edith." Laura hesitated by the door.

Edith stopped and Johannes pulled up abruptly so as not to run into her. "And check on Emma while you are there; she should be due to wake up from her nap."

"Of course, Edith," Laura said and gave Johannes a wink as he followed Edith into the room.

Charles was seated at a desk in the corner of the room near the window, bent over some papers.

"Mr Becker would like to speak with you, Charles."

Charles turned at his wife's voice. "So I am informed." He nodded at Johannes but didn't get up, nor did he ask Johannes to sit. Edith took a chair near her husband. "What is it you wish to speak to me about?"

Johannes clutched the brim of his hat in his hands. "I've …" His voice squeaked. He cleared his throat and began again. "I've come to ask your permission to marry your sister."

Johannes was startled by a low hiss from Edith.

Charles ignored his wife and stood. He was a big man, taller than Johannes, and carrying a lot of weight for a man only in his early thirties.

"I don't give it."

Johannes baulked at the sharp response. He had expected perhaps some resistance but not outright denial.

"Oh, well I'm sorry you—"

"We will marry regardless."

They were all surprised by Laura's interruption. She came to stand beside Johannes, slipped her arm through the crook of his and looked up at him with such tender adoration he was momentarily speechless.

"You will not." Edith was on her feet now, jabbing a finger in their direction. "Charles, tell her. She will not marry without your permission."

"You are not yet eighteen, Laura."

"I am old enough to make my own decisions." Laura gazed up at Johannes and his heart thudded harder in his chest. She looked back at her brother. "I love Johannes and I'm going to marry him."

Charles puffed himself up. "Laura, this is not in your best interests."

Johannes felt her grip on his arm tighten.

"Mine, or yours and Edith's?" she said.

"You little brat," Edith snapped. "I told you, Charles, this is what you get when you spoil children."

Charles narrowed his eyes. Johannes thought it made him look rather ugly.

"Laura, you will apologise for that remark. Edith and I took care of you after Father died. We have treated you as our own family."

Johannes shook his head. He had witnessed Edith's poor treatment of Laura but he had assumed perhaps Charles had been oblivious to it. Now he thought not.

"Laura *is* your own family," he said. "And yet you treat her like a servant."

Charles ignored him. "Laura, we want only what is best for you."

"If that were true you would wish me well." Laura tugged on Johannes's arm. "We should go."

"Where are you going?" Charles's face turned deep red.

"With the man who loves me."

Charles glowered at Johannes then at Laura as she turned away. "If you leave with this man you shall not be welcome back."

Laura paused at his words but without looking back she moved on swiftly down the hall and through the kitchen, where the youngest Wiltshire was beginning to stir. Once more she hesitated, this time looking into the cradle. Then she turned swiftly away from the sleepy-eyed child and pulled open the back door. "There are some things I would like to take with me," she said and went into her bedroom. He waited at the door, watching in case Wiltshire should come and try and stop her.

"Funny, isn't it? I moved out here after Father died. It used to be the guest room."

He glanced back. Laura was bundling clothing and personal items into the middle of her quilt.

"Really that's what I've become," she said. "A guest in my own family home."

She formed a bundle and tied the top with a ribbon. Johannes took it from her and tilted her face back to his when she turned for one last look.

"No, Laura. You weren't treated as well as a guest. You were a servant. You're my angel and I'll never allow anyone to mistreat you again."

He brushed his lips across hers and led her outside. They hurried down the side of the house and into the street. Johannes noticed the lady in her front garden next door looking at them closely. He took a few more steps then stopped.

"What's the matter?" Laura asked.

"We haven't thought this through. Now you have nowhere to stay and Charles is right. We can't legally marry until you're eighteen."

"Oh," Laura's face fell. "I can't go back."

"No, of course not." Johannes clicked his fingers as a solution came to him. "What about Mrs Prosser? She's very fond of you."

"I don't know."

"Your brother has evicted you from the family home. I am sure she would be happy to take you in if we asked."

"For a year?"

"It won't take long to pass and at least we could see each other. I will have more time to fix up our cottage."

"Our cottage?"

"It's only a shepherd's hut." As he said it his high spirits ebbed at the thought of the house she had given up for him. "It's just out of town. I have rented it and planned to make it a bit nicer before we moved in."

"Take me there," she said.

"Now?"

"Yes, I'd like to see it."

He took two steps then pulled up again. "Are you sure, Laura?"

"Positive," she said.

"Then I'll take you but first we should visit Mrs Prosser."

They set off again. At Mrs Prosser's door his bravado waned. Laura stood silently beside him. He held her hand and knocked.

"Hello, Johannes." Mrs Prosser smiled at him then turned. "Oh, and it's Laura. How are you, dear? I haven't seen you in a while."

"I'm well, thank you, Mrs Prosser."

"What's brought you both to my door?"

"We wondered ..." Johannes faltered. "Well at least I did—"

"I am no longer welcome at my brother's house, Mrs Prosser," Laura finished for him.

"Oh dear." Mrs Prosser stepped back into her house. "You'd better come in and tell me all about it."

An hour later, after two cups of tea and slices of Mrs Prosser's cake, they set off again. They had come to an agreement. Laura was to stay with Mrs Prosser in return for some domestic help — far lighter than the work she'd been doing for Edith, but enough that she would feel useful. Johannes felt a little better: she would have a roof over her head.

But first she insisted he show her their home. Mr Reynolds had allowed Johannes the use of his horse and small cart, so they went to the stable at the back of his yard. Johannes loaded two old chairs he had repaired for their sitting room then he helped Laura into the cart. It took little time to reach the cottage but then Johannes's spirits took another dive. The place looked lonely on the edge of a grassy plain, with only two nearby trees to break the flat landscape that stretched beyond it.

"It's not so far from town," Laura said as he helped her down from the cart. "I could walk there and back easily."

He strode ahead of her to the door. It needed a hard push to open.

"That's one of the things I have to fix."

She stepped into the middle of the first room, which had a large fireplace but was totally empty of furniture.

He took her hand. "The chairs will go in here. Come and see the kitchen." He led her through to the back of the house. The kitchen was small but he had spent some time cleaning it up. "The oven works — I've tested it already — and the table and chairs are sturdy." He flung open the door leading into another room. "This one is small but would be big enough for a nursery."

Laura looked around his shoulder then stepped back. "And where is our room to be?"

"It's the other front room." He led her back to the sitting room then came to a stop in front of the door that led to the bedroom. He was afraid to open the door. Not only because the room wasn't finished, but because it felt intimate and he wasn't sure what to say.

"Johannes?" She looked up at him with such love and trust. "Aren't you going to show me our room?"

With a quick turn of the handle he whisked the door open and she walked slowly inside. He had already installed a bed and mattress, a hanging rail for clothes and a small chest of drawers with a jug and bowl for washing, but that was as much as he had achieved so far. He watched Laura turn a full circle, taking in the details of the sparsely furnished room until she was facing him again. He held his breath, wondering what she would think.

"It's perfect," she said. "I have my quilt for the bed and there's a piece of fabric I can use for a curtain instead of the skirt I had planned. It will be just the right colour."

"There are bedsheets in the drawers. I have got more things to bring out. I will make it more habitable."

She reached up and gently put her hand over his mouth. "I will be able to do things too, and then when we're married this will be our little patch of heaven."

Johannes chuckled and kissed her fingers. "You are definitely my angel."

She wrapped her arms around him and nestled into his chest. Johannes wanted to hold her close but he didn't trust himself. They were not yet husband and wife. He carefully extracted himself from her embrace. "I will unload the cart."

"I can help."

While he carried in the chairs she was busy in the bedroom.

"Come and look." She beckoned him excitedly from the doorway.

He took in the bed, which she had made. She had draped a bath sheet across the window.

"You see." She took both of his hands in hers and gripped them tightly. "It looks cosy already." She stretched up and kissed him. "I wish we were married now."

"We will have a year to plan for it."

"No fuss," she said. "Just us."

"Have you no-one to stand with you?"

"I'd like to ask the Hemmings — they've always been good to me. But that might put them in a difficult situation with Charles." She put her head to one side. "Perhaps my friend, Margaret Hill, and Mrs Prosser of course."

"If it's all right with you I should like to ask William and Georgina Baker."

"Oh, Georgina is lovely." She put a hand to her mouth to cover her giggle. "You know Charles always fancied her as his wife but she married William instead. It caused such a stink at the time. I'd love to have them at our wedding."

"Very well." Johannes stepped back. Her close proximity made it difficult to control his emotions. "Now we must go."

"Oh no," she cried. "Not yet surely. Can't we spend a little longer here?"

He couldn't deny her, especially when she kissed him again.

They wandered the tiny cottage, and Laura looked in every nook and cranny as they talked about the future they planned together. It seemed to Johannes that her hand brushed his more times than could be accidental.

"I really must get you back to Mrs Prosser's."

Laura followed him to the sitting room where he'd left his coat over the back of a chair. Before he reached the coat she put a hand on his arm.

"Please let us stay just a little longer." Her grey eyes were wide and round. She slowly leaned in and kissed him. Not the sweet chaste kisses she'd given him until now, but a long, slow kiss that sent his blood racing.

"Laura, stop." He gently eased her lips from his. "You don't know what you're doing."

"I know I want to be your wife and I want us to be together now, here in our own little home."

"No, Laura." He was shocked but excited by her suggestion. "We're not yet married. I must think of your reputation, even if you won't."

She took his hand and placed it on her breast. "In my heart we are married already."

"Laura," he pleaded as he felt his defences slipping away.

She reached for his hand. "Please, Johannes. I feel as if I have waited for this moment for so long already. This is our house now. We don't have to worry about anyone else. I want us to be together properly, today."

As she spoke she was walking backwards, towing him towards the bedroom. He pulled her up. "Laura, are you sure this is what you want?"

She looked him directly in the eye. "I am."

His reserve crumbled. He scooped her into his arms and laid her gently on the bed. As he climbed up beside her she reached for him and he was lost.

Fifty-seven

January 1914

William adjusted the cushions on Johanna's couch before he beckoned Georgina to sit.

"Really, William, I've been sitting in the cart for nearly two whole days. I need to stretch my legs."

"That long? From Prosser's Run?" Johanna's eyebrows arched.

"The poor horse was allowed to do little more than amble."

"Doctor's orders, my love. We want to do all we can to keep that baby safe."

"Very well."

He took her hand as she eased herself onto the couch. They had left Prosser's Run in the cool of pre-dawn the day before and William had deliberately made the journey a slow one, so that Georgina was jostled about as little as possible. They had been lucky that the heat of January had abated a little but he had stopped during the hottest part of the day so that they could rest in the shade.

"This room and your bedroom are the coolest in the house." Johanna put a glass of cool lemonade on a small table beside her daughter.

"Thank you, Mother. I am fine really. Just a little tired from the long journey." She looked pointedly at William.

He smiled and kissed her forehead. He was as relieved as she was that the journey was over. He tried not to fuss but this was the first baby since Eleanor to survive this long. It was still a couple of months away but the doctor wanted her to stay in Hawker until the birth. He had suggested she stay at Mrs Ward's lying-in home but Georgina had insisted on her mother's house and Johanna had agreed. The doctor was just as close either way.

"Well you're here now, safe and sound," Johanna said. "How is Eleanor? You could have brought her."

"She would have driven you both mad cooped up here in the house," William said.

Georgina gave him a knowing look and he was pleased to see some spark back in her eyes. "William's right on this occasion, Mother. Eleanor wanted to come, of course, but I have put her in charge of the horses in my absence and she is perfectly happy. She loves the outdoors and would be no good here with us for two months."

"And she has her Uncle Robert to look out for her," William said.

"Dance to her tune you mean." Georgina chuckled and shifted her position on the couch. "She has him wrapped around her little finger."

"What about his new wife?" Johanna asked.

"Alice is there too," Georgina said. "They came a few days before we left and it was lovely to spend some time with them, wasn't it, William?"

"It was. We only met Alice for the first time at their wedding."

"She's rather shy," Georgina said. "But Robert adores her and she him, so that's all that matters."

"Perhaps Laura will call on you while you are here," William said.

"Yes, although her baby must be nearly due."

"I assume she's still an outcast from the Wiltshire home?"

"Of course." Johanna tutted. "It was only my plea added to Edith's that convinced Charles that Laura and Johannes must marry to avoid a scandal. He finally gave his permission but neither he nor Edith have spoken to her since. More people have boycotted their shop because of it."

Georgina looked at William. Her eyes shone. "I do know what it's like to want a man the family doesn't approve of."

"Really, Georgina." Johanna shifted in her chair and a sad look settled on her face. "What's done is done. I've learned my lesson. Helping Laura was my way of proving it."

"Johannes is a good man," William said.

"And Laura has made him the perfect wife," Georgina said.

"I saw her just last week," Johanna said. "We still take tea together when she comes into town. I enjoy her company. She was always a pretty girl but she has blossomed, and she is so excited about the baby." Johanna turned to William. "But perhaps you could go and fetch her in the cart. Johannes is often working away and she walks into Hawker and back from her house."

"Isn't she lucky she can take some exercise." Georgina swung her legs to the floor. "I really am too uncomfortable to lie here a minute longer."

"Why don't you come out to the front yard with me?" Johanna said. "It's cooler now and we can take a walk in the garden."

Georgina stretched, rubbed her back and then took her mother's arm.

William went to the window and watched them, mother and daughter, one grey head and one red head bent towards each other in conversation. It was early evening, the air was still and across the street, houses were glowing in the red and orange rays of the setting sun. They had been lucky with the weather for their journey but William didn't think it would be long before the full strength of the summer heat returned. He let out a long slow breath. He was relieved he had got Georgina safely there.

He turned and paced the room. Tomorrow he had some business to do. He would probably stay one more night after that and then he would return to Prosser's Run. They had just purchased their fourth windmill and it was to be put up near their drafting yards on the eastern boundary. While Robert was with him they would work on it together. William knew he would need to be busy every day to distract himself. He hated the thought of leaving Georgina but he was relieved she was close to the doctor. He hung on to the knowledge that Eleanor had arrived safely after nearly a full-term confinement. He prayed this baby would do the same.

Charles strode down the hall towards the noise. It had been an uncomfortably warm night, he hadn't slept well and now his head ached. The air was dry and outside the wind was picking up. He stepped into the kitchen and something wet hit him on the chin and dripped to his vest.

"What the devil?" he bellowed.

"Father," Victoria gasped.

Leonard lowered the spoon he had had just flicked and Grace gaped wide-eyed.

"Sorry, Father." Leonard's voice was contrite.

All three looked at him in alarm.

Charles took his handkerchief from his pocket and wiped his chin and then his vest. The break from school was interminably long. It also meant Edith was unable to help him at the shop. "Where is your mother?"

"In the wash house," Victoria said.

"Finish your breakfast quickly and go outside."

"But it's hot," Grace whined.

"You need some fresh air."

"Yes, Father," they chorused obediently.

The children ate in silence while Charles poured himself a lukewarm tea and served himself some of the porridge. He gave them one final glare. The sounds of giggling followed him into the hall. He shut the door and retreated to the dining room to eat his breakfast in peace. He had just settled over his paper when Edith burst in with Emma on her hip.

"Did you send the children outside?"

Her sharp tone grated. Charles took a breath. "They needed some fresh air."

She walked around the table and plopped Emma on his lap. "It's far too hot."

Charles took Emma's grubby grasping hands from his white sleeve and sat her on the ground. "They needed some air."

"There's a hot wind out there, Charles."

"I was only thinking of you, Edith." He brushed at the dirty mark Emma's fingers had left on his shirt. "Let them run around outside for a while. You are the one who will be home with them all day."

"Oh no I won't." Her hands were on her hips. "Leonard and Victoria can go with you this morning."

Charles frowned. Leonard was old enough to be useful but the two of them together would not be good. He shook his head but Edith was at him, her finger wagging before he could speak.

"It's all right for you going off all day. I am stuck here with four children. It's going to be a terrible day. I will have my work cut out managing the younger two." She plucked Emma away from the small table she had just reached. The child wailed and waggled her hands at the ornament she had been intent on grasping.

He sighed and picked up his paper. "Very well, Edith, but I should like to eat my breakfast in peace. Make sure they are dressed appropriately and ready to leave in half an hour."

Her face softened. "Thank you, Charles. It really is quite exhausting with all four of them home all day. If only I had some help—"

Charles gritted his teeth. He was not in the mood for Edith's complaints. "The shop is barely making us a living, Edith."

"I thought that now that you've sold that ridiculous horse and cart—"

"The bank took that money towards paying off our ongoing debt."

"I did suggest we go back to groceries."

"There are two other shops doing that now and I cannot ask the bank for more money to make changes."

"If only I had someone here, I could help at the shop, especially now you've let that young assistant go."

Edith sighed. "Mr Hemming and I are managing. Business has been slow since Christmas but I'm sure it will pick up soon."

"You should have tried harder to keep Laura here."

He fixed her with a cold stare. "What would you have had me do, Edith? Tie her to the kitchen?"

Edith sniffed. "I saw her the other day. She is large with child."

"That's no concern of ours. She made her choice. She is no longer my sister."

"But Charles, this house is hers. Now she will have a child to inherit it. If she ever finds out we'll be destitute."

Charles huffed out a breath and got to his feet. He was obviously going to get no peace this morning. "She won't find out. We are the only ones who know and the executor deals directly with me." Behind him the strengthening wind rattled the window.

"I'm going to work. Leonard and Victoria can walk down when they are ready."

He gave Edith a perfunctory kiss on the cheek. The ache in his head gripped tighter. He had that feeling it was going to be a terrible day.

Laura reached the shade of the post office verandah and leaned against the cool stone wall. She was momentarily protected from the hot wind and took the opportunity to draw her breath. Her back ached and she felt the weight of the baby today. Perhaps she should have stayed home, but she needed flour. Johannes would be cross with her — he was still away working on a building in the ranges to the north. She wanted to make sure the house was well stocked before the baby came.

She took a breath. Yesterday she'd had tightening sensations around her middle but they had stopped in the night. Now she felt it again.

The door to the post office opened and Mrs Crawford, the postmaster's wife, poked her head out. "Oh, Laura, it's you. I thought I saw someone out here." She leaned a little closer. "You look tired, dear — why don't you come in and rest for a moment? I'll get you a cup of water."

Laura licked her lips at the thought. She felt suddenly parched. "Thank you," she said.

It was much cooler inside the stone building.

"Bring a chair, Stanley," Mrs Crawford called to her husband.

They soon had her sitting down, a cup of water in her hands and Mrs Crawford pressing a cool cloth to her forehead and neck.

"I'm sorry to be a nuisance." Laura was glad there was no-one else there to witness the fuss.

"Not at all, Laura, my dear," Mrs Crawford said.

Mr Crawford studied Laura over the top of his glasses. "Oh, young Laura Wiltshire. I didn't recognise you."

"It's Laura Becker now, Mr Crawford." She put a protective hand over the bulge of her baby. At that moment a pain gripped her. She took a deep breath as the strength of it staggered her.

"What is it, dear?" Mrs Crawford asked.

Laura exhaled and the pain eased. "Nothing; I'm fine." She took another mouthful of water.

"Laura, of course. I have a letter for you." Mr Crawford hurried back around his counter. He rummaged underneath then came towards her waving an envelope. "I'm sorry it's been sitting here for some time and I had quite forgotten it. I didn't know where you had moved to, and the instructions on the front are that it should only be put into your hands."

"Thank you, Mr Crawford." Laura took the envelope, wondering who would be sending her a letter. She scrunched it tightly as another pain swept over her.

"You're not all right, are you?" Mrs Crawford said.

"I keep getting a pain but it passes." Laura forced a smile and stood up. She pushed the letter into the pocket of her dress. "I must get going."

"Where is your husband, Laura?" Mrs Crawford asked.

"He is away working."

Laura saw the concerned glance Mrs Crawford gave her husband then she gasped as the pain came again.

"Stanley, go and bring the cart to the front door." Mrs Crawford put an arm around Laura's shoulders. "We will take you to Mrs Ward's, my dear. I think your baby may be on the way."

"Oh." Laura put a hand to her stomach. She felt so silly. Of course that's what the pain would be. She had been so focused on making sure everything was prepared she had thought the pain was simply from being on her feet too long. "My husband. He should be back in a few days."

Mrs Crawford gave her a kindly smile. "Then he will arrive to a new son or daughter. I doubt your baby will wait for him."

Laura chewed her lip as another pain gripped her. She hoped Mrs Crawford was right. Two days of this pain didn't bear thinking about.

Fifty-eight

Something woke William from a deep sleep. He lay still, trying to work out what the noise had been. He reached out a hand for Georgina but she wasn't there. He sat up and as his eyes adjusted to the gloom he remembered they were at Johanna's house in Hawker, not at home.

Perspiration trickled down his back. The room was stuffy. They had gone to bed with the window shut against the hot wind that had raged outside most of the previous day and into the night. He opened it and felt a small relief as the fresher outside air flowed in.

William lifted his head at the sound of a moan and then the murmur of a voice. He stepped out into the sitting room. There was light glowing from under the door to the kitchen. Perhaps Johanna wasn't well. Then his heart skipped a beat: or Georgina. He opened the door to see his mother-in-law bent over his wife, who was seated in a chair, her head in her arms on the table.

He was by Georgina's side in an instant. "What is it?"

Georgina raised her head a little to look at him. Her face was pale. "I've overdone it, that's all."

On her other side Johanna shook her head at him.

"I'm going to fetch the doctor," he said.

"That's a good idea," Johanna said.

"No." Georgina's denial was followed by a sharp intake of breath.

Over the top of her William glanced at Johanna. The older woman was worried, and William knew her face reflected his own fear.

"It's not the baby." Georgina sat up. Her lip trembled. "I'm simply tired from the travelling and then that awful hot wind yesterday."

"The doctor won't mind coming to see you and then you'll be reassured," Johanna said. She pressed her hand to William's shoulder.

He bent and kissed Georgina's cheek. "I won't be long."

As it turned out he was back quicker than he thought, but as soon as he opened the back door he was greeted by more moaning from Georgina. This time she was standing in front of the kitchen bench, her head down and her hands propping her up.

"The doctor is out of town," he murmured for Johanna's ears only.

"Then we must take her to Mrs Ward's. She will know what to do."

"No." Georgina twisted her head to glare at them. "It's not the baby — it's too soon."

William could see the perspiration on her brow and the pain in her eyes. "Georgina, we must go. Mrs Ward is our only option." Before she could protest further he hurried to hitch the horse and cart.

Laura was near exhaustion but the racking pain would not leave her alone. How long had it been since the Crawfords had brought her to Mrs Ward's? She squinted through swollen eyes at the window. Around the edge of the curtain she could see a faint glow. It must be nearly morning. Dear Lord, she had been in this agony since yesterday. Why didn't Johannes come to help her? She moaned. He was away. He wouldn't even know the baby was coming. Mrs Crawford had said he would return to meet his new son or daughter.

She looked back at the two women who tended her. Mrs Ward and Helen, her helper, had both been so kind when she'd first arrived, telling her how lucky she was, but now they were the centre of her torture.

"I'm so hot," she moaned.

There was a moment's brief relief from the fiery heat as Helen mopped her brow with a cool cloth.

"You're doing very well, Laura," Mrs Ward soothed in her ear. "Nearly there, one more push should do it."

Laura turned her head to tell Mrs Ward she'd said that before, but the pain swelled again and carried her with it on a wave of agony.

Strong arms supported her and once more the women urged her to push and finally it was over. She heard a faint cry.

"Well *done*, Laura."

She opened her eyes.

Mrs Ward was wrapping the baby in a cloth. "You have a beautiful son."

Laura's lips cracked as she smiled. "Johannes?"

"Mr Crawford was going to try to get word to him."

"Sip this."

Helen's strong arms supported her and she tried to swallow. The cool water flowed into her mouth and over her chin. Mrs Ward laid the baby on her chest. She looked down at the scrunched face of her son and was instantly in love. If only the pain didn't still tug at her body.

She heard the two women murmuring together but her eyes were only for her son.

Mrs Ward put a firm hand on Laura's shoulder and smiled kindly at her. "I'll be back in a moment."

Helen remained at Laura's side. Laura wished she wouldn't. Helen's hands kept kneading her stomach and that made the pain return.

William looked up as Mrs Ward came back into the room. They had arrived in the dark in the early hours of the morning. Mrs Ward had already been up attending to someone else. She had examined Georgina while he waited outside. Then her assistant had come and hurried her away. William had entered the room where his wife lay on a bed. She had looked so pale against the white bedsheets and her eyes were wide with dread. He had sat beside her and taken her hand, feeling her hold tighten as each new pain gripped her body.

Mrs Ward smiled brightly. "How are we in here?"

"Not good, I'm afraid." Georgina's voice was stoic. "The baby is definitely coming, isn't it?"

"Yes." Mrs Ward took Georgina's other hand. "We are here to help."

"It's too soon."

William felt so helpless at the big tears that rolled down her cheeks.

There was a tap on the door. It opened and Helen popped her head around. "I'm sorry, Mrs Ward, but I need your help."

"I'll be back as soon as I can." Mrs Ward gave him one of her kindly smiles and followed after Helen.

The door opened wider for them to exit and William was alarmed to see blood on Helen's apron. Immediately he was back to his childhood and his parents' bedroom. His mother had died having a baby. Fear gripped his heart. He glanced down at Georgina and was thankful her eyes were shut and she hadn't seen it. Please Lord, he prayed. Don't let Georgina die.

Laura heard voices murmur and the relentless kneading of her stomach resumed. Her position was shifted by faceless hands and she felt a whoosh of warmth flow from her body and surround her. She struggled to open her eyes. Why couldn't they just leave her alone with her baby? Her eyelids fluttered. There was no baby on her chest. Had she dreamed him?

"My baby," she croaked.

"It's all right, Laura." Mrs Ward's breath was warm on her cheek. Laura had felt so hot and now she felt so cold. "Your son is safe in his bed. We will give him back to you soon."

A blanket was tucked around her shoulder and she nestled her head into its soft warmth. The voices were still talking but they were more distant now. Her lips tingled and her head spun. She was slipping, she didn't know where, but her body felt light. There was a faint cry. Johannes would be so pleased to have a son. Laura smiled. She relaxed and let herself float.

William could not stand the waiting. He wished he could be with Georgina, but they had ushered him outside. The sun had risen on a new summer's day, which would thankfully be cooler than the previous though still there was a promise of heat in the early-morning sunshine.

"Mr Baker." He stopped his pacing and turned at Helen's call. "You can come in now."

He was pleased to see the fresh apron she had donned to attend Georgina was still free of blood at least. He wanted to ask how his darling was, but Helen walked stiffly ahead of him along the hall.

He slowed as he approached his wife's door. Helen opened it for him, then shut it again as he stepped inside. Georgina was lying propped against some pillows, her face blotchy and her eyes wet with tears. His relief at seeing her overwhelmed him for a moment.

"William," she whispered.

Spurred into action by her sorrowful call, he strode to her side.

"Our son …" She turned her head to where Mrs Ward was bent over a small table in the corner of the room. "Our son was too small."

When Mrs Ward turned she held a tiny bundle in her hands.

"I'm so sorry, Mr Baker," she said. "He was just too early."

Georgina reached out her arms. "Let me hold him."

Mrs Ward looked on them with such a kindly gaze. He could see she shared their sorrow. "It's not a good idea."

"*Please,*" Georgina gasped.

Overcome by the desperation in his wife's plea, he went to the woman holding their baby. "Please, Mrs Ward. Just a few minutes."

"Very well."

She handed him the bundle; it felt so light he could barely believe there was anything inside. She lifted the corner of the blanket and tucked it under the tiny chin. William gazed at the wizened face of his son and felt his own tears warm on his cheeks.

Mrs Ward moved quietly from the room. William sat beside Georgina and she took the tiny bundle from his arms. He held her while she sobbed. They were both sitting quietly gazing at their baby when Mrs Ward returned to take him away. Once she had gone Georgina's body shook with her sobs. Helpless in the face of her deep sorrow he lay down beside her and wrapped her in his arms.

Johannes stood for a long while just staring at his wife. He always called her an angel and she looked like one now, laid out under a white sheet with her dark hair neatly brushed around her pale face. Finally, the tears came and he knelt at her bed, his head beside hers, one hand on her shoulder.

"My dear sweet, Laura," he murmured. "What have I done to you? I promised nothing would hurt you. I should have been here, and now it's too late. You've left me." He reached under the sheet for her cold lifeless hand, closed his eyes and wished he were with her.

Much later the door opened behind him, but he didn't move. A hand pressed gently on his shoulder.

"I'm sorry, Mr Becker, but we can't keep her here any longer." Mrs Ward squeezed his shoulder. "The undertaker is waiting."

Johannes closed his eyes, breathed deeply and struggled to his feet. His legs had gone numb and he began to fall. Mrs Ward's hand gripped his arm and she supported him against her shoulder.

"I have your wife's things in the sitting room, Mr Becker," she said. "Let me take you there. And I expect you will be eager to see your new son."

Johannes cast one last look at his dear sweet angel. The child she had so badly wanted had killed her. Pain knifed through his chest. He turned away and went with Mrs Ward to the sitting room.

She placed a cup of tea on the table beside his chair but he ignored it.

"Your wife was carrying this bag when she came to us, Mr Becker." Mrs Ward placed a calico bag on his lap. "We put Laura back in her dress, but there was a letter in the pocket which I have put in the bag with her boots and her locket. I hope you don't think me presumptuous, but I cut a small lock of your wife's hair and put it in the locket. I thought perhaps you might like that. Or the child."

Johannes stared at a flower in the pattern of the mat. He heard the words but they didn't sink in.

"Helen is bringing your son."

"No." The word came out more forcefully than he'd intended. "Perhaps later. I don't want to see him now."

"We must find someone to look after him."

"Yes." Johannes said. "Good idea."

"Have you family that could help?"

"No."

"What about your wife's family?"

Johannes felt himself rousing as if he had come out of a deep sleep. He lifted his gaze to meet Mrs Ward's worried look. "No. They will not touch one hair on the child's head." A sudden sense of urgency swept over Johannes. "Where is he?' He struggled to his feet, the bag falling to the floor. "Where is the baby?"

"He's here, Mr Becker."

Mrs Ward stepped back to reveal her assistant holding the baby. She beckoned her forward.

"I'm so sorry for your loss, Mr Becker." Mrs Ward gave him a gentle smile. "But you have the most beautiful son."

Helen lifted the baby and leaned towards him.

Johannes looked at the tiny face and once more the pain of Laura's loss ripped through him like a knife. Here before him was the reason she had left him.

"No!"

The anguish of his cry startled even him.

Johannes staggered backwards, gripped his head in his hands and sobbed.

A loud cry forced William's eyes open. He sat up and glanced back at his wife. He had been dozing but she was still in a deep sleep. The sun was bright behind the curtain. He put a hand to his eyes then edged himself from Georgina's side and went to the door. All was quiet out there now. He prayed the other mother and baby had survived.

He stepped back at a soft tap and the door opened.

Mrs Ward entered. "I'm glad you're still here, Mr Baker." She kept her voice low and glanced over his shoulder. "How is your wife?"

"Exhausted."

"Mentally though, is she a strong woman?"

William thought it an odd question. Did Mrs Ward think Georgina might lose her mind over her loss?

"In other circumstances I would say yes, Mrs Ward. She has lost so many babies and yet gone on. But because this baby kept growing we allowed ourselves to hope he might live. I don't know how she will recover from this."

"I understand, Mr Baker. This is such a terrible time, but I have an enormous favour to ask." She drew him closer. "I have a baby whose mother has just died giving birth."

William recalled the bloodied apron and his heart went out to the family that had lost their wife and mother.

"The baby's father has rejected it and I must try to do my best for it. I wondered if your wife might nurse it."

"Someone else's baby?" William was appalled. "After all she's been through. You can't ask my wife to do that."

"What's the matter?" Georgina struggled to sit up, her eyes blinking at them.

"Nothing, my love." He strode over and put a protective arm around her shoulders.

"What can't you ask me to do, Mrs Ward?"

William shook his head at the woman but she approached the bed.

"I have a motherless baby, Mrs Baker." She lowered her gaze then fixed it on Georgina. "And you are a mother without a baby. I had hoped you might consent to suckle the little mite."

William felt Georgina stiffen beneath his arm.

Mrs Ward went on. "The baby's father is inconsolable and has said he wants nothing to do with it. The family are friends of yours, I believe."

Georgina sucked in a breath. "Not Laura?"

Mrs Ward came to stand beside them. "I'm afraid so."

"Oh," she wailed and buried her face in William's chest.

"I'm sorry." Mrs Ward shook her head. "It's just the poor little babe could do with some love."

"You can't ask this of Georgina," William growled. "Not after losing her own."

"Can I see him?"

"Georgina." William removed his arm and stepped back from the bed.

"It's Laura's baby, William." She looked to Mrs Ward. "I don't know if I can do it. But perhaps if I see the baby ..."

"Very well." Mrs Ward turned on her heel and left the room, closing the door quietly behind her.

"Don't be angry, William," Georgina said.

He took her in his arms. "I'm not angry. I just can't bear the thought of you suffering any further."

"Perhaps this will help me."

"How can it?"

The door opened behind them and William stood back as Mrs Ward carried another small bundle to his wife.

They both leaned in to look at the baby. His hair was fine and fair with a hint of ginger. He had a button nose and his mouth opened in a yawn. Then his eyelids fluttered.

With that Georgina reached for him. "I'd like to try to nurse him."

"I shall stay with you and help." Mrs Ward turned to William. "Why don't you pop down to the kitchen, Mr Baker? One of the girls will make you a cup of tea."

Once more feeling totally lost William did as she suggested. He sat hunched over his mug at the kitchen table while two young women went about cleaning up after lunch. They had offered him food but he declined. His appetite had deserted him. There was so much sorrow in this house William wondered how Mrs Ward could stand her work.

Fifty-nine

March 1914

The first days of autumn were no different from the last days of summer. A heavy heat pressed down from a clear blue sky and Hawker baked.

Edith was dusting the glasses on the dining-room dresser. She felt tired and hot and was not making much of a job of it. At least the three older children were at school, and Emma was down for her afternoon nap. Charles had come home for lunch and was now dozing in his chair.

"If only I could sleep that easily," she huffed.

She saw a movement on the path outside just seconds before she heard the sound of footsteps approaching the front verandah. She peeped through the lace curtain, careful not to touch it. At the sight of the visitor she stepped back. Johannes Becker had come at last. They had heard about Laura's death of course, and the motherless child. Edith had immediately decided the boy could live with them.

Charles had been appalled at first. He had thought her ridiculous to want another child, especially one who was not theirs. Edith had quickly set him straight. If it was ever found out that their house was Laura's then surely they could continue to live in it if they cared for Laura's son. She had worried a while that Johannes would try to look after the boy himself, then she'd heard Georgina Baker, who had lost her baby, was staying at her mother's house and caring for the child. In desperation Edith had written to Johannes, saying Laura's baby should be looked after by family.

Over a month had gone by since then and she thought perhaps her plan had failed but here was Johannes Becker arriving at her door.

"Charles," she hissed. "Charles!"

He snorted and blinked bleary eyes at her. "What is it, Edith?"

"Wake yourself up. We have company."

By the time she had ushered Mr Becker inside she was pleased to see Charles standing, his shirt tucked in and a welcoming look on his face.

"Mr Becker has come to talk to us, Charles." She smiled back at their visitor. "Would you care to sit, Mr Becker?"

"I won't be here long."

Edith was taken aback by his sharp tone.

"How is your son, Mr Becker?" Charles came forward. "My sister's baby."

He peered down his nose at their visitor. Edith wished he wouldn't do that. There was no need to get high-handed. They had to negotiate the child's move to their home calmly. Convince Johannes it was the right thing to do.

"My son is very well. Unfortunately, my wife is dead. I must have missed your letter of condolence."

Edith gasped.

Charles puffed out his chest. "Now look, Becker."

"Don't bother to get yourself worked up, Charles. We wouldn't want you popping your braces. I have simply come to deliver this."

Edith's eyes opened wide as he drew an envelope from his pocket. Some kind of legal handover of the child, perhaps. She wanted to snatch it from his hand but she let Charles take it.

She watched his face eagerly as he read.

"What the devil?"

"What is it, Charles?"

Becker turned to Edith. His gaze was steady and cold. "It is your eviction papers, Mrs Wiltshire. It seems this house belonged to my wife. Bequeathed by her father."

Edith felt her throat tighten. She put a hand to her neck.

"As I was her husband it is now mine. And I have sold it."

"You've what?" Charles roared and lunged at Becker but the younger man side-stepped easily.

"You have two weeks to pack your belongings and move out. If you don't, I have arranged with the constable to remove you."

"You impudent—"

Becker put a hand in front of Charles's face. Edith watched as his lips turned up in a smile. It was a chilling smile that made her shudder.

"We have nowhere to go, Mr Becker." Edith hoped she had put on her saddest look. "Surely you wouldn't evict us. We're Laura's family."

"Well then perhaps you'd like to move to our cottage. I shall be returning to South Africa soon and I am sure the farmer who I rent it from would be happy for new tenants." He pushed the hat he'd been holding back onto his head. "Good day to you both."

The front door banged as he left and Emma began to cry.

"Charles." She looked to her husband, who had slumped to a chair. "What are we going to do?"

He looked up at her, crestfallen as a child who has lost a toy. "I suppose I shall have to contact Grandmother."

Georgina closed the door on the sleeping baby as her mother opened the front door to a visitor. Her heart gave an extra thump as she heard Johannes's voice. She had last seen him over two weeks earlier, when he had said he would return with a decision. She wished William were there with her. It had seemed so easy to agree to taking care of the baby to give Johannes time to recover from his grief and decide what he should do. Having his baby in her arms had someway eased the grief of the loss of her own but now she knew she would be devastated all over again if Johannes took his son.

"Hello, Georgina." He took off his hat as he stepped through the door and pulled a bunch of flowers from behind his back. "I've brought these for you lovely ladies."

"Oh, you are such a gentleman." Johanna smiled and took the flowers. "I'll find a vase for them. You two sit and I will bring some tea."

"Not for me thank you, Mrs Prosser. I can't stay long. But I will sit for a moment."

Georgina felt her heart quicken as her mother left her with Johannes and they both sat.

"Wherever did you get the flowers?" she asked, wanting to defer whatever he had come to say.

He smiled. It was so good to see after all the sorrow. "The lady who runs the boarding house. She always has something in her garden."

"Do you want to see the baby?" Georgina was halfway from her chair but he waved her to sit.

"Not yet. I want to talk with you first."

Georgina's heart was thumping so loudly she was sure he would be able to hear it.

He took a deep breath. "I have decided to return to South Africa."

She took a calming breath of her own. She had hoped that if he took the baby it would be somewhere local so she would at least still be able to see him. "I see."

"I have thought this over and over. Laura was my angel. I have been trying to think what she would want."

"She would want you to raise your child." Georgina knew she was right.

"But whenever I look at the baby—"

"Your son."

Johannes face drooped. "I find it hard to see him as anything more than the instrument of his mother's death."

She gasped.

"I'm not the man you think I am, Georgina."

She was puzzled by his words.

"My parents are ageing. My older brother has moved to India with his family." Johannes sat on the edge of his chair, moving his hat around and around in his hands. "I don't think I can give this child the love and the upbringing he deserves, not without … without Laura. I would be both honoured and grateful if you and William would adopt him."

"Johannes." Georgina's heart was thundering in her chest now. "Are you sure this is what you want?"

"As long as you both want the same."

"Oh, yes we do. He cannot replace the son we've lost, but you know he would be loved as our own nevertheless."

"I do. And that's why I think this is the right decision." Johannes got to his feet. "Can I see him now?"

"Of course." Georgina felt as if she floated across the floor to her bedroom where the baby slept.

They stood on either side of the cradle. Johannes trailed one finger down the baby's cheek. His little lips sucked in and out then he let out a long sigh.

"He looks very content," Johannes murmured.

"He is a happy baby." She drank in every feature of the child who was so different from her own. Every time she held him she couldn't help but compare him to the boy she had carried herself. This baby had a round face and fine gingery hair rather than the narrower shape of her son's face and his shock of black hair, but her dear son never took a breath and this little babe was healthy and strong. She raised her gaze to the man who was about to give up his son. "Are you sure about this?"

"I am."

"Then what would you like us to name him? We can't keep calling him Baby."

Johannes looked up. "You and William should name him. He is to be your son."

Georgina sucked in a breath. The pain of her loss never left her, but this baby needed her now. She and William had talked about what the baby should be called after Johannes first left him with them. Their own son had been named William. "Then we thought we would call him John after his father."

Johannes smiled. "Thank you," he said. "I think Laura would have liked that too."

When Johannes called back two weeks later to say goodbye, William was with Georgina at her mother's house. This time he felt able to hold the baby and take tea with them. It was strange looking into the eyes of his child. It was as if Laura were looking back at him.

He passed the baby to William. "He has his mother's grey eyes."

"I hope they don't change," Georgina said. "Babies' eyes often do after a few months."

Johannes lifted the small bag he had brought with him. "I have some things I would like to give you for John."

"Of course."

He reached in and drew out the locket. "Laura loved this locket. It has been in her family for generations. I think it should stay here with John. I hope one day he will find a wife to love and he will give it to her."

"Oh that's so sweet, Johannes." Georgina took the locket from his hand and he saw tears brim in her eyes.

Next he drew out the bank passbook. "I have opened an account in the name of John Baker. There is only a small amount of money in it."

"You don't have to do that," William said. "We will make sure he has all that he needs."

"I know you will but there will be a large amount of money from Laura's estate and I want John to have it. Perhaps when he's older. You will know what is right."

"Very well," William said.

"Mr Reed will see that the money is deposited once the sale of the house is finalised."

"But weren't you renting the cottage?"

"Oh yes. This money will be from the sale of the Wiltshire house."

William and Georgina both gaped at him and he chuckled.

"It turns out it was legally Laura's house but my sweet angel never knew it. She lived with her brother as if a servant in what turns out is ... was ... her own home."

William frowned. "How on earth?"

"After she died I found a letter in her pocket she had never opened. It was from a Flora Nixon."

"She used to be the Wiltshires' housekeeper," Georgina said.

"I see. Well evidently she had only recently heard of Mr Henry Wiltshire's death and she was concerned about Laura being in her brother's care."

"Rightly so as it turned out," William said.

"Yes." Johannes said. He felt a small stab of anger yet again over the Wiltshires' treatment of Laura. "The letter said Mrs Nixon knew her father had wanted her to have the house and she hoped that was the case. She wished Laura well and gave the name of the solicitor Henry Wiltshire had used. I followed up on that and it seems Mrs Nixon was correct. The executor of Henry's will was only too happy to help me, as he had obviously allowed himself to be duped by Charles into believing Laura had been aware of her inheritance. I found a buyer for the house immediately, then served the Wiltshires with their eviction notice."

"I'll be damned," William said.

"Is that why they are selling their shop?" Georgina asked.

"I assume it's the only thing they have left," William said.

"Not even that from what Mother tells me," Georgina said. "Mother heard—"

"Gossip," William cut in.

"I think there's truth in it," Georgina said. "Evidently they owe the bank a considerable sum and many people are taking their custom to other Hawker shops."

"What the Wiltshires do is no concern of mine." Johannes knew he was doing the right thing by his son, but the sight of him cuddled into William's arms was beginning to weigh heavily. It was time for him to leave.

Georgina gave him a hug and kissed his cheek. William shook his hand. Johannes smiled at the baby safely tucked into the chest of his new father.

Georgina put her arm around her husband. "Thank you for this precious gift, Johannes."

He gave them what he hoped was a reassuring smile and hurried from the sight of the happy family before he changed his mind.

Sixty

December 1914

Christmas day at Wildu Creek was warm, but no-one complained.
There were far too many of them even for Joseph and Millie's big
dining-room table so the men had rigged canvas between trees
outside near the creek, which still had water in it from some late
spring rains. An occasional puff of breeze helped keep the temperature down.

Thomas sat at the head of the long trestle table, which groaned
with the weight of abundant food. His weary bones felt better
than they had in a long time. He was surrounded by happy voices
and laughter, the squeals of children and the odd nicker of one of
Eleanor's horses. She had brought two with her for the children
to ride.

He looked up at the colourful bunting the women had strung
under the canvas and around the trees. Hooked on branches
were several lanterns ready to be lit at the end of the day. It was
much fancier than the outdoor room he had made for Lizzie, but
that part of the bank, the scene of many Baker celebrations, had
been washed away in the big storm. Trees, rocks, soil and even

the last of the old chairs he had made were lost as Wildu Creek had swollen and roared its way down from the hills to the plains below. He could count on one hand the number of times he had witnessed it flowing with such ferocity.

A touch on his arm made him look back at the table, where everyone was turned in his direction.

"We're ready for grace, Grandpa." It was William who had interrupted his reverie. Georgina sat beside her husband and gave Thomas an encouraging smile. From the other end of the table Joseph did the same.

Thomas knew they had much to be thankful for. The seasons of the last few years had been bountiful, William and Georgina had a new baby and Robert a new wife. Beth had recently been visited several times by a farmer from Cradock way. There would no doubt be another wedding to celebrate soon. Thomas had a wonderful family and good friends, a solid roof over his head and food to eat. How his dear sweet Lizzie would have loved this.

"Grandpa?" William's gentle call brought him back to the present again.

All eyes around the table were still watching him expectantly. Thomas cleared his throat and kept the grace short, after which there was an immediate eruption of voices again.

"You must be so proud of your family."

He turned to Johanna Prosser, who sat on his other side.

"I am, Johanna. And pleased that you are here with us as well." He smiled at the woman whose husband had been a thorn in their side for so many years. One could never tell how things would work out. "The new baby is a fine young chap."

"He's a darling," Johanna said. "And so strong. He's trying to walk on his chubby little legs. At least he's sleeping now so we can eat our luncheon without worrying he will drop off that bank into the creek." She chuckled and passed Thomas the platter of meat.

He put a sparse amount on his plate. His appetite was small these days in spite of all the different foods Millie tried to tempt him with. He did, however, take a larger serve of the jellied mint peas. He was rather partial to them.

William took another sip of the punch. "This is good."

Georgina raised her eyebrows. "You don't want to know all the things Millie put in it."

"I see the new people have totally renovated the Wiltshires' old shop," Robert said.

"Did you go in there?" William said.

"Why not? They don't own it any more."

"Did anyone hear what happened to them?" Clem asked.

"They've gone to live in Adelaide with Charles's grandmother," Georgina said.

Joseph shook his head. "He still lands on his feet, that man."

"I'm not so sure. I visited Harriet's shop years ago, when Henry was still alive," Johanna said. "It was a rather old-fashioned place with a little house out the back. I've no idea how they would all live there."

"She still has money," Joseph snorted. "He won't be living in poverty like he and his family have made others do."

"I don't think they'll be leading a charmed existence," Johanna said. "Apart from their small quarters he's nearly bled his grandmother dry over the years. Her business was in decline. It really relied on her and she's in failing health."

"I think we're finally rid of the Wiltshires after all these years," Joseph said.

William glanced at Georgina, who was looking at her mother. The formal adoption had been finalised, and John was now John Baker, not Becker. He hoped over time people would forget the baby's mother had been a Wiltshire.

"What do you say we purchase another windmill this year, Father?" It was time to change the subject.

"Do you think Father's all right?" Joseph murmured in Millie's ear.

His wife glanced down the table to where Thomas sat back in his chair, the food on his plate barely touched. "I'm sure he's fine. He loves days like this when we are all together, but he gets tired. He'll probably go off and lie down in a while."

Joseph leaned across and kissed his wife's cheek. "I'm so grateful I have you, my love."

Millie smiled. The creases around her dark brown eyes were deeper, but he was relieved to see her old sparkle had gradually returned as the years had gone by and their children had grown safely in her care.

"And yet you still keep that diamond as your good-luck charm."

Joseph patted his pockets in a grand gesture. "No I don't."

Millie raised her eyebrows.

"It's back in the earth."

"Really?"

Joseph grinned. "Well, in a box in the cellar. I don't need it any more. I really am very lucky without it."

Millie reached across and hugged him.

"Enough of that," Matthew said.

Joseph looked to his other side where Beth, Ruth and Matthew were all watching them.

"Matthew," Ruth chided her brother. "I think they're sweet."

Joseph looked at his wife in horror. "We're sweet?"

Millie laughed. It was a wondrous sound.

"Anyway, Matthew," Ruth grinned, "where's that young lady you were swinging around the shearing shed at the last cut-out dance?"

"Don't tease him, Ruth," Beth said.

"Pass him some more potato," Millie said. "Eat up everyone; we don't want leftovers."

There were groans from some and murmurs of delight from others.

"How do you think Alice is coping with her first Baker Christmas?" Joseph murmured in Millie's ear. Down the table his son looked like a giant beside his short wife.

"She's so shy she hardly leaves Robert's side, but I'm sure she'll get used to us."

"Robert is talking of enlisting," Joseph said.

"Surely not." Millie turned a worried look on her stepson. "The war is between Great Britain and Germany. It has nothing to do with us."

"I am too," Matthew said.

Joseph felt a chill go through him at his son's words. Along the table Jessie looked fearfully at Clem.

"No, Matthew," Beth gasped. "Tell him he can't, Father."

"Matthew can't what?" William asked from down the table.

"Matthew and Robert are going to enlist," Ruth said and the whole table went quiet.

Joseph noticed Alice lower her head as Robert's arm went around her shoulders.

"They must do what they think is best," Joseph said.

Millie's hand gripped his.

"England is our Mother Country." Johanna placed her napkin on her plate. "It's to be expected that our men support her."

"This is our country now." William glared across at Robert. "We were born here, not in England."

Silence settled around the table.

"They're offering six shillings a day for privates," Albie piped up, his scarred face twisted in a smile. "That's good money to tempt young fit men."

"Lucky you're not fit then," Clem joked and the tension around the table eased.

"We can only pray it will all be over soon," Joseph said. "Let's not spoil today with talk of war. Did you say there was pudding, Millie?"

She gave him a grateful smile. "Gather the plates please, children. We will clear the table."

"Ready to start again." Albie groaned, pulled a face and clutched at his stomach, making the children giggle.

The sun was lowering in the sky when William entered his grandparents' old cottage in search of his wife. Every bed in the big house was full, along with the shearers' quarters. William, Georgina, Eleanor and John were staying in the cottage, which was now much closer to the creek since a large part of the bank had been washed away in the last big storm.

Georgina was bending over John, who wriggled on the bed. He was half-dressed.

"Here you are," William said.

"He was wet through." Georgina shot out a hand to stop John rolling away. "Little scallywag won't lie still."

William held John while she collected the discarded clothes.

A scuffing sound behind them made them both turn.

"Hello, Grandpa." William smiled at the old man, who looked slightly bewildered to see them.

"I heard voices," Thomas said. "I forgot you were staying in the cottage."

He came into the room and looked around.

"You built a fine house, Grandpa."

"We love staying here," Georgina added.

Thomas crossed the room to the old chest of drawers.

William and Georgina looked at each other.

"Where did this come from?" Thomas asked, his back still to them.

"It's your old chest, Grandpa," William said.

"No, this." Thomas turned. He held John's locket in his hand.

"It belonged to John's mother," Georgina said.

"His mother?" Thomas's wrinkled face creased deeper in a frown.

Once more William and Georgina exchanged glances. Georgina went to stand beside the old man.

"You remember we told you our baby died and we adopted a baby?"

"Yes, yes I know." Thomas flapped a hand at her. "Who was his mother?"

William held his breath; they tried hard not to mention the Wiltshire name in this family.

"Mrs Becker." Georgina reached for the locket but Thomas kept it in his grip.

William watched the confusion on his grandfather's face. The room was quiet. The late-afternoon sun streamed through the open window. John was heavy in his arms. William looked down; the baby had fallen asleep.

Thomas suddenly looked to the window. "I'd like to sit outside," he said.

"Of course, Grandpa." William passed John to Georgina. "I'll bring you a chair."

"Can I hold the baby?" Thomas asked.

"I'm sure he'd love a cuddle with his great-grandpa." Georgina put her spare hand under Thomas's arm. "I'll walk out with you."

They settled the old man in a chair slightly back from the bank looking over the creek. He held the sleeping baby in his arms and clutched the locket in one hand.

"He seems to be quite taken with the locket," Georgina said as they retreated back as far as the little verandah.

"Strange," William said. "I wonder why?"

"It doesn't matter. Look how loving he is with John."

"Grandpa has always adored the children."

Georgina rested her head against his shoulder. "I hope—"

"Don't say it, my love," William cut her off. "We have two children now and if that's all we have we are luckier than some."

Georgina tilted her face to his, her green eyes mocking him. "I was going to say I hope there will be more children from your siblings one day. John needs some playmates." She nestled back against his shoulder. "Oh look, the baby is stirring and Grandpa is talking to him. What do you think he's telling our son?"

William hugged Georgina tighter and kissed the top of her head. His heart was full. "Probably how lucky he is to have the most beautiful mother in the world."

Thomas stared into the blinking grey eyes of the baby. "Hello, young John."

The baby's eyes opened wider. He yawned, stretched one hand up towards Thomas's chin then settled back into the crook of the arm that held him.

Thomas raised the locket up and the baby reached out to grasp it. "This belonged to my mother. You can see her initial on the front, *H* for Hester. It was stolen from me a long time ago by a man who may well have been your real great-grandfather. Now you've brought it back where it belongs. What a special Christmas gift."

The baby gurgled and pulled at the locket. Thomas shifted his gaze to the distant mountains. They were turning every shade of blue and purple. Below him Wildu Creek ran gently over rocks and tree trunks, wending its way south.

"Some things have changed since I first saw this land more than sixty years ago, young John." He lifted the baby higher in his arms. "One day it will be yours. You must learn to treat it well."

Thomas thought of his native friend Gulda who had first brought him here. He had passed on, as had Joseph's boyhood friend Binda. Millie's family had moved to the reserve and Millie and her children were the only local natives left.

Thomas sighed. The baby felt heavy in his arms. Movement across the creek drew his gaze to the sky. An eagle drifted on a current. Thomas clutched the baby a little tighter as the large bird circled closer. John continued to make happy sounds, playing with the locket Thomas dangled in front of him. The eagle dipped lower; its shadow swept up the bank and over Thomas and the baby, then it wheeled away. John flapped his hand in the direction he took.

"Wildu," Thomas said. The gully breeze strengthened, ruffling the hair of the old man and the baby, and stirred the tops of the trees while across the valleys and plains the sun bathed the land in its golden rays.

"We're here where we belong, Lizzie," Thomas murmured and closed his eyes.

Author's Note

The characters and places in this book are fictional with the exception of real towns and well-documented figures of the era. For example there really was a Mrs Ward who ran 'The Gables'. There was not always a doctor and with only the help of her daughters, she cared for many sick people and helped deliver hundreds of babies before the first Hawker hospital was opened in 1924. What a dedicated woman she must have been.

Millie and Jessie lived with the fear of their children being taken from them and this fear is based on the real events of the era. In South Australia the actual Protector of Aborigines didn't get the power to remove children of mixed race without a court hearing until the early twentieth century but I found reports of attempts to remove some children in the Flinders region before the turn of the century. The practice was stopped at that time due to resistance from the local Adnyamathamha people but it must have caused distress for many families. Where I have used indigenous names I have purposefully changed the spelling. My humble apologies if this means I have accidentally used the name of a deceased person.

My research took me on many tangents as I delved into the past and then there was the fun of disseminating the little gems, the variations and the historical facts into a fictional story. Trying to unravel the legalities of mining in the era was a definite challenge and I have taken some liberties with the rules. People have searched for diamonds in South Australia since they were first found near Echunga in 1859 by gold panners. The Flinders Ranges has had a lot of interest from mining companies since that time and diamonds have been found but not their elusive source. The search continues.

While this is a work of fiction and the main characters never existed, I hope that I have created a story which is grounded in past reality. I have had assistance from many quarters but as always, any mistakes are my own.

Acknowledgements

What a special journey it has been to write this series. The research that has driven the stories has been as addictive as my regular visits to the Flinders Ranges to soak in the scenery and the atmosphere. The characters have lived in my imagination for so long it is sad to let them go. I hope you've enjoyed the journey with us.

Love and thanks, as always to my husband, Daryl, who anchors the team, and to my children, their partners and grandchildren who all assist in a variety of ways, your encouragement is beyond measure. And to my wider family and dear friends who form such an important support network, my heartfelt thanks to you all.

I am so grateful to the wonderful publishing team at Harlequin Books who believed in this series and encouraged me to write it. I'd particularly like to acknowledge Michelle Laforest and Cristina Lee who were there from my first book. They have both moved on to other ventures now but were always special supporters. Thank you both.

There are so many at Harlequin who bring my books to life from the all-important cover designers to the sales team. Thank you to Sue Brockhoff who loved the initial idea of the series. To Jo Mackay and Annabel Blay, my sincere thanks for another job well done. Also to editor Kate O'Donnell who has a terrific eye for historical detail. It was great to work with you again. And to proofer Kate James, thank you for your dedication to your work. Adam Van Rooijen and his marketing team are always looking for new ideas to get my books to readers for which I am indebted.

My fellow writers come from diverse and widespread communities but your friendship, which can be anything from sharing a writing retreat to sending an uplifting text, is so valued. I love it when we catch up at fabulous events such as the Romance Writers of Australia Conference. If you're a writer looking for support this organisation is one of the best.

Finally to the wonderful book communities of publishing reps, booksellers, librarians and you, dear readers. Your messages of encouragement and anticipation for the next book are inspiring. I appreciate your warm support of this writer, thank you.

talk about it

Let's talk about books.

Join the conversation:

 on facebook.com/harlequinaustralia

 on Twitter @harlequinaus

www.harlequinbooks.com.au

If you love reading and want to know about our

authors and titles, then let's talk about it.

OTHER BOOKS BY
TRICIA STRINGER

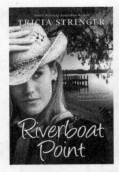

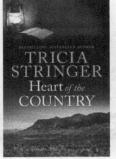

AVAILABLE NOW

Available where all good books are sold.
Or visit harlequinbooks.com.au